THE

Selecting a jar

Chinese paintbrush with a wickedly tapering tip, Heimdal the magician set about anointing Mara's glorious naked body. He traced the shape of a pentacle in the centre of her back; opening up her buttocks, he outlined an exquisite silver rose on the sensitive skin around her forbidden gate; with infinite patience, he traced a filigree pattern upon her beautiful heavy breasts.

'Now we must be joined,' he explained, fingering a stiff, silvered nipple. 'At the moment of climax I shall perhaps see into your past and future and maybe even see what has happened to your lover, Andreas.'

Heimdal's heart pounded as he began to pay homage to Mara's nudity – kissing each orifice in turn, pressing fingers into her most intimate places, anointing her with aromatic oils.

At last. At last he was going to have her . . .

Also available from Headline

In this series
Kiss of Death

The Lusts of the Borgias
Love Italian Style
Ecstasy Italian Style
Rapture Italian Style
Amorous Liaisons
Lustful Liaisons
Eroticon Dreams
Eroticon Desires
Play Time
Carnal Days
Carnal Nights
Hot Type
The Sensual Mirror
French Frolics
Claudine
Wild Abandon
After Hours
French Thrills
In the Mood
A Slave to Love
Amorous Appetites
The Blue Lantern
Sex and Mrs Saxon
Fondle on Top
Fondle in Flagrante

The Phallus Of Osiris

Valentina Cilescu

HEADLINE

First published in 1993
by HEADLINE BOOK PUBLISHING PLC

10 9 8 7 6 5 4 3 2 1

All characters in this publication are fictitious and any resemblance to real persons, living or dead, is purely coincidental.

ISBN 0 7472 4009 4

Typeset by Avon Dataset, Bidford-on-Avon, Warwickshire
Printed and bound in Great Britain by
HarperCollins Manufacturing, Glasgow

HEADLINE BOOK PUBLISHING PLC
Headline House
79 Great Titchfield Street
London W1P 7FN

Introduction

The Master is a vampire sorcerer who feeds and grows on human sexual energies, condemning his victims to join the ranks of the evil undead. Feared as the occult power behind Hitler, he was magically imprisoned by Allied sorcerers in a block of crystal at the end of World War II. He awakens in his prison, in the cellars beneath the country-house bordello of Winterbourne Hall, brought back to consciousness by the sudden emanations of sexual energy from the orgies in the Hall above. Immediately he sets about plotting his freedom and revenge.

His spirit seeks out the innocent but highly sensual psychic Mara Fleming and begins to manipulate her, with the hope of using her special powers to liberate not only himself but his long-lost Queen, an Egyptian priestess of Amun-Ra. Eventually, Mara discovers the crystal dagger and magical ring which are necessary to free the Master.

Cynical journalist Andreas Hunt becomes involved in the web of evil as he tries to investigate a series of bizarre sex-crimes involving MPs, media figures and other influential people. He becomes Mara's lover and – when she disappears in mysterious circumstances – he is determined to discover what has happened to her.

Andreas is tricked by the Master into following Mara to Winterbourne, where he witnesses many scenes of violence and sexual magic. The Master magically tricks Mara into stabbing Andreas with the crystal dagger, releasing his own evil soul into Andreas's body and condemning Andreas's soul to take its place within the Master's discarded and imprisoned body.

Suddenly emerging from her trance and seeing what she has done, Mara flees into the night, not realising that the soul of her lover lives on within the crystal . . .

1: Aftermath

It was dark in the room. Dark and strangely airless. But Mara felt no fear. She stretched out her hand and touched her unseen lover's hand. Although she could not see him, she knew he was standing by the side of the bed; that he was naked, and ready for her . . .

'Come to me . . .' breathed Mara. And her fingers moved from her lover's hand to explore his body – running down his flank, his thigh; searching eagerly for the warm weight of his testicles; seeking out his most sensitive and intimate places to tease and excite his flesh; and bring him to her.

She heard his breathing: hoarse and quickening now. And seconds later, she felt him sit down on the bed beside her, felt the soft coverings yield to his weight as he lay down by her side and pressed his hot nakedness up against her willing flesh.

He was by her side now, stroking her with knowing fingers that seemed to read her mind, divine her every dream and wish. His fingers slid down her body, as though taking the measure of her, mapping out the fullest extent of the bounty offered to them. They fluttered like butterfly wings, up from the firm roundness of her hips to the taut flesh of her tiny waist, and then up still further; until at last they found the swelling amplitude of her magnificent breasts, caressing their firmness appreciatively.

He was kneeling beside her: leaning over her, the better to toy with her. Mara gasped with pleasure as invisible hands cupped her breasts and kneaded their warm and yielding flesh. Skilled fingers searched out the budding hardness of her nipples and pinched them between finger and thumb, just hard enough to provoke an irresistible blend of pain and pleasure.

'Take me!' gasped Mara, reaching up and touching the hands which were so knowingly exploring her body. They were strong hands, hands she felt she knew well; hands that were strong and sinewy and capable of great violence – and yet gentle enough to tease, torment, arouse.

Strong, sinewy wrists and forearms . . . She could reach no further; so she stretched out her hand to the side, and felt for the body of her unseen lover. Her hand made contact with his thigh, muscular and covered with thick, coarse hair. She slid her hand upwards, upwards, letting her fingers glide softly over the hairs; and she felt her lover tremble at the exquisite torment of her touch. Bolder now, she let her hand move higher still, and shivered with delight as her fingers brushed against her lover's testicles.

They were heavy, vital, pulsating with a raw energy that communicated itself to her as she stroked their velvety pouch, weighing them in her palm. Then she let her fingers stray still further, and felt them slide deliciously along the smooth length of a hard and throbbing shaft that she knew yearned to bury itself in her.

And as she stroked it, she felt herself grow hotter and wetter, her juices welling up as though from some secret spring deep within her. It was as though she was melting from the inside outwards, as butter might melt in anticipation of the hot knife that would soon plough into its soft and willing depths . . .

The room was filled now with the fragrance of sex; the sweet, heady aroma of a cunt well greased, of a prick whose tip glistens with the first drops of semen, the first promise of the torrents to come. Mara slid her hand along her lover's shaft and ran her fingertips gently over its tip: it was already slippery with love-juice and she shivered again with the delicious anticipation of its entry into her most intimate places.

The shaft was thick, smooth, heavy; and it seemed to grow longer and thicker still as Mara stroked it, wanking it slowly up and down so as to titillate and tease her lover without bringing him to the point of no return. She could hear his breathing growing louder now, and more laboured. She knew he was close to his crisis and yearning for her.

At last, she felt his hand upon her own: a command – to stop, now, before it was too late. Silently, Mara's unseen lover drew apart her thighs. Mara did not even offer token resistance, for she yearned to feel his touch upon her womanhood, his prick within the depths of her belly. Once her legs were splayed wide apart, her lover knelt between them, as the faithful worshipper kneels silently to perform his devotions to the goddess.

He began by stroking between Mara's thighs, gradually working his fingers up from knee to thigh, from lower thigh to upper thigh, to that warm, moist crease where the thigh ends and the groin begins. He tormented her for what seemed an eternity, letting his fingers roam gently across her pubic hair, brushing it as lightly as a summer breeze playing across a field of thistledown.

'Harder, harder!' she groaned, trying to make him rub less teasingly at her pubis, to answer the call of her madly throbbing clitoris. But he refused to give her the release she yearned – pulling his hand away and retreating to the distant ground of her smooth inner thigh.

Not until she was almost weeping with frustration did her lover take pity on her and slide his hand once more up to her pubic hair, this time wriggling his fingers between her rosy cunt-lips and seeking out the throbbing button of her clitty.

Skilfully, he began to wank her, his index finger on her clitoris and his thumb burrowing into the hot depths of her vagina, which seemed to her like some steamy underground cavern whose walls were dripping with fragrant moisture. She felt the pressure of his knees against the inside of her thighs, and longed for him to come into her, ram into her soft vulnerability like a rutting animal covering a female on heat.

'Fuck me, fuck me!' she sobbed. 'Please, please . . .'

She thought she heard the merest breath of laughter, but no: her lover was silent still. Silent and strong and totally in control. She was entirely at his mercy, at the mercy of his pitiless finger and thumb, wanking her rhythmically and driving her to a distraction of desire.

Almost before she had realised what was happening, she felt another hand creeping up on her. But this hand was bolder still and knew no boundaries, no limits. This lewd hand was stroking the hidden valley between her arse-cheeks, as though it were looking for some secret entrance . . .

At last, it found what it was looking for. Fingertips nudged against the forbidden gate, seeking the concealed catch that would trigger it to open. Open sesame . . . yield, submit, give way . . . Mara heard herself silently praying for her arse to open up and welcome this eager, blessed visitor; to make it an honoured guest; to do its bidding in all things, no matter what it asked . . .

Her lover was scooping up the juices from her cunt now and using them to tease her perineum. Oh, how good it felt to have a finger skating smoothly across those secret places, to feel it gliding on a layer of slippery love-juice across her flesh.

'Come inside me, I beg of you . . .'

Mara's tone was almost panic-stricken now, filled with the hoarse urgency of unstoppable desire.

And her lover did not abandon her this time. With a deft thrust, he slipped his finger into Mara's arsehole; and she cried out at the sudden intrusion – a great, long cry of satisfied yearning.

He toyed with her for a while, moving his finger inside her with a circular motion, stretching the walls of her arse; amusing himself – and her – by letting the finger in her arse and the finger in her cunt enjoy a tactile communion with each other across the fragile partition which separated them.

And all the while he kept on rubbing slowly and lasciviously at Mara's clitoris, teasing and tormenting the swollen flesh and delighting in her groans of pain and pleasure.

And when Mara was once more on the point of tears, her lover withdrew his finger and thumb from her cunt and clitty, and – silencing her despair – thrust his magnificent manhood into her cunt, ramming it home up to the hilt, so that she writhed in an ecstasy of torment and began to babble nonsense like a mystic speaking in tongues.

For it truly was a mystical experience to have this massive and exquisite prick inside her: to feel it pressing against her cunt walls. And all the time her lover's finger was toiling away inside her arse, its thrusts keeping time with the rhythm of pulsating prick and cunt.

Silently, he fucked her. Silently, there in the darkness; his body moving against her, his prick within her cunt. And, thus joined, it felt as though his very soul was also within her, thrilling and stimulating and possessing her; climbing with her towards the very summit of pleasure, where joy explodes into a sunburst of many-coloured light.

As the orgasm tore through her body, Mara thought for a second that she saw the face of someone she knew, loved, yet did not quite remember: a man's face with closed eyes. Eyes closed as if in death . . .

Her lover withdrew from her and lay down by her side. Shaken, she lay for a moment in silence and then rolled over to switch on the bedside lamp.

She fumbled briefly for the switch; then the lamp clicked on, flooding the bed with a pool of sallow, yellowish light. Mara turned back to her lover, meaning to kiss him, but recoiled in horror.

For the man beside her, the man who had just fucked her passionately and brought her to ecstasy, wore the face not of her lover Andreas Hunt, but of one whose cruel, sardonic smile brought a terrible fear to her heart.

She was looking straight into the fiery-red burning gaze of the Master.

With a shriek of terror, Mara tried to pull away from him, but he had her fast, his claw-like fingers digging into the soft flesh of her tanned arm. And he took hold of her chin, forcing her to look at him, to watch and behold the gift which he had brought her.

As she looked on in horror, Mara saw the Master's face and form change horribly. This was no longer the darkly handsome face of seductive evil, but a grotesque caricature, a parody of sexual attraction. His face became the face of a demon: dark-skinned and ugly, his features distorted into a lewd grimace, saliva drooling from the corners of his lips, which drew back to reveal rows of sharply pointed teeth.

'No!' screamed Mara, struggling in his terrible embrace, the memory of his lovemaking still warm and trickling from her distended cunt. 'I will not submit to you . . . you cannot harm me . . .'

But all her white magic could not protect her now. For the Master was growing, his body expanding, swelling, deforming, until at last he towered high above her, filling the room, his evil eyes still fixing her with that fiery red gaze.

And as she watched, unable to turn away for he still held her fast, she saw the Master's prick also begin to change its form, swelling, lengthening, growing beyond all belief until it became the parody of a penis – a prick as thick as a man's torso and as long as a limb.

The Master's mouth opened and he began to speak, his voice hoarse and rasping, like the voice of a serpent turned into a cruel caricature of human form:

'Little slut,' he hissed, 'I have you now, and I have you for ever. You cannot escape me.'

'No, I will not do your will!'

'Silence, mortal whore! Lest I tear your body apart and feast upon your puny soul. Look at my penis. Is it not beautiful?'

He leered at Mara and she shivered but was unable to look away.

'My darling,' he hissed, 'it is all for you. Will you not take it into your cunt? Why so reluctant? You were eager enough for it but moments ago . . .'

And he presented his prick to Mara, thrusting it at her so that she could not avert her gaze, or see that it was now black, like polished stone, and gleaming as though exposed to the ethereal glow of moonlight.

As she screamed, the Master began to laugh. It was a humourless, chilling sound filled with evil and the foetid air of the tomb. His laughter echoed around her, bouncing off the walls and forming a web from which there seemed no escape.

Hands over her ears, Mara tried to shut out the terrible sound of the Master's laughter but, try as she might, it echoed on, growing louder and louder and more hysterical with pleasure, to see her in such terrified confusion.

The room began to spin and Mara's head was filled with a kaleidoscope of changing colours. The colours of fear . . .

As the room spun out of control and Mara fell sobbing on the bed, she heard a distant voice calling to her from very far away; a voice full of sadness and despair that, even as she heard it, faded away into the distance:

'Mara! Mara! Come back! Don't leave me here . . .'

The voice of Andreas Hunt.

With a final cry of terror, Mara felt her consciousness ebbing away. And all was darkness and release.

When Mara awoke she was dazed and disorientated. Where was she? Why was it so dark and cold? What had happened to her tormentor, the hellish chimera who had peopled her dreams and waking fears for so long? What had happened to her over the last couple of days? She could remember nothing save the terrible dream that had seemed so real.

Her eyes grew more accustomed to her surroundings, and she realised that she was not hemmed in by utter blackness after all. A glimmer of the palest light was filtering through a strange, twisted mesh above her head.

Moonlight. Moonlight filtering through a thick canopy of tall and ancient trees, casting strange patterns on the forest floor, awakening the nameless, formless shadows who dwelt within the deepest darkness and calling them out to dance before her on the night air.

Mara shivered, suddenly realising that she was naked. Her nipples were puckered hard with the cold and her smooth tanned skin had turned to gooseflesh under the chill breeze's incautious caresses. Reaching out and taking hold of a low branch, she struggled to pull herself upright. She winced, for she was stiff and sore, with the soreness that turns to many-coloured bruises in the light of day. Accustomed though she was to walking barefoot, sharp little twigs were digging painfully into the soles of her feet and her first steps forward were difficult and uncomfortable.

Stumbling, she put out her arm to stop herself from falling and the moonlight fell across her hand, delineating a strange dark shadow, like a black pool staining her fingers. She brought her hand up to her face and examined it. A dark, dried-on deposit. Mud perhaps. She sniffed at it . . . no, not blood. Something familiar, something coppery . . .

She put out her tongue and licked at the stain. Salty, unpleasant, sickening.

Her hand was covered in dried blood.

The vile taste of the blood filled her head with a sudden image: the image of something she had seen, perhaps something she had done. She could not quite remember. All she could see was the body of her lover, Andreas Hunt, lying on the ground at her feet – very still, very dead. And she looked again at the blood and began to weep slow tears. For although she could not remember what had happened, or how he came to be lying there, she suddenly knew that Andreas Hunt was dead.

And somehow, she knew not how, she had been responsible for his death.

She stood there, clinging to the tree, for a little while, until she became calmer. Confusion filled her mind. She had a vague remembrance of leaving Hunt's apartment, of walking down a deserted and dusty country lane; a faint memory of a big country house. But nothing more. It was as though some outside agency did not want her to remember.

Her thoughts began to crystallise. The autumn cold was eating into her nakedness. She must get help. Warmth and food and clothes. But which way to go? She looked around her, but there was no sign of light or habitation. She was utterly alone.

Instinctively, she placed her hands upon the trunk of the tree and directed all her thoughts into the heart of it, tapping into the earth's natural lines of magnetism.

'A sign, a sign,' she murmured. 'A sign to guide my steps, that is all I ask.' And the power entered her hands and flowed through her body like a warm tide of sweet wine. Its mellow warmth flooded her, calmed her and then began to excite her, and she felt as though she were being stroked and kissed by all the spirits of earth and air.

All her discomfort seemed to ebb away as she felt herself become as one with the earth-spirits, and she grew as warm and relaxed as if she were swimming in the clear waters of some tropical lagoon. Slowly, she began to shuffle her feet apart as she felt the heat kindle in her loins; pressing the magnificent swell of her breasts against the rough bark and delighting in the harshness of its rasping kisses on her nipples.

Her cunt was on fire now: a fire raging in her belly. And all the copious juices she produced served only to fan the flames, exciting her throbbing clitoris to new crescendos of desire.

Strange how she had not noticed it before . . . But, as she ground her pelvis against the rough bark, she felt a hardness pressing back against her pubis. She slid one hand down the bark and sought out this new presence. It was a deliciously smooth branch – perhaps eight inches long and as thick as any man's penis, jutting out obscenely from the trunk of the tree. Mara caressed it, and felt a surge of power, as she grew yet closer to the spirits she was evoking as her guides.

Knowing exactly what she must do next, Mara parted her legs still further, and eased herself onto the welcoming branch. It slid easily into her cunt, for she was deeply aroused and her womanhood was running with rivulets of love-juice. She gave a groan of pleasure and surprise as she felt the hardness slide home, pressing hard against the neck of her womb and sending shivers of ecstasy through her loins.

She lifted herself – just high enough to reach the very tip of the branch without allowing it to escape from her eager cunt; then lowered herself with a cry of joy as the hard surrogate penis filled her once more to the brim.

Her head was reeling as she used the branch to fuck herself. With each stroke of the curious dildo in her cunt she felt a picture growing in her head – at first indistinct, and then becoming sharper, more clearly defined. It began as a blur of light and then resolved itself into the image of something reassuringly familiar: a jumble of perhaps twenty caravans, nestling in the heart of the forest. As the picture grew more distinct in her mind, she felt a strong conviction that this was the nearest refuge for her, her best chance of finding what she needed.

Fucking herself faster now, Mara felt the climax building up in her loins. Her clitoris was aflame and she ground it ever harder against the surrogate penis within her. And it did indeed feel as though she had a penis within her – the hardness in her belly was the warm, throbbing hardness of engorged flesh, not the cold hardness of wood.

Gasping with ecstasy, Mara came to orgasm, her cunt opening and closing like some ethereal starfish upon the wooden shaft. And, as she withdrew, she was startled to see a flood of clear liquid gushing out of her cunt and trickling down her leg. Little droplets of the fluid were still glistening at the tip of the branch, and Mara tasted it. It was sap – the life-fluid of the tree, the spirit's gift to Mara, its supplicant and high priestess.

Warmed by the tree-spirit's gift to her, Mara turned three circles, clockwise, about the base of the trunk and then closed her eyes. Opening them again, she saw the direction she must take; and began to walk deeper into the forest.

* * *

The caravans were grouped together in a clearing in the forest, surrounded by a tumbledown fence of chicken wire and wood. The sign at the gate read: 'Deepdene Holiday Village'. It was illuminated by a single lamp which cast an eerie, yellowish light upon the gateway to the site.

'Maybe I'll find help here,' prayed Mara, hugging herself to keep out the cold and yet still afraid to walk through the gate. 'If I don't, I'll freeze to death in the woods tonight.'

Just inside the entrance to the site stood an unattractive wooden hut covered in peeling green paint. A hand-painted sign read 'Site Office'. A radio or TV was playing, and there was a light behind the dingy curtains.

Trembling, Mara made her way to the door and gave a timid knock. There was no response, so she tried knocking a little harder. After a moment, someone turned the sound down and she heard the sound of footsteps coming towards the door.

The door swung open. Shivering, Mara tried desperately to cover her nakedness; but the eyes were already drinking her in – enjoying her every curve, her every intimacy.

'Well, well – what have we here?'

The two men were in their mid-forties, clad in greasy overalls and smoking cigarettes. One was dark-haired, the other greying at the temples. Both had the look of men too long deprived of female company . . .

Mara's heart sank as she returned their lecherous gaze, wishing she had the courage to turn and run away, back into the forest; she merely stood there, rooted to the spot, shivering and begging for help and comfort. She knew that there would be a price to pay for such comfort: but the desperate do not name their price.

'Please . . . I need help . . . I – I was attacked in the woods,' stammered Mara, substituting a plausible lie for a truth so horrible that her mind seemed to have blocked it out almost completely from her consciousness.

'Come in, darling!' replied the grey-haired man, visibly bulging at the groin as he extended a lascivious paw of a hand to take hold of her shoulder and draw her into the hut. 'There's always room in here for a little darling like you.'

As he drew her inside, she felt his sickly sweet breath on the side of her face, his bear's paw hands brushing lightly against the flesh of her backside. And, in spite of her revulsion, her young woman's body began to awaken to the promise of much-needed human warmth . . .

The door closed behind her and she realised that there was no escape. She was between them now – the grey-haired man in front of her, his mouth agape with ill-disguised lust, and his dark-haired companion bringing up the rear. Already Mara could feel him pressing his burgeoning hardness against the full curve of her tanned backside. And she wanted to run, to scream, to push these monsters away.

And yet, and yet . . . Her treacherous body was awakening, her breath quickening; and it was all she could do to control the rising tide of lust within her. For there is lust sometimes in revulsion: the desire to indulge the most base of impulses, to live only by animal instinct and to find comfort in mindless, shameful pleasure.

The room was shabby, squalid even. A couple of rickety chairs and a Calor gas fire; an ancient black-and-white portable TV in the corner, on which Barbara Windsor was displaying her pneumatic tits in snowstorm effect. Half-eaten sandwiches and a pile of girlie mags on the office counter. The whole scene held a mesmeric quality for Mara, her brain numbed with cold and shock and her body only now beginning to return to a reasonable temperature.

'My, but you look cold,' remarked the dark-haired man, half-whispering the words in her ear. 'But I'm sure we can find a thing or two to warm you up.' And she felt him unfastening the buttons of his overalls, reaching inside, taking out something long and warm and so so hard . . .

'Yes, my dear – let us warm you up,' breathed her grey-haired tormentor, pulling out his own prick. Mara watched in horrified fascination as he began to caress it into impressive rigidity. For it was indeed a magnificent instrument, long and with a fine glistening purple head.

Then, with his prick still hanging out of his trousers, he began to stroke Mara's body, which was already warming in the ferocious heat from the gas fire, not to mention the sudden warmth of a prick thrust into her innocently unsuspecting hands.

'No . . .', moaned Mara, very faintly, as the grey-haired man forced her to wank his prick and began to tease her nipples with his greedy tongue.

But he just laughed; because he and Mara both knew that her resistance was a sham. That she could no more refuse the call of her comfort-starved body than he could stop his member leaping to attention at the sight of her glorious nakedness. He seemed as dazed as she: oblivious to the blood caked dry on her hands, to the mystical symbols and obscenities still painted on her poor, misused flesh.

And his dark-haired accomplice was no less single-minded. He of course had the advantage of surprise, his attack coming suddenly and devastatingly from behind. Without any pretence at preliminaries, he took hold of her softly rounded arse-cheeks and pulled them apart, nudging the tip of his short, thick penis against her arsehole and ramming it home in one, ungentle thrust.

Mara was too dumbstruck to cry out, too aroused to protest. And she found herself thrusting backwards, accepting and even welcoming this uninvited guest, somehow comforted by the rhythm of a stiff prick in her arse. Having her assailant's shaft inside her robbed her of the power of thought; and without thought there could be no sudden, terrifying memories, no pain. Only the slow, in-out, backwards-forwards movement of arse on prick, prick in arse.

As she joined her thrusts to his, the dark-haired man began to groan with pleasure, grasping at her hips and pulling her tightly to him, so that she must take every millimetre of his gift, every drop of his tribute.

The grey-haired man was still forcing Mara to wank his cock, his own hand on hers, dictating the rhythm. The motion was hypnotic, and Mara felt as though she were floating above her own body, looking down on this strange machine composed of cocks and hands and arses and pricks, all mystically joined in a harmony of movement.

The grey-haired man sucked harder at Mara's breast, tweaking her other nipple between finger and thumb. Then his hand left her breast and moved downwards, burrowing into the dark and glossy fur that graced her pubis, entering the warm and secret cave where so many had left their seed.

The touch of his finger on her clitoris awoke Mara to the reality of the situation, and for the first time she began to cry out, half in pleasure, half in anguish: trapped as she was within a spiral of pleasure and degradation.

And it was as though that electrifying touch also awoke the power that lay within the men's pricks for, as she raised her voice to cry out, they felt the spunk rising in their balls and prepared to jettison their foaming cargoes – one in Mara's hand, the other in her arse.

At that moment the door to the hut swung open and the newcomer was treated to the sight of a woman crying out in agony or ecstasy – he could not tell which – and trapped between the bodies of two disgusting middle-aged men.

'Leave her alone!' cried the young man, pushing away her two dazed assailants and seizing Mara by the arm. Then he turned to Mara and spoke gentle words to her: 'Come with me; don't be afraid. It'll be all right, I promise. I won't hurt you.'

Geoffrey Potter was renting a caravan on the Deepdene site in order to finish his novel in peace and quiet, well away from the nagging of his mother, his sister and her three revolting children. The novel was his big chance. He knew it had a good chance of making it big, if only he could finish it . . .

It was a horrible camp site – he'd expected as much when he'd seen the low prices – but it had everything he needed: peace, quiet and a roof over his head. He'd just popped in to the site office for a canister of camping gas, and what had he found? The two louts who worked in the office practically raping a poor naked girl who looked like she'd been through a pretty terrible ordeal already.

Summoning up reserves of chivalric bravery that he had never dreamed he had, Geoffrey had rescued the damsel in distress and brought her back to his caravan. The only question was: what was he to do next?

'Are you OK in there?' he enquired timorously, neck craned towards the tiny shower cabinet which graced the otherwise Spartan van.

'Fine, thank you,' Mara called back. 'I'm so grateful to you for bringing me here. I don't know what would have happened to me if you hadn't come along just at that moment.'

I do, thought Geoffrey, blood boiling with righteous indignation as he thought of those two scoundrels and what they had been doing to this poor girl. Not that he could blame them for desiring her though. She was a most attractive young lady . . . He shivered slightly as he recalled the warmth of her naked skin against his arm as he had half-led, half-carried her back to his van.

At that moment, Mara emerged from the shower cubicle, pink and flushed and clean, the towel wrapped round her torso barely concealing her nipples and the dark, glossy bush of her pubic triangle. She had washed her long black hair and was busily towelling it dry.

She smiled as she saw Geoffrey doing his best not to look at her too closely.

'Don't be shy!' she urged him. 'After all, what is there to see that you haven't already seen?'

True, thought Geoffrey, remembering her magnificent nakedness and wishing profoundly that he didn't.

'And you must have seen dozens of women naked – a good-looking young man like you!' she continued, folding up the towel and hanging it over the rail.

You must be joking, thought Geoffrey gloomily, recollecting that the nearest he'd ever come to losing his virginity had been that time on the works outing when the women from Packing and Despatch had torn down his trousers. And even then, his sister had come along at the crucial moment and spoilt his chances of being ravished.

'Actually . . . no,' replied Geoffrey hoarsely. 'So I hope you won't mind my being a little embarrassed at seeing you . . . well . . .' He blushed crimson, and looked away.

'Naked?' Mara was smiling now, could not resist the irresistible upturn of the corners of her mouth. 'And what is so terrible about my nakedness, pray? Am I so very dreadful to look at?'

'Terrible? Oh no, not terrible at all!' stammered Geoffrey, in complete confusion now. 'I only meant . . .'

'Don't worry. Everything is all right,' Mara soothed him, sitting down beside him on the single bunk bed, and putting her arm around his shoulders. She felt him start at her touch, his breath quickening, his heart racing. 'I'm so very grateful to you; I want you to know that. Let me show you just how grateful.'

And she began to undress him, very gently and slowly, as a mother might undress a beloved child; kissing each inch of his flesh as she exposed it; licking and stroking and loving his body with every ounce of her gratitude.

Geoffrey could scarcely believe his amazing good fortune. Here he was, in a grotty caravan on a seedy camp-site, and now a beautiful young woman was making love to him. A woman was making love to him for the very first time in his young life.

'Lie down now,' breathed Mara, removing the last of Geoffrey's clothes. He had a nice body, she mused: making love to him would not be a chore.

He obeyed, stretching his lithe frame out on the narrow bunk bed, oblivious now to the grubby blankets, the lumpy mattress and the creaking springs beneath him. He gazed up into the clear pools of Mara's violet eyes and longed to drown there: to immerse himself in their liquid light and never more emerge to do battle with the uncharitable world.

Slowly, she began to stroke him from head to toe, missing not an inch of his smooth young body. His flesh had the ivory whiteness of a young noblewoman's, sensitive and cool to the touch, but with a hint of muscle beneath the smooth lines of thigh and forearm and calf. His skin was taut, firm, with a downy covering of very blond hairs: the bloom on a firm, yet ripe and juicy, peach.

'What . . . what are you going to do with me?' gasped Geoffrey, his words barely masking the urgency of his hopes and desires.

'I am going to teach you,' replied Mara softly, running her tongue down his breastbone to the waist, and then turning back to let it twist and turn deliciously about each nipple.

'Teach me? I don't understand . . .'

'I'm going to teach you how to touch a woman. How to caress and kiss and fondle and fuck her. Geoffrey, I am going to teach you how to fuck like a real man.'

And, before he had a chance to say a word, her lips were upon his, stifling his cries, his moans, his sighs. And her tongue was inside his mouth, circling the depths of its moist dark cavern like some lascivious serpent.

At last she withdrew from him, leaving him panting and gasping on the bed. But there was no time for him to catch his breath. For Mara was kissing him more intimately now, running her tongue down his body from waist to thigh, taking the greatest delight in teasing the sensitive flesh of his inner thigh with her lewd tongue.

He groaned appreciatively as her tongue worked its way further in, burrowing its pointed, muscular tip into the fold of his groin. How wonderful, how unimaginably wonderful it felt to have her pleasuring him like this. He thought back to the thousands of times he had resorted to his own fingers and a sordid girlie mag, and a wave of anguish swept over him for all the missed opportunities, all the pretty girls he had left unfucked . . .

But there was no time for remorse now. There were too many new and wondrous sensations to be enjoyed. The sensation of a moist pink tongue on his bollocks, making the little curly hairs stand erect as though straining, like his penis, for release. The sensation of teasing and tormenting fingers, smoothing and awakening his yearning flesh, making his prick rear its head like a fiery thoroughbred longing for the chase.

And now another sensation, even more miraculous: the incredible sensation of a hot, moist mouth bearing down upon the swollen tip of his penis, engulfing it, swallowing it down as a snake gulps down its helpless prey.

And then, slowly and carefully, releasing the prisoner for a fleeting moment, so that the serpent's lithe tongue might circle about the glistening head of the prey and make it long once more for the dark cavern that awaited it.

Slowly and with infinite care, Mara sucked and licked at Geoffrey's prick, judging exactly how far she could take him without precipitating his crisis and bringing a premature end to their innocent game. As her mouth worked upon his shaft, her fingers toyed playfully with his fine, downy bollocks, enjoying their growing heaviness, the way they were tensing up as though gathering all their strength for the final assault, the final push . . . the final spurt of white creamy joy into the abyss of ecstasy.

But Mara had other plans for Geoffrey. Silencing his protests with a kiss, she rolled him onto his side and then lay down in front of him, working her backside against his pelvis so that his straining prick began to nuzzle its way between her arse-cheeks.

As quick as lightning, Mara took hold of Geoffrey's prick and pressed its tip against the entrance to her cunt. With a deft wriggle of her backside, he was inside her, crying out in surprised delight at this wonderful new world of sensations.

'Fuck me, fuck me!' whispered Mara, taking hold of Geoffrey's hands and placing one upon her breast, the other between her thighs. 'And play with me, to give me pleasure, too.'

An eager learner, Geoffrey was quick to comply, tweaking Mara's nipple so deftly that she gasped with pleasure, and working his hand into her most intimate crack so that she cried out loud for the joy of having his finger on her clitoris.

They came together in an explosion of lights and colour and fell asleep still locked together on Geoffrey's bed. When they awoke, they fucked again, first with Geoffrey on top of Mara, and then with Mara astride him like a steed, spurring him on to the peak of ecstasy.

In the morning, they fucked again and then breakfasted together like great friends who have known each other for years. Then Mara put on the clothes which Geoffrey had offered to lend her – a pair of old cords and a jumper – and, bidding him a cheerful farewell, set off in the direction of the nearest village.

When she had gone, Geoffrey sighed and sat down to begin work on his novel once again. Somehow he felt more inspired than he had done for months. Something told him that this novel was going to be a blockbuster.

Out in the depths of the forest, in the shadows which even at noon the sunlight never quite dispels, a dark and evil presence watched Mara set off along the track that led to Devlingham. She would not be quite alone on her journey.

2: Dawning

The Japanese setting was perfect in every last detail. Delgado had worked hard to provide exactly the right ambience in which to welcome Mr Takimoto and his colleagues to Winterbourne. It was so important that they should feel relaxed, at home, off their guard . . .

The Master was well pleased; not only that Takimoto had accepted an invitation to attend one of Winterbourne's orgies, but with life and the world in general. He had not yet quite come to terms with the unbelievable sense of release – for, after nigh-on fifty years of darkness and imprisonment, he was at last free.

And the body he had chosen was also pleasing to him. It amused him greatly to have taken the body of the journalist Andreas Hunt and possessed it, pushing out his puny little soul and condemning him to the same horrible fate which the Allied magicians had imposed on him. It amused him even more to know that he had forced the white witch Mara to obey him, even to the point of plunging the crystal dagger into her own lover's heart. And now here he was inhabiting Hunt's body, delighting in its strength of sinew, its youthfulness, its lusts.

His powers were growing by the minute. Soon they would be infinite. And to what lengths could he then drive the witch Mara in his quest to find and resurrect his lost queen, Sedet?

The Master glanced around the Great Hall, and nodded his approval to Delgado:

'You have done well, yet again,' he smiled. 'Why, I might

almost think I was in some whorehouse in Yokohama. You shall be amply rewarded.'

'There is only one reward I crave,' replied Delgado. There was a hint of pain behind his fanatical eyes. 'And that is to serve you as others do, as an immortal.'

The Master sighed. Delgado was a good servant, a faithful slave with a thousand uses. But it seemed he could not understand that the imperfection of his body marked him out as irredeemably unsuitable for the Master's grandiose schemes. Only the physically perfect or politically influential were fit to be initiated into the new kingdom which he was preparing. Delgado, a mere underling with a twisted leg, would be sadly out of place in such an immaculate world. It was a pity though, for Delgado's soul was an impressively black one, extremely receptive to evil thoughts and seething with lusts which demanded continual satisfaction.

'I shall think on it,' he replied, addressing Delgado once again. 'It is possible that if we can find you another, more suitable body . . .'

There was no time for Delgado to plead or protest, for at that point the Ethiopian Ibrahim entered to tell the Master that the evening's guests were arriving. Takimoto and six of his senior executives from Japan's number-one producer of computer systems, who were currently working on an artificial intelligence project which interested the Master more than a little. Why, the potential for corrupting young minds through the computer screen was infinite and so exciting that his new and vigorous body developed a hard-on straight away.

The Master surveyed the scene. The Great Hall had undergone a radical transformation since the Egyptian orgy at which his growing empire had gained so many new recruits. In place of the hieroglyphics and tomb paintings, the hall had now been decorated in the style of a Japanese villa, divided up with many paper screens and with its own temple and garden. The sunken pool in the centre of the hall was filled with water-lilies, and a little bridge crossed it.

Three naked Japanese maidens sat on the bridge, their tiny feet dangling in the water, combing each other's glossy black hair and toying with each other's bodies as innocently as children exploring the wonderful world of naked flesh.

In the garden, whores in the guise of Japanese noblewomen were walking and talking or sitting on low benches; the only sign of their false nobility the way their kimonos parted at the front as they walked or crossed their legs, revealing smooth, slender limbs naked to the thigh.

The temple area consisted of a three-sided structure, opening onto the hall so that spectators and other participants at the orgy could have a perfect view of what was going on. Inside, a number of shaven-headed young monks were at their devotions and flower-garlanded girls were wafting sweet incense skilfully concocted from aphrodisiac herbs and spices by Madame LeCoeur, Delgado's trusted assistant.

The centrepiece of the scene was the Japanese villa, a large and sprawling structure made entirely of opaque paper screens, within which lights glowed dimly and shadows moved lewdly and sinuously with the promise of delights to come.

Beside the ornamental pool Delgado had arranged an area perfect for a formal tea ceremony, so that the guests could watch all the entertainments around them and still enjoy the tranquil pleasure of this ancient Japanese custom . . . with a difference.

All in all, concluded the Master, Delgado had indeed done well – for a mortal. He nodded to Delgado to proceed.

'Let the ceremonies begin.' Delgado clapped his hands and Madame LeCoeur drew back the exquisite curtain of painted silk which covered the entrance to the hall.

The procession entered the hall: Takimoto and his six henchmen, clad in traditional Japanese robes, followed by seven beautiful oriental maidens, immaculately dressed in kimonos and wooden sandals, with dark formal wigs covering their hair. Their eyes were downcast and they walked with tiny steps, their hands demurely folded before them. There seemed nothing at all improper in this traditional scene. But Delgado smiled to himself, for he knew that there would be surprises in store before the evening was over.

The Japanese businessmen sat cross-legged upon bamboo-leaf matting, which Delgado had had specially imported from Kyoto, and the ceremony began. The Master and Delgado took up positions beside their guests.

Beside each of the businessmen sat a beautiful oriental whore: each one hand-picked by Delgado from the international network of whorehouses which he had built up throughout Europe, North Africa and the Far East. They had beautiful faces, knowing fingers and a love of the most perverse sexual practices; and Delgado was confident that they would prove pleasing to these transitory masters.

The paper screen slid across to reveal three more girls. The first was clad in traditional dress, and carried the equipment necessary for the tea ceremony, whilst the other two carried stringed musical instruments rather like lutes. They were also quite naked, apart from little bead necklaces and anklets. The businessmen stared at them open-mouthed, bulges appearing already in the front of their robes; and their female companions began, very slowly, to caress them – at first through the silken fabric, but then growing bolder and slipping tiny, delicate hands through the front of their robes and searching out their eager penises.

The two musicians began to play, and their companion set about serving tea to her illustrious guests in the most delightfully formal way imaginable. As she knelt before Takimoto and bowed before him, he could not help noticing that her kimono was rather loose at the front and afforded him an excellent view of the rosebud breasts within.

In silence, the businessmen strove to maintain their distance and dignity, even though the handmaids' delicate caresses were driving their engorged pricks to distraction.

They began to fantasise about fucking these little temptresses with the doe eyes and succulent lips, who knew how to drive their masters wild with the merest touch, or the hint of a sidelong glance from beneath long, sweeping eyelashes.

For the Master, too, this was a tormenting experience. After so long trapped in darkness, within a useless body, he was hungry for sensations; hungry for the taste of a woman's cunny, for the soft moist delight of her belly, the heavenly hell of her arse. He too longed to throw down the girls, one by one, upon the hard floor and abuse them, fuck them till they cried out for mercy and not listen. Never listen. Never show mercy. Only fuck, fuck until their life's energies flowed into him and they lay spent beneath him, whilst he grew stronger and more invincible by the second.

And the Japanese had, after all, been promised an orgy . . .

'I grow impatient,' remarked Takimoto at last. 'This is a passing imitation of our Japanese tea ceremony, and the girls are comely enough; but I am disappointed by the extent of the entertainments you have provided. Were we not promised more than this, Mr LeMaitre?'

The Master nodded graciously and smiled.

'I fear I must have misled you,' he replied, his smooth, melodious voice like a silken garotte about their throats. 'For this is but the beginning of our night's entertainment. These girls are here merely to amuse, to titillate, to awaken your appetites and your senses, so that you may more fully enjoy what follows next. If you will graciously allow me, I shall show you some more little scenes of . . . artistic merit . . . which I feel sure will delight you.'

Mollified, Takimoto nodded; and unfastened the front of his robe so that his whore might more easily handle and stimulate his penis as he watched.

At a nod from Delgado, the fun began.

One of the naked girls on the bridge over the pool sighed and stretched her arms in a parody of boredom.

'Oh, I am so weary,' she sighed. 'I do so wish the Lord

Koto would come to us and fuck us.'

'Ah yes,' sighed one of her companions. 'It is wearisome being the Lord Koto's whores when he has so many other women to pleasure.'

'Then can we not make our own pleasure?' suggested the third girl. 'May we not pleasure each other, to lighten the burden of our wearisome days?'

The other girls seemed to think this an admirable idea; and the first girl immediately fell to kissing the second warmly upon the lips, whilst her hands strayed to her breasts, teasing the pert little nipples into stiffness whilst grinding her own pelvis against her sister's.

The third girl, no doubt feeling rather left out of the proceedings, came up behind the first and began to run her tongue over her back and buttocks, an action which drew the most lascivious moans from her sister whore. Then she pulled apart the girl's buttocks and wriggled her tongue into her arsehole, causing the girl to cry out in surprise and delight.

'Oh, do it to me!' she cried, her eyes widening with incredulity and pleasure. 'Do it to me, put your fingers inside me!'

Her sister whore obeyed promptly, licking two fingers as lasciviously as if she were taking a man's cock into her mouth; and then ramming them unceremoniously into the girl's cunt from behind, causing still more moans and sighs of pleasure.

Meanwhile, the first girl was now licking and biting the girl's nipples, whilst her right hand had strayed further down, and was toying with her glossy black pubic bush, winding the curly black strands about her fingers and pulling hard enough to draw sharp little cries of pain from her willing victim. Then, emboldened by her own and the girl's desires, the whore pulled apart her victim's protruberant cunt-lips and sought out her clitoris, pinching and rubbing it so skilfully that the poor girl quickly came to her crisis and felt a great flood of cunt-juice inundating her thighs.

The businessmen, previously so impassive, seemed most interested in this picturesque little scene on the bridge, and willingly lent their pricks to the skilful ministrations of the handmaids who knelt to handle them with the loving attention of true enthusiasts. Delgado was very proud of the fact that all his whores were as perverted as their clients: no girl came to work at Winterbourne who did not dearly love to lend her body to the vilest and most imaginative perversions.

Not that they had to work particularly hard: for the aphrodisiac concoction which Madam LeCoeur had instructed to be mixed with the green tea was already having its desired effect – producing impressive erections which would not soften for many hours, no matter how many orgasms the subject might enjoy.

The Master required no whore to handle his cock: he had already unzipped his trousers and was manipulating it with true delight – the delight of one who has but recently awoken to discover he has been given the wonderful gift of a new and enthusiastic body.

And the best of it all was that Andreas Hunt's old body, now the home of the Master's evil, immortal soul, had become heir to all the powers which had formerly belonged to the Master: the power to travel astrally; to assume another form; to influence minds and abuse bodies and endow its victims with the same living death which the Master had enjoyed for so long. And more than this: the power to fuck endlessly, to come to orgasm once, twice, a thousand times and never tire. Life – or was it death? – was getting better all the time.

As the three naked girls on the bridge dived into the lily-strewn waters of the pool, there to continue their lascivious games, attentions were shifted towards the rock garden, where the two lovely noblewomen were engaged in ladylike pursuits – reading, walking, talking, playing Go. It was an idyllic scene, almost silent but for the sound of birdsong.

What could possibly happen to interrupt the calm of this peaceful Japanese idyll?

A series of blood-curdling cries rent the air and the silken curtain was once again wrenched back, to reveal three outlandish figures: three Samurai warriors, in full battle costume. They were magnificent, their muscles rippling beneath their armour as they strode into the hall, their swords held aloft above their heads.

Seeing these new intruders, the noble ladies forgot their gentle pursuits and, screaming, sought to run away. But their assailants were too swift for them, pursuing them and capturing them in seconds.

'Mercy, mercy!' cried the taller of the two women, clad in a yellow kimono embroidered with multi-coloured dragons. As she knelt before her captors, her skirt parted to reveal two delectable naked thighs and the shadowy suggestion of a dark triangle. No underwear . . .

'We shall show you no mercy,' replied the leader of the Samurai raiding party. 'You are our prize and we shall do with you exactly as we please.' With a swift, swishing movement of his sword, he slit the yellow kimono from neck to hem, slicing through the cummerbund which held it tight beneath her breasts; and the cut fabric fell in tatters to the ground. She was then bound hand and foot, and cast onto the ground to watch what the attackers would do to her companion.

Seeing what was happening, the second lady attempted to escape: but her attackers threw her face down to the ground and pulled her blue kimono up around her waist, exposing the prettiest pair of rounded buttocks for all to see. The watching businessmen nodded appreciatively, and one of them came in a flood of pearly white seed, just at the sight of so much beautiful naked flesh. To his amazement, within a few moments he was hard and yearning again, and his handmaid recommenced her ministrations with renewed vigour.

As the lady squirmed upon the gravel of the rock garden, the leader of the Samurai signalled to his companions to hold her down. Taking a bamboo cane from his belt, he flexed it approvingly, took aim and brought it down upon the lady's backside. This evidently caused her much pain, and she leapt up – but was forced back down onto the gravel by the two Samurai. Looking on, the Master felt the spunk boiling in his balls, and forced himself to hold back for a little while so that he could enjoy the full pleasure of the lady's humiliation.

The bamboo cane whipped down again and again against the lady's soft flesh, and she cried out lustily and twisted and turned with all her might; but her tormentors held her fast and nothing she could do would allow her to escape from the hail of blows. Her poor backside grew redder and redder. And then a miraculous thing happened. The lady stopped struggling and her cries became gradually quieter, until at last they became a low moaning which might have been construed as the soft murmuring of a creature in ecstasy.

For the vicious searing of her backside had begun to be transformed into the deep, exciting warmth of carnal desire, radiating out from the centre of her being to inflame cunt and arse, and make the lady's nipples stiffen and her breath quicken. She began to wriggle her legs apart, little by little, until there was an appreciable gap between her thighs – a gap amply wide enough to admit a bamboo cane . . .

How she started and cried out as her Samurai warrior thrust his bamboo cane into her cunt, as lustily as any true swordsman might run his opponent through with his well-honed weapon. And she writhed again, but this time she was endeavouring to impale herself more completely upon the bamboo shaft which was invading her soft wet cunt.

'Whore!' cried the warrior. 'Thou art no lady! Thou art a little slut who likes nothing better than for a stranger to violate her upon the stones of her husband's garden!'

Taking off his armour, he began to strip for the fray. His body was quite magnificent: well-muscled and glistening with the fragrant oils Madame LeCoeur had massaged into his flesh before the ceremony – secret, exotic oils which had their own very special function in hardening the prick and prolonging sensual pleasure.

His prick was beautiful, too: a full eight inches long and curving proudly upwards as though it were some deadly eastern scimitar.

Once naked, he signalled to his companions and they turned over the lady so that her legs were splayed wide apart, displaying the priceless treasures of her cunt to the watching businessmen. She gave token resistance, but her captors were implacable and overwhelmingly strong. Kneeling between her thighs, the Samurai leader gave a mighty thrust and rammed his cock into her, ensuring that at the same time he pushed a finger up her arse to make his ascendancy over her complete.

Thus humiliated and degraded, she lay still upon the ground and suffered the thrusts of the Samurai's prick, feeling its hardness opening her up and wetting her despite herself; and she came with a great cry of anguish, inundating him and triggering off his own orgasm.

Meanwhile, the taller woman, who had already been stripped of her kimono, lay helpless upon the ground, watching in horrified fascination as her companion was abused and fucked before her. She now saw the warriors turning their attentions towards her once again, and cried out in terror as she saw that their leader's prick was already returning to its former rigidity, his balls swinging heavy and hypnotic between his well-muscled thighs.

Still bound hand and foot, she found herself hauled to her knees, and forced to kneel there with her hands tied behind her back. Before she had time to wonder what her tormentors intended to do with her next, she felt cruel fingers prising apart her lips and something hard and salty being forced into her mouth.

Try as she might, she could not free herself of the prick which had so lately been toiling inside her companion's cunt, and which was now forcing its way down her throat, half choking her.

She was forced to suck upon it, nonetheless; and was rewarded for her efforts with a flood of milky white semen which she had to fight hard to swallow, so abundant was the tide.

If she had thought this was the end of her torment, she was soon to be disabused. For the other two Samurai were undressing now, exposing their equally magnificent bodies and cocks which were nothing if not eager for the fray. Their weapons were unsheathed and glistening, and it only remained for them to dispute who should have her first. Since neither would concede that right to the other, the solution was clear: they must take her together.

Takimoto and his aides watched in delighted silence as the whores rubbed their pricks, gently but so arousingly, whilst they were treated to the spectacle of an apparently high-born lady, being laid down on her side on a rough gravel path so that two magnificently endowed Samurai warriors could violate her cunt and arse with their spunk-filled pricks.

'Most satisfactory,' was the only comment Takimoto allowed himself as the warriors gave a final thrust into the girl and the spunk overflowed and ran down her abused flesh. 'Do you have other entertainments for us?'

The Master smiled:

'My dear Takimoto-san,' he breathed in a voice as seductive as double cream. 'The night is young; the entertainments have only just begun. First you shall watch, so that you are at the peak of arousal; and then you yourselves shall become part of this great pageant which we have created to serve your needs and desires.'

He nodded again to Delgado, who signalled to the monks in the temple that this part of the orgy should now begin.

The temple was an ornate structure which had taken weeks to design and construct, decorated with erotic pictures taken from Japanese mythology. Before the altar knelt two shaven-headed monks in saffron robes, the bare flesh of their shoulders oiled and supple.

Before the temple danced a troupe of lithe young girls, clad in diaphanous veils and with their white-powdered faces garishly painted to represent the heads of mythical beasts. Their bodies were small-boned and slender, their breasts like rosy bobbing apples behind their gauzy robes. They performed their dance before the Master's illustrious guests – a knowing dance, in which they exposed their bodies in a series of lewd, sinuous movements calculated both to inspire and to excite.

Takimoto and his henchmen watched entranced, their eyes glazing over with lust unsatisfied, lust which demanded its price. Lust which would serve the Master very well . . .

Dancing into the temple, the girls began to remove their veils one by one, letting them flutter to the ground like the many-hued leaves of a tree as the autumn breeze catches its branches. The monks knelt silent and still at their devotions, their heads bowed as though in mute reverence.

But the dancing girls had other plans for them. Their leader, a tall, willowy girl with her face painted to resemble a dragon-beast, came towards the monks and addressed them:

'Brothers, will you not rise and do battle with us? For we are the demons of lust and you must overcome us if you are to attain true spiritual perfection.'

The monks turned round and replied:

'You cannot overcome us, unclean spirits. For we are pure of heart. We accept your challenge.'

At this, the dancing demons seemed greatly pleased; and they swooped down upon the hapless monks, plucking at their robes and in a moment undressing them. Then, as if from nowhere, they produced disciplines with supple leather thongs, which they used upon the monks' backs and buttocks.

'Mortification of the flesh!' breathed the dragon-woman, fire in her eyes as she brought the whip down once again upon the proffered flesh. 'Only through the path of suffering shall you attain purity!' And she laughed wildly as she chastised her victims with the cruel discipline.

At last, the monks slumped to the ground, breathing

heavily and their flesh reddened from the lash. The dancers rolled them over onto their backs, and it was plain to see that they were not indifferent to their punishment. Indeed, they were most eager for it to continue, to judge by the turgid state of their pricks.

And the dancing demons fell upon them with lips and fingers and teeth, teasing and tormenting and exciting their flesh until they could take no more. They lay broken before their tormentors, panting and moaning as their cocks strained for release. And the demon-dancers laughed to see such sport, such humiliation of the holy and the pure.

Two of the dancers straddled the monks, taking their hard pricks easily into their well-greased cunts – for Madame LeCoeur had prepared them well for this lavish display, douching their intimate parts with sweet and aromatic oils which mingled now with the ready moistness of their own desire. Other dancers sat astride their faces, forcing them to smell their heady fragrance and lap up the sweet and abundant juices as they cascaded out of their cunnies. The remaining demon-dancers fell upon each other with cries of lust, licking and biting at each other's flesh, probing deep into secret places with fingers and practised tongues.

And the watching Japanese businessmen observed with impassive faces, though their cocks told a very different story: twitching and spurting forth their pearly foaming tribute again and again, only to return almost instantly to a state of rigidity so painful that the only way to relieve it was to come once again . . .

And to their silent ecstasy were added the shrill, agonised cries of the monks, ravished so perfectly that at last their pricks fell into flaccidity upon their tormented loins, for even Madame LeCoeur's alchemy could not last for ever.

The delightful pageant over, the dancers and their victims lay panting upon the temple floor, wave upon wave of incense wafting through the Great Hall until the watchers' brains grew dulled, their thoughts confused by the overwhelming tide of lust which was filling their bodies, driving them to one single thought, one single impulse: they must fuck, fuck, fuck and be fucked – and if they fucked until they died, that would not be long enough to quench the lusts which had taken over their minds and bodies.

The Master looked on, well satisfied. For in the glazed expressions of Takimoto and his aides, he read what he had hoped to read: the abandonment of control, the loss of will, the total victory of lust over reason. Now he could make his move.

'Takimoto-san,' he breathed in the businessman's ear. 'Let me show you the next part of our entertainment. I promise you that it is more exciting, more satisfying than everything you have seen so far.'

'And shall I . . . shall I fuck?' gasped Takimoto, his erect penis sliding rhythmically between the silken fingers of the lotus-eyed girl still kneeling beside him.

The Master smiled. When he smiled, his face was transformed utterly: he was no longer the living image of Andreas Hunt. For his was a smile imbued with the most radiant, flawless, magnificent evil.

'You shall know the most exquisite pleasure,' he replied. And he did not lie. His only sin was the sin of omission. 'Come with me.' And, signalling to the geishas to bring the other guests, he took Takimoto's hand and led him towards the mysterious geisha house, whose inner shadows seemed to gather together expectantly as the little procession wended its way towards the door.

They entered the house and the panel slid shut behind them, leaving them apparently alone, in an empty room. But there were dancing shadows around them, in the rooms beyond, like the phantasms created by a mind enslaved by unstoppable but unattainable desires. The Master guided Takimoto until he found himself standing in front of an apparently blank and featureless screen wall.

'I . . . do not understand,' stammered Takimoto, his shaft throbbing now with the pain of denied release, for his geisha companion was highly skilled in the games of love.

'Strike three times upon the gong,' replied the Master, handing Takimoto a wooden drumstick, padded at one end. Uncomprehending, Takimoto obeyed, striking the stick three times against the tiny gong which stood beside the screen.

As the last reverberations died away, a small panel slid across in the centre of the screen, and a pair of hands appeared. They were tiny hands, exquisitely manicured and with long, painted nails, each one bearing a miniature erotic picture in the traditional Japanese style. The hands took hold of Takimoto's straining prick and pulled him gently towards the screen, so that his prick passed through the panel and into the unseen world beyond.

The inscrutable mask falling away, Takimoto gasped out his delight as soft, moist lips fastened about his prick and a hot, muscular tongue flashed across the tip of his yearning hardness.

'Suck me . . .' he breathed; but his unseen fellatrice needed no instruction. She was already working upon him with all the skill and devotion of a high priestess, her lips and tongue stroking and moistening his shaft whilst her exquisite hands lavished knowing caresses upon his balls.

She seemed to know all the arts of love; all the ways to bring a man to the very brink of orgasm and hold him there, refusing to allow him the mercy of release. And surely therein lay her power, her delight: to have a man in the palms of her hands, the soft wet cave of her mouth; and to know that he was hers to reprieve or to condemn as her fancy took her.

Takimoto knew that he was in the woman's power but he no longer cared. His arrogance had deserted him. He was no longer anything more than a throbbing prick, a bundle of sensations begging to be allowed expression.

And when, at last, she pressed the tip of her perfect tongue a little harder into the weeping eye of his prick, he came to a huge and shuddering orgasm with all the gratitude of a penitent whose soul has been spared damnation. He could have wept for joy. If only he had known what awaited him next he might have wept for very different reasons . . .

As his crisis ebbed away, the screen slid back and Takimoto saw with horrified realisation the whore who had brought him to such a crescendo of pleasure: not, as he had thought, a beautiful woman, but a beautiful boy: a naked boy with kohl-rimmed eyes and painted fingernails, with a thrusting prick and such sharp teeth . . .

Weakened and dazed by his orgasm and by the aphrodisiac drugs, Takimoto had neither the will nor the strength to save himself as the boy's teeth buried themselves in his groin. Strange how he felt no pain. Strange how a dark strength seemed to seep into him like storm clouds pushing back the sun. Stranger still how he welcomed the transformation . . .

Before they had quite realised what was happening to their leader, Takimoto's companions heard the gentle swish of paper screens sliding back, and turned – too late – to find that they were surrounded by the most exquisite of oriental whores: the most beautiful and skilled that Winterbourne could offer. Almond-eyed women with pert breasts and flat bellies, their glossy pubic hair scented with aphrodisiac oils; and the prettiest of boys, slender-framed with delicate hands and heavy balls, surmounted by arrogant, curving pricks.

Why, so bedazzled were they by this feast of nubile flesh, that Takimoto's companions hardly noticed the sharp little teeth behind the rosy red lips, the pure and exultant evil behind the Master's ingratiating smile.

The sudden surge of energy hit him like a bolt of lightning, as though someone had suddenly flicked on his consciousness like a light-switch.

Oh my God, thought Andreas Hunt. Where am I? Who am I?

What am I?

He couldn't see, couldn't hear, couldn't move – no matter how hard he tried to, his body wouldn't respond.

And was it his body? No, don't be bloody daft, of course it was his body. And if it wasn't, whose was it, for fuck's sake?

He was panicking. Mustn't panic. Got to work this one out rationally. You're a journo, remember? Don't lose your cool now, Hunt, you old bastard.

What happened? He couldn't quite remember. Wait a minute though . . . He remembered the big house – Winterbourne, that was it. He'd come to rescue Mara. And he'd found her, at last, but there was something wrong with her, he couldn't get through to her. And suddenly there was a sharp pain in his chest and . . . nothing.

Just the fear. The darkness. The wondering.

Mara. She had looked so afraid, so . . . different. He knew she was in terrible danger. He must help her. But how? He didn't even know where he was. Maybe he was dead. But he didn't feel dead. He felt alive and if not kicking, well, bloody angry anyway.

There was just one question that kept on nagging at him. His body. What had happened to his body? Because he couldn't feel it. He couldn't feel anything except the pain. The pain of being imprisoned within a body that wouldn't respond, wouldn't do his bidding, wouldn't even let him see or feel or hear, for pity's sake! A body that, for some unaccountable reason, just didn't seem to fit . . .

There it was again: a sudden surge of energy, like plugging your fingers into the mains and feeling the electricity fizzing and bubbling through them.

Hunt couldn't feel his fingers, though. Maybe they weren't his fingers anyway.

As the energy surged through him again, he wondered in anguish what was happening to him, if this was perhaps some message to him from Mara, Mara in trouble, Mara needing him desperately and he wasn't there. Mara with the luscious breasts and delectable thighs and warm, wet, welcoming cunt . . .

'Mara!' he screamed. And he wondered if she would ever be able to hear him again.

* * *

'I still don't understand why we have to bring these foreigners into it,' grumbled Sir Anthony Cheviot, sitting down in the comfortable leather armchair and parting his legs so that Madelon could suck his cock more easily. She was pinching his bollocks quite delightfully, such a talented girl . . .

'I don't quite understand either,' agreed Meredith Parry-Evans, his hands thoughtfully caressing the blonde head of the girl who was fellating him. 'I thought we were going to keep this strictly to ourselves.'

'Have you no imagination?' replied the Master, whose cock was already halfway down the delectable throat of Anastasia Dubois, currently his favourite whore and certainly an enthusiastic one: keen, but with that touch of aristocratic hauteur which flattered his self-importance. Her tongue, her lips, her fingers . . . all felt diabolically good on his new and vigorous flesh. He gave a sigh of resignation and continued: 'The global power which we seek to achieve will only be ours through diligence and cunning. With Takimoto's artificial intelligence corporation at our disposal, we shall have the potential to control millions through the power of the computer screen.

'You are men who have both achieved a certain . . . pre-eminence in your own country,' the Master went on, urging Anastasia to ever-faster movements of her pretty little tongue across the tip of his agreeably turgid prick. 'And power excites you – you cannot deny it. Whether it be the power of a tyrant over his subjects or of a libertine over his favourite whore, it matters not. What matters is the immense pleasure of the power itself: the way it swells your prick to see terror in the eyes of those who must obey you.

'Imagine then, if you will, the satisfaction you will experience when this, my kingdom, extends across every continent, and there is no authority but mine: an authority in which you, as my trusted followers, shall share. Now that Takimoto and his colleagues have been initiated into our cause, we are one great step nearer to achieving our aims. This time, I shall not fail.'

It felt good to talk of such things. Meredith Parry-Evans gasped with the anticipation of orgasm as the Master graciously filled his obedient mind with pictures of a new world of infinite darkness: a world in which he, Parry-Evans, would be responsible for dispensing pleasure and pain. Cheviot, whose tastes were rather less straightforward, contemplated the exquisite enjoyment to be had in a regime which would allow him to be both the master and the slave, the torturer and the victim.

Reading into the foetid darkness of Cheviot's perverse imaginings, the Master smiled and bestowed upon him a deliciously vivid vision: Cheviot saw himself standing in a dimly lit dungeon, as naked as the woman before him, held by chains spreadeagled across the damp stone wall. He was whipping her naked flesh with a bundle of birch twigs, and with each shrill cry he felt his prick grow harder and more eager for the fray. Most delicious of all, a naked girl in leather mask and spike-heeled thigh boots was kneeling before him, sinking her glossy red talons into the tender flesh of his testicles, and preparing to take his prick into the depths of her hungry mouth.

The pleasure of the pain was so enormous that Cheviot felt his spunk rising and groaned in ecstasy as it pumped out in great white gobbets onto Madelon's waiting tongue.

The Master grabbed Anastasia's head and forced her to take his prick deep into her throat as he came to a thundering, seismic orgasm; shuddering slightly but giving no other outward sign of his immense enjoyment. He heard the girl give a low growl of pleasure as she tasted his sex-fluid and knew that, like him, Anastasia was still basking in the invigorating energies which had been released during the Japanese orgy.

The businessmen had provided the Master and his followers not only with an entertaining diversion – how he had laughed to see the blood spurting out of Takimoto's groin as the boy-whore bit into him, bestowing upon him that most precious gift, the kiss of death – but also a supply of the sexual energy which was so vital to their continued growth and ultimate victory.

Cheviot and Parry-Evans left for the House of Commons, to take part in an important vote. That evening, on the Master's instructions, several more influential MPs would receive a personal invitation to one of Winterbourne's very special entertainments. It was happening at last. The Master's powers, so long dormant, were beginning to fulfil their true potential. And, now that he had come into possession of Andreas Hunt's fine young body, there could be nothing in the whole world powerful enough to withstand the force of his will. The realisation of his ambitions, the satisfaction of his appetite for power: all were within sight now.

But there was one ambition which craved fulfilment above all others; and that was the Master's desire to renew his sacred union with his chosen queen, the Egyptian priestess Sedet, who had been so cruelly sacrificed to a hell of living death four thousand years ago.

For a few brief moments, when his soul had entered Delgado's body, the white witch Mara had brought his queen to him, for Sedet's soul had possessed Mara's body; and through the sexual agency of their stolen bodies they had once again enjoyed the ecstatic mingling of their evil souls.

But the glory and passion had been short-lived. Too soon, Sedet had been called back to her imprisonment, and he had lost her once again. Without her, his rule would be incomplete. He must find her. But still he knew not where her body lay, between life and death; for the spell which had bound her had also masked her from his sight. Sometimes, he could hear her soundless screaming, echoing across the astral plane.

The only way to find his queen was through Mara, he knew that now. Only she had the gift of sight, the psychic powers necessary to the quest. And now he had discovered, to his delight, how responsive she could be to the skilful touch of a true Master . . .

He smiled grimly to himself. It would not be easy to

manipulate the witch, for her powers were almost a match for his own. But he would use her and obtain what he craved; and then he would break her, as easily as he might break an inconsequential little whore who had displeased him. Already, he had experienced the delight of forcing her to plunge the crystal dagger into her own lover's heart – the fatal thrust which had damned Andreas Hunt to the crystal tomb, and freed his strong young body for a worthier guest.

But the pain of Mara's gradual realisation was as nothing compared to the pain that she would suffer when the Master had used her and cast her aside. Why, the delightful prospect of her future sufferings was so potent an image that the Master felt his prick swelling in delicious anticipation; and he called to Anastasia Dubois to come and part her sleek white thighs, so that he might slide his hardness into her wet and willing cunt.

'Mara!'

Mara awoke with a start, to find that she was lying on a sofa, naked and only half-covered by the blankets, most of which had slipped to the floor during what must have been a turbulent few hours' sleep. Afternoon sunshine was filtering weakly through the light chintz curtains.

A moment's confusion and then she recalled the encounter with Geoffrey, her walk to the village and the friendly village constable and his wife who had taken her in, offering her their sofa to sleep on until she felt strong enough to tell them the rest of her tale.

Constable Donaldson had been particularly kind to her, and she had almost begun to feel safe with him. Noticing the constable's obvious interest in her body, she had even been prompted to offer him her favours in return for his kindness.

But he had hushed her and told her to concentrate on assembling the details of her story. If she could only remember what they were . . .

Why had she awoken so suddenly? She could have sworn

she heard a voice calling her name, calling to her desperately, as though in terrible agony.

The voice of her lover, Andreas Hunt.

But Andreas Hunt was dead.

Shivering with sudden cold, Mara gathered the blankets around her shoulders and tried to coax some warmth back into her frozen limbs. It was odd, really. There was a fire roaring away in the grate, the sun was shining through the window . . . and yet the room seemed in the grip of a preternatural coldness which owed nothing to defective central heating . . .

'Mara!' This time, the voice was so loud that it seemed to explode inside her head in a sunburst of pain and bright lights. She shook her head, convinced that grief was playing games with her head, muddling her psychic powers. But the voice echoed on inside her head, and the confusion of lights began to resolve itself into a picture.

A picture of a big house, dark and sinister against the evening sky. Of a naked girl, her flesh torn and bruised, crossing the threshold and entering into the darkness within. Entering into something unspeakably evil.

And another picture, very brief this time: little more than a snapshot. A picture of a tall man with a crystal dagger protruding from his chest, glinting blood-red as it caught the last rays of the setting sun. A glimpse of Andreas Hunt, standing before the door of the great house and beckoning to her, his mouth opening in silent supplication: 'Mara!'

With a great rush of agonised realisation, Mara remembered Winterbourne Hall and what had happened to her there – the ways in which Delgado had abused her body; the ways in which the Master had manipulated her psychic powers; and worst of all, the ceremony at which he had tricked her into taking up the crystal dagger and . . .

Forced her to kill Andreas Hunt.

The rest, she did not understand. Somehow nothing else mattered very much. If Andreas really was calling out to her from beyond death, then she must somehow find a way to answer his call.

* * *

'The woman Mara has left for London, sir. I thought you'd want to know.'

'Thank you, Constable Donaldson,' replied the Master. 'You have done well.'

This helpless young woman was no match for the awesome power of the Master. He summoned Ibrahim and watched him ram his magnificent ten-inch penis into a succession of pretty boys and girls, delighting in the growing heaviness in his own balls. Takimoto would be arriving soon, and the Master looked forward to watching Ibrahim fuck him, too. Why, he might even join in.

Things were looking good.

3: Heimdal

Mara closed the door of the flat wearily behind her and went into the bathroom to wash her face. A discarded sock hung limply over the side of the bath, reminding Mara of that last crazy evening when they had pounced on each other like wild beasts in the rutting season. That was one of the great things about Andreas Hunt: he might be less than enthusiastic about washing his socks, but he was never half-hearted about sex.

The empty whisky bottles; the half-eaten peanut-butter sandwich, now curling at the edges; the girlie mag lying open at a sex aids advert . . . all details that made it seem impossible that Andreas Hunt would not be coming home.

Despite the melancholy jumble of Hunt's possessions, Mara felt better, surrounded by his things. They reinforced the feeling she had – the feeling that Hunt's death might not be quite as final as it seemed. It didn't make sense – once you're dead, you're dead, Hunt would have scoffed – but that's how it felt. Mara knew she had to get some expert help.

Exhausted from the events of the last twenty-four hours, Mara went into the bedroom, undressed and lay down on the bed where she and Andreas had enjoyed such enthusiastic sex so often. The sheets still bore the heavy scent of that last night's lovemaking. She recalled the feeling of his beautiful stiff cock burrowing into her, his fingers skilfully teasing her clitoris to another orgasm, and another . . .

The memory of fucking with Andreas was so powerful that Mara closed her eyes and tried to imagine that he was there. With a little effort of imagination she could really believe he was lying on the bed beside her, his hot eager flesh touching hers, his breath urgent in her ear:

'Want to fuck?'

And already, without waiting for her so-predictable yes, Andreas was upon her, his lips fastening on her right nipple whilst his fingers toyed with the left. He knew how much she loved him to play with her breasts – it made her crazy with lust for him, sent her cunt-juices into overdrive. She could feel the familiar prickling sensation just before her clitoris began to swell into a taut pink flowerbud, as sweet and firm and juicy as any fragrant young rose.

'Fuck me, Andreas, fuck me . . .' Her lips formed the words instinctively. She could feel his arms about her now, his hands stroking her large firm breasts, tracing the generous curve that led from breast to tiny waist and flaring out again into womanly hips. With her own fingers she simulated the sensation of Andreas's touch, caressing her in ways that were known only to them.

A hand insinuated itself between her thighs, moving slowly and slyly upwards until at last the edge of the palm lay against her dark and fragrant curls. It pressed so insistently that she sighed with pleasure and, smiling, parted her legs to make room for its incursions.

Fingers; bold, exploring fingers that opened up the petals of her blossom and revealed its pulsating heart: a trembling pistil waiting for the male to come and fertilise it. The butterfly touch of fingertips now, and then something even subtler: his tongue. Andreas was licking her clitty, and she was laughing and shouting now; shouting at him to stop – no, never to stop, for she wanted this exquisite agony to go on for ever.

And at last, his low, lustful growl as he climbed astride her, his prick knowing instinctively where to find its home: one hard thrust and he was inside her, fucking her like no one else had ever fucked her in her life.

With one finger on her clitty and the other inside her hot, wet cunt, Mara frigged herself to a warm, expansive orgasm that seemed to last for ever, each successive wave carrying her a little further out to sea; until at last she came crashing back on the final breaker that left her washed up on the shore, dizzy and helpless with pleasure.

Opening her eyes, she was at once transported back to the reality of an empty bed, a lonely pillow, an empty space – and a gaping cunt which yearned for a stiff prick to end its loneliness. Her thoughts turned to the recurring dream which had started just before she awoke in the wood, and which returned now every time she fell asleep: a dream of fucking the unspeakably evil creature she knew only as the Master.

She knew that it must be some kind of warning: her psychic powers telling her to be careful, to beware endangering herself; for she sensed that, if Andreas had met a terrible fate, her own escape had been achieved more through luck than design. And yet – what could the Master possibly want of her now? He had tricked and abused her and succeeded in getting what he wanted. Surely she was safe from now on . . .

She showered and washed her long dark hair. As she dabbed the towel over her wet skin, she eyed herself critically in the mirror. The ordeal of the last few days had left a few marks upon her flesh – bruises on her arms and thighs where the guards had handled her roughly; a few scratches on her legs and sore feet from her trek through the woods; but the woman with the extraordinary violet eyes who gazed back at her was still the same Mara Fleming who had merrily fucked her way from Glastonbury to Stonehenge a dozen times and left her men wanting more.

Mara had always lived life according to her own rules. She wasn't going to start playing by someone else's now. She had a score to settle with the Master, and if there was any way that she could help Andreas, she was going to find it out and do it – no matter what the danger or the cost to herself.

Pulling her dark green velvet cape tighter about her shoulders, Mara stepped out of the front door of the apartment block and into the watery autumn sunshine.

Jürgen Kaas lived the sort of playboy lifestyle that was more typical of pop singers and film stars than psychics. When not away at his country mansion, he held court in his Notting Hill pied-à-terre – two Georgian mews cottages knocked into one – and boasted at least one princess among the wealthy and famous who beat a regular path to his door.

Kaas – or Heimdal, as he was known professionally – was a millionaire psychic with an even more lucrative sideline: his own unique brand of psychic sex-therapy. Bored housewives whose rich husbands were too tired to raise more than a smile; couples whose sex lives had lost their spark . . . Heimdal received them all with a smile and a promise to help them – for a fee.

It was congenial work. Some astrological mumbo-jumbo, a ceremony with crystals and incense; and then he would get down to some serious screwing, which was really all they wanted from him. It was a pity really seeing as, ironically enough, he did have some genuine psychic ability.

But, let's face it, he did have a beautiful cock. Long and thick, even in repose, it twitched at the merest thought of sex and swelled into a mighty wand of which any magician would be proud.

Heimdal stood before the mirror and gloried in his own nakedness. A blond giant well above six feet, his broad shoulders and well-formed muscles testified to successful careers in professional wrestling and modelling before he had found his true vocation. He smiled as he slid the palm of his hand down his hard, well-toned stomach and under his testicles, which were large and heavy and hung low between his stocky thighs.

He cradled his bollocks and enjoyed the growing sense of heaviness in his loins as he recalled the job he had once had in a Hamburg nightclub, where he had been billed as 'Heimdal the Destroyer' – a key role in the midnight sex show. It had been easy work. All he had been asked to do was what he did best: fucking.

Just before midnight a circular space was cleared in the middle of the dance-floor. This served as a stage, and some small attempt at scenery was made: a few cardboard mountains and a little Astroturf helped to create the overall impression of some fairly vague Aryan rural paradise. And, in the midst of this bucolic homeland, two little blonde milkmaids in dirndl skirts sat giggling together on a grassy knoll, their too-short skirts giving tantalising glimpses of the delights beyond their stocking-tops. Anachronistic and just plain daft, but the punters loved it.

This sunny scene changed suddenly, as the lights dimmed and the Club Za-Za was launched into the middle of a wonderfully theatrical storm: thunderflashes, distant rumbling, sudden flashes of multi-coloured light across a dark sky, and glitter dropped from the ceiling to imitate rain.

Oh, how the silly little girls squealed as this was joined by other, distinctly wetter rain, soaking their flimsy little frocks and drenching their frilly blouses. And how the wet fabric clung to their bra-less breasts, which were ripe and heavy as every good Teutonic maiden's breasts should be.

Whilst the girls were fooling around, trying to pat each other's breasts dry with their aprons and handkerchiefs and generally making matters worse, the *pièce de résistance* was being prepared up above the audience. The thunderclaps grew louder and rainbow-flashes of lightning illuminated something mysteriously large and bulky, being lowered down on heavy chains from the ceiling.

This mystery object was in fact a wire cage, decorated to resemble a thundercloud. And in the middle of the cage stood Jürgen Kaas – now metamorphosed into Heimdal the Destroyer – the very picture of Teutonic wrath.

Heimdal remembered how he had loved that moment when the audience realised what was happening, saw him above them and gasped as they realised the full magnificence of this blond god who was descending among them. He had certainly presented an imposing sight:

horned helmet crowning long blond hair and beard; chest bare and well oiled to show off his musculature to best effect; golden bracelets on his arms and goatskin leggings strapped from ankle to knee. His loin-cloth was bulging already with the excited anticipation of the fray.

The 'cloud' descended to the ground and Heimdal stepped out onto the stage, his double-headed axe held aloft, and roaring with predictable ferocity as his eyes lighted on the two succulent milkmaids.

The girls made a feeble attempt to run away, but Heimdal always succeeded in catching them without the slightest difficulty. With a few deft swishes of his axe – which was quite genuinely sharp and required an expert's touch – he succeeded in divesting the maidens of their flimsy robes – not too quickly, as the punters loved to see the girls struggling to cover their protesting modesty with the remaining vestiges of their shredded garments.

When both were naked, Heimdal made great play of choosing between them: feeling the plumpness of thigh and upper arm, looking at their teeth as though selecting prime livestock, squeezing their firm titties and even slipping a hand between their thighs to judge the size of their cracks. In point of fact, it mattered little how well endowed the fräuleins were, since Heimdal's prick was big enough and fat enough to stretch even the most spacious of cunts.

Having selected his first victim, Heimdal would throw the other girl into the cage and lock her inside it with an immense golden key. He would then turn his attentions to the first girl.

Stripping off his loin-cloth, he would make sure that everyone in the club got a really good look at his mighty weapon. Why, he had even the blokes longing to feel it thrusting into them – it was enough to make you want to turn gay. And Heimdal was pretty adaptable. He'd screw anyone – or anything – for a price. He loved his work.

Casting aside his axe, Heimdal set to work on his chosen victim. Generally, he made great play of forcing her to suck him off, roaring oaths at her: 'By the mighty cock of the great Thor!' he would cry. 'Your lips are like a butterfly's upon my manhood! Suck me harder, faster, or I swear you shall suffer . . .'

He did not usually allow the girl to swallow down his semen, as he liked to withdraw at the last moment and wank himself to orgasm, watching the spunk fountaining out in triumphant spurts all over the girl's face and breasts.

To give himself time to recover, he would then indulge in a little pantomime of spanking and light torture, biting and pinching the girl's breasts, sticking the handle of his axe up her cunt, which she would obligingly display for all the world to see. By this time, most of the audience were wanking too; and the lucky ones, who had brought a sexual partner with them, were getting ready to have sex. The management of the Za-Za Club were extremely tolerant about such things, and indeed outside the front door of the club the manager had displayed a series of explicit colour photographs of the punters fucking and buggering each other. It was great for business.

After abusing the girl for a while, Heimdal would sling her into the cage and drag out the other girl instead. This one would put up a stiffer resistance, and for her pains would receive a thorough beating, plus a taste of Heimdal's whip up her arse. Strangely, this seemed not to chasten but to excite her . . .

The climax of this little playlet came when Heimdal asked for volunteers from the audience to restrain the little vixen whilst he gave her a really good seeing-to. There were always plenty of volunteers, several of them women; and soon the poor girl would find herself spreadeagled on the Astroturf, with her legs held as far apart as they would go by willing volunteers. Heimdal would then fuck her as though his life depended upon it, and would sometimes follow this up by buggering her for good measure.

The sex-show went down best of all on the nights when the manager succeeded in finding a real live virgin willing to be deflowered on stage in return for a fat fee. More often than not, this meant scouring the Hamburg schools, or tracking down an unscrupulous mother happy to sell her daughter's virginity. Virgins were pretty hard to come by, even in those days.

Happy days, thought Heimdal, wanking himself up to a quick climax and growling with satisfaction as he watched the creamy spunk spurt out. Happy, yes; but not as happy as these days . . . He collected the semen carefully in a small green glass bowl, for it was a valuable fluid, of great power and significance in magic rituals. Heimdal was no longer a sex-show stud; no longer a two-bit Tarot reader; no longer just a minor psychic, even. These days, Jürgen Kaas was a serious magician too.

One day, around five years ago, Heimdal had had a psychic experience whilst fucking one of his mistresses. At the moment of orgasm, he had had a vision of her past and future. Highly sceptical, he had told her what he saw and, to his amazement, the events of his vision had proved to be true. Within a week, the poor girl from the East End had won a top modelling contract with a major international agency. Other paranormal experiences followed; and suddenly the bizarre events and feelings of his childhood had begun to make sense.

Heimdal realised that he had psychic powers and that he had two gifts in particular: that of divining the past and future through sexual conjunction; and that of locating missing objects and people. The second gift brought him fame through his successes with the police – helping them to catch a notorious serial killer, in particular, as well as locating several important caches of stolen property.

The tabloids had loved him ever since: this Nordic giant with the steel-blue eyes and the long blond beard; a man who had enormous sexual attraction and – it was rumoured – equally enormous physical accoutrements. His use of sex in magical rituals, and in particular his gift for fortune-telling through sex, had made him an instant hit on the society scene. Overnight, everyone wanted a session with the great Heimdal, if only to find out if the rumours of his wondrous sexual potency were to be believed. Heimdal liked to think he never sent anyone away disappointed.

One person who had been there at the very start, when he was only just becoming aware of his powers, was the white witch Mara Fleming. He owed Mara a great deal. She had taught him how to understand his powers, how to channel them and not simply become their victim. A deeply sensual young woman herself, she had spent many hours with him, exploring his body and teaching him to explore hers.

But, oddly enough, for all their intimacy, he had never fucked Mara Fleming. He would have liked to fuck her. She had told him that, at that time, when his powers were at a nascent stage, it would have been wrong for them to have joined their bodies; for the superior strength of her psychic energy might have destroyed his own before it had even had a chance to develop fully.

And now she had made contact with him again. A mysterious message, saying very little. She needed his help, that was all. And he would be glad to help her, if he could. Nevertheless, Heimdal couldn't help wondering vaguely if this time, the rules would be different. This time, now that he was a fully fledged magician, would Mara let him fuck her?

Mara stood outside Heimdal's mews cottage and rang the doorbell, shifting uneasily from one foot to the other. It was a long time since she had seen him, heard from him, even. How could she expect him to remember what she had done for him now, after all those years?

The door opened, and Mara was surprised to see not Heimdal but an elderly woman.

'Miss Fleming? Herr Heimdal is expecting you.' Seeing Mara's questioning look, the woman smiled and explained: 'I am Frau Kluger, his housekeeper. Please follow me and I will take you up to his consulting room.'

Mara followed Frau Kluger obediently up the intricate wrought-iron staircase, marvelling at the wealth so much in evidence around her. When she had last seen Heimdal he had been struggling to find the rent on a tatty flat in

Camden: now he was rubbing shoulders – and no doubt other, more intimate parts of himself – with the glitterati.

They reached a door on the first floor landing: it was painted glossy black, with an exquisitely enamelled miniature from the Kama Sutra inlaid into the wood. It had been cleverly positioned at eye level, just like all the other erotic pictures which Mara had noticed lining the stairwell. Tasteful, but explicit enough to arouse even the most frigid of maiden aunts. Why, despite her anxieties about Andreas's fate, Mara was beginning to get the hots . . .

Frau Kluger knocked on the door, and a familiar voice answered, powerful and resonant as a mighty foam-flecked wave rolling onto some northern sea-shore:

'Enter.'

The old woman indicated to Mara to go in, and then turned and wended her way slowly back down the staircase. Mara wondered what on earth brought a respectable old *Hausfrau* to work in a place like this.

She pushed open the door and stepped into another world.

The room was a shrine to the act of sexual union, and to the magical arts in which Heimdal had immersed himself during the past five years. All around were fetishes, paintings, bottles filled with sweet oils, and the air was filled with the heavy scent of burning incense – a fragrance which Mara recognised instantly as one used by her own coven to produce sensual awakening.

At the far end of the room stood a small altar consisting of a plain hexagonal plinth about four feet high, with what appeared to be four silver snakes coiled about its length. There was a shallow depression in the top, in which wood was burning beneath a dish of sweet-smelling liquid. The walls were hung with erotic pictures and ornate gilded mirrors, and painted in deepest crimson.

'The colour of living flesh, of passion, of the beating heart,' explained Heimdal, signalling to Mara to take a seat beside him on a pile of softly padded cushions and animal skins. His steel-blue eyes surveyed her appreciatively from beneath his mane of corn-blond hair. 'You are more beautiful even than I remember you, Mara Fleming.'

Mara was accustomed to compliments, but was nevertheless surprised to feel herself blushing. She gave a little cough and changed the subject:

'I need your advice. If you're willing to give it.'

Heimdal laughed: the genial roar of a contented bear, and the warm sound melted the ice between them. 'Could I ever refuse you anything? You were always able to wrap me round your little finger.'

He caught hold of her slender hand and pressed it lightly to his lips. She shivered with the sudden pleasure of it. Too long without the touch of a friend, she responded quickly to Heimdal's uncomplicated warmth.

'Now, tell me what ails you, little pussycat. You sounded very distressed on the telephone.'

Haltingly, Mara began to tell Heimdal all she knew: the sense of a dark presence stalking the edges of her dreams; her meeting with Hunt; her ordeal in an unknown house of pleasure and pain; awakening amid naked, blood-spattered bodies beside a massive sarcophagus, with Hunt's dead body slumped at her feet – her only certainty the conviction that the Master, this mysterious face of evil which haunted her waking and sleeping, had somehow tricked her into murdering her lover.

'I don't remember it all – only glimpses of what happened, like snapshots of something I can't quite recall. I think perhaps I don't want to. I remember looking down at Andreas, seeing the dagger sticking out of his chest. And his eyes were still open, gazing up at me. He looked . . . surprised, as if death was the last thing he'd expected at my hands. Oh God, I killed him. I must have killed him.'

Her head in her hands, she wept out the fear and the pain for the first time since she had fled the scenes of carnage in the cellars at Winterbourne.

Heimdal put his arm around her shoulders. *Mein Gott*, he thought as his fingers brushed lightly against her flesh, she's got the most wonderful titties. He stole a sidelong glance at them and felt his ever-eager cock leap to attention at the sight of those boldly swelling curves, standing proud above a tiny waist, taut belly and womanly hips.

Her legs were crossed, so that her wrap-over skirt fell like stage curtains on either side, revealing the entirely diverting spectacle of a pair of tawny thighs, still tanned and bare-skinned, despite the autumn weather. She was a morsel fit to whet any Norseman's appetite. The memories came flooding back now, reminding him of just how he had felt that first time he saw her, clad in that diaphanous sari and not much else.

He wanted her then. And he wanted her still. The difference was, this time he was going to have her.

'So tell me: what do you want from me?' He raised a quizzical eyebrow.

'I don't understand it really . . . but somehow, I feel Andreas is . . . not dead. I don't think it's just wishful thinking. I'm convinced I've heard him calling out to me for help.

'I know you have an ability to read the past and the future, and also that you have ways of finding missing people. I want you to look into my soul and read my past, tell me what really happened to Andreas and what – if anything – I can do to help him now.'

Heimdal nodded gravely. *Himmel*, it was difficult hiding that broad inner smile. It really was turning out to be his day. First the randy TV producer who wanted to do a documentary on him, and now this! Not only was he going to be able to help her – he was going to get what he wanted as well.

'You know my methods?'

Mara nodded.

'But I have to remind you of what you told me at our last meeting, all those years ago. You told me then that my psychic powers were insufficiently developed to permit us to join our bodies and souls – such an unwary conjunction would harm me, perhaps even overwhelm me and destroy my powers.'

'You were a mere novice in those days,' replied Mara. Was that a note of desperation in her voice? Why, she'd be begging him to screw her before he'd finished. 'Your powers were in their infancy. But you are now a magus, a scholar magician. Your psychic energies are the equal of mine now. In some respects they are superior – and that is why I have come to you for help. Won't you help me?'

If he had had any genuine misgivings (and let's face it, Heimdal knew darn well his psychic abilities were too lucrative to risk losing them) they melted clean away as Mara gazed deep into his steely eyes and began to undress before him.

The velvet cape she had already cast onto the floor, revealing a long-sleeved shirt in softest woollen cloth, which held her delicious body snug as any lover's embrace. Her generous breasts pressed against the fabric, straining it so severely that the pearl buttons seemed to sigh as she released them, one by one.

She peeled the shirt down over her shoulders, and dropped it to the floor. Braless as usual, she was wearing only a tiny blue T-shirt underneath, moulding her firm breasts like a second skin. Her large nipples were already stiff and clearly visible through the thin cotton fabric, and Heimdal longed to tear off that T-shirt with his teeth, rend the fabric until it fell away in tatters and then bite on the nipples as though they were ripe hazelnuts. He imagined their toughness between his teeth, the expression of discomfort and pleasure on Mara's face as he pinched and nipped at her sensitive flesh; and his manhood yearned for release from his tight leather trousers, through which the outline of his massive erection pulsed frantically.

Mara took hold of the hem of the T-shirt, and without further ado pulled it up over her head. Her breasts sprang into view, jiggling delightfully as they popped out from under the tight material. They were even more beautiful than Heimdal remembered: lightly tanned and firm, yet as soft as clouds to the touch. Heimdal recalled the nights he had spent exploring those breasts with fingers and tongue . . . but never had she allowed him to fuck her, not until now.

'Do you like them?' breathed Mara, as though echoing his thoughts. 'Do they please you?' She placed her hands underneath them, as though offering her twin delights to him upon some exotic platter.

'Beautiful . . .' murmured Heimdal under his breath; and he put out his hands to touch them, but Mara drew back.

'No, no,' she hushed him with a kiss upon the forehead. 'Remember the ceremony. We must do everything according to the ceremony.'

Heimdal shook himself mentally, remembering that he was supposed to know what he was doing. He sat back on the pile of animal pelts, his crotch aching with lust, and prayed that she would stop tormenting him, undress quickly and let him get on with what he really wanted to do. A thousand times he had fantasised about sticking his big stiff cock up into her tight wet womanhood.

Mara kicked off her shoes and then turned her attentions to the cotton wrap-skirt, knotted over her left hip. The knot seemed to take an age to yield and, when it did, there appeared to be yard upon yard of material wound around her. At last she peeled away the fabric to reveal – to Heimdal's delight – that she was wearing nothing underneath.

Some things never change, he thought to himself, giving his cock a surreptitious rub as he remembered the first time she had undressed for him, and the delicious shock of discovering how much she hated underwear . . .

'Are you ready?' asked Heimdal, working hard to keep his voice steady and not betray the desperate tide of lust rising in his loins.

'I am ready.'

'Then kneel before the altar, and I shall perform the first of the sacred rites upon your body.'

Heimdal was proud of his ritual altar, which he had designed himself to look as much like an erect penis as possible, whilst retaining a superficial air of decency. He found that covert sexuality and heavy symbolism were a massive turn-on for the rich and repressed ladies who formed a large part of his clientele. Not that he needed to resort to such tactics with Mara: she was already an adept in all the rituals of lust.

Mara knelt before the altar, resting her hands upon the top edge, to brace herself.

Still fully clad and wishing heartily that he wasn't, Heimdal slipped a hand down the front of his trousers and adjusted his cock to a more comfortable position. Then he drew back a curtain to reveal a rack containing a variety of magical paraphernalia: wands, magical vestments, jars and bottles of many-coloured potions and a range of instruments of torture and restraint, which Heimdal found most efficacious when used on his less co-operative clients.

He selected a jar of a shimmering silver liquid, a fine Chinese paintbrush with a wickedly soft and tapering tip, and a wand made from priceless medieval glass tipped with silver, which was said to have been owned by the magus Abra-Melin and to be endowed with strong magical powers.

Touching Mara's naked flesh with the tip of the wand, Heimdal began to intone the rite.

'Azriel,' he began. 'Me teket tekorem.' And he took up the jar of silvery pigment and dipped in the tip of the paintbrush. Very carefully, he began to trace the shape of a pentacle in the centre of Mara's back. The silver paint gleamed alluringly against her perfect golden skin. She shivered with a mixture of surprise and delight as she felt the fine hairs skating across her flesh.

The pentacle complete, Heimdal set about drawing a silver unicorn on either shoulder: both animals had huge horns and enormously erect penises.

'Ezriel: te tekem tekorim,' intoned Heimdal and, sensing that this was the moment, Mara rose to her feet before him. Opening up her buttocks with the tip of the glass wand, Heimdal applied the tip of the sable brush to the sensitive skin around her forbidden gate. Mara squirmed delightedly as, very delicately, he outlined her arsehole with silver, turning it from an amber rose into an exquisite silver one, its heart quivering with eager, impatient life.

Glitter-eyed silver serpents wound about Mara's long, tanned legs, their darting tongues yearning for the dark and secret delights of her womanhood. When Heimdal was satisfied with his artistry, he turned her round to face him, and set to work on her beautiful heavy breasts. With infinite patience, he traced a filigree pattern of silver upon each perfect globe, finishing off his handiwork by painstakingly colouring each nipple so that it seemed he was gazing upon two exotic trinkets, enclosed within delicate lace bags, woven from the finest silver thread.

Moving down Mara's belly, he adorned her with magical symbols: a pentacle, the Eye of Horus, mystical numbers half-concealed by the sheltering shadows of her breasts. A mighty serpent slithered forth from her navel, uncoiling its thick silver body down the length of her taut golden belly, and darting its ferocious tongue deep into the midnight-black forest of her pubic hair.

Kneeling before Mara, Heimdal once again parted her flesh with his silver-tipped wand. Opening up her plump cunt-lips, he revealed the rosy delights within; and, his breath quickening with every stroke of the sable brush, the mage Heimdal set about his work with a will. With relentless patience, he traced the inner cunt-lips with his brush, covering her with a pigment made from purest silver, mixed with aromatic oils and an aphrodisiac root. Though he worked assiduously, he could barely make the silver paint adhere to her cunt, so moist had Mara grown at his light but lascivious touch.

At last, when every nook and cranny had been silvered, Heimdal turned his attention to her last unconquered citadel. With the tips of his fingers he found what he was looking for and, sliding back its fleshy hood with a gentle touch, he exposed Mara's clitoris and gasped with rediscovered pleasure, for he had forgotten how large and beautiful a clitty Mara had. Fully three-quarters of an inch long, it stood forth like a tiny penis, longing for the touch of a maiden's lips or the depths of her virgin cunny.

With light but lingering strokes of the soft brush, Heimdal coated Mara's clitoris with the silver pigment, making sure to tease her most intimate place with the tapering brush-tip, so that she twisted and turned in his grip, her body contorted in a silent agony of pleasure, as torrents of juice flooded out of her tormented cunt.

'Ara tekim mahete,' breathed Heimdal, rising to his feet and completing his handiwork with a kiss upon Mara's forehead.

Mara knew that this was her cue to perform a similar rite upon Heimdal. It felt curious to be in the position of pupil and postulant – she who had taught Heimdal so much of what he now knew. And yet she had already begun to feel the power within his touch, the power emanating from his fingertips and into her own body: a power that was not merely sexual, though it struck long, ecstatic reverberations from her flesh and made her clitoris throb with uncontrollable desire. No: the power within Heimdal was the power of a genuine seer. She began to hope anew that he might be able to help her.

'Azriel, mehe takim,' she whispered. And she began to undress Heimdal, unfastening each button of his shirt with the most loving care, bestowing kisses upon each inch of flesh revealed as she peeled back the fabric. Casting his shirt upon the ground, she pulled off his sandals and set to work on his tight leather trousers.

Her fingers fumbled clumsily with the belt-buckle: the head of a Nordic sea-monster, cast in solid gold. Heimdal was doing well for himself.

Finally she succeeded in unfastening first the belt buckle, and then the button on his waistband. Button flies, she noticed with pleasure: she had always loved men who wore button-fly trousers. There was something so sensual in the act of unfastening the buttons, one by one, revelling in the gradual unveiling of the delights within.

The last button unfastened, she peeled away the skin-tight leather to reveal the briefest of G-strings, a tiny pouch in metallic silver-grey fabric, stretched to bursting by the bounty within. Mara smiled inwardly, for she remembered not only the surpassing beauty of Heimdal's penis, but the vanity with which he had regarded it.

Heimdal stepped obediently out of his trousers and cast them to one side. Mara was already unfastening the bows which held the G-string tight against Heimdal's crotch. First one yielded, then the other, and she stripped away the tiny triangle of fabric.

Heimdal's cock was every bit as magnificent as Mara remembered it: appreciably longer than the average and thicker too. But, more than that, it was magnificently formed: smooth, white, blue-veined like the finest marble, and curving upward like some mad, ethereal bow, waiting to shoot forth its pearly arrows.

And there was something new which made Mara's eyes linger on Heimdal's impressive shaft. For there was now an exquisitely carved jade ring adorning the tip of his pierced penis: a ring in the form of a sea-serpent, whose gleaming green body passed through the flesh of his prick before emerging to seize its tail in its own ferocious jaws. The mythical sea-serpent, Jormungandr, who encircled the earth and who would, in his rage, bring poison and destruction upon mankind. A fitting ornament for Heimdal the Destroyer . . .

Mara touched the ring and moved it gently, feeling Heimdal shiver with the pleasure each movement produced. Evidently the ring was not there to serve some purely mythical purpose.

She longed to take the ring into her mouth; to tease it with her tongue and provoke Heimdal to ecstasies as she toyed with him. But she must not dwell on pleasure: she was here to help Andreas and she knew what she must do.

Taking from the cabinet a brush and a jar of golden pigment, Mara set about adorning the seer's body. Speaking words of power, she began by painting suns and moons on his shoulders and decorating his nipples with little crests of gold. Then she painted a great serpent emerging from the base of his spine and encircling his waist before returning to take its tail into its own mouth. His limbs and chest she adorned with beasts of prey: a lion, an eagle, a tiger.

And then, as a final tour de force, she painted Yggdrasil, the World Tree, sprouting forth like a massive phallus from the luxuriant thicket of his pubic bush.

Kissing the tip of his penis, which she had also decorated with golden paint so that it gleamed like some unearthly sword, Mara drew back and lay down upon the pile of animal pelts before the hexagonal altar. Casting a handful of sweet herbs onto the smouldering embers, Heimdal then turned to Mara and knelt between her thighs.

'The ritual is of my own devising,' he explained, bending to kiss Mara's silver-tipped breasts. 'First I shall pay homage to your body and then we must be joined. According to the laws of Tantra, we must lie together unmoving until the sweet herbs and woods have burned away; and then, and only then, may we complete the act of coition. At the moment of climax, I shall perhaps see into your past and future. Perhaps I shall even see what has happened to your lover, Andreas.'

His heart pounded as he performed the ritual acts of homage to Mara's naked body; kissing each orifice in turn, and pressing fingers and tongue into her most intimate places, anointing her with warm, aromatic oils. At last. At last he was going to have her . . .

At last, he came to her cunt. The flood of warm oil mingled with the fragrant juices already flowing from Mara's belly, for she was excited beyond endurance by this wild-eyed, blond giant with his magnificent, insistent prick.

Dazed with desire as she was, Mara was taken by surprise as, with one mighty thrust of his pelvis, Heimdal entered her, the exceptional thickness of his shaft forcing apart the delicate fleshy curtains of her cunt and causing her to gasp with the intensity of the sensation.

And then he lay still upon her belly, waiting for their abstinence to empower the ritual.

Mara's flesh cried out to be satisfied. She wanted to

scream out, 'Take me, fuck me, fuck me!' but she knew that she must have patience and endure.

The sensations flooded through her: a cascade of sense-impressions so intense it felt as though her entire body had been robbed of the top layer of flesh, all its nerves exposed and screaming together, half in pain, half in ecstasy. Heimdal's prick felt fiery hot inside her belly – no, icy cold – she could no longer tell the difference. All she knew was that the power was surging between them in some cosmic interchange she could barely grasp, and that above all other feelings and desires screamed out one, greater than all the others.

The overwhelming desire to move, to thrust, to fuck.

They lay there, fused together like some obscene two-backed beast, for what seemed an eternity. Frustration reached a screaming-point and Mara opened her mouth to cry out in agony, but at that very summit of caged lust something miraculous and breathtaking happened.

It was as though a flood-gate had been opened: a flood-gate beyond which swelled and surged a great maelstrom of psychic energy and sexual desire. As the energy flooded through their bodies, Mara was overwhelmed by something she had never felt before: an entirely new kind of orgasm – an orgasm not only of the body, but of the mind and spirit. A seemingly endless roller-coaster ride of the most intense pleasure Mara had ever experienced.

At the moment of crisis, Heimdal's mind was filled with a vision of what had happened to Mara in the cellars at Winterbourne Hall. Her sexual torment; the orgy at which so many had given themselves up joyfully to the service of the Master; the beginnings of the ceremony . . .

But it was an imperfect vision which flooded Heimdal's mind. He could not understand it – normally the picture was so clear, so comprehensible. All he was getting now were the briefest flashes of images – intense colours and light interspersed with blackness and what sounded like very faint, very distant laughter.

It was as though someone – or something – was trying

to stop him seeing what he sought; flashes of dazzling colour were zig-zagging across his sight now, almost blinding him and – like electrical interference on a television screen – preventing him from quite perceiving what was happening before his eyes.

A crystal dagger. A ring. Mara plunging the dagger into Andreas Hunt's chest . . . Andreas Hunt dead . . .

Andreas Hunt rising to his feet, plucking the dagger from his heart . . .

And nothing. No more. With a great cry of frustration and pleasure, Heimdal felt his cock twitch, and a flood of semen gush out of him, leaving him exhausted and weak.

And, at that same moment, Mara heard it once again: the voice of Andreas Hunt, far far away, calling to her with the voice of a soul damned for ever:

'Mara! Don't leave me . . .'

They lay together for a long time, unmoving; unable to speak; their heads reeling.

At last, Mara found the strength to speak.

'Did you . . . see anything?' she gasped.

'Hunt . . . I saw Hunt, his body alive and walking – but no soul behind his eyes.'

'Andreas lives?'

'His body lives. But his soul is not within his body. I believe that it now dwells within the crystal dagger which you were forced to plunge into his heart. His body walks the earth as an empty shell, a prey to evil, and I fear for him, I fear for him greatly.'

Mara's face was ashen with horror.

'Is there nothing I can do to save him?'

'I believe that you must find the crystal dagger which contains Hunt's imprisoned soul; and, if you are able to touch his flesh with the dagger's point, you may yet succeed in reuniting his soul with his body. It is your only hope.'

'But how . . .?'

'I shall do all I can to help you. Trust me.'

And Mara trusted him, for in Heimdal she recognised Andreas Hunt's only chance of salvation.

* * *

He was dreaming again; dreaming of Mara. Her violet eyes and sensuous lips and large, firm breasts filled his thoughts. And thoughts were all that remained to Andreas Hunt, imprisoned he knew not where or how or why.

His mind wandered between consciousness and sleep. A dim, dank alleyway; that's where he was. A dark alleyway whose walls towered up on either side of him. He looked upwards, but the night-sky was obscured by heavy grey clouds that let only a mist of moonlight through. This place felt like a prison.

He felt a crunching sensation beneath his feet and glanced down. Broken glass littered the ground as far as the eye could see, glittering like a million malevolent eyes in the sickly moonlight.

He wanted to run but something prevented him, made his limbs as heavy as lead. They refused to obey him; though he strained with all his might to race away and out of the alleyway, he remained locked to the spot, the shards of glass crunching and grinding beneath his imprisoned feet. And, as he watched, the level of the glass seemed to grow higher, piling up around his shoes, his ankles, the bottoms of his trousers. My God! He was going to be buried in glass . . .

Panic overtook him. And then he heard a voice calling from behind him and a hand tapping him on the shoulder . . .

'Andreas! Andreas! It's me . . .'

Mara! Mara was here!

In his excitement, Andreas tried to turn to face her, and the strangest thing happened.

With a ghastly feeling reminiscent of a rickety roller-coaster, Andreas felt himself torn away from the time and place that held him prisoner and whirling into a vortex of coloured lights and confusion. Suddenly, he realised that he could see again.

But he was nothing more than a helpless, homeless spirit: a floating, incorporeal presence, looking at the inside of the cellars at Winterbourne; looking down on the dusty surface of a polished granite sarcophagus he recognised only too well. Looking down with sickening realisation at the place of his own imprisonment. And the words of the old song ran through his mind again and again, like a mocking chorus: 'I ain't got no body . . .'

A hissing sound made him look towards the corner. A rat was staring at him, beady eyes almost popping out of their sockets, teeth bared in a grimace of terror.

Why was it so afraid of him? What had happened to his body? Why was he so bloody scared?

It was the briefest moment of freedom. A few seconds, and it was over. The dizzy vortex drew him in, sucked him down, dragged him back beneath the lid of his granite prison. He could almost have imagined it had all been part of the dream.

A few moments, and darkness closed over him once more. Deaf, dumb, blind and shit-scared, Andreas Hunt wondered if he would ever fuck Mara Fleming again.

4: Mind-games

The Master was in an excellent mood. He was enjoying the day's entertainment enormously. His new acolyte Igushi Takimoto had presented Winterbourne with two of Japan's finest geishas, and the Master had spent a diverting morning watching through a two-way mirror as Professor Andrew McNulty learnt about Japan the hard way.

For these were geishas with a difference: trained not in submissiveness but in all the arts of retribution. Divine retribution . . .

'Rising Sun' was the name of the room in which they plied their trade, for it had been decorated to mimic a Japanese tea-house. But the subtlest of modifications had been made, to fit it for a more lascivious purpose. The hapless professor had been swiftly trussed up and was now suspended by his wrists and ankles, belly down, from the sturdy bamboo trellis which covered the ceiling. Silken ropes bound each hand and foot, and a leather mask and harness held his head up, forcing him to peer before him through the gaping eye-holes. He looked for all the world like some bizarre starfish, limbs spreadeagled, dangling helplessly from the ceiling.

He was completely naked, his middle-aged body surprisingly lithe and fit for its age. His straining muscles bulged and glistened with sweat as the delicious pain of his torment permeated every nerve and fibre of his being. The contours of his face, unseen behind the leather mask, were as unimportant as his identity: here, in the chamber of the Rising Sun, all men became the faceless, nameless hosts of overwhelming pain and desire.

The Master saw with approval that McNulty was fully appreciating the personal attention which he was receiving: for his not-insubstantial cock was satisfyingly hard and dancing jerkily beneath his belly, whilst his bollocks were as firm and round as two ripe plums in a velvet bag.

Since all forms of lust were equally appealing to the Master, and all depravities to be welcomed, he gazed upon the professor's nakedness and allowed his mind to wander – experiencing in his thoughts the exquisitely novel pleasure of standing behind his victim, taking out his cock and buggering him – whilst the unfortunate professor could do nothing but gaze before him and moan his feeble protest. To amuse himself he casually projected this thought into McNulty's mind and, in a lightning reflex, the professor began to writhe about in his bonds, as though trying desperately to escape the unseen tormentor he imagined looming up behind him.

The Master smiled and signed to Anastasia to wank him harder: he was so enjoying these moments of leisure and relaxation. This new body was proving to be most satisfactory. It was wonderful to know once again all the sensations of fucking and wanking and buggering and being sucked off; and he had built up a great hunger – a fifty-year hunger – which he knew would take the whole of eternity to satisfy. More than eternity, perhaps. Sex was his food, his drink, his life-energy – the more he surrounded himself with it, the stronger he would become. And so, with each successive orgasm savoured or shared or observed or felt, he would take another step closer to his ultimate and inevitable triumph.

Soon, all power will be mine, he exulted. And the thought made the spunk seethe in his balls.

Just as he had planned, once the foolish and easily influenced professor's attentions were fully taken up with trying to escape the imagined threat from the Master, the two geishas peeled off their robes and mounted their own surprise attack upon him, thrashing his naked flesh with bundles of springy birch twigs.

The assault came upon McNulty as a complete and terrifying surprise, and he cried out in pain as the twigs bit into the soft flesh of his belly and buttocks.

Excellent, mused the Master, his own fingers closing tightly around Anastasia's as he felt his crisis approaching. Make him suffer, make his flesh bleed: his spunk will flow more freely if his blood flows first.

Indeed, the professor's prick grew ever-stiffer with each successive stroke of the birch twigs. His flesh grew redder and great weals began to appear on his belly, buttocks and legs. Sometimes the twigs were manipulated with exceptional skill so that they fell upon the tender flesh of his bollocks, causing him to shriek with the pain of his punishment. But, try as he might, he could not disguise the mounting pleasure in his loins.

Judging the moment with expert skill, the two geishas left off beating their victim and set to work on pleasuring him in gentler ways, first massaging him with soothing oils – paying the greatest attention to his loins – and then applying their butterfly-soft fingers and tongues to his mortified flesh. How he groaned as tiny fingers probed his arse and a wily tongue wound itself about his spunk-filled bollocks.

The girls finished off their victim with as fine a display of fellatio as the Master could remember seeing: taking turns to engulf the professor's hardness in their eager throats. They prolonged the torment for as long as they could but the professor was already in a paroxysm of pleasure from which there was only one way out. He came in a flood of spunk and with cries of pleasure which soon turned to a very different blend of agony and ecstasy as he felt the sharp little teeth piercing his flesh, and the warm, delicious blood spurting out . . .

With a grunt of satisfaction, the Master at last allowed himself to climax, watching the semen gush out all over Anastasia's hand and breasts with a fascination born of so many long years of deprivation.

Another recruit to the cause.

Turning away from the mirror, the Master left the geishas to sort out what to do with the inert body now hanging apparently lifelessly from the bamboo trellis – a dead spider entrapped in its own silken web . . .

He projected his thoughts with relaxed and consummate ease and Delgado was by his side in a moment.

'Master?'

'I have been monitoring the witch, Mara Fleming,' replied the Master. 'She now believes she has the key to her lover's death and salvation. Poor, foolish little slut – so talented, and yet so easily misled.'

'What would you have me do, Master?'

'Soon she will be setting out on a quest – a quest of discovery. Ensure that things are not made too . . . difficult for Miss Fleming.'

'It shall be done'.

'Oh yes . . . and I'd like you to arrange for a certain Mr Jürgen Kaas to receive a little visit . . .'

'What do we do now? We must do something,' pleaded Mara, gripping Heimdal's hand very tightly.

'Don't worry, Mara,' replied the seer, stroking her hair as one might stroke a fretful child's, to pacify it. 'The vision has convinced me that Andreas Hunt's soul is now imprisoned in the crystal dagger. What we must now do is locate the dagger's current whereabouts. One thing is certain: its master will have hidden it well, for he will be anxious to foil any attempt to reunite the soul of Andreas Hunt with his body.'

'And how . . .?'

'We must perform another ceremony, now, before the energies of our coupling are dissipated. First, you must describe the dagger to me in as much detail as you can. Every last detail of the inscription, the shape of the dagger – everything. I shall then make an effigy of it in wood, and we shall use it in our ceremony. If all goes well, the crystal will tell me where you can find the dagger.'

The details of the dagger were etched for ever in Mara's

mind: the silver hilt, adorned with hieroglyphs; the wicked, slender blade cut from a single perfect crystal. Only now, whenever her thoughts turned to the dagger, she saw it with its cruel blade sullied with the blood of Andreas Hunt.

Heimdal worked quickly, fashioning as faithful an image of the dagger as he could from wood said to be taken from the World Tree. It was an imperfect representation: rough-hewn and inelegant, in sharp contrast to the evil beauty of the crystal dagger. But it was the best they could hope for.

'It will serve,' decreed Heimdal. 'Now, please lie down upon the floor, part your thighs and draw up your knees . . . yes, exactly like that. I shall speak a spell of location, devised to show the magician the hiding-place of a lost item. Then we shall proceed to the sexual ritual.'

He spoke the words of the incantation; and it seemed to Mara that the world began to spin, that the light in the room became dimmer and that everything around her began to blur, to sink out of focus, until at last she hardly knew who or where she was. Her strength ebbed away, to be replaced by the insistent throb of irresistible desire . . .

Heimdal was kneeling between her feet now, feeling deftly for her clitoris with his left hand whilst, with his right, he masturbated his penis, his movements machine-like and efficient. Dizzy and disorientated, Mara felt that her identity had almost disappeared. Now she was little more than a dully throbbing clitoris, a body of desire that was, and yet was not, herself; and when her orgasm came, despite its raw power, it felt as though she was no more than an observer, privileged to share in the sensations enjoyed by some other woman who was almost exactly like her.

As he wanked himself to orgasm, Heimdal ensured that the warm droplets of semen fell onto the blade of the wooden knife, inundating it and spreading the love-juice with his fingers so that the entire surface glistened. Then he took hold of the rough-hewn dagger and inserted it, gently, into Mara's cunt, which was now dripping with moisture. He thrust it in and out of her, so that the blade was well covered with her juices, and then took it out and reversed it, to ensure that the hilt was also moistened.

Removing the dagger from Mara's cunt, Heimdal rose unsteadily to his feet and walked slowly to the table on which stood a crystal ball. Carefully, he gripped the dagger in both hands and held it before him at arms' length, lowering the tip until it rested on the top of the crystal globe.

'Azarte!' he cried, and at once an immensely bright mist of light filled the room, like a fluorescent fog. Through it, Mara could just perceive the massive, shadowy figure of Heimdal, the point of the dagger now in his left hand and the hilt in the right, with its blade laid flat across the top of the crystal globe.

He was peering down, deep into the heart of the crystal, and seemed to be in incredible pain for his entire body was trembling and cries of repressed agony escaped like the distant hiss of steam from between his clenched teeth.

'I . . . I see it!' he cried and fell to his knees on the floor, the wooden dagger discarded by his side and his head cradled in his hands.

At once the mist began to fade, and Mara felt the dizziness and weariness subside. Struggling to her feet, she staggered over to where Heimdal half-sat, half-lay, still shaking his head as though trying to rid himself of a lingering bad dream. She laid a trembling hand on his shoulder.

'Are you all right?' gasped Mara, seeing the rivulets of mingled blood and sweat coursing down his brow.

He nodded.

'I saw it, Mara; I know where the dagger is now.'

She gripped his hand tightly and stared deep into his eyes:

'Tell me, Heimdal. Now. Tell me where it is.'

There was a look of utter bewilderment on his face.

'I know this is going to sound ridiculous, Mara; but the dagger is somewhere in the British Museum!'

The door of the penthouse flat swung open and a smartly

dressed young woman ushered them inside. The Master noted that she had extremely fine legs and a promising bosom, and felt the beginnings of a surge of interest in his loins. She looked at him with large, baby-blue eyes and smiled.

I won't forget you, thought the Master. You'd be a real asset to any organisation . . .

'I'm Sir Charles's private secretary, Madeleine Gorton,' she explained. 'Follow me, please. He's expecting you.'

She led them down a corridor lined with Manets, Seurats and a couple of Berthe Morisots. All originals, of course. Sir Charles Forton didn't have to worry where the money was coming from. His main worry was working out what to spend it all on.

Art and politics were his main hobbies and Sir Charles was reputed to be the single largest contributor to Tory Party funds. An extremely influential man, mused the Master. About time I took steps to improve our acquaintance. He stole a glance at Anastasia Dubois, walking silently by his side, her face a mask of sensual innocence.

Sir Charles was working in his book-lined office, gold-plated fountain pen hovering over a pile of letters for signature. He glanced up as his secretary ushered the visitors in, dismissing her with a cursory nod.

A few moments passed whilst Sir Charles finished signing the letters. Evidently, he didn't intend leaving the Master in any doubt as to who was boss. The Master and his companions waited in patient silence, broken only by the steady ticking of an eighteenth-century grandfather clock.

At last Forton put down his pen, folded his arms, and looked the Master up and down. His steady gaze presented not so much a welcome as a direct physical challenge.

'Let's get one thing straight, Mr LeMaitre: I'm a very busy man. I don't have time for con-men and charlatans, nor for time-wasters. You said you had something to show me – something that would be to my advantage. I'm warning you: it had better be good.'

Oh, it is, thought the Master, smiling to himself. It's so good, it's going to change your whole life . . .

He stepped back to reveal Anastasia, who peeled back the sides of her sable coat to reveal that she was gloriously naked underneath.

Sir Charles's jaw dropped. All the juices that he had thought long dried-up began to flow at the sight of such delectable young flesh; and he felt an irresistible stirring in his loins that made him forget for a moment just who and where he was. His hand strayed, absent-mindedly, to the unexpected bulge in the front of his hand-sewn trousers.

'Sir Charles,' continued the Master, 'I'd like you to meet Miss Anastasia Dubois. She'd like to show you a few things which I'm sure will interest you.'

Half-hypnotised already by the Master's commanding gaze, Sir Charles submitted eagerly to the cool, manicured hand slipping incautiously down inside his silk boxer-shorts. My God, he thought, I'm interested already.

As she took down his pants and teased and sucked and fucked him, there on his own office floor, Sir Charles surrendered to her with all the unquestioning wonderment of an infatuated boy – though he was fleetingly curious why she seemed so intent on planting passionate kisses on the pulsing flesh of his proffered throat.

Mara and Heimdal had spent an entire, and completely fruitless, morning wandering around the British Museum. Nothing. Nowhere could they find any trace of the crystal dagger. Had they ever really expected to?

Only as they entered the Egyptian galleries did Heimdal begin to sense the trail once again.

'It has to be here,' he hissed, pressing his fingertips against the glass case and feeling the vibrations of a distant power. 'I can sense its presence. The dagger is definitely somewhere in this building. Its power is overwhelming, intense, incredible . . .'

'Can you sense nothing else, beyond the fact that the dagger is nearby?' Mara pressed her fingers to the glass but, although she felt the distant echo of a faraway power, she could not tap into the pulsing artery of its central energy source. For the first time, she felt truly in awe of Heimdal's powers.

'Only . . . only the fact that there seems to be a lot of . . . paper nearby, a lot of knowledge, all gathered together. Books?' He turned to Mara quizzically, hoping for enlightenment.

The realisation hit Mara so suddenly that she almost laughed.

'Paper, knowledge gathered together in one place, books . . . don't you see? It's obvious. This building doesn't just contain the British Museum. It houses the British Library, too!'

Oh God, thought Heimdal, watching her running out of the Egyptian Room, her bum wobbles delightfully when she runs. I wish we could just go home and have a good fuck . . .

'But what would a crystal dagger be doing in a library?' he protested, striding faster to keep up with Mara, who was already racing before him through the echoing corridors.

'I haven't a clue,' she panted, turning and grinning at him. 'But I'm going to find out!'

Andreas was beginning to realise that something very odd indeed had happened to him. He wasn't properly dead, he wasn't unconscious and, as far as he could tell, he wasn't dreaming. The things that were happening to him couldn't have been conjured up by his own mind. After all, his editor always said he had no imagination. So what the bloody hell *was* going on?

His encounter with the rat had not been the end of his strange experiences: in fact, it had been the beginning. Since then he had felt his spirit float free of its place of captivity several times, and each time he had experienced brief periods of lucidity when he had been fully conscious of his surroundings and able to see what was going on as though he were some sort of peripatetic spirit.

Am I a ghost, then? Good God, man – pull yourself together. You don't even believe in ghosts. Mara's always telling you you're an irredeemable old sceptic.

Mara.

He pulled himself together as best he could and tried to think about it all logically. There was one encouraging factor, at least. During his brief periods of consciousness and sight, he had recognised where he was. The cellars, the Great Hall, the bizarre theme bedrooms with their erotic paraphernalia and their gorgeous whores . . .

He was at Winterbourne. Somehow – and God knows, it was beyond him to understand how – his spirit was able, from time to time and for periods of perhaps a few minutes at most, to witness the events within Winterbourne Hall. And he couldn't help noticing that these periods were getting longer. He was developing some sort of ability to control them, to resist the terrible force which dragged him back to the dark helplessness of his imprisonment.

The weird thing was, it was almost as if sexual activity acted as a magnet for his spirit, for each of the experiences he had had so far involved watching people having sex. The last time it had happened he had found himself looking at two people in the Outer Space room at Winterbourne. He recognised the room as one of those he had searched through in his quest for Mara, that fateful night at the Hall. It was fitted out like a space capsule, with two soft leather seats and lots of flashing coloured lights.

One of the people was someone he half-recognised – a TV personality, yeah, that was it. The other was a big blonde girl, tall and busty and dressed in a silver space suit. Her statuesque, Nordic figure looked damn good in all that skin-tight silver lamé. And those tantalising little zips, strategically placed over her titties, her cunt, her arse . . .

If Hunt had been capable of it, he would have developed a huge hard-on. Instead, he had to watch – apparently completely unseen – as the TV personality sat in one of the reclining seats and got himself well and truly fucked by the big blonde in the space-suit. Out of this world . . .

And then, just as the guy was spurting into her, Hunt had seen her lunge for his neck, as though to sink her teeth into it . . .

At that moment, he had felt himself dragged back into darkness, to mull over what he had seen. All he could do was watch, listen, try to understand. Maybe something of what he learned would turn out to be of help to him. Or to Mara. He wished he knew what had happened to Mara. He had to do something to help her . . .

It was happening again. With a silent cry of pain, Hunt felt his spirit wrenched free of its prison. When consciousness came, it was with a dazzle of bright lights and a riot of sound and smell.

He was in the Great Hall, watching an orgy being acted out. The hall had been decorated to resemble a North African bazaar, in the centre of which was a large wooden raised platform on which young women dressed as slave-girls were standing, half-naked and linked together with heavy chains. They looked afraid, terrified even. Hunt couldn't tell if they were really scared, or just great actresses. Sitting at the foot of the platform, men were shouting out sums of money. They were drinking a thick, syrupy liquid with a heavy scent, and seemed excited – drugged.

A slave-market: Winterbourne's exclusive clientele were bidding for the favours of the girls on the dais. One was being unchained and flung roughly into the arms of her purchaser, an elderly man with a pot-belly who immediately threw the girl to the ground and pulled out a surprisingly hard, enthusiastic penis. Forcing apart the girl's legs, he took no account of her struggles and cries of protest, and flung himself upon her, ramming his hardness into her right up to the hilt. The girl's cries of anguish seemed genuine . . .

Sickened, Andreas turned away and found he was looking down at a pair of hands. Nice, well-formed hands, tanned and smooth-skinned. And a pair of legs and feet. And a bulge in the front of his trousers which must be an erection.

He could feel the spreading warmth in his loins.

He could feel!

But they were *not* his loins. And this was not his body. Suddenly, he felt a tide of nausea overwhelm him as he realised the overwhelming evil of the body his spirit was inhabiting, smelt the stench of its age-old corruption.

The shock of his revulsion was sufficient to break the link between body and spirit, and Hunt felt himself spinning back, spiralling into the vortex which led inexorably back to the darkness of his captivity.

Oh my God, he thought, as the darkness closed over him once again. What evil is this that surrounds me? And what evil have I abandoned Mara to?

Not surprisingly, when Mara and Heimdal asked to see the Chief Curator of the British Library, he was officially 'in a meeting'. But his secretary could not hold out long in the face of Heimdal's animal magnetism. While he amused her – and himself – by getting his hand up her skirt and giving her a good shagging across the desk, Mara took full advantage of the diversion to push open the door to the Curator's office and slip inside.

She shut the door behind her as quietly as she could. The Curator was sitting in a swivelling leather armchair beside the window, a small table carrying books, a portable telephone and an intercom at his elbow. He was miles away, engrossed in a report, and Mara was able to get quite a good look at him before he noticed her.

He was a surprisingly youthful man – early forties, perhaps. A real careerist, no doubt of it. Tall, slim, tanned (lots of ski-ing holidays at the taxpayers' expense?) and with a shock of sandy brown hair. A second or two after Mara entered the room, he glanced up – half in anger, half in surprise.

'Who the . . .?' He reached for the intercom to buzz his secretary.

'I wouldn't bother,' interjected Mara. 'She's . . . otherwise engaged at the moment. Look, all I want is a quick word. Won't you listen?'

The Curator sighed, laid the report on top of the pile of books, and settled back into his executive leather armchair, legs comfortably crossed, fingers interlaced and hands resting on his knee.

'You'd better get on with it, young lady,' he said, 'and thank your lucky stars you're such a good-looking woman. I don't interrupt a morning's work for just anyone, you know.'

'I'm looking for some . . . stolen property. I have reason to believe it may be here. A crystal dagger with a silver hilt. It was stolen from my family a little while ago.'

'My dear girl, what possible use could I find for a silver dagger?' The mocking grey eyes stared back into hers and she could feel his desire. It was filling her, swelling into her like a poison gas, choking her.

He wanted her, wanted her; and for some reason all her psychic senses told her that she must resist him, for he was evil. Something told her that he had designs on more than just her body . . .

'Is there something wrong?'

Mara did not reply. For, out of the corner of her eye, she had seen it. The dagger was on the other side of the room, lying on the desk, its crystal brilliance half-concealed by a pile of opened letters.

So that was it. The priceless crystal dagger that held the soul of her lover was being used as a common or garden letter opener. No doubt this was the Master's idea of a good joke. But how to get the dagger, how to take it away? She must have it . . .

She realised that the Curator was staring at her, his watery grey eyes boring into the side of her face, scanning the undulations of her body beneath her thin sweater. The pale glimmer of afternoon sunlight filtering through the blinds turned his sandy-coloured hair into a misty halo about his head, so that it seemed as though he were truly on fire for her.

And his desire was burning her now, consuming her, so

that, like slowly melting glass, she was losing the memory of her shape, her identity, her mission.

Mara rose to her feet and walked across the room to the Curator. Every step was leaden and unwilling, yet she knew deep down, for her instincts told her, that she must use her body – use it to barter for the soul of her lover as she would use any other coinage.

She stopped a few feet away from the Curator: she would go no further. He must make the next move, the ultimate move. She would not submit to him so easily. Standing there before him, she took hold of the welt of her sweater and pulled it up over her head, revealing the glorious twin swells of her naked breasts. It was an act both of challenge and of submission. Come and have me if you dare: and the winner takes all.

'Lovely . . .' breathed the Curator and Mara was reminded of the seductive hiss of a cobra, about to mesmerise and fell its prey. 'Come to me, my lovely one . . .'

Fighting the urge to let her mind sink into the oblivion of submission, Mara unfastened the button on her skirt, and let it fall in bright swathes about her feet. As usual she wore no panties, and the Curator drew in his breath sharply at the sight of her glossy black triangle of curls.

Kicking off her shoes, Mara stood naked before him, watching and waiting for her moment. The Curator seemed to sense that it was his turn to respond, and he rose slowly to his feet, sliding down the knot on his painted silk tie. He peeled off his jacket and tossed it carelessly over the back of the chair, then began to unbutton his shirt. His chest was broad, sun-tanned and covered in a thick carpet of sandy hair, and Mara found herself longing to sink her fingers into it, twisting and turning them until they were held fast, like . . .

Like a drowned corpse, held fast by long tendrils of water weed . . .

Like a mummified body, suffocated and imprisoned by its bindings . . .

What – or who – was putting such macabre thoughts into her head? For a brief moment, she recalled the faded memory of a dream; a dream of a girl within a coffin, bound up like a mummy yet still alive and silently screaming . . .

And then it was gone again, like a breath of frost in July, leaving only the desire, the desire to fuck. The real reason why she had come here was receding into the back of her mind; now, she was here only to fuck, and to defeat the will of this man who was so eager to possess her.

He had taken off his shoes and socks and his hands were on his belt-buckle now, unfastening it, sliding the belt out of the loops and letting it fall to the ground. Now the button at the waistband; the zip, sliding down like a sigh of desire; and he was stepping out of his trousers, out of his underpants.

He stood naked before her and Mara heard her own desire echoing around her head, as though someone . . . something . . . was putting her feelings into words:

'Got to fuck you; got to feel your cock in my cunt; got to make you shoot your load . . .'

He had a good body: tall and slender, with broad shoulders and a narrow waist. His taut belly led down to a crop of sandy-brown curls, surrounding a fine, thick penis which was already arcing upwards like a bow, straining for release. His testicles were large and pendulous, and she began to breathe more quickly with the thought of how much semen must be gathering in their fleshy sac, how much white, foaming delight just waiting to pump into her . . .

The Curator held out his arms to her, in the promise of a lover's embrace, and whispered:

'Come to me . . .'

Although her body cried out for her to obey him, Mara raised her hands to her own breasts and began to toy with her nipples, teasing them into ever-greater wakefulness, and sliding her cool palms over the softly swelling flesh of her bosom. She knew that the Curator must see, and be infuriated by, the pleasure which she was giving herself. So she pulled up a chair and sat down on it, facing the Curator, drawing her legs wide apart.

Silently, and smiling like an angel of destruction, Mara pulled apart her cunt-lips and began to masturbate herself. Not too hard, not too fast; for she didn't want to come too quickly. She wanted the Curator to get the full benefit of the show she was staging just for him.

She returned his burning gaze boldly, though inwardly she trembled at the power she sensed within him: a power so dark that it seemed as though she were looking into some vast black abyss which she dared not enter, and yet from which she had not the will to draw back. All her psychic senses told her that the evil she sensed within him must be part of some other, much greater, evil.

She knew that she must fear him, must beware of his seductive voice, his sensual lips, his hard, purple-tipped penis which would slide oh so beautifully into her well-oiled cunt . . .

Summoning up all her courage, Mara continued to gaze back at the Curator, all the while rubbing and displaying herself ever more lasciviously.

Look, she seemed to say, take a look at these hot, wet delights which I am offering to you if only you will submit to me. See: here is my clitoris. Is it not beautiful? Is it not bigger and more magnificent than any other clitoris you have ever seen? Why, it is fully three-quarters of an inch long – can you see? I am sliding away its little pink hood so that you can get a better view.

Would you not like to take this little rosebud into your mouth, moisten it, and feel it throbbing on your tongue? I am rubbing it now – see how much pleasure I am giving myself; if you were rubbing it, could you give me more pleasure? Why should I submit to you when I am so self-sufficient in pleasure?

See: now I am opening up my arse-cheeks and grinding my naked, intimate flesh against the fabric of the chair. How good its roughness feels upon the sensitive flesh of my arse. Oh, if only you could see how my tight little arsehole is opening and closing like the mouth of some greedy starfish. It is longing, yearning to be filled. Could you fill it, more expertly and more pleasurably than I can fill it with my finger?

And here is my vagina: isn't that a cold, clinical word for something so hot and wet and willing? Here: I am pulling apart my cunt-lips so that you can see a little of the way into my hot, wet hole. It's dark and juicy in there – running with rivulets of moisture, like some magical cave; see – I'm sliding my finger in and out of it. Can you hear the delicious squelch it makes?

And now I'm taking my finger out so that you can see the wetness glistening on it. And putting my finger to my lips, so that I can see, taste, smell the fragrant wetness which I and I alone have produced. Tell me: could you truly give me more pleasure than this?

So effective were the words she spoke silently, within her own mind, that she felt the sudden onrush of the orgasm which she had sought to delay. Unable to prevent it, she rubbed harder still at her clitoris and great waves of pleasure crashed over her. Love-juices trickled out of her and moistened the rough fabric of the chair.

As she closed her eyes in orgasm, the Curator could resist her no longer. When she reopened them, he was before her, towering over her and brandishing his stiff cock like some deadly weapon.

For all his aggression Mara knew that she had won the first round of their contest. He had come to her, she had not submitted to him.

She opened her lips willingly to accept the tribute of his stiff, yearning flesh. His cock throbbed with pent-up spunk, and yet it felt surprisingly cool – like sucking the cock of some obscene marble statue. She cradled his balls in her hands, marvelling at the way they tensed at her touch in readiness for the spurt of love-juice which would bring ecstasy and the renewal of desire.

He thrust into her eagerly, holding her breasts, teasing her nipples with his long, cool fingers. Her cunt grew wetter and wetter as she sucked him, pulsating with yearning to be filled up and satisfied.

She felt his shaft grow stiffer still and then a flood of semen gushed out into her mouth, half-choking her in its profusion. She swallowed it willingly but with a tinge of regret – believing that he would not now be capable of fucking her.

But, to her amazement, the Curator's recuperative powers were unusual in the extreme. His body was in a curious way like some sophisticated mechanism, some perfect, perpetual-motion machine dedicated only to sex. For, within a couple of moments, his penis was ready and willing once again – if anything, it seemed even stiffer and more eager than before.

With surprising strength, the Curator slipped his arms under Mara's backside and hoisted her waist high, so that her legs wrapped themselves behind his back and his stiff penis slid comfortably into her wet cunt.

Mara could not suppress a little cry of pleasure as she felt his hardness entering her, filling her up and pressing deliciously against the neck of her womb. Her cunt tightened possessively around the invader, welcoming it in and unwilling to let it escape.

'I'm going to fuck you till you cry out for mercy,' hissed a quiet voice in her ear. 'I have you now and there is no escape . . .'

For a moment, Mara saw that it was true: that she had foolishly allowed herself to become this strange, evil man's prisoner in spite of her better judgement; that she had deluded herself that, in making him come to her, she had exerted some power over him.

He held her fast now. There was no point in struggling. And, what's more, she had lost all desire to resist him. All she wanted to do was submit to the tightness of his embrace, the hardness of his delectable prick. Thoughts of her own damnation – and Andreas's – had slipped far away, pushed back into the furthest recesses of her mind, she knew not how or why. Some superior force was at work, manipulating her mind, playing games with her desire, making her its victim.

Its willing victim.

He fucked her, bouncing her up and down on his prick as though she weighed no more than a tiny child. And she cried out as loudly as she dared for the pleasure and pain of his possession. A second and a third time he brought her to orgasm and – as his semen pumped into her and she almost fainted away with the power of her fourth climax – she hardly noticed the way the Curator was nuzzling into the crook of her neck, as though looking for some special place . . .

No! cried a voice inside the Curator's head. You shall not bite the witch Mara. Not yet, not yet. Have I not forbidden it? She has other uses. Let her go, I command you! Let the white witch go free or you shall feel the burning agony of my wrath. You are my creation and only I can destroy you . . .

For a moment the Curator seemed to hesitate, but then he shook off the power of the voice within him and bent once again to Mara's throat, teeth bared in a parody of a smile.

At that moment he lost consciousness – felled by a blow to the back of the head from a marble statuette which Heimdal had picked up from a plinth by the door. He collapsed into a crumpled heap on the carpet, Mara half-beneath him.

'What . . .?' Mara was dazed and weeping as Heimdal picked her up and checked that she had come to no harm.

'He was trying to bite you! That madman was trying to bite your neck!' Heimdal was incredulous. 'Are you all right?'

Mara nodded, leaning on Heimdal as he took off his jacket and slung it around her shoulders, regretfully veiling the twin delights of her magnificent bosom. He really had the hots for her today . . .

'The dagger: I saw it,' exclaimed Mara, returning to her senses. 'It's over there, on the desk. What happened to me, Jürgen? What's happening to my life?'

But Heimdal could not answer. He picked up the dagger and thrust it into his belt.

'Hurry up and get dressed,' he said. 'There's no time to lose.'

5: Reunion

Andreas was dreaming. Dreaming of Mara – of fucking her as he had fucked her so many times on their big, soft bed. Or on the warm, sandy beach, with a gentle breeze playing on their naked bodies. He remembered with anguish the glorious warmth of her well-lubricated cunt; the way she had loved to take his yearning hardness into her mouth and tease him to ecstasy with the very tip of her lascivious tongue. The thrilling tightness of her willing arse . . .

But the dream was changing. Where was Mara? Don't run away . . . There – there she was, still naked and walking towards him. She was smiling at him and her arms were outstretched in welcome.

'Come to me, come to me, my darling; and fuck me . . .'

Oh yes, breathed Andreas within the agonised prison of his mind. Let me join with you and fuck your beautiful body.

And she was yet closer now, still smiling, still stretching out her arms to him. Soon she would be close enough for him to touch her, hold her, fuck her.

As she reached him, he stretched out his hand to touch her. But his hand passed straight through her as though she – or he – were no more than an insubstantial phantom. And Mara carried on walking, still smiling, still holding out her arms to someone.

In the agony of his dream, Andreas turned to see where she was going and saw that she was walking towards another man. A man who stood in the distance, waiting for her and smiling – but not so far distant that Andreas could not make out his features.

A man who looked exactly like Andreas Hunt.

Mara lay upon the hard wooden bench, its surface rough against her naked skin. The crystal dagger lay upon her belly, its wickedly sharp tip pointing down to the perfumed garden of her pubic hair. She felt its coldness flooding through her, as though within its heart it burned with an icy flame; and she wondered how such a cold, evil, malevolent thing could hold the soul of her lover. Its evil touch froze her blood and yet also excited her, for the essence of its evil was sexual – she had felt that as soon as she touched it again – and in her, it sensed a pulsing, vibrant heart of physical passion.

The heavy velvet drapes were drawn across, and the room was in complete darkness, save for the blood-red candles which burned at the head and foot of the bench. Heimdal stood beside her, his face seeming awash with blood in the ghastly candlelight.

Mara could feel the power of the dagger already, knew that she had not been mistaken in fearing its touch. But there was pleasure, as well as fear, in the touch of that bright, crystal blade, that engraved silver hilt.

Her clitoris warmed and began to tingle, as it always did when it swelled in anticipation of a lover's touch – or her own. For Mara was skilled in all the arts of love, including the subtle art of masturbation, which she had refined since adolescence, until she was now able to control both the timing and the quality of her orgasm. As one of a long line of white witches, Mara knew and respected the power of sex; believing that through sexual pleasure and activity of all kinds, a mystic might attain greater powers and develop clearer astral vision.

She reached out her hand and touched the dagger's silver hilt, her fingers lingering on the strange hieroglyphics carved into the metal – signs and symbols which she had not the learning to read but which she knew instinctively were words of great power. Great power and great evil. And, as she smoothed the cool blade with her hand, she wondered if Andreas was aware of her, could feel her trying to communicate with him.

Heimdal's voice brought her back to her senses.

'I must utilise your psychic energies now,' he explained. 'You are the person closest to Hunt. Your own soul has sought out his in locating the dagger; and now you must send it out onto the astral plane, there to search until it finds the whereabouts of Hunt's body. There is no time to lose: for without the immortal soul which ennobled it, his body will be prey to any and all evil powers.'

'I shall do whatever you say,' replied Mara. 'I am ready.'

Unzipping his trousers, Heimdal took out his prick and began to masturbate it skilfully into rigidity. In fact it took little effort since the sight of Mara's body, once again naked before him, had already caused Heimdal's prick to twitch into insistent life.

As he rubbed at his shaft, he looked down and admired the loveliness of Mara's sweet young flesh. Even now, in the mournful depths of autumn, her skin was a uniformly golden colour, without telltale lines or white patches – testifying to the amount of time she spent naked. Heimdal's cock surged into life as he imagined her stretched out in the sun like some exotic cat, stretching those long, slender limbs and rubbing coconut oil into her smooth, elastic flesh.

It really was a remarkable body, as perfect as any he had ever seen, and in his long career as sex-show stud and, latterly, magical sex-guru to the rich and bored, Heimdal had seen an awful lot of very nice bodies. The most delightful aspect of Mara's physique was that it combined slenderness with amplitude, firmness with graceful curves. Her belly was muscular and flat, her legs smooth and slender, and her waist tiny in proportion to her gently flaring hips.

Most striking of all were her magnificent breasts, which soared above her taut belly like the graceful flying buttresses of some fairytale Gothic cathedral. Like some fantastical triumph of medieval architecture, their firm fullness defied gravity, and they seemed intent only on rising still higher, their long, hard nipples straining upwards as if towards not only physical but spiritual fulfilment.

Heimdal was hard now and throbbing. He knew it would not take long to bring himself to the climax which he required in order to empower the ritual.

Letting go of his shaft for a moment, he picked up a jar of ointment which he had prepared especially for the ritual. It had a heavy, almost hypnotic scent, for it contained a dozen costly Eastern incenses and many other secret ingredients with aphrodisiac qualities. It was most important that Heimdal – and especially Mara – must attain a peak of sexual desire so that, at the climactic moment of the ritual, the energies released might combine to produce a vision of Andreas Hunt.

Dipping a finger into the scented unguent, Heimdal smeared it liberally over the tip of his penis, his throbbing shaft and his spunk-filled balls, which felt already as if they were about to burst. He could not suppress a groan of pleasure as he felt the ointment begin to take effect.

Next, he scooped up more of the ointment and bent over Mara. She felt a sudden coolness as the ointment touched the tips of her nipples, followed by a tingling and then a delicious, smouldering warmth which made her writhe with unexpected pleasure.

Heimdal's skilled fingers moved on, smoothing the ointment all over her breasts, then moving down her belly and foraging in the secret garden of her pubic hair; sliding further down and searching out the heart of her womanhood. Mara began to tremble as she felt the ointment slide over the delicate membranes of her cunt, kindling her flesh and making it pulsate with desire.

And now he was smoothing the ointment over her clitoris, and she was crying out with the terrible, unbearable pleasure of it; the hellish, heavenly sensitivity of the little button of flesh as it caught fire and sparked into sudden, tempestuous life.

Paying no heed to her cries, Heimdal took the dagger

from her belly, seized her by the shoulders and made her roll over onto her front; whereupon he pulled apart her buttocks and set to work on her arsehole with his devilish ointment.

As Mara writhed beneath his fingers, Heimdal felt his own desire reaching unbearable new heights. How he longed to do what would have been so simple: just to hold her arse-cheeks apart and spear her with his mighty prick. He imagined how hot and tight her arse would be, how welcoming it would feel as it caressed his cock; and he almost spurted at the mere thought of it.

With a desperate effort at self-control, Heimdal succeeded in restraining himself. He must not weaken. For Mara's sake, he must see the ritual through; he must conserve and direct his psychic energies.

'Lie on your back,' he instructed her, hardly able to speak for the all-consuming feelings of lust which were throbbing and surging through him like forest fire.

Mara obeyed, almost crying with the exquisite torture of her body, awakened and enslaved by the aphrodisiac ointment with which Heimdal had anointed her.

It was as though her nipples, her breasts, her cunt, her clitoris, her arse, had all been sparked into a new and infinitely more exciting life of their own; as though they were independent of the rest of her body and, from their new position of infinite power, were now dictating to her their terms for peace.

Fuck. There will be no peace for you until you have fucked, little Mara. You know that what we tell you is true. Touch yourself, and *feel* that what we say is true . . .

'Touch yourself,' gasped Heimdal, touching her clitoris with the point of the crystal dagger and then laying it once more upon her belly. 'Masturbate yourself. Hold back for as long as you can, to maximise the energies that will gather in the dagger. I too shall masturbate, and when my semen spurts out onto the dagger, you must make yourself come to orgasm.'

Mara slid her finger between her cunt-lips, and moistened

her clitty with a little of her copious cunt-juices. But when she tried to place her fingertip more firmly upon her clitoris, she cried out in pain – for it had become so sensitive that anything but the merest hint of a touch was now agony.

She tried again, this time only brushing gently against her clitty; and felt the most delicious, overwhelming sensations flooding through her loins, extending upwards and outwards throughout her whole body, so that her clitoris felt like the nerve-centre of some vast and complex network, whose only purpose was pleasure.

Seeing the expression of wonderment on Mara's face, Heimdal warned her:

'No, Mara, not yet.' Sweat was coursing down his face as he strove for self-control, desperate not to climax too soon. 'You must hold out a little longer or the power will not be sufficient. Be patient, patient; fight the urge – overcome it with your own power. Allow your own psychic force to achieve mastery over your physical desires . . .'

But, even as he spoke, he was gasping with the superhuman effort required to hold back from the brink of orgasm. A little longer, just a little longer . . .

He looked down and saw to his amazement that the blade of the dagger was glowing with a strange inner phosphorescence, like bluish-white fire. It seemed to be pulsating, ebbing and flowing in time to Mara's quickening breathing.

It was happening. It was happening.

'Now!'

He rubbed his cock a fraction harder and the world seemed to slip out of focus, blurring at the edges as he fought to maintain concentration.

'Now, Mara! You must come now!'

Looking down, he watched in fascination, almost detachment, as the flood-tide of pent-up semen gushed out of his penis and onto the bluish-white blur that was the dagger's blade.

Obediently, Mara applied a little pressure to her clitoris and felt the abyss of pleasure open up before her, like a multi-coloured chasm into which she leapt joyfully with no thought of fear.

The crystal dagger flamed into life, a blinding bluish-white light surrounding and engulfing both it and Mara.

She cried out in fear, caught in the midst of the blue-white mist which felt as cold as ice as it swirled about her naked flesh. She was snow-blinded by the brilliance of the light, and at first saw nothing beyond the swirling mist.

But it began to clear and, blinking in confusion and disbelief, Heimdal made out the blurred image of a man.

A man, expensively dressed and getting out of a long, black limousine. Talking to two men. Walking with them towards an ornate, Gothic-style building. Turning back to say something to his companion . . . A man with a look of pure, cold evil in his eyes.

'No, no!' cried Mara. 'The pain – it's too much!' And she fell back, unconscious, upon the wooden bench, the dagger cold and lifeless upon her belly. Her flesh seemed to shimmer like a frosty pavement in the candlelight, and when Heimdal touched her he found that her body was covered in tiny, white ice crystals.

He wrapped a blanket around her to bring warmth and life back into her body and drew open the curtains, still troubled by what he had seen. When Mara at last revived, still cold and shivering, he told her the news:

'Andreas Hunt's body is alive, Mara. I have seen him. I don't understand . . . but he is at the House of Lords. You must go there quickly, today: now is your chance to save him.'

Anastasia Dubois stepped elegantly out of the limousine, nodding to the driver to pull away. She opened her handbag and took out lipstick and a mirror. She had to look her best if she was to carry out the Master's instructions to his complete satisfaction.

Such a hunger raged within her. But soon it would be sated. Those who followed the true Master were never allowed to hunger for long.

Got to fuck.

Heimdal's mews cottage was just around the corner. She unfastened her top button and checked that the seams of her stockings were straight. Her dark hair fell in seductive waves about her shoulders and her nipples pressed urgently against the tight fabric of her thin, gauzy blouse. She never felt the cold, not any more.

She was looking good. But she had no time to waste now – mustn't be late for the appointment the Master had arranged for her. The appointment with Heimdal. Heimdal the Destroyer.

She laughed. For destruction does not always present itself with a fiery sword. Sometimes it has firm breasts and a tight, wet cunt. Sometimes it has succulent red lips and sharp little teeth.

She rang the doorbell and waited for the maid to answer. And the November sun shone cheerfully in a powder-blue sky, as though trying to convince itself that nothing was amiss.

Heimdal had given Mara all the instructions she would need. All she had to do was persuade or trick Andreas into holding the crystal dagger, and his soul and body would be reunited.

It seemed too easy somehow. Flawed, because it was just too flawless. All Mara's instincts shouted out that there must be more to it than that – but she did not want to hear. Everything was going to be all right at last. Soon Andreas Hunt would be restored to her and they would once again fuck in Andreas's king-sized bed.

She crossed the road outside the House of Lords, the dagger cold and inert in the pocket of her coat. For the first time it struck her that she really hadn't the faintest idea how she was going to carry out her plan – if you could call it a plan. What if they searched her? How was she going to explain away the crystal dagger? How was she going to get into the House of Lords? And if she did get inside, how would she find Andreas?

Not that it was Andreas. Not the real Andreas. She shivered to think of her lover's body, zombie-like and empty of the spirit that had been Andreas.

She wondered what evil could have enslaved it and pressed it into service. What purpose could it have in luring Andreas Hunt's body to the House of Lords?

The Master put away his pen and closed his briefcase with an authoritative click.

'So I can be sure of your support, gentlemen?' He scanned the figures sitting round the polished mahogany conference table.

Heads nodded.

'I am sure it will be a mutually beneficial arrangement, Mr LeMaitre,' replied Lord Westfield, who had a crumbling stately home and was always short of ready cash. 'Money from your . . . charitable foundation will come to us for . . . good works; and in return, we will undertake to support you in any candidacy for public office.'

'You will not lose by the arrangement.' The Master was on his feet now and Lord Amberley was helping him on with his cashmere coat. 'And, as a mark of the great respect and gratitude which I feel towards you, I should like to invite you all to a little soiree I have planned in a couple of weeks' time. Dinner and an evening's entertainment at my country estate – Winterbourne Hall. My personal assistant will send you the details. And now, gentlemen, I must bid you good day.'

As he turned to leave, a hand caught his sleeve.

'I hope you won't mind my mentioning it, but you do remind me very much of a journalist who interviewed me once,' remarked old Lord Spenthorne, amiably. 'Can't quite remember the fellow's name . . . Hunter or Huntley or something. You wouldn't be a relative of his, by any chance?'

The Master's frozen smile left the decrepit old peer rooted to the spot and wondering what on earth he had said to upset him.

Mara had almost given up hope of getting into the House and saving Andreas when she glanced up and saw a tall familiar figure coming out of one of the side entrances. The clothes were all wrong – far too smart, too expensive; and there was no light or warmth in the blue-grey eyes. But there was no mistaking him.

Andreas!

He had not seen her standing there and Mara knew that she must exercise the utmost care if she was going to be able to carry out her plan. She mingled with a crowd of camera-wielding American tourists, intent on getting a lot closer to Andreas before she risked being seen.

But he was moving away from her now – towards a long, black, shiny limousine parked beside the kerb. Frantic not to let her opportunity slip away, Mara struggled to break free of the jostling hordes and run after him, throwing caution to the winds.

As she pushed and shoved her way out of the crowd, Mara felt a burning sensation gnawing at her hip. Glancing down, she realised that it must be emanating from the dagger in her pocket. Unthinking, she plunged in her hand and pulled it out.

Its hilt was glowing red with heat and she cried out in pain, letting go of it and clutching her burned fingers. The tourists glanced at her momentarily, then carried on taking pictures as if nothing had happened.

The dagger fell to the ground with a clatter and, as Mara watched in horror, it glowed incandescent red and began to melt. In seconds it was reduced to a few drops of a molten, glass-like substance, soiling the paving stones.

Shocked to the core, Mara stood in silence for a few moments, unable to pull herself out of her trance. Then she remembered Andreas and looked up, searching frantically for his familiar outline beyond the hordes of tourists.

As she watched in silent desperation, he turned for a moment and she found herself looking straight into his face, into the cruel eyes that were not his, set in a face she had known so well. And he opened the door of the limousine, climbed inside, and was gone.

'I'm so pleased to meet you, Mr Heimdal,' breathed the glossy-lipped brunette, easing down his zip and insinuating a cool, delicate hand through his flies. 'I've heard so much about you.'

She smiled and, as her lips drew back, he couldn't help noticing how her teeth glistened with saliva. Curious little pointed teeth she had, like some beautiful carnivorous beast. A handsome, sexy woman like her had no need of a magician to conjure her up a sex-life. Heimdal wondered vaguely what bizarre whim had drawn her here.

He kissed her and her flesh was cool and smooth as alabaster.

'May I suck your cock, Mr Heimdal?' Already she was on her knees before him and her tongue was teasing the tip of his eager member.

He needed no further prompting.

6: The Phallus of Osiris

It was Heimdal himself who opened the door to Mara. Mara sensed immediately that there was something strange about him but nothing that she could quite define. He had the same easy manner and tireless sexual charm but for a moment she thought she glimpsed a disturbing, almost fanatical, look in his eyes.

She was imagining things again. Obviously her shock had unhinged her more than she thought.

'Come up to the studio,' said Heimdal. 'You look as if you need a drink.'

Mara nodded dumbly and followed him up the spiral staircase to his studio.

Over a double whisky and soda, Mara explained what had happened to her at the House of Lords. Heimdal nodded gravely.

'Clearly some force more evil than I had anticipated has intervened to prevent you reuniting Andreas's soul with his body. We shall require great perseverance and ingenuity to save him now.'

'I'll do anything, anything!' protested Mara and Heimdal seemed pleased by her determination. 'But tell me, please, what has happened to Andreas's soul? Was it not destroyed forever when the dagger was consumed?'

Heimdal shook his head.

'Evidently the destruction of the crystal dagger has freed his soul to wander as a shade in the realms of the underworld,' he replied. 'He is neither living nor dead but cut off from his own body, unable to be reborn within another.

'The only way we can save him is to follow our original plan of reuniting soul and body. And to accomplish this we must consult my own spirit-guide, Hermodr, who has great knowledge of the life that dwells beyond death.

'The spirit of Hermodr dwells in certain natural phenomena. He is a proud spirit and cannot be contacted, save by those who are in tune with the green heart of nature. He is a spirit of vegetation, fertility, of rebirth out of death. It would be fruitless for us to attempt to make contact with him here, in my studio, where we are surrounded by inanimate objects.

'So we must travel to one of the places in which I have felt his presence most strongly. And there we must both undergo ordeals which will test our reserves of sexual energy to the full. Are you willing to undertake the trial of Hermodr, Mara?'

His eyes burned into hers with a ferocious intensity.

'I am willing,' replied Mara, her mouth dry with anticipation. She had seen so much already; been through ordeals which even she, a practitioner of the occult arts, could never have imagined.

After all that she had seen and experienced, after all that her fragile, naked body had undergone, surely nothing could shock or harm her now? She dared not believe otherwise.

Heimdal's hand was on her breast now, cupping it like a ripe fruit, palpating the flesh as though he were judging it for sweet, juicy ripeness. The touch was comforting, though his hand felt oddly cool through the fabric of her shirt. He bent to kiss her throat and it was a strangely restrained kiss, as though it took a mighty effort of will not to go further, to be carried away by some much baser, primeval urge.

'Don't be afraid, Mara,' he whispered, his tanned, muscular fingers toying with the erect stalk of her nipple. 'It'll be all right now. I'm here to help you . . .'

A sudden, inexplicable surge of fear clutched at Mara's heart. But she knew it was just foolishness. She had been a true friend to Heimdal in his days of doubt and exile and now he was merely showing her his gratitude: repaying her with kindness and the offer of practical help.

Besides which, she realised with a brief stab of pain, Heimdal was her only hope. He was the only person she knew of in the entire world who had the powers necessary to help her rescue Andreas's soul from its shadowy prison, his body from its walking death. She raised her eyes to Heimdal's and smiled as bravely as she could.

'Let's go,' she said. 'We mustn't waste any more time.'

The wheels bit into the soft mud as Heimdal manoeuvred the Range Rover amongst the trees. Mara blinked apprehensively in the coppery twilight created as the watery sunshine filtered through multicoloured autumn leaves.

Mara shivered and was not quite sure why. She had spent many a day – and night – in woods just like these; her coven met regularly in a woodland clearing and danced naked in the moonlight. But ever since she had woken in a wood very like this ancient Hampshire forest, her body naked and bloody after her unspeakable ordeals, Mara had found it difficult to feel comfortable in the whispering cathedrals of nature.

She was being foolish again. Hadn't the tree-spirits helped to guide her to safety, that time in the forest? It seemed so long ago now . . .

Heimdal got out of the car and began to unload a collection of magical paraphernalia: a small altar, with two chafing-dishes filled with sweet woods, which he lit and set at either end of the altar; a large sheet of red velvet, which he spread over the damp ground; a small leather bag which he laid down on the velvet; and a bottle of fine white powder, with which he set about describing a circle around the altar and the velvet cloth.

Mara jumped down from the Range Rover and stood shivering in the clearing as Heimdal busied himself with his work, intoning words from an ancient grimoire as he did so. He seemed lost in his preparations, oblivious to Mara's existence. She hugged her shawl about her, and wondered what would happen next.

At length, Heimdal was satisfied that all was ready; and he took Mara by the hand and led her into the circle.

As Mara watched he began to undress, not exuberantly, as Mara had so often seen him, but with a ritualistic – almost mechanical – precision, folding each item of clothing and laying it carefully upon the top of the altar.

'This is the symbolic casting-off of old life,' he explained. 'For I am about to journey beyond life, beyond death even, into the world where the undead dwell.'

Mara noticed for the first time the blemish on the side of Heimdal's neck: a small, dark redness, rather like a love-bite, in the centre of which were several tiny puncture wounds.

'You've hurt yourself!' she exclaimed, stepping forward to get a better look at the injury.

But Heimdal put out his hand to stop her.

'It's nothing,' he said. 'Just a little accident. One of my clients yesterday insisted that I dress her in bondage clothing before the ceremony and, whilst we were fucking, she got carried away and injured me with her spiked leather collar. It's an occupational hazard.'

As if eager to change the subject, Heimdal silenced Mara's protestations with a kiss and explained what they must both do to empower the ritual:

'In order for me to travel to the kingdom of the undead, we must both shed our prejudices and preconceptions and transcend these frail vessels of flesh, so that my spirit may roam free and find the enlightenment we both seek.'

So saying, he stretched out a hand and began to unfasten the buttons of Mara's blouse. She stood before him, meekly submitting to his touch, allowing him to strip her clothes from her and lay them, with his, upon the altar.

'First, we must empty our bodies of sexual desire,' Heimdal went on, stroking her nipples gently with his strong, muscular fingers. 'We must exhaust our passions, glut them with physical pleasure, so that there is no impediment in my mind to prevent my spirit guide from entering and leading me towards enlightenment. We must fuck until we are both entirely spent, for only then shall we rise above our sensual world, our twin psychic energies combining and endowing me with the power to enter the world of the spirit.

'If you have desires, Mara, you must articulate them,' he continued, gazing deep into her eyes. 'And we shall then exorcise them together. I, in turn, shall voice my own desires, and you shall assist me to experience them to the full, thus banishing them as impediments to our work. And when our desires are spent, we must go further: travel beyond desire and perform outrages upon each other's bodies, accomplishing the final death of mortal fleshly desire.

'Speak, Mara: tell me the lustful secrets of your heart.'

At first, Mara was somewhat taken aback. Seeing her discomfiture, Heimdal opened the leather bag, took out a bottle and poured a little honey-scented liquid into a green crystal glass, instructing her to drink it down in a single draught. It tasted cloyingly sweet, with a half-hidden aftertaste of bitter herbs, and it obviously contained a powerful drug for Mara felt an immediate warmth spreading through her veins, inflaming her desires and loosening her tongue.

'These are the desires of my heart, Lord Heimdal,' she began, toying with her own nipples and enjoying the sensation as they grew ever-harder and more erect. 'I desire that you should force me to submit to the whip; that you should fill up my every orifice until I cry out for mercy; that you should bind me with thongs and chains and fuck me and bugger me till I can take no more.'

Heimdal's cock was swelling hugely in his pants; and Mara could clearly make out the outline of his massive hardness through the skin-tight leather of his trousers.

'For my part,' began Heimdal, 'I desire that you should mortify my prick and balls with your teeth and nails, and then suck me to a climax and make me spurt out all over your face and breasts. When I have buggered you, I desire that you should make me lick my semen out of your arse. I desire that you should sit upon my face and masturbate yourself to orgasm and force me to drink down the fruits of your self-love and the juices of my own loins.

'Come to me,' he commanded, and held out his arms to Mara, who stepped hesitantly towards him, shaking with cold, with fear, and with desire.

'Kneel, Mara; get on all fours, and thrust your arse towards me, to receive the consequences of your desire.' She obeyed, supporting herself on knees and hands as she waited for him to begin. The damp chill of the sodden ground was soaking up through the velvet, and she felt as though she was sinking, very slowly, through pack-ice into a frozen sea.

The first stroke of the lash bit into her flesh and made her arch her back with pain. The memory of her experience at Whitby Abbey still haunted her, and with each stinging blow she recalled the pain she had felt as the Master's arm rose and fell, raining pitiless blows upon her borrowed flesh.

Pain, yes; but also an insidious pleasure, which began as the spreading heat from savaged buttocks and soon grew in intensity and scope until it filled her whole body and mind, and seemed to focus on the throbbing bud of her clitoris. Mara gave a sigh of recognition as she felt the pain ebb away, leaving only the delicious warmth of irresistible desire, the pulsating pleasure of a hot, wet, cunt which longs to be satisfied.

Instinctively, Mara shuffled her knees apart, so that the lash fell not only on her buttocks, but on the moist and tender furrow within. She writhed in an agony of pleasure as its fiery tongue began to lick at her arse, her gaping cunt, and ventured as far as her clitoris, tormenting it into savage, ecstatic life.

At last the rain of blows ceased and Mara slumped gratefully to the ground, her erect nipples grinding into the damp red velvet.

'Well done, Mara,' breathed Heimdal, a little out of breath after his exertions. 'Can you not feel the power generated by your sexual energies, by your pleasure and pain? Can you not feel it all around you?'

And in truth there was an electricity within the circle, like static crackling across the damp night air. And there was a presence, like an unseen, watching eye; like a hooded figure half-glimpsed before it vanishes round a corner; like dark shadows at the edges of her vision . . .

Heimdal reached into the leather bag and took out leather thongs and chains. Mara wondered vaguely how he could have known the desires she would speak before him. Were his powers greater than she had thought?

'Lie on your back.' Mara obeyed, and Heimdal fastened her wrists in heavy iron manacles, linked together by a long chain. He attached a leather thong to either wrist and tied each to a ring set into the base of the heavy altar.

She now lay before him, spreadeagled and utterly helpless; her most intimate places offered up to him like some delectable human sacrifice.

If she had expected him to fuck her there and then, she was to be sorely disappointed. For Heimdal turned back to his leather bag and, this time, he took out a strange assortment of objects: a long, bleached-white thigh-bone; a wand made from green malachite; and a dish containing an assortment of wild berries.

He turned to Mara and smiled: a chilling, inhuman smile now, which both terrified and excited her. It reminded her so acutely of the Master's cruel smile . . .

'Animal, vegetable, and mineral,' explained Heimdal, laying out the items in the red velvet triangle between Mara's legs. Together, they symbolise the wholeness of creation.

'In inserting these items into your body, I shall be bringing us closer to the nature-spirit who shall be my guide.'

He took hold of Mara's thighs and forced them further apart, making her draw up her knees, the better to display the treasures of cunt and arse.

Taking the bone, he crushed some of the berries onto it and smeared the juice over the smooth, white surface. Then he slid his finger down through Mara's intimate crack until he found the hidden gateway to her most secret place.

The bone was thick and Mara's arse was tight, despite the mingling of cunt-juice and crushed berries which Heimdal used to lubricate it. Seemingly indifferent to her discomfort, he prised open her arse with his fingers and inserted the tip of the bone, pushing it home with one long thrust. Mara cried out with the pain of it, but as it lodged deep inside her she realised that the sensation was beginning to be pleasurable.

Next came the stone wand, gleaming in the car headlights which Heimdal had left switched on to illuminate the scene. He felt for Mara's cunt and slid the wand between her outer lips. It slid home without resistance, for Mara's cunt was dripping with natural moisture.

This done, Heimdal turned his attentions to his own prick. He took the rest of the berries and crushed them onto his stiffened flesh, letting the juice run down the shaft. Then he knelt astride Mara's face, facing her feet, and teased open her mouth with his fingers.

His shaft slipped easily into Mara's welcoming mouth. The crushed berries and their juice slid onto her tongue, mingling their piquant taste with the salty tang of his prick, already well lubricated with its own juice.

Bending forward, he took hold of the malachite wand and began to thrust it in and out of Mara's cunt, working it up and down like the piston of some phantasmagorical engine. She could not cry out at his roughness, for his shaft filled her mouth and throat, and all she could do was suck on it as a babe sucks at the breast.

Her juices flowed as he masturbated her; and her arse began to pulsate in time with the rhythms of her cunt, opening and closing on the bone which distended its delicate tissues. She felt herself coming to orgasm and thrust her hips upwards to meet the stone wand which was gratifying her.

Coming with a muffled groan of pleasure, Mara fell back onto the sodden velvet and received the salty tribute of Heimdal's spunk, which flooded her mouth and almost choked her.

Heimdal climbed off Mara, took the wand from her cunt and unfastened the thongs which held her fast to the altar. But, far from letting her go, he merely flipped her onto her stomach and then fastened her once more with thongs attached to her manacles.

The bone was still protruding obscenely from Mara's arse, like some ghastly skeleton penis, its white surface stained red with a liquid which might have been berry-juice or blood . . . Heimdal took hold of its end and began to move it in and out of Mara, manipulating it with expert skill. He knew just how much pleasure to give, just how much pain . . .

And then, almost before Mara had realised what he was doing, he had withdrawn the bone and cast it to one side and he was upon her, his cock searching for her, finding her secret entrance, forcing its way in through the bruised curtains of her martyred flesh. And she could hear a far-off voice – her own voice – screaming:

'Bugger me! Yes, bugger me!'

He rode her as though she were some pretty boy he had picked up off the streets: a pretty boy who would fuck any man in return for a meal and a few pounds to pay the rent. He buggered Mara hungrily but without passion, as a starving man might accept and devour any meal that was placed before him. And he paid no heed to her cries as he rode her beyond the barriers of suffering, into the realms of delirious, forbidden pleasure.

With a roar of satisfaction, he poured his second tribute into her, and they lay for a few moments, locked together, panting with exertion.

Heimdal released Mara from her chains and drew her to

her feet. Rivulets of semen and berry-juice stained her lips and were trickling down her thighs, soiling the flesh of her buttocks and her face. She swayed a little, and held onto him for support.

'Now you must exorcise *my* desires, Mara,' whispered Heimdal. 'You must take my body and purge it of its need to fuck and be fucked.'

Still half-dazed, Mara watched as Heimdal lay down upon the ground and beckoned her to him. Amazingly, his cock was fully erect once more, and its magnificence began to awaken new depths of lust within her. She knelt between his parted thighs and, remembering the desires which he had confessed to her, began to work upon his cock and balls with her teeth and nails. To her surprise, his desire seemed not dampened, but heightened, by her savagery: the harder she bit him, the deeper she sank her nails into the flesh of his balls, the harder his penis became. It began to dance deliriously against his belly, as though the spunk within were desperately struggling to pour forth its bounty.

At last, she took pity on him and began to suck the tip of his prick – all the while digging her fingernails into his scrotum. Within a few seconds he came: spurting copious amounts of creamy-white sperm into her willing mouth.

She gave him no time to recover – kneeling on all-fours before him, and ordering him to lick his own spunk from her arse. The sensation was quite new to her and its novelty was entirely pleasurable. It felt as though a tiny warm, wet, wriggling creature was burrowing its way into her most intimate places and the thought set her clitty throbbing once again with unsatisfied desire.

She felt the tip of his prick nudging against her buttocks but diverted it from her arse and repositioned it at the entrance to her cunt.

'Fuck me,' she commanded Heimdal.

He thrust into her and she took hold of his right hand and guided it to her clitoris.

'Wank me off.'

He rubbed at her juicy little rosebud and she felt her cunt

begin to throb with the urgent need for orgasm.

'Harder, harder!' She thrust out her buttocks and he understood and began to fuck her with all his might, burying his shaft in her up to the balls.

When they came, it was in unison, in a great flood of spunk and cunt-juice that seemed to make the whole world spin around them, divorcing them from the everyday laws of time and space. They slumped to the floor and Mara wearily rolled Heimdal onto his back, mindful of the one last task she must perform before the ritual could proceed.

Climbing astride him, she pressed the juicy flesh of her cunt against his face, so that he was forced to feel and taste and smell her heady womanhood. With her right hand, she began to wank herself, realising that – far from being spent – her desire had now reached its peak and must flower in a final, overwhelming orgasm.

Beneath her, Heimdal tasted the ever-greater flood of cunt-juice mingled with berries and spunk, and knew that her crisis was near. Putting out his tongue, he made contact with her clitoris and began to tease it.

With a loud shriek of pleasure, she exploded into a rainbow-bright orgasm and fell forward onto Heimdal's belly.

In her half-conscious state, Mara hardly noticed as Heimdal laid her gently upon the velvet cloth, her legs wide apart and her hands crossed upon her breasts, like the hands of a corpse.

'From death to rebirth,' whispered Heimdal.

When she opened her eyes and looked up, she saw a fearsome sight. Heimdal was towering over her, ferociously erect and hungry for her cunt. But the mighty weapon thrusting forth from his loins was horribly changed; upon it, he wore a thick leather sheath, covered in large metal studs. She wanted to run away, but somehow could not find the strength.

'Be not afraid,' soothed Heimdal and his voice was as smooth as honey. 'It is all part of the ritual. As we lie together, our loins fused, we shall enter the limbo between life and death. There, I shall meet my spirit guide and together we shall go forth into the land of the undead, where I shall meet with the soul of your lover, Andreas Hunt. But first, there must be pain. Pain and pleasure . . .'

And with these words, he lay upon her, belly to belly, prick poised at the gateway to her cunt. He looked down at Mara, and saw that she was weeping quietly. There was a faraway smile on his face; an unfamiliar, cruel twist to the corners of his mouth. Without further ado, he pressed the massive studded sheath against the entrance to her womanhood and thrust into her with one mighty movement of his loins.

She tried to cry out but could not. The sound seemed to catch in her throat. And she was no longer sure if she was feeling pain or pleasure. The metal studs felt huge inside her, pressing cruelly against the walls of her cunt, distending her womanhood, threatening to tear her fragile flesh. Yet they were also intensely arousing . . .

And she was floating now . . . She could hear the faraway voice of Heimdal, intoning a Nordic spell she could not understand. The world was spinning and she was falling, falling, into a many-coloured vortex where only her cunt existed.

For a moment, she thought she saw a pair of glowing eyes staring down into hers, thought she heard the sound of distant, cruel laughter. And then came a far-away voice, a terrifying voice that seemed to come from the very wastes of Hell, a voice that spoke words she could not understand:

'Seek the Talisman of Set.'

When she blinked and opened her eyes, she saw that Heimdal was still above her, gazing down at her with apparent concern. He was shaking her by the shoulders and she could feel the sting of a slap across her face.

'Mara! Are you all right? For a moment, I thought . . .'

She nodded, though she scarcely knew if it was true. Heimdal climbed off her, the studded sheath still gleaming on his penis. She sat up, shivering with the sudden realisation of the cold. Her cunt felt sore but otherwise she seemed fine.

'Andreas . . .?'

Heimdal nodded. 'I have spoken with my spirit guide. As I feared, your lover's soul walks with the shades in the underworld, alone and afraid. But have no fear, there is yet a way to save him: a key which will unlock his prison and restore his soul and body to the world of the living.

'I cannot tell you about it here – there are things I must show you. Secrets I must tell . . . Get dressed and get into the car. We're going back to London. I will tell you everything there.'

Heimdal took the weighty, leather-bound volume from the shelves and laid it carefully on his desk.

'This is a rare Victorian translation of the Egyptian *Book of the Dead*,' he explained. 'More properly, it is called the *Chapters of the Coming Forth By Day*. It is, as I am sure you know, the most sacred book of the ancient Egyptians.'

Mara nodded, at a loss to imagine what relevance it could have for her present plight.

Heimdal leafed through the book until he came to a chromolith depicting the gods and goddesses of ancient Egypt, then turned the book round so that the illustration was facing Mara.

'This is Osiris, god of vegetation and rebirth,' he continued, pointing to a human figure with a greenish-black face. 'And here is his wife and sister, the goddess Isis. Many scholars believe that Isis and Osiris were not formless spirits but real people who ruled Egypt in pre-Dynastic times. This,' he indicated a black figure with a malevolent expression, 'is the god Set, Osiris's brother, who envied him his power and wished to govern Egypt in his place.

'Such was Set's envy of his brother that he plotted to kill him. He invited him to a great banquet whose centrepiece was an ornate box fashioned in the shape of a coffin. Set invited his guests to try the box for size. One by one, they all tried in vain to fit into the box and at last it was Osiris's turn. He of course fitted into it perfectly and when he was inside, Set locked up the box and had it thrown into the Nile. Eventually the box containing Osiris's dead body was recovered by Isis, but it was stolen again and the body carved up into thirteen pieces, which were distributed throughout the land.

'Eventually, Isis succeeded in tracing all but one of the pieces of Osiris's body: his penis. In despair, she fashioned one out of wood, and added it to the reassembled body – with such success that, by copulating with it, she was able to conceive a son, Horus.

'The missing penis, mummified but still magnificent, was lost to the world for centuries. Think how great its power must have been, if even a poor wooden representation of it could impregnate Isis! Magicians have known for millennia that the Phallus of Osiris – or the Talisman of Set as some call it – has great powers of life and death and they have pursued it across the globe. Many false imitations have been made to deceive the foolish but the true phallus still exists somewhere in the world.

'It is this which you must seek if you wish to restore Andreas Hunt to life, to reunite his soul with his body. For only the Phallus of Osiris contains sufficient power to raise the dead.'

Mara looked crestfallen.

'But how am I to find this . . . talisman, if so many magicians have tried and failed? Where am I to begin?'

Heimdal smiled reassuringly and laid his hand upon hers. His flesh was cool, almost amphibian, and for a moment she flinched. Then the power of his gaze began to warm her once again, moistening her cunt with reluctant desire.

'Have no fear, Mara. For I know of the Phallus's last reported location. During the last War, Allied and Nazi magicians strove relentlessly to acquire the Phallus, which they were convinced would endow them with the power of life and death, and perhaps even ensure victory. Eventually it was acquired by Hitler and kept in his personal museum of magical artefacts, in his bunker deep beneath the streets of Berlin.

'Unfortunately, no one seems to know – or admits to knowing – what happened to the Phallus at the end of the war, when the Russians invaded Berlin. You must go to Berlin and seek out some of the magicians who used their powers for – and against – Hitler: only they can help you now. I have the names and addresses of a few sorcerers who may be able and willing to offer you their assistance.'

The colour drained from Mara's face.

'Berlin? But that's crazy! I have no money, no resources. I don't even speak German! How can I just set off for Berlin?'

Heimdal was closer now and more attentive than ever, his hand sliding down from her shoulder to her breast, fingers skilfully unbuttoning her shirt and slipping inside, cupping the firm, warm flesh and beginning to stimulate the nipple into yearning hardness. Mara's breathing was becoming hoarse and he noted that she had relaxed her knees and they were moving slightly apart.

'I could give you money aplenty,' he breathed into her ear. 'But you will have no need of money. For I have a gift for you which will protect and assist you throughout your quest.'

Smiling at Mara's questioning expression, Heimdal reached into his pocket and took out a crystal pendant, very similar to the one which Mara had lost in her confusion and terror at Winterbourne. Swiftly and silently, he slipped the chain over her hair and let it fall into place round her neck, multi-coloured light flashing from its many facets as it swung, invitingly, between her magnificent, tawny globes.

'Trust in fortune,' he breathed 'and it will smile upon you. Trust in the power of this crystal amulet and it will bring you all that you need upon your journey. No need will be left unsatisfied. No need . . .'

And, feeling the urgency of his own need, Heimdal finished unbuttoning Mara's shirt, his enormous prick straining against the tight leather of his trousers. His right hand slid along Mara's thigh and up to the delicious surprise of her naked cunt. No knickers. Good. Fragrant, warm and wet from her ordeal in the forest. Still better. He reached for his zip and tugged it down, so that his prick sprang out, exuberantly ready for the fray.

He lifted up her skirt and picked her up bodily in his strong arms, easing her thighs around his hips and lowering her gently onto his soaring prick, feeling her shudder with silent pleasure as his hardness forged deep into her belly.

'Don't worry, Mara,' he whispered in her ear. 'You won't really be alone on your journey. There'll always be someone watching over you . . .'

'You have done well, Heimdal,' remarked the Master, inviting the magician to choose a whore and avail himself of her soft wet mouth or tight, tender backside. He himself was settled in his favourite armchair and enjoying being fucked by a tall Zulu warrior-woman, who was sitting on his lap and raising and lowering herself upon his penis.

'Thank you, Master,' replied Heimdal, casting an eye round the room and selecting a tall, leggy whore with waist-length waves of blonde hair.

'Go to him, Sonja,' the Master instructed her. 'Give him all that he desires.'

Sonja crossed the room obediently to where Heimdal was standing, and peeled down the front of her strapless dress, so that he could enjoy a preliminary feel of her small but juicy tits.

'Bend over,' Heimdal commanded. 'I want to bugger you.'

Obediently, Sonja leant against the back of an old leather armchair, and thrust out her buttocks. They were lily-white and as smooth as satin. He peeled apart her arse-cheeks and was delighted to see that she had a very tight, very tiny hole which would take quite a lot of forcing before his mighty weapon could enter. Heimdal was going to enjoy himself.

'Because you have done well,' continued the Master, making a conscious effort to retard the moment of orgasm to increase its eventual intensity, 'I shall explain the significance of what you have done.

'Through skilful deception, you have convinced the witch Mara that her lover's soul dwells in the underworld and that, in order to reunite it with his body, she must find the Phallus of Osiris. It was a nicely staged deception, and I particularly enjoyed the mumbo-jumbo in the forest.

'Naturally, my true intent is to use her considerable psychic abilities to locate and raise the body of my lost queen, Sedet, who sacrificed herself for me so many thousands of years ago. For only the Phallus of Osiris has the power to raise her inanimate flesh and restore her to her rightful place beside me.

'It is my belief that this woman, Mara, is the only one capable of performing these tasks. Already, she has shown that she has a latent ability to communicate with Sedet and I have found none other with this gift. For the time being she is useful to us. We must ensure that she comes to no harm.'

But, as he spurted his semen into the Zulu girl's cunt, he was thinking to himself:

How I despise the witch Mara Fleming. How I long to destroy her, and the powers she carries within that frail little body. When she has served me, I shall allow myself the considerable pleasure of watching her die. But for now I must be patient and use her as my pawn.

Heimdal entered Sonja Kerensky like a bull mounting a cow: without gentleness, but with a raw sexual power which made the girl roar with the pleasure of his violation.

It was a pity about Mara, he mused. But let's face it: the girl had expected way too much from him by way of gratitude. In the world of magic she was a mere amateur, trying to play in the big league. And her death would simply be the inevitable consequence of crossing swords with Heimdal the Destroyer.

7: Berlin

Mara walked down the steps of the plane at Tempelhof Airport and got onto the bus with the other passengers. As they rattled across the tarmac towards the airport buildings, she pondered over the incredible good fortune which had accompanied her on her journey so far.

Heimdal had had his work cut out, persuading her to come on this wild goose chase. Even at the last minute, as he bundled her into the taxi, she had had serious misgivings. In the end, she had arrived at Heathrow with barely enough money in her pocket to pay for a standby to Berlin. Mara smiled to herself. She was becoming as cynical as Andreas Hunt. And, of course, Andreas Hunt was the reason she had come.

She checked in at the desk and put her name down for a standby economy ticket on the morning shuttle. Then she went off to buy a coffee. As she was about to pay for it at the counter, a hand touched her lightly on the shoulder.

'Can I buy that for you, Miss Fleming?'

She turned round and found herself looking into the warm brown eyes of a Lufthansa pilot, his flight bag slung over his shoulder. She had never seen him before in her life but he was smiling at her as though she were a long-lost friend . . . or a lover.

'I read your article on crystal therapy in *Oracle* magazine,' he explained, his voice full of genuine enthusiasm. 'Very scholarly, very impressive. And your photograph – stunning! Though, of course, it did not do you justice. I would have recognised you anywhere, Miss Fleming – may I call you Mara?'

She nodded, and he went on speaking as they carried their coffees over to a table by the window. The thick, plate-glass windows only just managed to mask the deafening whine of jet engines as planes taxied past and manoeuvred onto the runways.

'My name is Ralf Westerhof,' he explained. 'But you must call me Ralf. All my friends do.

'I was walking past the check-in desk, and I heard you ask for a standby ticket to Berlin. Surely such a beautiful woman should be travelling first class!'

'I wish I could afford to!' laughed Mara, making circles in her coffee with her spoon. He was a very attractive man, and she could feel his desire for her burning into the side of her face. She could hardly bear to look at him, for fear of trembling and lapsing into gibberish.

'Well, I think I can arrange it, Mara,' Ralf reassured her, abandoning any pretence of drinking his coffee and placing his bear's paw of a hand upon hers. 'If you'll allow me to! You see, I can arrange anything for a . . . friend.'

She looked up at him and the magnetism crackled between them as though they were two electrical terminals.

'I was wondering – would you like me to fuck you, Mara Fleming?'

By way of reply, she stood up and lifted his hand to her breast, so that he could feel the budding nipple stiffening and straining under the soft cashmere of her sweater.

'Come with me,' he breathed, taking her by the wrist and leading her out of the restaurant and across the tarmac. 'I know somewhere where we can be alone.'

It still seemed so unreal, when she looked back on it now, hours later. First, Captain Westerhof had arranged for her to have a seat in First Class, complete with champagne breakfast. And then, whilst her mind was still reeling and her body still yearning for him, he had taken her out to the aeroplane – the very one she had been planning to travel on.

The plane was deserted, with an hour to go before the crew were expected. Ralf ushered her on board, past the ranks of mechanics and cleaners who were fussing about outside, and closed the door behind them. It was eerily quiet inside the plane – warm and soft and silent – except for the gentle, rhythmic hum of a nearby tanker. It was just like being inside the belly of some fantastical beast.

He had kissed her passionately, then laid her down gently on the lush, red-carpeted floor of the First Class cabin and unfastened her blouse, so that her ripe, unfettered breasts sprang out for the joy of freedom and fucking.

With the gentlest of movements, he stroked their smooth, tanned surface, then knelt between her thighs and bent to kiss her nipples. They sprang into obedient life, enraptured by the velvet touch of his muscular but gentle tongue; and Mara could not help but relax and allow herself to float away on the swelling tide of sensual pleasure.

Sliding his hand down from her breasts, Ralf took hold of the hem of her skirt and raised it high above her waist, revealing the naked beauty of her loins.

'Such loveliness . . .' he gasped and, parting the lips of her cunt like the petals of some exotic flower, he bent to savour her fragrance, to drink at her ever-renewing spring of secret nectar.

'Fuck me,' sighed Mara. 'Please fuck me. I need to feel you inside me . . . now . . .'

'Patience, little one,' he replied and continued to stimulate her clitoris with his knowing tongue. 'All in good time.'

And it was not until Mara was almost sobbing with frustration that Ralf unzipped his pants and took out a good-sized, throbbing prick whose glistening tip bore witness to the urgency of his own desire. Mara's thighs were wide apart now, straining to welcome him in, and her cunt glistened with little rivulets of agonising desire. Ralf thrust fingers knuckle-deep into her soft wetness and ground them into her flesh. She flinched a little as his signet ring bit into the walls of her cunt but the discomfort only added to the pleasure, the excitement.

Ralf could wait no longer. Using his fingers to prise apart her sweet, soft flesh, he slid his hardness into her in one long thrust. He groaned with pleasure as he rammed into her, feeling her silken cunt-walls tighten instinctively around his shaft like iron fingers in a soft glove. And she responded to him as a thoroughbred filly who knows and obeys her master's innermost desires.

He rode her time and time again to a shuddering climax; and, when she thought he had sated her of all pleasures and desires, he flipped her over onto her belly and buggered her with all the enthusiasm of a man who has been deprived of sweet flesh for many months.

As he climbed off her and his semen flooded out of her, soiling the expensive red carpet, Mara sighed contentedly, almost forgetting the pain of loss and fear which tore intermittently at her heart.

Ralf helped her to her feet and she cleaned herself up a little before taking her seat in First Class. Only a few moments later, the cabin door swung open and the first of the crew members arrived. They exchanged knowing glances as they passed the beautiful woman sitting alone in the First Class cabin. She must be another of Captain Westerhof's 'close friends' . . .

The plane soon filled up with passengers and before Mara had time to think they were taxiing down the runway. They were on their way to Berlin.

When she tired of looking out of the window at the dwindling trees and houses beneath them, Mara turned her attentions to her fellow-passengers. She found she was sitting next to a tall, quite distinguished-looking man who was working away busily on a laptop computer. As she watched him out of the corner of her eye, he looked up at her as though aware of her gaze.

'Oh, I'm sorry,' stammered Mara. 'I hope I didn't disturb you.'

'Not at all,' replied the businessman affably, logging off and snapping shut the lid of the laptop. 'I was just entering in a few sales figures – very boring stuff, but it has to be done. I have an important Board meeting this afternoon so I must be well prepared.' He spoke excellent English, but with the faintest hint of a German accent.

He held out his hand. 'Heinrich Kröll,' he announced. 'I'm very pleased to meet you.'

'Mara Fleming.' She felt very shabby and out of place in her simple sweater and cotton skirt.

He leaned over her, as though to look out of the window, but instead whispered to her in conspiratorial tones:

'You have very nice tits, Fräulein Fleming. *Very* nice tits indeed . . . In Germany, we know how to appreciate a beautiful woman, how to pleasure her body . . .'

To her amazement, she found herself responding with uncharacteristic boldness:

'And I should not be at all surprised to find that you have a fine, fat prick inside those hand-stitched trousers, Herr Kröll. I see that it is getting quite hard. Would you like me to suck it for you?'

She heard a little sound, like a sigh of anticipation, as Herr Kröll's hand strayed briefly between her thighs before returning to his lap. When he spoke, it was in such a quiet, matter-of-fact voice that Mara could hardly believe it was the same man.

'Come to me in the toilet in five minutes' time.'

Kröll stood up, smoothing the creases from his trousers, and strode off down the gangway towards the lavatory. Mara looked after him, appreciating his tall, spare frame, his tight arse, the easy grace of his walk. She saw the door open and close and the sign flick from green to red.

Her heart was pounding. She had fucked in many strange places before but never on an aeroplane. And yet, since sex was an essential part of her psychic growth, perhaps there was some psychic significance in her sudden upsurge of desire? Perhaps her psyche sensed that it needed more sexual energy to see her through the trials and tribulations of her quest? And if there was no mystic significance to the invitation, surely there could be no harm in a little innocent enjoyment?

She checked her watch again. Another two minutes. One. The second hand ticked round the face with agonising slowness. Now it was time. Picking up her handbag, she stood up rather shakily and walked the longest few yards she had ever walked. Everyone seemed to be either asleep or engrossed in magazines and in-flight movies – but she still felt as though all eyes were on her. Had they overheard her brief conversation with Herr Kröll? Could they have guessed that this ordinary-looking young woman was going to the lavatory to fuck – to spread her legs for a complete stranger?

She knocked gently on the door.

'It's me.'

After a moment's pause, the door swung open, just wide enough to let Mara slip inside.

'I'm glad you decided to accept my little invitation.'

It was a tiny, hot, airless cubicle, reeking of stale piss and disinfectant. Heinrich Kröll was sitting on the only available seat – the lavatory – with his flies unzipped and his prick protruding through the gap in his trousers.

It was quite a nice prick, mused Mara, kneeling down silently before him on the damp vinyl floor and slipping her fingers through his flies, insinuating them inside his underpants and cradling his twin love-apples. A nice prick, good and stiff, and big enough to stretch my cunt agreeably. I'm still hungry for a good fucking. I shall enjoy having him inside me.

Odd, that. All she could think about was fucking, fucking, fucking – like an animal. Mindless and entirely physical. It felt as though some quite different person had taken charge of her mind and was filling it with all manner of lewd thoughts. Where was the spirituality which she had always so prized in her sexual activities? She was so hungry for sex that she began to wonder if she might be turning into a nymphomaniac. It felt almost as though some external force was using her body for its own ends. For its own pleasures . . . With a twinge of unease, she recalled that she had encountered this feeling before . . .

She shivered as she recalled the demonic possession of her body at Winterbourne Hall; the many men who had used her and mocked at her frailty; the evil female spirit which had briefly entered her and used her for its own physical delight. What did it all mean?

Anxious to banish these dark thoughts from her mind, Mara set about sucking Herr Kröll's cock with energy and enthusiasm. It was an appreciative subject, twitching and swelling and hardening under the touch of her tongue, her lips, her sucked-in cheeks.

She felt his bollocks harden and knew he was close to coming.

'No.' He stopped her with a hand on her shoulder and drew his cock out of her mouth. She looked up at him in surprise. 'That was most agreeable, Fräulein Fleming. However, I have a fancy to come to orgasm in your cunt. I take it you have no objection?'

Mara shook her head, bewildered, and stood with legs wide apart, waiting for him to enter her. It was a tight fit, getting two people into this tiny compartment – let alone for those two people to fuck standing up.

Kröll flexed his knees, adjusted his prick so that it was precisely positioned at the entrance to her cunt, and then straightened his legs. His cock slid up into her wet tunnel like a knife into butter and she had to hold on tight to her lover to prevent her knees from giving way with the sheer pleasure of it all. It felt wonderful.

He slid a finger round behind her and burrowed it into her arse, completing the pleasure-circuit which triggered off an enormous orgasm. As the last, titanic waves rippled through her cunt, she felt Kröll spurt into her and she collapsed forward into his arms. Fear ebbed away in the glorious warmth of physical pleasure.

When they had tidied themselves up and returned – separately, of course – to their seats, Kröll got out his computer and started tapping away again. Mara began to wonder if she had simply dreamed the whole thing: but her cunt was still dripping with Kröll's semen and her clitty still throbbed dully with the memory of the orgasms he had given her.

As they landed at Tempelhof Airport, Kröll turned to her and smiled.

'My dear Fräulein Fleming, such a pleasure meeting you and . . . doing business with you. As a mark of my gratitude, I hope you will accept a little gift.'

Seeing the questioning look on her face, Kröll went on:

'I am the owner of a rather fine hotel in Berlin – the Hotel Kaiserhof. This card will entitle you to free board at the hotel for as long as you wish to stay.' And he pressed the card into her hand and was gone.

All in all, mused Mara, as the bus decanted its passengers at the airport buildings, this has been a lucky day. Wonderful sex, a first-class air ticket, and now free board and lodging in a luxury hotel! Perhaps Heimdal had been right. Fingering the crystal medallion, she felt a surge of power crackle through her fingertips. She wondered if luck like this could hold out for ever . . .

The room was every bit as luxurious as Mara had hoped, and she spent a lazy hour wallowing in a hot bath, scented with the jasmine bath oil she had bought at the airport.

Strange how, just when she thought there was no more money in her purse, she would put in her hand and take out another ten-mark note – a hundred, even. Someone – or something – really was watching over her.

After her bath she rang round the contact numbers which Heimdal had given her. The first two sorcerers turned out to be dead; the third had moved to Stuttgart and become a dentist; but the fourth showed some interest and said he would ring back later.

What to do now, while she waited? She tried to read a magazine, but the words just seemed to dance in front of her eyes. In the end, she took off her bathrobe and lay down on the bed, making the most of the centrally heated luxury.

She was feeling sexy again. Very sexy. She closed her eyes and let her hands roam over her freshly bathed skin. It was still damp and fragrant, as though she had been swimming in a perfumed sea. Her mind wandered and she became a mermaid, swimming naked through a scented ocean, her long dark hair streaming out behind her.

She pressed a finger to her clitoris. It was hard and almost painful to the touch. Lubricating her finger with her own cunt-juices, Mara returned to it a second time, this time rubbing so gently that her finger passed across it almost like a whisper, or like warm, fast-flowing water.

Her desire grew more urgent and she rubbed harder. Now she was back in her own, familiar body, but still naked and swimming amongst the coral and the sea-anemones. The warm water showered lascivious caresses upon her, awakening clitty and nipples to new heights of sensual desire. Shoals of multi-coloured fish wove patterns around her. Here was one fish, larger than the rest and more audacious, passing between her thighs and now burrowing into her pubic fleece, nibbling greedily at her little clitoris. How delicious it felt!

As her orgasm approached, a strange vision entered her head and would not be banished. She was swimming into a patch of coarse, dark seaweed, and there was something caught up in it. Something . . . a long, narrow wooden box; a box large enough to contain . . . She came closer, and stretched out her hand to touch it, and the lid slid across, and floated away into the darkness.

Her orgasm was almost upon her now, she could feel the mounting tension in her loins, the delicious suspense before the fireworks . . .

She bent over the open box, curious to see what lay within. And as the orgasm took hold of her body, racking it with delicious, agonised spasms, her mind screamed silently for the horror of what she had seen:

A dead man, his flesh greenish-black with decay. A dead man only just recognisable as Andreas Hunt.

The phone rang, and she shook herself back into wakefulness, almost sobbing with fear and exhaustion. Trying desperately to control herself, she picked up the receiver and answered in a trembling voice:

'Hello . . .?'

'*Guten Tag*, Fräulein Fleming. Did you find your interlude agreeable? I most certainly did! Though I was a little confused by your underwater exploits . . .'

'What do you mean?' demanded Mara, suddenly aghast.

'Come now, my dear Miss Fleming. I am, as you well know, a magician with many years of scholarship behind me. I am also a seer, a true seer like yourself. I simply tuned in psychically to your thought-waves.

'But enough of this idle banter. I have considered your proposition, and I am willing to meet with you. Meet me at the Cafe Kranzler, on the corner of the Kurfürstendamm and Joachimstaler Strasse at two-thirty this afternoon and we shall discuss the matter further.

'But . . .!' protested Mara.

'*Auf wiederhören*, Fräulein Fleming!' A tiny click, and the phone went dead.

Mara glanced at her watch. Almost one-thirty already. No time to lose. Throwing on a few clothes, she grabbed a warm shawl and set off for the Kurfürstendamm.

The Cafe Kranzler, once a hotbed of radical intellectuals during the 1848 revolution, looked more like a harmless tourist-trap than the sort of place where two magicians might meet to discuss the most powerful magical talisman the world has ever known.

It was a chilly day and most of the cafe's patrons were huddled inside the building, hands wrapped round a steaming cup of coffee, or drinking endless beers to help them forget November and the approach of winter.

But Mara had arranged to meet Otto Helsing on the terrace where there was less chance of their being overheard. Scanning the other patrons, she saw only two women with young children and a handsome man in his mid-thirties who seemed to appreciate her obvious curves. No sign of him yet, then. She sat down at one of the tables, drew her shawl round her and prepared for a long wait. Perhaps he wouldn't turn up at all. A white-aproned waiter brought her coffee, and she let her mind wander as she sipped the scalding liquid.

'Have you changed your mind, Fräulein Fleming? Do you no longer wish to speak to me?'

The familiar, mellifluous voice brought her back to her senses and she looked up to see the handsome young man smiling down at her, a little patronisingly, she thought.

'I don't know what you mean,' she replied. 'I'm waiting for someone.'

'As am I.'

'Who *are* you?'

'Otto Helsing, at your service.'

Mara's jaw dropped. Otto Helsing? But he had worked as one of Hitler's black magicians. At the very least, he must be nudging seventy . . .

'I can see that you are sceptical, Fräulein Fleming. And that is understandable. After all, I do not "look my age" as you English say – is that not so? Well, Miss Fleming, do not look so disbelieving. I am a magician, after all. There are secrets which even you, my little white witch, are not privy to. Dark secrets which would curl your beautiful black hair, my lovely . . .'

He patted her hair with his too-smooth, too-perfect fingers and she wanted to recoil from him, from this abomination of a man who had devoted his entire life to working for evil.

But she must be strong, resolute. Now that she knew of his telepathic powers, she must block him from her mind, so that he could not fathom the lies she was about to speak. She remembered Heimdal's words: 'Trust to fortune and it will smile upon you. Trust in the crystal . . .'

Surreptitiously, she slid her hand beneath her shawl and touched the crystal lightly. She could tell from the sudden look of bafflement on Helsing's face that he was having no success in reading her mind.

'Herr Helsing,' she began. 'I am a member of a neo-Nazi group and have been entrusted with a mission of vital importance. I must find the Talisman of Set – the Phallus of Osiris – in order that we may bring the body of the Führer back to life.'

Helsing's eyes narrowed.

'The body of the Führer was destroyed by the Allies in 1945, my dear. Burned after death in his bunker, along with the corpse of his little slut, Eva Braun. Any fool knows that.'

'So everyone thought until recently. But it has now been revealed that those loyal to the Führer succeeded in smuggling his body out of the country and it is now being preserved within a magically protected coffin somewhere in Bolivia. Only a privileged inner circle knows exactly where. Sorcerers have determined that the Phallus of Osiris may have the power to restore our beloved Führer to life.'

'I see,' replied Otto. 'And just supposing I did have information on its whereabouts, what would be the benefit to me?'

Mara slipped the shawl from her shoulders, to reveal the low-cut blouse which she had carefully selected.

'I think I can persuade you that it's worth your while,' she heard herself reply.

Helsing paused for a moment, as though weighing up the bargain, and then beckoned to the waiter to bring the bill.

'Come, my little temptress,' he said, his thin lips curling into a smile. 'And we shall see if the wager is worth the game.'

Otto Helsing lived in a small house beside the Grünwaldsee, on a path which led from Pücklerstrasse into the dense pine forests of Wilmersdorf.

He parked the car beside the lake, got out and unlocked the front door to the house, which looked as though it had once been a huntsman's or ferryman's lodge.

Inside, it smelt odd: like a museum. The air was full of the mingled scents of ancient things, of half-forgotten incense, of magical and alchemical substances whose origins were too horrible to bear contemplation.

Eye of newt . . . Mara shivered, and allowed herself to be

ushered into the main sitting room, which had been converted into a black-magic shrine. Above the black-draped altar hung a Nazi flag, tattered and stained with brown patches which Mara realised must be dried blood.

'The standard which the Führer himself blessed before it was carried in the Münich putsch of 1923,' explained Helsing. 'It was carried by Horst Wessel and after he was killed it was used to wrap his body. It is a very potent symbol . . . and a very evil one, of course!'

Mara surveyed the scene with horror. Black candles, an inverted crucifix, the stench of blood not long ago shed – all of these signs told her that she should run, try to escape the madman and his piercing blue eyes.

'Our bargain. Remember our bargain,' whispered Helsing, slipping an arm round her waist and sliding his hand upwards to clutch at the firmness of her right breast. 'If you want information – and I know that you do, desperately – then you must give yourself up to me, utterly, to do with exactly as I please.'

She nodded, and began to undress.

'For the good of the Fatherland, I shall obey you . . .'

Helsing had already unbuttoned his flies and was fondling his prick before her, as though daring her to admit that she could not go through with what she had promised. And yet she must. And . . . he was a handsome man, though his eyes were filled with evil. It would not be unpleasant to have him enter her body – if she could banish the fear from her mind, the fear of what perverse fantasies might seize control of those strong, cruel hands . . .

Without warning, he was upon her, scratching and biting her delicate flesh, and making her cry out with terror and pain. His fingers seemed to probe into her every nook and cranny, each orifice explored and defiled by sharp fingernails which tore and bruised as they satisfied their prurient curiosity.

And then he forced her to her knees, sobbing, and prised open her mouth, thrusting his tool between her lips and making her gag as its head touched the back of her throat.

'Swallow it down, little whore!' he cried. And when Mara looked up at him, she saw not the blue eyes of Otto Helsing, but the mad, burning coals which had illuminated the Master's evil face. She tried to escape, to draw away, but he was relentless. His cock rammed into her again and again, until at last she felt it judder and semen flooded her mouth, tasting bitter on her tongue.

And she knew that this was just the beginning.

That afternoon, Mara underwent sexual humiliation the like of which she had never imagined. Helsing buggered her with his ornate black candlesticks, buggered her till she bled and begged for him to stop. He stuffed her cunt and arse full of candles and stretched them beyond endurance, bruising and tearing the delicate flesh – until at last pain became pleasure and she came to an enormous, crashing orgasm which left her lying, spent, upon the floor.

'Foolish girl,' smiled Helsing, zipping up his flies and buckling his belt. 'Did you really think you could fool me with your childish lies? And did you really think your arguments, even if true, could sway me?

'Child, I have only two things to say to you. The first is that I hated Adolf Hitler and would do nothing to further his cause. His relics I cherish for their magical power but the man . . . he was a jumped-up corporal, with the mind of a peasant.

'The second thing is this, and it is the truth. I tell you the truth because I like you, for all your pathetic trickery, and I like your spirit, Fräulein Fleming. I do not know what became of the Phallus of Osiris, but I should dearly love to own it. If you succeed in finding it, remember that you will not get a better price for it from anyone.'

He gathered together Mara's clothes and hauled her to her feet. Opening the front door, he pushed her out, dazed, naked and sore, into the chilly November afternoon.

'Go, foolish girl. I have enjoyed our little games. But remember: you must not come back unless and until you have found the Phallus of Osiris. Otherwise, be very sure that I shall destroy you.'

* * *

The following morning Mara awoke to the sound of a gentle knock at her door. She sat up in bed, wincing as she remembered the previous day's ordeal and the painful, humiliating games that the seductively evil Otto Helsing had played with her body.

Drawing the covers up round her naked breasts, she called out:

'*Komm*!'

The door swung inwards and a young boy tottered in, trying desperately not to spill the tray of orange juice, coffee and fresh rolls.

'*Guten Morgen*, Fräulein Fleming,' the young lad greeted her, blushing to the roots of his fair hair as he saw that, beneath the sheet, Mara was naked. 'I hope that you have passed the good night?' Mara smiled at his confusion, thinking how different he was from Otto Helsing. He had an open, honest face.

'I slept very well, thank you,' she replied; and she pointed to the bedside table. 'Perhaps you could put it down there? I wouldn't like you to drop it!'

The lad obeyed and was turning to go when Mara patted the bedcovers beside her.

'Why not sit down? I could do with a chat.'

She could see from the front of his uniform trousers that the youth was already excited by what he could see of her body, so she took hold of his arm and pulled him down, forcing him to sit on the bed beside her. Then she dropped the sheet, exposing her magnificent breasts to his disbelieving gaze.

His jaw dropped open and he began to babble incoherently in German.

'It's all right, it's all right,' soothed Mara, silencing him with a kiss full on his trembling lips, her tongue wriggling impishly into his mouth and seeking out his. 'I won't harm you . . .'

Taking hold of his hands, she placed one on either breast and showed him with gentle circular movements how he could pleasure her and make her nipples stand erect. As he toyed with her titties, she leaned forward and took hold of his zip, tugging it down and feeling inside for the gap in his pants that would lead her to his penis.

She found it and pulled it out with a little cry of girlish delight. He was whimpering now, his face buried between Mara's breasts as he continued to play, almost mechanically, with her nipples.

It was a good-sized prick, nice and firm – as you would expect from a sixteen-year-old lad – and circumcised. Mara allowed herself a little shiver of pleasure: there was something wicked about a circumcised prick – the way you could run your tongue over its every nook and cranny, exploring it without any modest little cloak of flesh getting in the way. She began to manipulate it – and the inevitable happened. He gave a convulsive shudder, and came all over her hand.

Immediately he tried to pull away from her, deeply ashamed of what had happened.

'I . . . I am so sorry . . . please don't tell anyone.'

'It's all right, nothing bad is going to happen to you,' repeated Mara, unfastening his trouser belt and pulling his trousers and pants down below his hips, the better to toy with his manhood. 'We'll soon have you ready and willing again.'

And she bent and took his half-erect penis into her mouth, savouring the salty taste of fresh semen on her tongue, fondling his balls and wondering at their mobility within their little velvet sac. As she sucked she felt his shaft stiffening once more into eager rigidity with all the swiftness of extreme youth.

'I want you to fuck me, little boy,' she whispered in his ear. 'Do you understand me?'

He nodded, too embarrassed or too overcome to reply – she couldn't tell which.

'Tell me truthfully: have you ever fucked before?'

He shook his head.

'I . . . I have never seen a woman naked before. I touched

my Aunt Gerda's breasts once . . . no more.'

'Then I shall guide you.'

Mara pushed back the covers and signalled to the youth to lie on top of her. But he was clumsy and his untried penis could not find its way to her rapidly moistening crack. Gently, she took him in hand and guided him to her hole.

'Now!' she whispered.

He thrust into her, clumsily but with the great energy of a young animal in its first rutting season: the juvenile stag mounting his first hind and discovering that it is wonderful, and that no matter how long it goes on it can never be long enough.

Mara answered his awkward thrusts with her own: slower and more sinuous, controlling his movements so that he would not come until she was ready for him. He felt pleasingly large in her tight cunt and her own orgasm was hastened by the delicious thought that her cunt was the first this eager little ramrod had ever breached.

'I . . . I'm coming!' cried the youth, and poured out his tribute, just in time to feel the rhythmic contractions of Mara's cunt as she climaxed beneath him.

He left with apologies and thanks, and a damp, darkening stain on his uniform trousers.

When he had gone, Mara noticed a slim brochure lying on the tray underneath the glass of orange juice. Strange – she could have sworn it wasn't there before. She picked it up and read it. It was a guide for visitors to the Berlin Ägyptisches Museum – the Museum of Egyptology.

Why not? she thought to herself. Since nothing is going right, I might as well do some sightseeing. Maybe the museum will give me some clues about the Phallus of Osiris.

And she got up and went into the bathroom to turn on the shower.

Mara liked museums. Not the modern sort, with interactive displays and mechanical dinosaurs; but museums of the old school. She loved the musty smell, the glass-fronted mahogany cases, the feeling of being in a time warp.

She liked the Ägyptisches Museum. As she laid her hands upon the glass fronts of the cases she could feel some of the vibrations coming from the objects within them, her psychic powers bringing her once more into contact with the past. Two simple statuettes entitled 'A married couple' . . . she touched the glass and a vision of sun-burned sand filled her head; a vision of a man, naked to the waist, fashioning the figures from wet clay. She moved on and the pictures changed. A child's toy, food dishes, funerary trappings that filled her head with pain and her lungs with the suffocating stench of death.

But nothing to give her any clues about what she was seeking.

At last, she stopped in front of the museum's most famous exhibit: the sublime, painted head of Queen Nefertiti. A beautiful woman's portrait in clay, only half-finished before the craftsman abandoned his task. The head gazed back at her, its one painted eye seeming to dare her to unravel the mystery. She stretched out fingertips to touch the glass . . .

And a hand touched her shoulder.

'Fräulein Fleming? I think I may have information which is of interest to you.'

8: The Tomb

Mara suppressed a gasp of surprise and turned on her heel.

She found herself looking into an old, wrinkled face with twinkling dark-brown eyes. A face framed by a straggling white beard and a small skull-cap. He wore the sombre black garb of an elderly Jew.

'My apologies for startling you, Miss Fleming. I had no wish to alarm you. My name is Abraham Weits. I do not think that you will have heard of me.'

Mara shook her head, still dazed from the shock.

'Herr . . . Weits? How do you know my name? And what is this information that you are offering me?'

Weits laughed and Mara glimpsed the brownish stumps of broken teeth, lurking like crooked tombstones in the black cavern of his mouth.

'Offering, Fräulein Fleming? Yes, I have a proposition to make to you but I am not offering the information to you as a gift. Shall we call it barter, a fair exchange? For it is plain that each of us has something that the other wants . . .'

He rested his gnarled hand on Mara's sleeve and she wanted to push him away, to tell him that she did not need his information. Instead, remembering the importance of her quest, she made an effort to smile and replied:

'State the nature of your proposition, Herr Weits, and name your terms.'

'Patience, my dear Miss Fleming. First, I have a little something to show you. If you would be kind enough to wait a moment?'

He glanced around to verify that they were alone in the gallery, then rummaged in the pocket of his faded black jacket and took out a key – rusty with age and rather insignificant in its design. As Mara looked on in amazement, he took a step towards one of the mummy-cases which stood against the wall and moved it a fraction to the right – just far enough to expose a small section of the oak-panelled wall. He appeared to insert the key into it – though Mara could see no sign of a lock.

With an almost imperceptible whirr, the panel slid back, revealing a short passageway, at the far-distant end of which Mara could see a yellowish light burning. She shivered and drew back, suddenly remembering the hidden room in Winterbourne where she had suffered so many terrible ordeals.

'Enter,' invited Weits. 'There is no need to be afraid. I will not harm you. After all, as you can see, I am just a frail old man – what could I do against a strong and beautiful young woman like you, Fräulein Fleming?'

Although she did not trust him for an instant, Mara knew that she had no choice, she would have to play his game. She stepped through the hole in the panel and into the passageway beyond. Weits followed, and the panel clicked shut behind them. They walked down the murky passageway and entered a brightly lit room in the middle of which stood a comfortable leather armchair. The walls were lined with books and a table at one end of the room seemed to serve as an altar. In the middle of the stone floor a chalked pentacle surrounded a silver swastika.

'This is my realm,' explained Weits. 'For almost half a century I have lived here, within the very walls of the museum. The fools! They have forgotten all about the secret rooms and passages. Not one of them has ever asked himself why the layout of the museum does not quite match up to their mathematics.

'Yes, I have lived here since my beloved Führer's death in 1945 and I have continued to carry out the duties with which he entrusted me.'

Mara stared at him in confusion. Weits read the expression on her face and explained with a dry laugh:

'Yes, Miss Fleming, I am a Jew. But I am also a devoted disciple of our beloved leader; for, hearing of my mystical powers and occult scholarship, he saved me from certain death in the camps and appointed me the keeper of his collection of magical artefacts. A job which I have continued to carry out until this very day . . .'

He took Mara's chin in his hand and stroked her cheek gently. His breath was hot and acrid on her skin.

'I know what you seek, the object of your quest. You seek the Phallus of Osiris.'

Mara's heart was racing. 'And you have it?'

Abraham smiled. 'Patience, my dear. All in good time. But follow me and you shall see the evidence of my good faith.'

He pushed open a narrow door and ushered Mara inside. The room itself was long and very narrow, and Mara surmised that it must be located within the thick stone walls of the museum. The walls were lined with glass cases, each containing a magical item, painstakingly labelled. Seeing that Mara was baffled by the German, Weits translated the labels for her:

'This one here is the foreskin of Napoleon, jealously guarded by the ex-Empress Josephine until her death and then bequeathed to a magical brotherhood in Paris. The next, there, is a fragment of the Spear of Destiny, sadly shattered and its fragments dispersed in an ill-judged magic ritual in the First World War. Whoever succeeds in recovering all the fragments and restoring the spear shall hold the key to world dominion. And this silver reliquary, in the jewelled casket, contains the ashes of the great magician Abra-Melin. All are relics of the most supreme magical significance.

'And so you see, my dear Fräulein Fleming, that I am truly what I say I am. And what I offer you is a chance to obtain what you seek.'

Her knees trembling with fear, Mara forced herself to answer his piercing gaze.

'I will do anything for a chance to find the Phallus.

Anything, Herr Weits. Simply name your price.'

'It is a simple exchange, my dear,' he replied. 'Your body – which I crave – in return for my co-operation, which I see you are most anxious to obtain.'

He had no need for sorcery to persuade his victim. For already Mara was undressing before him, there in the dimly lit treasure-store where Abraham Weits had for so long hoarded the magical spoils of a corrupt regime that refused to die. Abraham Weits – an old man, his body warped with age and his mind with the blind devotion of a victim for his torturer. A man who was now eyeing her with unconcealed lust; and whose trembling fingers were rubbing the swelling front of his rusty-black trousers.

Mara slipped off her sweater and dropped it onto the stone floor and stepped out of her shoes. She shivered as she felt the iciness of the stone flags seeping up into her feet. Though she usually scorned underwear, something had insinuated its way into her subconscious and told her that today she should dress the whore.

And now she stood before Weits clad in black silk French knickers, black seamed stockings and suspenders, and a lacy black underwired bra which thrust her magnificent breasts upwards and seemed to offer them to him like twin juicy fruits at a banquet. The crystal amulet nestled in her cleavage, casting out multi-coloured flashes of light whenever she moved.

'Beautiful . . .' sighed Abraham Weits, seizing her by the hand and leading her through yet another door, into a tiny room almost entirely occupied by a carved wooden bed.

She sat down obediently on the edge of the bed and waited for him to join her. He began to undress, carefully folding his shabby but immaculate clothes and placing them on a table at the foot of the bed.

His body was old, yet there was a glittering vigour in his eyes. His prick curved upwards with all the enthusiasm of a young man's, its circumcised shaft glistening with the moisture of intensifying desire. His bollocks were large and, to Mara's surprise, almost hairless. Their twin globes hung like sap-filled fruits between desiccated thighs – almost as though all the life left in this aged body had become concentrated in the genitals, that last outpost of youthful vigour.

Opening the lid of an oak chest, Weits took out a collection of leather thongs, an Arab strap, Japanese love-eggs and a large ivory dildo, carved with Eastern designs. Anticipating what Weits intended to do to her, Mara made to lie down on the bed and offer herself up to the torture. But Weits shook his head.

'No, no. You don't understand. I wish you to use this . . . equipment . . . upon me, upon my body, for my pleasure.'

He lay down on the bed, and stretched out his naked body, closing his eyes, the better to enjoy all the sensations. Rather taken aback by this twist of events, Mara busied herself with sorting out what he had given her.

Taking up the thongs, she discovered that there were sufficient to bind him hand and foot; and she set about attaching his wrists and ankles to the carved bedposts. He evidently enjoyed this process, for he urged her time and time again to bind him more tightly, to make the thongs bite more cruelly into the flesh.

'Bind me tightly – pull the knots as tight as you can . . . I want my desire to bleed for you . . .'

When he was secured, Mara took up the love-eggs and put them into her mouth, to wet them with saliva. Then – feeling beneath him for his backside – she insinuated first one finger, then two, then several, into his tight arsehole. He growled with pleasure as she forced open his intimacy and began to press home the love-eggs, ensuring that they went into him as deeply as she could possibly manage.

His cock reared up even more implausibly as she fitted the Arab strap about his shaft and balls: it was a little leather harness which she could adjust until it exerted just the right amount of pressure to provoke his prick into soaring rigidity.

'Tighter, tighter!' cried out Weits, twisting and turning in his bonds as she buckled on the harness and watched the leather straps bite into his most tender flesh. 'Now bite me – sink your teeth into my flesh. Make me bleed!'

Baffled by Weits's preferences, Mara bent to take his shaft into her mouth and nibbled gently at the very tip, terrified that she would hurt him.

'Harder! Bite me till I bleed!'

Horrified, Mara obeyed, and was rewarded by a sigh of ecstasy as droplets of blood began to ooze out of the martyred tip of Weits's penis.

Out of breath, she drew away and wiped the unpleasantly metallic taste of blood from her lips. Weits was still groaning with pleasure beneath her and babbling incoherently about blood and mortification. She began to understand dimly that he wanted her to do something with the dildo – but what?

Aroused, in spite of herself, by this bizarre interlude, Mara climbed onto the bed and astride Weits's face. She pulled aside the gusset of her French knickers and – parting her plump cunt-lips – forced the ivory dildo up into her moist and fragrant cunt.

Weits was watching her now: gazing up, wide-eyed, at her cunt and watching the surrogate penis disappearing into the moist pink flesh. And it felt good, felt so good to feel the cool, rough surface of the carved ivory rubbing away at her cunt. With her free hand she exposed her clitoris, sliding back the fleshy hood so that Weits could not help but see the throbbing bud beneath.

She wanked herself with enthusiasm and, when she came, Weits put out his tongue and lapped up the fragrant juices which oozed out of her crack.

'Fuck me,' he pleaded. 'Have pity . . .'

In a moment of inspiration, Mara forced the head of the dildo between Weits's buttocks, sending it to join the love-eggs in his forbidden tunnel. It must have caused him the most intense and delicious pain, for he moaned and almost spurted off before Mara had had time to sit herself down on his rampantly erect penis.

She rode his shaft expertly, knowing that with each thrust of her hips she was forcing the dildo further into his arse and causing him more of the pain which he so desperately needed in order to obtain sexual gratification. Sinking her fingernails into the flesh of his bollocks succeeded in finishing him off; and his prick jerked convulsively as it poured forth a load of watery spunk into her cunt.

Weits lay in silence for a while, his eyes closed and his chest rising and falling rapidly as he fought to regain his breath. At last he opened his eyes.

'You have done well, my dear,' he smiled.

'Will you then keep your side of the bargain, and give me the Phallus of Osiris?'

He laughed, and his yellow, parchment-thin skin seemed in danger of splitting, of giving way under the unnatural strain.

'Give it to you, my dear? Would that it were mine to give! But I am an honourable man and I will give you what I have, which is some valuable information.

'Many years ago, during the war, the Führer did indeed obtain the Phallus and entrusted it to me to safeguard until such time as his trusted inner circle of magicians might use all of the magical objects in his collection to ensure victory over his foes, the eternal rule of the Third Reich, and immortality for his own blessed body.

'Alas, Hitler's entourage included many unprincipled magicians who thought only of their own glory. Although the Führer sought to keep the existence of his collection a secret from such men, some had begun to suspect. And one – Diedrich Theophanau – stumbled by accident upon the existence and location of the Phallus. In the confusion surrounding Berlin at the end of the war, I was not able to prevent this odious, self-seeking man stealing it from me.

'Although Theophanau professed devotion to our beloved Führer, he despised me; and I knew also that his apparent devotion concealed a simple desire to acquire greater power and knowledge for himself. He saw clearly that the war was about to end in disaster for Hitler, stole the Phallus and fled into hiding. That was the last I saw of him or of the Phallus.'

Mara's face fell. 'And so that is all you can tell me – that the Phallus was stolen by this man and taken away from Berlin?'

'Not quite all, my dear. This much I know: that Diedrich Theophanau fled to Lyon. It is there that you must go if you wish to seek the Phallus of Osiris.'

It was all very well, thought Mara, telling her to trust in fortune: but how on earth was she supposed to raise the money to get to Lyon? She had searched her purse and all her pockets, but no hundred-Mark notes offered themselves obligingly for her salvation.

At Tempelhof Airport she had discovered, to her despair, that the plane fare was quite simply out of her league – and no obliging pilots or hoteliers leapt to her rescue with offers of free flights and lodging. Hitching would take for ever and hiring a car was out of the question. Even the train fare was astronomical. Things were not looking good.

There had to be some other way.

Sitting in a cafe off the Unter den Linden, Mara pondered her next move. Cars rolled by and she began to fantasise about one of them stopping – a handsome man offering her a lift to Lyon in return for a few favours, easily and painlessly granted. The prospect was quite exciting. Her ever-eager clitty began to tingle with anticipation and when she came back to her senses it was with the keen disappointment of discovering that reality does not always match up to the substance of our dreams. If luck intended to bail her out – well, it was taking its time.

A group of English and American students were laughing and joking at the next table. They'd evidently had a little too much cheap wine and the conversation was becoming bawdy. Mara watched with interest and amusement as one of the girls took her shoe off and insinuated her foot between the thighs of the young man sitting opposite her. She was an attractive girl, dark-haired and slender, and with full, red lips which reminded Mara of her own sensual mouth.

The girl's boyfriend slid down a little in his chair, to make it easier for her. Mara remembered with a pang of sadness how she and Andreas had seduced each other in the reading room at Whitby library and ended up fucking under the table, only yards away from where the spinsterly librarian was cataloguing Mills and Boon romances.

The other two were playing with each other now, oblivious of the sidelong glances of the other cafe patrons. Were those looks of disapproval, or of envy? The boy had succeeded in wriggling his hand surreptitiously inside his girlfriend's jumper and was now stroking her right nipple, which showed clearly through the thin woollen fabric.

Meanwhile, the girl – a stunning blonde whose long, shapely legs were encased in tight black jeans – had unfastened her boyfriend's zip and was quite blatantly playing with him inside his underpants. Mara remembered her own student days, not so very long ago, and the time she had almost been arrested for fucking on a Greek beach in the middle of the afternoon. But the policemen could be so understanding when you knew the right way to approach them . . .

Mara wondered idly if the girl would take out her boyfriend's prick and suck it right there, in view of all the other diners. That fat old man over there – the one with the briefcase and the battered trilby – he'd choke on his Bratwurst if she did that.

But at that moment one of the boys leant across and suggested that they move on. Why didn't they go back to the hostel? There'd be nobody there at that time of day . . .

And the four students staggered to their feet, tidied themselves up, collected their belongings and left – walking unsteadily round the corner into the Unter den Linden and out of sight.

It wasn't until several minutes later that Mara noticed it. It was a small, blue vinyl wallet, like the ones meant to carry credit cards, and it was lying on the ground underneath the chair where the dark-haired girl had been sitting. What was it?

Curious to know what the girl had left behind, Mara picked up the wallet and opened it. It contained a student union card, with a photograph of the girl smiling out at her. She looked astonishingly like Mara. She read the girl's name: Maria Fenning. A couple of deft pen-strokes and that could easily be made to read: Mara Fleming. And with a student card, she could buy cheap rail travel. Maybe her money would just stretch far enough for a rail ticket to Lyon?

She knew she ought to hand in the card to the authorities, own up that she'd found it. What would the girl do without her card? But somehow it just seemed so inevitable.

She paid the bill and took a taxi to the Bahnhof-Zoo.

The 135 Deutschmarks Mara miraculously found in her purse did indeed buy her a one-way ticket on the overnight train from Berlin to Paris. Nothing luxurious – just a couchette in the standard class accommodation – but at least she would be on her way.

She boarded the train just after six in the evening, and stowed her luggage in the compartment she would have to share for thirteen and a half hours with a garrulous family from Aachen. In an attempt to escape their well-meaning but noisy company, she decided to squander a little more of her money on a proper evening meal in the restaurant car.

Dinner was served at eight and Mara was engrossed in the menu when a pleasant voice broke into her reverie:

'*Excusez-moi*, mademoiselle: do you mind if I sit here?'

Mara looked up and saw a tall, red-haired woman with greenish-brown eyes and soft, full lips. She was smartly dressed in a suit and Mara guessed that she must be returning to France after a business trip.

'No, not at all . . . Please, do sit down.'

The woman hitched up her tight pencil skirt and squeezed into the seat opposite Mara. She was a most attractive woman, athletic, yet with a hint of womanly curves beneath the tailored green jacket and skin-tight skirt.

'*Je m'appelle* Sophie Delaine,' smiled the newcomer. 'And you are called . . .?'

'Oh . . . my name is Mara Fleming. Are you travelling on business?'

Sophie nodded and picked up her menu. 'I do so hate these international trips – they leave me feeling so tired. And the men! Businessmen are so tedious! A few days of talking money with them and they leave me longing for some intelligent female company.'

The significance of her smile was lost on Mara until Sophie reached across and touched her hand: her fingers lingered longer than they ought to have done on her tanned flesh, as though they were seeking to establish some deeper, more intimate contact.

Mara returned the smile and felt a treacherous warmth spreading through her loins. Almost without thinking, her hand strayed to the top button of her blouse and unfastened it, presenting her new acquaintance with an excellent view of the bare, tanned cleavage beneath. At the same time, quite unconsciously, her knees began to move apart, as though begging to embrace someone, something . . .

She watched with mounting interest as Sophie ordered dinner for both of them, the very point of her moist, pink tongue passing over her lips as she darted glances at Mara.

As they were sitting back, waiting for the meal to arrive, Sophie gave an exaggerated sigh of annoyance.

'See what I have done!' she cried. 'How silly of me – I have dropped my purse under the table.'

And Sophie slid down onto the floor, ostensibly to pick up her purse. But she did not simply retrieve the purse and then regain her seat. Instead, Mara felt butterfly-soft fingers stroking her ankles, her calves, her knees; easing apart her thighs and working their way up her thighs, towards the inevitable discovery of her glossy black pubic hair, her naked cunt's only covering.

Glancing around her furtively, terrified that someone would see what was going on, Mara nevertheless felt her body gradually abandoning itself to Sophie Delaine's angelic caresses. Her hands felt so cool, so very cool against her flesh as they worked their way up between her thighs and brushed, gently but insistently, against her pubic curls. Mara could sense the woman's delight as she realised that her conquest was wearing no panties beneath her short skirt; and a few seconds later, she felt her cunt-lips being gently pulled apart and a warm, muscular tongue insinuating itself in between.

As the woman lapped at Mara's clitty, her fingers went on another short journey, at last discovering what they had set out to find: the hot, wet tunnel of Mara's cunt. And two of the woman's fingers disappeared inside, so smoothly and sensually that Mara almost cried out with the ecstasy of the feeling.

It took all of Mara's considerable energies to maintain an expression of relative calm, in the hope that her fellow-diners would not realise what was going on. Would Sophie stay down there for ever? Would she not abandon this madness and return to her seat opposite Mara?

Evidently the woman intended to make the most of her position of advantage, for she was now working her fingers in and out of Mara's cunt, wanking her and licking her with an almost fanatical zeal. And Mara was trembling and helpless beneath her caresses, unable to push her away or to make her excuses and leave.

The orgasm, when it came, tore through Mara's body with all the ferocity of the Mistral shrieking across the marshy wastelands of the Camargue. Desperate not to cry out, she bit into her lip and a little trail of blood trickled from her mouth.

Her task accomplished, the lascivious Sophie emerged from beneath the table, with not a hair out of place. She was brandishing her purse.

'It took me a while but I got there in the end!' she remarked enigmatically as the waiter arrived with their *soupe de poissons*.

Sophie toyed for a while with her soup, apparently not

hungry; and then got up from the table, scribbling a note which she pressed into Mara's hand.

When she had gone, Mara read the note. It said:

'CABIN 501. HALF AN HOUR.'

Scarcely able to take stock of this new and bizarre development, Mara finished her meal in thoughtful silence.

'Chérie! I thought you would never arrive!'

Mara stepped self-consciously into the sleeping-compartment, and Sophie closed and locked the door behind her, before returning to her bunk and slipping between the sheets. She was naked, save for a diaphanous nightgown that emphasised far more than it concealed, and an ornate collar studded with crystals – which stirred something deep but formless in Mara's memory.

'I wasn't sure whether or not to come,' replied Mara. And it was true. Although she had enjoyed the occasional lesbian liaison, and thought nothing of it, she felt a nagging sense of doubt about the perfect and devastatingly attractive Sophie Delaine. It was nothing that she could quite define but something – perhaps her psychic sixth-sense – told her that Mademoiselle Delaine was not all that she seemed and indeed was rather more than she professed to be.

But Mara had been instructed to follow the dictates of fortune; besides which, the succulent French business-woman had stirred deep longings within Mara: the longing to lie naked against soft flesh, to worship and be worshipped.

'*Couche-toi, chérie.*' Sophie lifted the covers and wriggled over towards the wall, making a space for Mara to lie down beside her. 'Take off your clothes, my dear, I shall keep you warm.' And, as if to show her the way, Sophie lifted her own nightgown off over her head. She had a slender, almost spare frame, but her breasts were unexpectedly full and womanly. She looked almost regal, sitting up in bed dressed only in her jewelled collar.

Mara felt an irresistible stirring in her cunt and her hands hastened to free herself of her impeding clothes. Off came the sweater and the skirt, off came the shoes, and she was naked once again: naked, as she loved to be.

She climbed into bed beside Sophie and was surprised to feel how cool the Frenchwoman's flesh was against hers. It was evidently Sophie who needed warming up, not Mara.

'Lie close to me,' whispered Sophie, her fingertips roaming over Mara's lithe nakedness. 'Lie close, so that I can adore your loveliness.' She turned until she lay on her right side, with her left leg across Mara's body, the knee drawn up onto her thigh. Then she took hold of Mara's right breast, very gently, and slipped the long nipple into her mouth. It hardened instantly and Mara gave a long sigh of delight as Sophie worked her tongue round it, teased it with her teeth, sucked on it like an innocent babe.

Sliding her knee down Mara's belly, she insinuated it between Mara's legs, forcing her to open her thighs and allow her cunt to be titillated. Sophie's own thigh made contact with Mara's pubic hair and with the fragrant inner sanctum between her plump cunt-lips; and for the second time that evening, Mara felt her clitty swell.

Sophie was on top of her now, playing the man. Her right hand was exploring between Mara's thighs, acting out the part of the eager penis, searching out its home. Her legs were between Mara's thighs, the tips of her breasts rubbing against Mara's nipples.

She found Mara's hole and slipped her finger inside. A second finger disappeared into Mara's arse and she lay beneath her lover, as helpless as any child, while Sophie brought her skilfully to orgasm.

As the climax ebbed away, she became vaguely aware that Sophie's tongue was between her lips; she seemed to be lapping at the remains of the congealed blood around the wound made by her teeth. The sudden thought made Mara feel slightly sick but Sophie was growing more and more excited. Her kisses were moving down the side of Mara's face now, towards the crook of her neck and Sophie was babbling quietly to herself:

'Ah, *ma pauvre chérie*! *Tu t'es blessée* . . . you are

wounded. See, see the blood, taste it . . . it tastes good, good . . .'

Sophie opened her mouth wide, as though preparing to bite.

But a voice in her head spoke like thunder and fiery eyes burned into her soul:

'No! Do not harm her! I have forbidden this . . .'

And, with a tiny whimper of distress, Sophie drew back, rolled away and, with her face to the wall, fell into a deep slumber.

In the morning, they were awoken by a steward's knock at the door. If he was surprised to find two young ladies in a bed made for one, he did not remark upon it; and he simply went off and fetched another breakfast tray.

'Where are you going when you get to Paris?' asked Sophie.

'To Lyon . . . to look up some old family friends,' lied Mara, wary of divulging too much about the real purpose of her trip. 'Have you any idea where the train leaves from? I must go and buy a ticket.'

Sophie laughed, setting aside her croissant, untouched. 'No need, *mon petit ange*. For I am travelling down to the Midi! I left my car at the station in Paris and I would be delighted to drive you down to Lyon.'

Although Mara had serious misgivings, she could not think of a polite way to refuse.

As luck would have it, the journey down to Lyon proved uneventful and Sophie made no mention of the delights they had enjoyed together in the sleeping-car. The little red sports car devoured the miles between Paris and Lyon, and within three hours they had arrived.

Sophie drove Mara to the address Abraham Weits had given her and then drove away, with a cheerful wave and a smile that revealed the perfection of her little, white, pointed teeth.

Taking a deep breath for courage, Mara slung her embroidered bag over her shoulder and walked up the drive to the house. It was a large villa, tall and square, and standing in the middle of its own grounds. Like so many other buildings in Lyon, it was topped off by a terracotta pantiled roof which seemed to contain all the lost sunshine of a half-forgotten, ancient summer.

The windows were shuttered, and when Mara pressed the bell the sound seemed to echo for miles. Maybe there was no one at home. Maybe the house was uninhabited. Mara rang again. Still no answer, so she turned away and had taken a couple of steps back down the path when the front door swung open.

Turning round hastily, Mara was greeted by a thin woman in a black dress and white apron, her grey hair scraped back into bun.

'*Je . . . je suis Anglaise. Je voudrais voir Herr Theophanau . . . il est chez lui?*'

The woman shook her head, and called out into the echoing twilight of the house:

'Brigitte . . .'

A younger woman arrived and the old woman explained what had happened. '*Elle est Anglaise,*' she added and then padded off bad-temperedly, back to her kitchen.

'You must, please, excuse my mother,' explained Brigitte. 'She lives constantly in the past and has vowed never again to leave this house. She believes that her life has lost its meaning since Herr Theophanau died.'

'Died? Theophanau is dead?' Mara could feel her hopes evaporating before her eyes.

'It is almost twenty years since he passed away. In his will, he left the house to my mother on condition that it was kept exactly as he had left it, with nothing disturbed. We have carried out his wishes to the letter.'

Mara was about to go, when she had a sudden inspiration:

'Do you know where Herr Theophanau was buried?'

'Yes, of course. He was interred with his most valued possessions in the family vault of some old French friends, in the main Lyon cemetery. We do not visit any more – the memory is too painful. We like to remember Herr

Theophanau as he was in life . . . But perhaps you would like to pay your last respects?'

Explaining that she was an ardent admirer of the great Herr Theophanau, Mara accepted the directions, and hitched a lift to the cemetery.

A light drizzle was falling, and she pulled her long cloak around her more tightly as she walked through the gate and into the cemetery. The grass in this part of the cemetery was neatly cropped and the headstones well tended. But as she walked further on she came to an older part which seemed to have been almost totally neglected. The grass grew waist high around and over the graves, and broken stone littered the ground, testifying to some recent acts of desecration and vandalism.

Mara's heart was thumping as she made out the shape of what she was looking for, half-buried among the overgrown vegetation: a low, stone building with angels flanking the door and an iron gate leading to a flight of stone steps. She had the key to the gate in her pocket, having 'persuaded' the sacristan that she was not only a very desirable young lady but a thoroughly trustworthy one, too.

As she got nearer, Mara realised that she was not going to need the key. For the gate was swinging gently on its one remaining hinge, the gentle breeze playing a plaintive dirge on the rusty metal.

She approached, and saw that the damage was worse than she had feared. Vandals had evidently broken into the tomb some time ago, for the graffiti on the walls had faded and the top of the steps was strewn with rubbish.

Profoundly grateful that the sacristan had offered her his lantern to supplement the feeble light filtering in from the outside world, Mara switched it on and walked gingerly down the stairs. A sleek rat with glittering black eyes ran past her foot and she almost cried out in alarm.

Reaching the bottom of the steps and turning the corner into the main burial chamber, Mara gave a shriek of horror. The inside of the vault was a mess. The coffins had been splintered or overturned and the floor was littered with a mess of bones. No one had bothered to come in and tidy them up. Perhaps no one even realised what had happened.

Theophanau's coffin had evidently occupied a stone ledge, recessed into the wall, for a brass plate still bore his name and the date of his interment. The mahogany cabinet which had once held his most prized magical items had been looted, and glass shards glittered on the dusty floor.

Only one item remained. Mara bent to pick it up. It was a mirror, framed in silver gilt and decorated with the heads of howling demons. Its glass was cracked straight across, as though the thieves had dropped it in their haste to flee this place.

Instinctively, Mara looked into it. And to her astonishment she saw, not the reflection of her own, full-lipped face and violet eyes, but the face of Andreas Hunt, alive and afraid, and calling out to her.

'Mara! Mara! Why did you leave me here? Save me . . . come back to me . . . bring me back to my body . . .'

Suddenly, the mirror began to tremble in her hand. As she looked on in horror, the glass crazed over and turned to a fine, pearly white dust which a sudden rush of cold air caught and carried far, far away.

9: Vannes

'My dear Mr LeMaitre,' replied the Bishop, his fingertips pressed together like the steeple of his own cathedral, 'I simply cannot endorse your candidature unless I know a little more about you. It is true that I have a certain . . . influence in Court and Government circles but I must be sure that I am using that influence for good.'

His voice was as rich and sickly as warm golden syrup and the Master's hatred of him was growing by the minute. Soon, sooner than you might think, my Lord Bishop, you are going to be enjoying a very different sort of communion from the kind you are accustomed to . . .

He forced an ingratiating smile and topped up the Bishop's sherry glass.

'So tell me, my Lord, what do you think of our little sociological research centre, here at Winterbourne? Would you be interested in perhaps participating in one of our research projects?'

The Bishop's eyes registered a flicker of interest. Although no one seemed to know exactly what went on at Winterbourne Hall, he had heard one or two rather intriguing rumours. And the Bishop was not averse to a little extra-diocesan activity . . .

'What exactly had you in mind, Mr LeMaitre?'

The Master gave an inner sigh of relief. This one was going to be easy. He pressed the bell on his desk and Sonja Kerensky entered the office.

'My Lord Bishop, this is Sonja, one of our . . . research assistants. If you would like to follow her, she will take you and show you round our . . . laboratories.'

The Bishop could hardly help noticing how shapely Miss Kerensky was beneath her crisp white blouse and short navy-blue skirt. Why, her breasts were thrusting against the fabric fit to burst her buttons and those slender, black-stockinged legs seemed to go on forever. He felt a sudden, unholy urge to seize her by her long, blonde mane, throw her to the floor and ravish her. He could almost hear the fabric tearing as he ripped off her blouse, exposing those lovely breasts . . .

Eagerly, he levered himself out of his chair and followed Sonja out of the room.

Mara steadied herself against the stone wall and took time to calm herself down. A shattered mirror, that was all. And she had, at last, received a message from Andreas! Perhaps things were going to go her way after all.

As she leaned against the stone ledge where Theophanau's coffin had once rested, she felt something give way underneath her hand.

She looked down, and saw that she had accidentally tripped a tiny concealed button and a small drawer had sprung out of the apparently flawless wall. She held up the lantern, illuminating the yellowed pages of a pile of old notebooks lying in the drawer.

Diaries. Could these be the diaries of Diedrich Theophanau? Mara wondered how much they would be worth to a collector of Nazi memorabilia. She picked one up and ran her fingers wonderingly over the smooth surface. Each of the four notebooks was bound in dark leather, embossed with the swastika and eagle of the German Third Reich. Wonderingly, Mara began to turn the pages. Instantly, despair filled her heart, for of course they were written in a spidery gothic German and, save for the occasional word, they were quite incomprehensible.

Just as she was about to give up in frustration, she felt a strange warmth around her throat. Glancing down, she saw that the crystal talisman was glowing and, as she watched, it began to spin very fast over the pages. To her amazement, the script began to alter, at first imperceptibly and then completely. She was reading the diaries in English!

Not daring to question the miracle, Mara leafed frantically through the notebooks, searching for something – anything – of significance among the painstaking accounts of Theophanau's magical experiments, his involvement with the Führer and his hatred of Abraham Weits.

She read on, despairing of ever reading what she needed to know. Then she remembered the words of Jürgen Kaas: Trust in fortune . . . Picking up one of the diaries, she opened it at random. At first, she read nothing of interest, but then one of the last entries caught her eye:

'It is too late for me now. The curse has worked its worst, and I shall die. My magic cannot save my mortal body, and I shall now direct all my efforts into preparing a safe haven for my immortal soul.

'Some of my prized possessions, I have decreed are to be buried with me in the Jeanmaire family vault. But my most prized possession of all – the Talisman of Set, which I stole with such ease from the foolish Jew Weits – I must send away, into safety, with a brother magician.

'For this task, I have chosen Alain Kerriel, a Breton priest and mystic who has served the Reich well in clandestine operations, both as a magician and as an agent of espionage. His black heart will guard the treasure well, until such time as it can be restored to a fourth, glorious Reich.

'Kerriel will arrive from Vannes tomorrow, and I must survive at least until then. My strength grows weak, and I can write no more . . .'

As she finished reading the entry, the words began to dance and blur once more upon the page, and when they resolved into readable print they were once more in German gothic script.

Outside, the wind was howling around the cemetery as though the enraged soul of Diedrich Theophanau sensed that his prize was in danger.

* * *

Standing on the main road out of Lyon, with a tattered piece of card marked 'Bretagne,' Mara began to wonder if fortune had deserted her after all. The rain was pouring down the back of her neck and her shoes were letting in water. She had almost run out of money and it would soon be dusk.

She had tried buying a train ticket, but she couldn't raise sufficient cash. The plane was out of the question for the same reason. And the bus service was quite simply beyond her comprehension. So – like it or lump it – it was hitching or nothing.

She stood on the hard shoulder, desperately trying to look sexy for the benefit of the passing motorists. She hitched up her skirt a little and was rewarded with wolf-whistles from the open windows of a passing minibus. But the driver didn't stop.

Bedraggled and despondent, Mara was wondering if it wouldn't be wisest to make her way to the nearest *auberge de jeunesse* and beg a night's accommodation, when she noticed a car with a British numberplate bearing down on her.

The car, a bright red BMW, cruised to a halt beside her, splashing her ankles with muddy water. The window wound down and a familiar face smiled up at her:

'Hello, Mara. Going my way?'

'Geoffrey Potter!' exclaimed Mara. 'What on earth are you doing here? And what are you doing in a BMW? You haven't stolen it, have you?'

'Climb in,' he replied, with a grin, 'and I'll tell you.'

As they sped off down the autoroute, Geoffrey related the incredible tale of what had happened to him since she left him that morning in the woods. How he had finished his book with an energy and originality which he had never dreamed of before. How the first agent he approached it with had snapped it up. The day, only a week later, when he got the phone call telling him that a major transatlantic publishing house had accepted his novel and were offering him an advance of half a million. And now he was using the money to travel round France, researching ideas for his next book.

'All this, and success with the ladies too!' he joked, slamming his foot down hard on the accelerator.

Mara was astonished at the change in him. Gone was the timid, almost wimpish figure who had been overwhelmed by her sexual openness. Gone were the shabby, shapeless clothes and the deferential manner. He was confident, stylish, and – she had to admit it – pretty desirable.

Geoffrey reached out and laid his hand confidently upon Mara's knee. The heater was full on but his hand felt cool against her flesh. Yet she could feel the insistent rhythm of his pulse and it was racing through her, exciting her, and at that moment she could almost believe that she wanted him more than anything else in the world.

'It's a long drive up to Vannes,' remarked Geoffrey, with perfect casualness. 'I thought we might put up for the night in a little auberge I know.'

And Mara had to agree that this was a terribly good idea.

They arrived at the Auberge du Cerf Blanc at around ten o'clock, too late for dinner, and Mara was starving. She accepted the innkeeper's offer of sandwiches gratefully and was astonished when Geoffrey professed not to be very hungry. He nibbled unenthusiastically at a chunk of baguette but hardly seemed to eat enough for a sparrow.

Afterwards, they went up to their room.

'I think I'll have a shower,' sighed Mara. 'Travelling always makes me feel so hot and sticky.'

She took her towel into the bathroom, and turned on the water. When it reached exactly the right temperature, she undressed, taking off everything except the crystal pendant. If it really was a powerful protective talisman – and circumstances were beginning to make her believe that it was – then she must not risk removing it, even for a moment.

Mara stepped into the shower, and was about to reach out and draw the curtain when a voice whispered:

'Mind if I join you?'

She opened her eyes and saw that Geoffrey was standing there, stark naked and obviously pleased to see her. His cock was larger and more beautiful than she remembered it and it was thrusting out of its glossy brown bush like a pillar of living stone.

She reached out her hand and touched it. It was pulsating with vibrant life, swollen with love-juice that just longed to spurt into the depths of her.

'Plenty of room for two . . .'

Mara stood aside, and Geoffrey stepped into the shower-cubicle, drawing the curtain behind them. Now they were alone in their own private world of lust. Mara was amazed at how strongly she felt, how agonising were the pangs of desire which shot through her, awakening every millimetre of her luscious young woman's flesh.

'I want to fuck you, Mara Fleming. I want to fuck you and make your flesh sing with desire, cry out with ecstasy. I want to fuck your cunt and your mouth and your arse, Mara. I want to take you to a forbidden land where all pleasures are sacred and nothing is denied.'

He took her in his arms and they stood beneath the spray of warm water, letting it play over their naked bodies. Geoffrey's hardness pressed insistently against Mara's belly, demanding entrance to the delights within.

Taking up a bar of soap, Geoffrey worked up a lather and then began to spread the soap bubbles over Mara's body, beginning at her smooth, tanned shoulders. She shivered with pleasure as his hands slid over her neck, her shoulders, her back; and then moved forwards to glide over the magnificent swell of her breasts. He was most attentive to these perfect globes, ensuring that their entire surface was enrobed in soap suds, so that she looked for all the world like a statue formed from snow.

Mara began to breathe more quickly as he paid special attention to her nipples, soothing and teasing and pinching them into hardness; and weighed her firm, full breasts in his hands like ripe melons, using the soap suds like some exotic massage oil as he smoothed his hands over their flawless, tanned surface.

As his hands moved from her breasts and began to work their way down Mara's belly, she felt the juices within her well up from their own internal spring and instinctively she slid her feet apart on the smooth ceramic floor.

The shower spray played upon her breasts and warm water trickled down her body, sending rivulets of soapy liquid coursing between her thighs, as though a dozen invisible lovers had spurted their semen into her belly and were now watching silently as it flooded out of her cunt and down her slender, tanned thighs.

'I want you, Mara Fleming.'

The whispered words seemed to echo around the tiny cubicle, as though they were not really spoken by Geoffrey at all but by some great and terrible power within him, that fired his belly and stiffened his cock and chose his words for him.

His hands were at the base of her belly now and working their way down, through her pubic hair. Her clitty! Please let him find her clitty, and rub it . . .! But he was inexorable in his exploration of her body: no nook should remain untouched. He slipped his hands round behind her once again, and began to rub the bar of soap across her buttocks.

And now he was insinuating the bar of soap between her buttocks and sliding it down, down; pressing the corner of it into the tight rose of her arsehole, and she was writhing in delight at the boldness of his touch.

When he was well satisfied that he had finished with her backside, Geoffrey at last turned his attentions to Mara's cunt. Before she had a chance to protest, or even to realise what was going on, he had pushed the bar of soap right inside her.

It was a sensation of mingled pleasure and discomfort. The harsh, perfumed soap stung the delicate membranes of her sex and she almost cried out for the pain of it. But the sensation of being filled up, forced apart, was exquisite; and when Geoffrey began to masturbate her roughly with his fingers, she did indeed cry out – this time with pleasure.

She climaxed in a few moments. As her cunt-juices welled up, the bar of soap became dislodged, and she giggled as it began to slide out of her cunt, finally falling to the floor with a soft thud. Before Geoffrey had time to resume his torments, Mara took the initiative, bending down and picking up the soap. It was redolent with the mingled fragrances of cheap perfume and cunt-juice.

Silently she began to massage his penis with the soap, rubbing the bar across its tip, so that it stung his sensitive flesh and made him even stiffer, even more anxious for her.

Seizing the bar of soap, Geoffrey threw it to the ground and forced Mara to lean her hands against the wall of the shower-cubicle. Warm water cascaded down her hair and into her eyes and she began to imagine that she was drowning, drowning in an ocean of fragrant sperm and cunt-juice . . .

Geoffrey prised her buttocks apart in a moment and pressed the tip of his soapy prick against her arsehole, ramming into her without gentleness. The violence of his entry only served to excite Mara, who began to thrust backwards, greedy to take in every inch of his eager tool.

He buggered her expertly: so expertly, that Mara began to wonder how he could have learned such sexual skills in such a short space of time. A few short weeks ago he had been a gauche boy – a virgin, whom she had had to teach to fuck her. And now he was a libertine, a man of the world, a stallion with a red BMW and a go-faster prick. He buggered like a man who has spent all his life learning the art, not like a young man who, weeks ago, had to have his prick guided to a woman's cunt.

He shot his semen into her and within a few moments was stiff again, pushing Mara to her knees and forcing his hardness between her lips. As he thrust in and out of her, she stroked his balls, feeling them tense as they prepared to shoot their load into her mouth.

As she toyed with his bollocks, Mara noticed two tiny scars on his groin: hardly visible, really – and certainly nothing worth remarking upon, except for their location . . . and the fact that they looked uncannily like the scars of two tiny puncture-wounds. Two tiny teeth-marks . . .

He came with a shuddering groan, clasping the back of her head so that she could not deny him the fullness of his pleasure. She swallowed his second load of semen and resigned herself to having to masturbate to orgasm. But not so. To her utter astonishment, it took only a matter of minutes for Geoffrey's prick to become serviceable again.

Not stopping to turn the water off, or to grab hold of a towel, Geoffrey picked Mara up in his arms and carried her, dripping wet, to the twin beds which they had pushed together. Throwing her onto the soft mattress, he was on top of her and inside her cunt within seconds.

'Fuck me, Geoffrey, fuck me!' cried Mara, not caring if the whole world heard the bedsprings creaking as they fucked. And Geoffrey was only too happy to oblige. His penis ploughed into her and as he rode her to orgasm, he pinched the tips of her nipples with great savagery.

The sudden pain was sufficient to bring Mara to her crisis and she seized Geoffrey's buttocks, pulling him into her to crush him against her pulsating clitoris.

He pumped his seed into her and they lay together for a long time, water and semen dripping from their exhausted bodies.

The following morning they got up early and set off for Vannes. Geoffrey still didn't seem to be eating much and Mara began to be worried about him. Was he ill?

'Don't worry, Mara!' laughed Geoffrey. 'I've had a bit of a stomach bug, that's all. I'm a bit off my food. I'll be right as rain in a couple of days. In fact, I'm feeling better already.'

As if to prove a point he chewed his way laboriously through a croissant at their next stop but Mara couldn't help feeling it was just an exercise, staged entirely for her benefit. For some strange reason, Geoffrey just didn't seem to be hungry any more.

They set off again, entering Brittany by lunchtime, and drove into a thickly wooded area where the recent rain seemed to have washed every speck of grime from the trees and their multi-coloured leaves glistened in the autumn sunshine. Mara was just beginning to feel good again.

The winding road led between dense plantations of pine forest, the low sunshine darting from between the trees as the red BMW sped past, like the flickering from an old movie camera. Mara felt the hypnotic effect of the flickering lights dulling her brain, disorientating her, and she turned to Geoffrey, placing a hand gently on his arm:

'Please slow down, you're making me feel nervous.'

He flashed her a brief smile and Mara saw that his pupils had shrunk to tiny black specks in a mass of grey. He seemed to be looking, not at the road ahead, but at something beyond, something Mara could not see.

A sudden unease swept over her, she could sense something. Something bad that was going to happen if she didn't stop it.

'Slow down, Geoffrey – please . . .'

His response was to slam his foot down onto the floor, making the BMW leap forward like a beast of prey. They roared on into the forest, Geoffrey wrenching the wheel from side to side on the bends as though he relished the closeness of danger.

'Geoffrey, don't: you'll kill us both . . .!'

But Geoffrey simply smiled that same fixed smile, teeth clenched, corners of his mouth turned up in a defiant rictus.

The white deer appeared before them quite suddenly, stepping into the middle of the road, turning its beautiful eyes towards them as though pleading with them to stop.

Frantic, Mara tried to seize the wheel but Geoffrey brushed her aside with more strength than she had ever imagined him to have within him. And he could easily have avoided the deer. It was standing stock-still in the middle of the road, almost defying them to harm it: all he had to do was swerve a little to miss it.

But Geoffrey put his foot down, aiming the BMW as

though it were some deadly missile, ploughing into the deer with a horrible, soft, sickening thud that threw its inert body through the air. It fell by the roadside in a crumpled heap, obviously dead.

Mara stared in horror at the blood-spattered windscreen, too shocked to speak. Geoffrey threw back his head and laughed. It was the manic, humourless laughter of the irredeemably damned.

They came to the level-crossing about half an hour later and Mara seized her chance. As the car stood waiting for the train to pass she wrenched open the door and – before Geoffrey had a chance to stop her, even if he had wanted to – she was away and sprinting across the fields for all she was worth.

The lorry driver peered down from his cab at the long-limbed beauty with the glossy cascade of black hair and the astonishing violet eyes. His Gallic prick was already stirring into furious life and he stuck his hand down the front of his trousers and adjusted it. He made no attempt to conceal the gesture. He wanted the woman to be under no misapprehensions . . .

'M'selle?' He pushed his képi back on his head and tried to make sense of Mara's rather sketchy French. *Mon Dieu*, but she had nice titties.

'Vannes!' exclaimed Mara, thumbing ineffectually through the pages of her phrasebook. '*Je voudrais* . . . I want to go to Vannes.'

'*Ah, c'est donc ça que tu veux, ma p'tite? Alors, monte là-bas, avec Pierre et Jean-Louis. Ils t'acceuilleront de bonne grâce, je t'assure! Tu veux un peu d'ça, hein*?' Mara could not understand his words but there was no mistaking the meaning when he unzipped his flies and pulled out his prick. '*Tu veux suçer mon zob, p'tite Anglaise*?'

He laughed and shoved his cock back into his trousers. '*Alors, ça c'est pour plus tard* . . . how you say? We save 'im for later, yes?'

His toothless grin was hardly appealing but Mara allowed

him to help her up onto the back of the lorry, an ancient ex-army vehicle, complete with canvas top. The inside was half-filled with a large pile of artichokes and most of the rest of the space was taken up by two men – presumably Pierre and Jean-Louis.

'*Bonjour . . .*' began Mara, hesitantly. The two men were eyeing her up with obvious interest and she would have preferred to keep to her own end of the lorry but – short of sitting on the artichokes – she had no other option. She would have to accept their leering offer of a place next to them . . .

The lorry was rumbling down a deeply rutted country lane and she stumbled across the artichokes, half-falling into the arms of the older man, who had a grey moustache and was brandishing a half-empty bottle of cheap red *vin de table*. He took full advantage of the opportunity to give Mara's tits a really good grope.

'*Tu as de la chance*, Pierre!' exclaimed his companion, a swarthy man in his thirties. And he too began to explore Mara's body. She put up some slight resistance but Pierre began to pour the red wine into her mouth and silenced her protests. Half-choking on the vinegary liquid, she realised that Jean-Louis was busily unfastening first her jacket, then her blouse.

His hand was inside now and she could feel the excitement trembling through his fingertips as he rejoiced in the fact that this tasty little morsel wasn't even wearing a bra. His rough, calloused hand passed across the tender flesh of her nipples and, in spite of herself, Mara felt them grow hard and erect at his touch. She could not find the will to resist as he peeled off her jacket and blouse, leaving her naked to the waist.

Pierre, meanwhile, was trying to fathom the intricacies of Mara's belt. He fumbled for a while with the buckle, then lost patience and reached for his pocket-knife. With one swift movement, he cut through the leather. Next the button, then the zip, and Mara's skirt slipped down her hips to the floor. Her bare, tanned thighs and dark pubic triangle slid into view and Mara's suitors began to talk to each other in excited whispers.

Although she spoke little French, Mara had no difficulty in understanding what they were talking about. They were discussing her – what they were going to do with her, who was going to have her first, and how.

To her surprise, Mara found herself excited by the prospect of becoming these men's plaything for a while. She was inexplicably turned on by the thought that she was at the mercy of two uncouth French farmers, who did not speak her language and who were at this very moment deciding her sexual fate.

They tugged off her skirt, leaving her clad only in her leather knee-boots and the crystal pendant. Sitting her down on the floor between them once again, they took turns to stimulate and tease her flesh.

Whilst Pierre bit into her nipples, causing her a delicious pain which set the love-juices trickling out of her cunt, Jean-Louis pulled out his prick and urinated in a corner. It was obviously an exercise entirely for Mara's benefit, for his dick was the largest she had ever seen: so large, in fact, that she wondered if it would hurt her to have him inside her. As he turned to her and wanked himself to hardness, Mara began to shiver with delicious anticipation and exquisite terror.

She imagined that massive baton of flesh forcing its way into her, opening up the tightest and most secret pathways of her body, making her shriek with mingled pain and ecstasy. A terrible, wonderful burning sensation spread through her clitoris, making her desperate for him, desperate to be fucked by the filthy peasant who owned that wonderful prick.

His little display finished, Jean-Louis relieved his companion, who had succeeded in making Mara so excited that she had inadvertently forgotten how she had meant to clench her thighs, keep her knees held tightly together.

Jean-Louis's hand slipped stealthily between Mara's thighs and worked its way slowly and steadily up towards her cunt. When it reached the outer lips, it pressed hard against them and, quite unable to resist such an assault, the fleshy petals parted. Mara gave a little cry of pleasure as the side of Jean-Louis's palm bit into her tender flesh, pressing hard against the burning bud of her clitoris. He began to work his hand back and forth between her cunt-lips, causing her the most exquisite discomfort and pleasure, inextricably mingled.

Her mind numbed by insistent pleasure, Mara willingly allowed herself to be dragged onto hands and knees and Pierre's hard little prick thrust into her mouth. She was vaguely aware that Jean-Louis was standing behind her, but it was not until she felt a dreadful pain that she realised what he was doing.

Jean-Louis was forcing her with his enormous prick, not thrusting into her cunt – which would have been a tight enough fit – but violating her arse, which was resisting with all its might as he sought to bugger her.

'No! *Non*!' she tried to scream, wrenching her head away from Pierre's cock, but the men simply laughed and made her suck on it afresh and the sound of the lorry's engine drowned the sound of her cries. Jean-Louis stuck his two thumbs into her arse, and began to enlarge it by pulling his thumbs relentlessly further apart. Mara tried to wriggle away but it was no use. He held her fast. And Pierre, at her head, was far too excited to allow her to escape now.

Jean-Louis's second assault on her arse met with more success. With a vigorous thrust of his pelvis he penetrated her. It felt as though she were being torn in two and tears of pain and humiliation began to flow down Mara's face. At that moment, Pierre gave a grunt of pleasure and ejaculated into her mouth, filling it with a flood-tide of semen which she knew she must swallow.

Pierre withdrew, panting, and watched Jean-Louis pumping into Mara, his enormous prick buried up to the hilt in her toothsome backside.

Mara was half-sighing, half-sobbing as he reached round underneath her and felt for her clitoris. With a groan, she felt her orgasm breaking over her like some irresistible ocean swell, and the spasms of her cunt communicated themselves to Jean-Louis's cock, making him come to a massive, pulsating orgasm.

The men took turns with Mara all the way along the road to Vannes, and when they tired of the sport they hung her by the wrists from two old hooks in the iron framework which supported the canvas canopy. The lorry halted for a while on a lonely country road and the driver climbed into the back of the truck, smiling that same, repulsive, lecherous smile which had been on his face when he first saw her.

His cock was already out and his fingers were fondling his own bollocks lovingly. He was evidently both amused and excited by the spectacle of Mara, naked and hanging helplessly from the roof, and he wasted no time in taking off his belt and using it on her bare backside.

When he had reddened it to his satisfaction and drawn more tears and sighs from his victim, the driver pulled Mara's legs apart and fucked her pitilessly until both he and she were exhausted.

They drove into the outskirts of Vannes just as dusk was falling and they paused briefly in a side-street to unload Mara, her clothes and baggage, before rattling off into the distance.

Aching and exhausted, Mara looked around for a map, an *agent de police*, a passer-by: anyone or anything that could tell her the way to the centre of town, and the nearest cheap hotel.

As she looked around, her gaze fell upon a poster, newly pasted to the wall opposite, and bearing a large picture of the head of Tutankhamun. She walked over to it and tried to make it out, but it was all in French.

At that moment, she heard footsteps and, turning round, was startled to see a figure standing right behind her.

'For God's sake, Mara, what the hell did you think you were doing, running off like that?'

'Geoffrey!' Mara wasn't sure whether to be pleased or

scared. He had been behaving so oddly . . . 'Look, I'm sorry about that. I . . . I was shocked by what happened with the deer. I don't know what came over me . . .'

Geoffrey slipped his arm round Mara's waist, and gave her right breast a playful stroke. Even after her ordeal, there was plenty of sexual energy still there within her, just waiting to be awakened. Maybe she'd been hasty in her judgements about Geoffrey . . .

'It's OK, Mara. I understand. But it was just a silly accident – you understand that, don't you?'

She nodded, not really knowing whether she believed him or not.

'Look, Mara, I'm here now. I'm here to protect you and help you in whatever way I can.'

'Then translate that poster for me, would you?'

Geoffrey peered at the poster in the half-light, and read:

'It says: "Sale of Egyptian antiquities from the collection of the late M Alain Kerriel, 4 p.m. Thursday, Hôtel Lion d'Or." Why?'

'I'll explain later,' replied Mara. 'But for now, could we go to a hotel? I'm so worn-out, I feel like just going to bed.'

'So do I, Mara,' grinned Geoffrey, running lascivious fingers across her breast. 'Believe me, so do I.'

10: Discoveries

In the end, she'd had to tell Geoffrey everything and, surprisingly enough, he hadn't called her a crackpot or a crazy woman. Funny that: Andreas was always calling her a New Age weirdo, and yet Geoffrey's constant, polite attentiveness was far less easy to take. In fact, it sometimes made her flesh creep. She was afraid to let her psychic powers tune in to him in any way, in case she discovered something she couldn't cope with.

Andreas. She missed that cynical smile, the jumble of half-empty whisky bottles, the way he used to rip off her clothes and make mad, passionate love to her on the balcony, in the woods, in the bath – anywhere.

The memory of his troubled face in the shattered mirror was as clear in her mind as it had been that day in Theophanau's tomb. The images played back constantly in her head, like a videotape loop with no 'off' switch. Andreas was calling to her, he could see her – she now knew that, wherever his soul was, he had been able to see her.

She reached her hand into her pocket and touched his watch, which she had carried with her ever since that fateful night; and the psychic vibrations were once again reassuringly strong. Andreas's soul might be in torment, it might be beyond her reach for the moment, but it was resolutely and defiantly alive.

Geoffrey was not easy to shake off but Mara did finally manage to persuade him that she was quite safe on her own and that he could afford to leave Vannes on business for a few days. She would be quite OK by herself. Fortune was smiling upon her, after all . . .

On the day before the auction, there was to be a public viewing of the articles on sale, in the function room at the Lion d'Or. However, unusually, not all the items were to be released to the public gaze. Some, considered to be of 'special occult significance', were offered for viewing and sale by invitation only. Mara knew that, if the Phallus was indeed being offered in the sale, it would be among these occult items. She knew that, somehow, she must be among those invited to the private viewing.

Luckily, one of Mara's occult friends had moved to Paris a few years earlier to take up a prestigious post in parapsychology; and she was able to ring him and ask him to exert a little influence with the auction house and executors of Kerriel's estate.

'No problem,' he replied. 'I'll just ring up the auctioneers and tell them you're going to be at the auction, bidding on my behalf. That should do the trick.'

And so it was that, on Wednesday morning, Mara found herself among an internationally renowned group of occultists, sorcerers and witches, at the offices of Meisterlinck & Co, the executors of Kerriel's estate.

Such was the apparent value of the occult items on sale that the visitors who wished to view the pieces were admitted separately to the basement of the building, which housed an enormous safe. When it came to Mara's turn, she was ushered down a steep flight of stone steps into a dimly lit room dominated by the huge safe at one end.

'We keep the lighting at an absolute minimum,' explained M Meisterlinck, 'So as not to risk damaging these precious items.'

Mara nodded knowledgeably as she was taken to stand in front of a glass viewing-booth and articles were passed before her one by one. In this way, she was able to see each item, but could not touch any of them.

A shrunken head, set with an enormous diamond; bones said to be those of the sage Nostradamus; all manner of paraphernalia used in Satanic rituals . . . evidently M Alain Kerriel had been a distinctly unpleasant man.

'I'm sorry, Monsieur Meisterlinck,' sighed Mara, 'but I seem to have wasted my time. The article I am seeking is not here. There is nothing else?'

The executor's eyes narrowed.

'There may, perhaps, be certain other items, which I am not at liberty to discuss, mademoiselle . . . they are for sale by private treaty and the contract is soon to be signed.'

Mara's heart began to pound.

'A painted box, around a foot long and three inches wide? Do you have such a box and its . . . contents?'

The executor smiled enigmatically.

'As I have told you, Mademoiselle Fleming, I cannot discuss the nature of such items.'

'Then perhaps I can persuade you?'

Mara felt recklessness clutch at her heart and threw all caution to the winds. Walking to the door, she closed it softly, shutting out the world above. She was alone with Meisterlinck, in this subterranean world of black magic and gloom. Only the sightless eyes of a shrunken head stared at her, seemingly indifferent to whatever she might get up to.

She took off her jacket and threw it over a chair.

'It's getting hot in here, Monsieur Meisterlinck. Mind if I cool off a little?'

Meisterlinck's eyes were like saucers as he watched Mara's slow striptease. First the jacket – don't forget the gloves; that's right, peel them off ever so slowly so as to tantalise him. Throw the jacket over the back of the chair, then kick off your shoes.

The sweater now. Not too quickly, or you'll spoil the surprise for him. Let him wonder for a while – is she, or isn't she? What is she wearing underneath . . .?

Nothing, Monsieur Meisterlinck. I am wearing nothing underneath my little white mohair sweater. See how beautifully tanned my breasts are, even though it is winter.

I walk naked in the wind and rain and sunshine for as many months of the year as I can bear, monsieur. That accustoms the flesh to freedom and I never lose my tan. When I am with my coven, I perform naked rituals even in the snow – did you know that, Monsieur Meisterlinck?

Do you like to think of the pretty picture of Miss Mara Fleming, dancing naked in the snow? Do you like to think of her tanned flesh growing rosy with the cold, her nipples hardening, the flesh on her breasts tensing and the tiny little hairs erecting as the wind plays upon her skin?

She knew that the thought-messages were getting through to him. She had seen that he was a sensitive, the very first moment she had set eyes on him. Yes, a sensitive; but one who had for years denied and suppressed his powers. And now those very powers were exerting their right to exist and today they would bring about his downfall.

The skirt now. See my fingers toying with the buttons. It's a button-through skirt, do you see, monsieur? There are lots of very tiny, very shiny mother-of-pearl buttons that go all the way down the front. I think I'll start unfastening them from the bottom and work my way up . . .

Look: you can see my legs now, through the gap in the front of my skirt. They're bare and brown, too. Do you like my legs, monsieur? They are very long, very slim, very strong. My thighs now: they are strong thighs, that long to crush you between them, squeeze all the spunk out of you and make you cry out for release.

And see: yet one more treat is in store for you, for I am wearing no panties beneath my skirt. My pubic hair is thick and black and glossy, and if you were to kiss it you would find that it is fragrant, too. It smells of my womanliness, Monsieur Meisterlinck. Of my womanliness and of my womanhood.

Would you like to kiss my cunt, monsieur?

At these last, silent words, Meisterlinck was unable to control himself any longer. He hurled himself at Mara's feet, embracing her naked thighs and burying his face in her pubic hair, breathing in the heady fragrance of her sex.

Mara shuffled her feet apart and allowed him to wriggle fingers and tongue into her intimacy, delighting in the clumsy ways in which he sought to pleasure her. Evidently Monsieur Meisterlinck, although possessed of certain psychic abilities, was no adept in the arts of love.

That's it, monsieur. Fuck me with your fingers. Feel how wet I am. Search out my clitty and tease it with your tongue. It's hard and it's throbbing for you – just for you. Can you feel it?

Despite his clumsiness, Meisterlinck soon succeeded in bringing Mara to orgasm; and he cried out with pleasure as he felt her cunt open and close like the mouth of some exotic sea creature about his fingers.

That was nice, monsieur. Very nice. Now – what shall we do next?

Would you like me to suck your penis, Monsieur Le Notaire? Would you like me to pull down the zip on those so-sensible, so-anonymous pinstripe trousers, and feel inside and see what you have to offer me? I'm a greedy girl, monsieur: I don't want to be disappointed.

Meisterlinck allowed himself to be pulled to his feet, and Mara took up her place on her knees before him, unzipping him and feeling for his penis in his underpants. She was not disappointed.

Nice prick, Monsieur Le Notaire. Nice prick. I think I shall suck it, after all . . .

Meisterlinck's gasp of amazement as she took him into her mouth was sufficient to tell Mara that this was a first for him: no peroxide whore had ever taken his prick out of his pants in some darkened back-alley and given him a local; no grim-faced wife had ever softened her resolve and allowed herself to be persuaded to suck his cock in the darkness of the conjugal bed. No: today was going to be a real treat for Monsieur Meisterlinck.

Not so fast, monsieur. Don't get so excited, or you'll come too quickly. Just relax, and let me take control. You'll soon see how much fun it is when I'm in control, monsieur. I can suck away at you all day, if you want . . .

She kept him on the brink for as long as she could, and then slipped her fingers under his testicles and gave them the gentlest of squeezes.

Instantly she was rewarded with a mighty gush of semen

which spurted out so suddenly that she was taken unaware and almost choked. She felt Meisterlinck's whole body shuddering with the terrific force of his orgasm.

No – don't pull away from me, monsieur. There is more to come. Let me play with you a little and we'll soon be able to enjoy some more fun.

Mara amused herself by licking and nibbling at Meisterlinck's testicles, and placed his hands upon the wonderful ripeness of her breasts. Within a few minutes, he began to grow hard again and Mara ran her tongue over the tip of his penis, savouring the salty aftertaste of the semen which was drying on the glistening purple flesh.

Now, monsieur, now I think you are hard enough and we can play another, very wonderful game. In this game, you lie on the floor and I get astride you – yes, that's it: perfect! You are such a quick learner, monsieur.

Meisterlinck lay beneath her and moaned gently as Mara lowered herself, very slowly and very carefully, onto his rigid penis. It slid into her with exquisite ease, for she was very, very wet.

Slowly, ignoring his pleas to ride him recklessly, Mara slid up and down on Meisterlinck's penis. She knew she could not hold him for long, for already she could feel him twitching, ready to shoot forth his load. But she was determined to make it last as long as she could, and it was not until she could feel that her own orgasm was almost upon her that she finally let go and allowed Meisterlinck to spurt his semen up into her cunt.

They collapsed together in an untidy heap and for several moments neither of them had the strength to move or speak.

Eventually, Mara raised herself up on one elbow and looked into Meisterlinck's eyes.

'Will you tell me now, monsieur? And show me what it is that you have been concealing from me?'

'What . . . what did you do to me, Mademoiselle Fleming?' demanded Meisterlinck, the blood strangely drained from his usually florid face. 'Such power, such an infinity of control. I am afraid of you: you must indeed have great occult powers . . .'

Greater than I had imagined, thought Mara to herself. For which I am eternally grateful.

'Tell me what I need to know,' continued Mara, 'And you shall come to no harm. In fact . . .' she stroked his already stirring penis with gentle fingers, 'you shall experience my very special form of gratitude . . .'

'I shall show you what I have,' promised Meisterlinck. 'If you will only fuck me once again . . .'

It was a request which Mara hardly knew how to refuse.

The items in the private sale were kept in a locked cabinet in Meisterlinck's office under a twenty-four-hour guard and a combination lock.

'Only two people in the world know the combination,' he explained, 'I and my partner. These items are of such tremendous importance.'

Mara waited in impatience as Meisterlinck punched in the combination and the door swung open. Inside were several smallish objects: three piles of parchment and one parcel, oilskin-wrapped, about a foot long and three inches thick . . .

'Open that one!' gasped Mara. 'That one – and hurry!'

Meisterlinck obeyed, baffled as to why the girl was so disinterested in the priceless manuscripts. He unwrapped the layers of oilskin and revealed a small, plain wooden box.

Plain, thought Mara. The box I am looking for is painted. But it's not the box I'm really after . . .

'Open it!'

The lid slotted into the top of the box. Meisterlinck lifted it off, to reveal a cylindrical object within. He lifted it out.

'The original parchment scroll of the first book of secret Hermetic teachings,' he announced proudly, holding it out to Mara. 'Priceless! Isn't it wonderful . . .?'

And Mara didn't know whether to laugh or cry.

The suburban backstreets were quiet and almost deserted as

Mara walked disconsolately back to the hotel where she and Geoffrey had taken a room. Try as she might, she could not get over the immense disappointment. How easily arrogance can lead to downfall! She mused with some amusement upon the irony of her discovery: in normal circumstances, she would have been amazed, thrilled, delighted, to have been in the same room as that Hermineutic scroll.

But circumstances were far from normal.

As she walked, she gazed disinterestedly into the windows of the few tatty shops which lined the street. She had insisted that they stay in this quiet, almost run-down part of town, because something told her not to draw attention to herself. Geoffrey, of course, with his new-found affluence, had been dismayed. She had liked him a lot better that night at the camp-site.

A tatty boulangerie, a horse-meat butcher's shop, a thoroughly unsavoury bar . . . not much to interest the casual observer. And then, all of a sudden, her eye was caught by the jumble of objects in a tiny shop window.

It was without a doubt the grottiest, tattiest bric-à-brac shop that Mara had ever seen. Its window was filled with rubbish – a plastic duck, an old bicycle wheel, one or two books with half their pages torn out . . .

But at the front, almost hidden underneath a pile of yellowing magazines, lay a curious little wooden box.

A box roughly twelve inches long and three across. A box whose painted hieroglyphics were only just visible beneath a thick layer of dust.

11: Journeys

Mara hammered on the door of the shop for what seemed like hours. Surely it couldn't be shut? Did they have half-day closing in Brittany? Oh come on, come on, open up!

At last, when she had almost given up hope, she detected signs of movement in the gloom at the back of the shop. A sudden glimmer of light as a door was opened and closed again. Slow, heavy footsteps dragging across a bare and dirty floor.

A key turned in the lock, and the door swung open. A dried-up, wrinkled face greeted Mara with a grimace of annoyance.

'*C'est quoi que vous voulez, hein? Fichez-moi le camp*!'

'Please . . . *s'il vous plaît* . . . can I come in?'

'Ah . . . English!' The grim face cracked into a toothless smile. 'You were good to my Raoul in the war. You may enter.'

The old crone shuffled back into the shop, reaching for a switch on the wall. Dull, yellowish light filtered into the room through a greasy, fly-specked lightbulb, hanging on a frayed flex above the counter. The shop was filled with the most overwhelming stench of dust, mildew, decay and incontinent cats.

Mara gave the shop no more than a cursory glance. She rushed to the window, and began rummaging through the rubbish that littered her way.

'Mais, *qu'est-ce que vous faites* . . . Mademoiselle!'

'The box, the box!' exclaimed Mara. 'I must have it – *la boîte* . . .!'

The door to the back room opened again, and two more

women entered: the first, a woman of perhaps forty-five, clearly the old woman's daughter, and the second, a pretty girl of no more than twenty. All had the same dark eyes, the same strong features. Mara felt a chill of psychic recognition run down her spine as she felt their presence envelop her.

These women were more than they seemed. Neither good nor evil, yet with powers that transcended Mara's as emphatically as hers transcended those of the common herd of fortune-tellers and two-a-penny prophets.

They gathered round her as she searched for the box, standing silently and just watching, watching. Mara could feel their dark eyes burning into her back, the strength of their will exploring her mind, searching out the hidden truths.

Who were these strange women, who were not of this world, not of this time . . .?

Their whispers rose like the buzzing of insistent bees, intermingling in Mara's mind:

'La boîte . . . elle veut la boîte . . . elle la cherche là, à la fenêtre . . . tu vois? La boîte . . . elle est venue chercher la boîte . . .'

And suddenly many hands reached out and touched Mara. She started as the fingers ran down her spine, smoothed across her hips and buttocks, reached around her waist and slid up to stroke the magnificent curve of her breasts . . .

Somehow, it was not an altogether unpleasant touch. There was a raw energy in these women's fingers, as though they carried a low-voltage electric charge; and this energy flowed into Mara's body as they stroked her, exciting her in spite of herself, and making her want to open herself to their tactile exploration of her body.

There it was! There, beneath a pile of rubbish, at the very front of the window, down in the left-hand corner. Mara reached out for it, just as the hands began to pull up her skirt and toy with her naked buttocks.

'Nue . . . elle est toute nue! Regarde qu'elle a de jolies fesses . . . !'

Torn between the desire to submit to these women's lewd advances and the need to have the box at any price, Mara made a final lunge forward and succeeded in wrapping her fingers round the box.

She pulled it in triumph from the window and turned to face the three women, who were all smiling at her in a most disconcerting way. She looked down, and saw to her embarrassment that they had pulled up her skirt and tucked it into her belt so that she was naked from the waist down. And yet, she had not the will to cover her nakedness, for there was something in the women's eyes, their need for her, which matched a need within her own body.

Mara found herself sliding her feet further apart, so that the entrance to her cunt was no longer barred to her tormentors. Their hands stretched out to her again, and this time they began to stroke her legs, her hips, the inside of her thighs, the incredibly sensitive spot where thigh meets the margin of the cunt-lips.

The old woman smiled toothlessly at Mara and for a second it was as though in the old woman's eyes she saw the faces of all three women, all three ages combined in one, suddenly ageless, face.

'Open it, my lovely,' whispered the old woman. 'Open the pretty painted box, my darling . . .'

'*Ouvre-la, ouvre-la* . . .' whispered the younger women.

Mara gazed down at the box. Her hands were trembling, not only with fear and sexual arousal, but with the power which was undeniably flowing into her from the box itself.

Could this really be it? Could she at last have found the box containing the Phallus of Osiris?

The box was about twelve inches long and obviously very ancient, for the wood was parched and cracked and the unwieldy hinges rusted almost solid with age. The painted surface was faded and worn away in patches, but the brightly coloured Egyptian paintings were still clearly visible: a tree, with a box caught up in its branches; a weeping woman straddling the dead body of her husband, a wooden penis sliding up into her cunt; a human figure with a greenish-black face and a huge penis, weighing the soul of a dead man.

Osiris. Osiris, lord of the underworld, god of rebirth. All-powerful Osiris, give me back the life of my undead lover . . . Surely this *must* be the box . . .

The old woman's eyes were burning into her. Hands were sliding up her thighs, fingers exploring her cunt, probing deeper, toying with the swelling bud of her clitoris . . .

Taking a deep breath, and trying desperately to clear her mind of the clouds of sexual desire, Mara seized the lid of the box and pulled. At first nothing happened, for it was stiff with age. She tugged harder, and the lid snapped open.

The scents of age and the sickly sweet aroma of embalming oils rose up to meet her. Naked figures danced in bright profusion across the painted wooden interior, couples fucked and buggered each other in colours untainted by age.

But the box was empty.

In an agony of disappointment, Mara tried to fling the box to the ground. But it felt as though it were fused to her hands by some irresistible force; as though it recognised that here was its home, its rightful owner from whom it would not easily be parted.

And, as the lascivious fingers explored her cunt and arse, and pulled at her blouse, liberating her naked breasts, Mara felt a mist of confusion begin to surround her, making strange images swim before her eyes.

As physical pleasure overwhelmed her, Mara was borne away into a multi-coloured kaleidoscope of pictures and sensations which she only dimly understood.

The mist cleared and she realised that she was no longer in the tatty little shop on the rue de Velay. She was in a strange, white room with smooth walls and no windows. White walls and a rough, concrete floor. A single, flickering bulb swung slowly from the low ceiling, as though stirred by the distant rumble of heavy guns.

She was lying, naked, on a rickety iron bedstead, her legs outspread and her cunt gaping. Looking down at her body, she saw that her skin was snow-white, and long blonde tresses fell over her shoulders and arms. This was not her own body . . .

A tall, blond man in an SS uniform was standing at the end of the bed, his flies unbuttoned and his erect penis in his hand. He watched her with a cruel smile as she tried in vain to extricate her wrists and ankles from the leather straps.

'Lie still, *Liebling*,' he sneered. 'It will be the better for you. The Führer has chosen to share his sacred seed with you. You, my darling slut, have been chosen to be the bearer of our beloved Führer's sacred line.

'You must show you are not unworthy of the Reichsführer's trust. Terrible things happen to those who cannot show themselves to be worthy, my little dove . . .

'And whilst we await the Führer's magnificence, shall we amuse ourselves in some agreeable preliminaries? You have such a pretty little cunt – but so very tight. It would be an act of Christian charity for me to grease it well for my Führer's cock, would it not, *Liebchen*?'

Mara tried to scream, but the SS captain placed his leather-gloved hand over her mouth, silencing her cries. Tears began to well up and spill onto her cheeks.

'You must not weep, my pretty,' hissed the captain. 'Tears might spoil your looks for the Führer. And he might wonder what I had been doing to you to make you so unhappy. Hold back your tears, tender one, or I shall be obliged to have you killed . . .'

Mara fought back her tears, her breath coming in painful gasps. The SS captain was upon her now. She could smell the mingled scents of leather, motor-oil and stale beer upon him, and his rank breath almost choked her as he pressed his face close to hers. His hard leather gloves chafed her sensitive skin as he gripped the flesh of her forearms, raising fierce red welts. But she dared not make a sound, for fear that he would take out his Luger and press it against her temple.

His penis pressed insistently against her groin, searching for the entrance to her palace of desire. And indeed she felt desire mounting within her, in spite of her revulsion. She could not suppress the sudden pulsing of her cunt as it anticipated the imminent invasion, releasing a flood of pent-up cunt-juices.

The captain let go of her right arm for a moment and fumbled for his prick. With a swift, savage movement, he steered it towards Mara's hole and pressed it home. The vicious thrust made her moan quietly, for he tore into her without gentleness.

He took his pleasure quickly, like a man who is afraid of being caught fucking his master's wife, and paid no attention to Mara's throbbing clitoris. Pumping into her with a series of long, hard strokes, he pulled out at the very last minute and watched his semen spurt out all over Mara's belly. Clearly his courage did not quite match up to his boasts and he was careful to wipe away the evidence of their copulation.

Mara lay panting and unsatisfied on the bed, gazing up resentfully into the face of her tormentor. He was still wearing the same cruel smile.

'Now, my *Liebling*, let us see how well we can prepare you for your moment of glory. I see that your cunt shows a proper respect for our Führer, for already it is running with juice. Let us see if we cannot make you even readier for your moment of ecstasy.'

He took the whip from his belt, and Mara began to cry out in fear:

'No, please, no: don't hurt me . . .!'

'Silence, my sweet little fount of corruption: and taste the delights of pain!'

He brought the lash down hard upon her right breast, and her body convulsed as the pain stung her. Again and again he whipped her, so skilfully that the pain was always mingled with the beginnings of a terrible, fearsome pleasure. As the lash fell between her thighs, Mara felt a delicious burning in her clitty and knew that this monster of depravity was taking her to some terrifying new summit of pleasure which she had never known before.

But, just as she was sure of the approach of her orgasm, he stopped whipping her and put the lash down.

'You are ready now,' he decreed. 'It is time for you to meet your destiny.'

He opened the door and went out, leaving Mara alone in her bare, white cell, shivering with mingled fear and desire as she listened to the sound of the guns. They were distant, but they were coming nearer.

After what seemed an age, the door opened again and a rather insignificant man walked in. Insignificant but for his eyes, which gleamed with a fanatical zeal. He looked old and tired and his uniform stank as though it had not been changed for weeks.

Hitler. Adolf Hitler. And he was going to fuck her.

He spoke not a word but examined his prize minutely, peering intently at her most secret places and verifying that she was, indeed, worthy of being joined with his flesh.

Then he reached into his pocket and took out a small bottle, filled with a pearly white fluid. Semen . . . And he opened the leather bag he had brought with him, and gently removed a box, about twelve inches long and three inches thick. A painted wooden box, very ancient and whose hinges were almost rusted shut.

He opened up the box and took out a object which, although Mara had never seen it before, she recognised instantly. It was almost a foot long, greenish-black and shiny, and as hard as polished leather. At one end were two wrinkled, leathery pouches. It glowed with a greenish luminescence.

The Phallus of Osiris!

Almost forgetting her fear, Mara watched intently as the Führer smeared the tip of the phallus lovingly with the semen from the bottle. His own semen? What was he going to do next?

Taking up the talisman as though it were a sacred chalice, the Führer approached the bed on which Mara lay.

'*Nicht zu spät . . . es muss nicht zu spät sein . . .*' he murmured.

Silently, he climbed onto the bed and knelt between Mara's thighs. He made no attempt to kiss or fondle her, and approached her with an almost businesslike coldness.

The phallus gleamed more brightly as he brought it closer to Mara's cunt and she shivered – half in fear, half in fascination – as she gazed upon it. So this was what she had been searching for, for so long! This was what she needed to rescue Andreas – and it was still beyond her reach . . .

Her cunt was still pulsating with the desperate need to fuck, and it grew wetter still at the approach of the sacred Egyptian phallus. Though she twisted and turned in an attempt to evade her torment, Mara's body longed for the touch of that massive hardness, for the feeling of delicious fullness as it violated her fragile womanhood.

The semen-drenched tip of the phallus nudged against her labia, and instantly Mara felt a terrible pain coursing through her body. A terrible pain, mingled with a desperate yearning for more, for the pain was the precursor of the most exquisite pleasure.

The Führer pulled apart Mara's cunt-lips, and with a single thrust the phallus was inside her. Though she knew her life might depend upon her silence, she could not suppress a scream as the fiery dart lodged in her belly, kindling her wildest and most base desires.

Her lips parted and she heard a voice which was not her own whisper:

'Fuck me, mein Führer. Fuck me, for the destiny of the Fatherland . . .'

The dizzying currents of pleasure and pain which racked her body culminated in a series of ferocious spasms, which tore through Mara and left her exhausted and near-unconscious.

When she opened her eyes again, she was looking upon a very different scene.

A sumptuous room: the grand hall, perhaps, of some noble house or palace. The gleam of carved and polished oak was everywhere, and golden light filtered in through tiny panes of irregular glass.

She was kneeling before a tall, red-haired woman on a large, gilded chair, and they were alone save for two men in archaic dress who guarded the door. She glanced down and saw that she, too, was dressed in the same fancy-dress costume. Her waist was tiny, tightly nipped-in, and long full robes of silver-grey satin, embroidered with pearls, flowed around her knees. She could barely move her head for the stiffly starched ruffle about her neck.

A door opened at the far end of the room and a tall, darkly handsome man strode in. On seeing the woman, he removed his feathered cap and bowed low.

'Your Majesty.'

And Mara heard the woman reply:

'My dear Sir Walter. And what have you brought to show us today? What glittering treasures have our new dominions yielded for our royal pleasure?'

'Your Majesty, a treasure far beyond my power to name its price. A treasure which, I have no doubt, will appeal to Your Majesty's supremely sensual nature.'

A flicker of interest passed across the Queen's face, and she turned to the two guards:

'You may leave us now. Wait in the ante-room and ensure that no one disturbs us.'

Mara made to rise to her feet and leave but the Queen stopped her:

'No, not you, child. You shall remain with us. We may have other uses for you. Now, Sir Walter, show us this marvel that you have brought for our amusement.'

The bearded man smiled and reached into the large leather travelling pouch slung from his belt. He took out a painted box which Mara recognised instantly.

'This is a pretty toy from the land of the Pharaohs,' announced the explorer. 'But it has been lost for centuries, and has only now been discovered, in a pagan temple in the

New World where it was being used in a crude fertility rite.'

He opened the box and revealed the phallus within, its phosphorescent glow eerie against the spring morning sunlight.

The Queen's face lit up with sudden, unfeigned interest, and she reached out a ringed hand to touch the gleaming surface.

'Tell me more of this strange relic,' she commanded. 'And of its purpose and function.'

'Your Majesty, this is the lost Phallus of Osiris, the penis of the Egyptian god, severed by his brother Set and lost for generations. It has great magical properties. It is said that all who possess or use it shall enjoy long life and the power of life and death over others. It also endows the user with great physical pleasure – and knowing, as I do, how much you value your reputation as a virgin queen, Your Majesty, methinks this little gift may find favour with you . . .'

The Queen took the box from Sir Walter and removed the phallus, which she began to stroke and explore with her eager fingers. It seemed to hold an infinite fascination for her and Mara could see her trembling with excitement.

After a few moments, the Queen turned to her visitor again and announced:

'We shall not fuck with you today, Sir Walter. Today we shall watch you fucking with the Countess Derby. Methinks this shall inspire us . . .'

With a gracious bow, Sir Walter laid down his cap upon a convenient chair and unfastened the buttons which held up the front of his breeches. Out sprang a most impressive prick, worthy of a great explorer, for Mara could see that it craved the scent of new flesh to explore.

'Unfasten your bodice, Countess. We wish to see Sir Walter playing with your bubbies,' instructed the Queen. 'Fie! You are too slow!' And she drew Sir Walter's sword from its hilt and used it to slice through the laces of Mara's bodice. Dutifully, she pulled back the sides of the material, so that her breasts would be exposed to the Queen's critical gaze.

'The flesh is agreeably white and taut. Have you been massaging them daily with rosewater and oil of cloves, as we instructed you?'

'Yes, Your Majesty. And I have been masturbating as you taught me, to increase the power of my desires and strengthen the muscles of my womanhood.'

'Good, good. Now we wish you to offer your bubbies to Sir Walter for him to suck. And whilst he is doing that, you may toy with his prick a little – but beware: you must not provoke him to his crisis until we give you the sign that we are ready. Do you understand?'

Mara nodded and turned to Sir Walter, offering him her breasts like exotic sweetmeats for the tasting. He took her right breast between his hands and felt it, not ungently, doubtless enjoying the touch of firm white flesh between his fingers. Then he bowed his head and took the nipple into his mouth, crushing it a little between his teeth before beginning to suckle like a greedy babe.

Mara realised what was required of her and slid her hands down to Sir Walter's groin. His prick was already agreeably hard, its tip moist and weeping slippery tears of unsatisfied desire. Mara released his stones from their breeches and squeezed them carefully, just hard enough to cause him a frisson of delight.

'Egad!' cried out the explorer. 'You have taught the hussy well, Your Majesty! She is indeed her mistress's pupil! For I can feel the firmness of your touch in her fingers.'

'We have spent many long hours instructing the Countess in the ways of the flesh,' replied the Queen in self-satisfied tones. 'She is an apt pupil and an excellent cunt-licker. There are no limits to the girl's depravity. She is a born whore.

'Why, we have set her to sucking the cocks of all our courtiers, and yet she does not tire of it. It is a diverting sport and we have spent many amusing afternoons with

Lord Essex, watching the jade sucking off half the court, one after the other.

'We have bound her hand and foot and commanded her to fuck with the filthy beggars and cripples who ply their trade outside the palace gates, and there seems no end to the pleasure she derives from it.'

Such talk would normally have revolted Mara but in this new body she felt the woman's excitement at the remembrance of her depravity: the way the blind beggar had pawed at her and whimpered as she straddled his foul, ulcerous body; her delight when she had been tied and bound and buggered by the Queen's brutal guards; and the enormous orgasms that had shuddered through her as the soldiers violated her frail woman's body, again and again.

To Mara's consternation, the memory of such horrors did not sicken her; rather, it excited her – and she felt her cunt growing hotter and wetter beneath her heavy silk robes. Sir Walter was bringing her such an intensity of pleasure that she forgot who she really was and slipped seamlessly into this borrowed life of joyful depravity.

Sir Walter's prick grew still stiffer in her hands and at length he drew away, mindful of the Queen's commands.

'So, my little jade, you like to fuck with brutes and beggars? I have a fine, fat prick – will you not fuck with me? Is it too rich for you after a pauper's pizzle?'

'I will fuck with you willingly, sir,' replied Mara, pulling up her skirts to reveal creamy-white naked flesh beneath. 'And to judge from the size of your pizzle, I have no fears of disappointment.'

'Since it is my lady's pleasure to fuck like a common slut, we command you to fuck her as a dog would fuck a bitch,' announced the Queen, evidently greatly enjoying these spicy frolics. 'And whilst you are entertaining us, we shall make good use of this new gift which you have brought us, Sir Walter.'

Sir Walter pushed Mara onto her hands and knees and lifted up her skirts, so that they rested on her shoulders like the upturned petals of some libidinous flower. To her mingled delight and dismay, Mara found that she was longing for him to enter her and she thrust out her creamy buttocks to accept his assault.

'Excellent!' exclaimed the Queen, as Mara felt Sir Walter's prick ram up into her, its eager head battering against the neck of her womb. 'Show the jade no mercy, Sir Walter, we command it.'

So saying, the Queen pulled up her own skirts, revealing a very pretty pair of thighs and a tight little cunt, fringed with chestnut curls. She picked up the phallus again, still marvelling at its greenish-black luminescence, and began to use its tip to toy with her clitoris.

'Ah!' she sighed. 'Truly you have brought us a marvellous gift, Sir Walter.'

Mara watched entranced as the Phallus slid slowly and deliciously up into the Queen's cunt, each stroke of Sir Walter's prick mirroring the regular movements of the Queen's hand as she thrust the Phallus in and out of her womanhood.

Mara felt her orgasm upon her and, with a cry of ecstasy, she thrust backwards, the spasms of her cunt stimulating Sir Walter's cock to spurt its semen into her belly. When she looked up, she saw that the Queen, too, had been brought to the peak of pleasure. The Phallus lay in her lap, glistening with moisture, and little rivulets of love-juice were running from her cunt as though she, and not Mara, had drunk in Sir Walter's seed.

'You have done well, Sir Walter,' announced the Queen, smoothing down her skirts and putting the Phallus back into its box. 'This gift which you have brought us is a true instrument of power and we are greatly pleased with you.

'Sadly, we fear that this gift is too momentous to risk anyone ever hearing of its existence. Therefore, Sir Walter, we must regretfully condemn you to death. You shall submit yourself to be taken to the Tower this very day.

'And as for you, my little whore,' she smiled, taking Mara's chin in her hand and forcing her to gaze up into her cruel eyes. 'You know too much and must also pay the price of your depravity.' So saying, she took Sir Walter's dagger from his belt and pressed it against Mara's throat.

That was the last thing Mara remembered until she opened her eyes once more and saw that she was no longer in the magnificent Elizabethan throne-room, but lying on the floor of what seemed to be a mud hut. It was cold and she shivered, realising that she was naked save for a woven belt of grass and sea-shells about her waist. She looked at her hands and saw with a start that they were smeared with a bright blue dye.

She pulled herself to her feet and turned to look for a way out. But the only doorway was blocked by two guards, clad in long woollen robes and carrying spears.

Hearing movement inside the hut, they turned and saw that Mara was awake and addressed each other in a language Mara could not understand.

A few moments later, reinforcements arrived, led by a tall, dark-haired man in a rust-coloured woollen cloak, under which he was completely naked. From the authority which he was shown by the others, Mara guessed that he must be a chieftain or high priest.

On seeing Mara, he smiled, and his prick began to rise to attention. He seized her roughly by the arm and began to poke and prod her flesh as though she were some domestic beast, an ox or a horse, whose quality he was trying to assess.

At length he seemed satisfied, and his prick certainly seemed to approve of Mara's naked loveliness. He clapped his hands and the guards took hold of her arms, half-dragging her out of the hut and across the damp grass towards a rough platform, made from woven branches. Yoked to it were several naked boys, playing out the role of a team of oxen.

Throwing Mara down onto the hurdle, the guards set about lashing her to it, arms and legs splayed wide. Once they were satisfied that she was securely tied, they began to paint her breasts and cunt with a bluish pigment, which stung as it touched her sensitive flesh.

Almost weeping with cold and terror, Mara felt the hurdle begin to move. She was being dragged off across the marshy grass, she knew not where. All she could see was the lowering grey sky and the lustful, vicious smiles of the tribesmen who were pursuing her.

Her journey ended at last, as the team of young boys dragged the hurdle into the middle of the marsh. The tall man in the cloak came towards her, carrying a box. Even before she really saw it, Mara knew what it was. He was opening it, taking out something greenish black. It was glowing faintly and all about her the tribesmen were falling to their knees in terror and adoration.

He was in front of her now, the Phallus in his hands, pointing towards her. And he was kneeling on the marshy ground before her, and pushing the Phallus up into her cunt.

'No, no!' cried Mara; but the words turned to dust in her throat. And the exquisite pain of the Phallus flooded through her body, awakening the power of sensations too terrifyingly acute to bear.

The orgasm came swiftly, her cunt sucking greedily on the Phallus and floods of cunt-juice running down her thighs. The tribesmen were on their feet now and smiling, laughing, congratulating each other.

Their chieftain was cutting her bonds with his dagger . . . were they going to let her go free?

And then she felt the noose as it was slipped over her head and tightened round her neck. They were dragging her across the grass to a place where the marsh was deep and treacherous. If she fell in there, she would never get out alive. No one would ever find her body. Perhaps they didn't want anyone to . . .

The noose tightened around her throat and her consciousness ebbed away.

When she came to, it was not to the sight of cold grey skies and fathomless marshes, but to the warmth of a hot noonday sun upon lithe brown flesh.

Mara opened her eyes and rolled over onto her side. The

Nile waters were blue and inviting before her. If she just walked a few yards further, through the papyrus reeds, she would be there, at the water's margin, and could cool her parched flesh in the limpid blue depths . . .

The white robe fell about her in diaphanous folds as she got to her feet, her tanned breasts and dark pubic triangle clearly visible through the gauzy fabric. Tiny insects buzzed through the sunlit air and the warmth of the day soaked into her flesh, dulling her brain but awakening her senses. Her clitty began to throb gently and her nipples hardened like ripening fruits in the summer sun.

The sound of voices awoke her from her reverie and she looked away into the distance, towards the temple of Ra, to see a procession of priests and priestesses approaching the river. They were wearing ceremonial animal masks and were naked to the waist, the women's breasts bobbing invitingly in the sun, glistening with the sacred oils they massaged daily into their flesh.

As they approached, the main body of the party turned right and went down to the river, where they took off their robes and began to wash each other in the river. But two of the priests – a man and a woman – came towards Mara, walking past where she stood, apparently unaware of her presence as she stood among the reeds watching them.

They were wearing jackal masks which concealed their faces and lent them the air of mythical beasts. They undressed and laid their belongings on the river bank and Mara saw that their bodies were lithe and youthful, their flesh deeply tanned, supple and glistening with sweet oils.

The priest stepped thigh-deep into the warm, shallow water and beckoned to the woman to follow him. She did so, bringing with her an embroidered cloth which she dipped in the Nile waters and used to wash the priest's powerful body. She began at his shoulders, chanting as she washed each new part of him, and began to work her way down towards his waist.

He had a flat belly and powerful thighs, between which hung a magnificent penis and two firm, hairy balls which were clearly bursting with spunk.

Mara had the curious impression that she had seen those balls before, cradled their wrinkled purse in the palms of her hands, and felt the flesh tense; that she had felt that thick, hard penis burrowing its way into her soft, willing flesh. Her cunt began to ooze love-juice as she watched the priest's prick grow increasingly erect at the priestess's careful caress.

As she reached his prick, the priestess dipped the embroidered cloth into the river once again and this time squeezed it over his flesh, so that the warm, clear water ran in rivulets down his shaft, dripping into the river and forming little eddies around his calves. Little droplets clung for a moment to his testicles, glittering briefly in the fierce sunshine, before they evaporated and were gone.

Mara felt desire rise in her loins as the priestess took out a small bottle of oil and poured a few drops into the palm of her hand, using it to smooth across the tip of the priest's penis; and she pulled up her shift and, standing with feet apart on the burning sand, she began to finger her own clitoris.

The priest's prick was glistening with oil now, and seemed on the point of pouring forth its semen. But at the critical moment, he pushed away the priestess's hand and instead began to anoint her body with the oil, beginning with her plump, firm breasts and working his way down her taut belly until he reached the pleasure-garden of her loins.

His hand worked its way between her thighs and she moaned softly as his finger worked away tirelessly at her clitoris. Mara, too, had to work hard not to cry out, for her own desire was reaching a peak and she longed to be satisfied by the priest's fingers, by his straining prick.

Without warning, the priest waded to the shore and picked something up from the pile of belongings on the sand. Mara recognised the box instantly, and mingled fear and longing washed over her as he took out the Phallus, its smooth surface gleaming in the powerful noonday sun.

Intoning words of power which Mara could not

understand, he slid the Phallus between the priestess's thighs and she gave a low cry – of pain or pleasure? – as the massive shaft slid home and the priest worked it in and out of her with grunts of lustful determination.

The priestess's sudden ecstasy shook her body with terrifying spasms as Mara felt the approach of her own crisis bring the juices flowing into her cunt and down her thighs. She watched the priestess fall forwards into her lover's arms, her red-painted talons digging into the flesh of his shoulders as she clung helplessly to him.

When he slid the Phallus from her cunt, it was dripping wet and glistening.

Coming to her own crisis, Mara gave a little involuntary cry of pleasure and the priest and priestess turned their heads swiftly towards her hiding-place, suddenly alerted to her presence.

They were upon her in seconds, ripping off her robe and pinning her to the ground, where she gazed up at them in terror as they slowly removed their masks and began to force apart her unwilling thighs.

Their faces terrified her even more than the power of the Phallus. For she was looking up into the eyes of the Master, and of the young and beautiful priestess whose terror she had so often looked upon in visions, as the woman was violated and buried alive by vengeful priests. The priestess who wore the face of Mara Fleming.

And Mara screamed in terror as the Phallus slid into her cunt and the pain surged through her body, washing away the last vestiges of her consciousness.

The coffin drifted down the river and Mara stood on the riverbank, watching helplessly as it floated out of sight. The dying cries of the man inside filled her mind. Osiris was dying, Osiris was screaming for help, Osiris was struggling for air and the water was filling his lungs.

Silence covered the Earth. A great blackness filled Mara's mind and the chill of fear clutched at her heart.

Osiris was dead.

And Isis would never find that most precious, most sacred, most potent fragment of his dismembered body.

Only the Master knew where to find the Phallus of Osiris.

As the pictures faded, Mara was left with one final vision, clearer and more enduring than all the rest: the picture of a deserted mountain village, huddled defensively beneath a lowering black sky, yet ringed with a mantle of purest power. As the dizziness caught her, and flung her through time and space, she wondered what it might signify . . .

'*Elle souffre . . . regarde, qu'elle souffre!*'

'*La pauvre petite . . . elle a mal au con . . .*'

'*Sois sage, sois tranquille, rien de mauvais ne va t'arriver, ma belle . . .*'

The voices wove a net around her and as she opened her eyes Mara felt their presence like an impenetrable barrier between herself and escape.

A wetness in her cunt testified to the sexual pleasure which the three women had given her. Had they drugged her? Or had the pictures she had seen truly been visions of the past life of the Phallus?

Mara struggled back into consciousness, into the world of reality, where visions are only hallucinations, and where three strange women display nothing more sinister than a remarkable family likeness.

'What happened . . .? Please, tell me where you got the box . . . *comment . . . obtenu la boîte . . . je vous en prie. C'est tellement important . . .*!'

The old woman smiled.

'Have no fear, child. You are a true seer. There are always answers for those who truly seek.

'The box came to us only a little while ago, brought to us by travellers from Budapest. *Et voilà tout* . . . that is all we know, *ma belle enfant*.'

'How much . . . *combien – pour la boîte*?' she gasped, pulling down her skirt over her knees.

The old woman took her hand and kissed it, her dry

reptilian lips making Mara shudder with repulsion.

'You are a true mystic, a true seeker, *ma belle,*' she replied. 'Take the little box, and may all the great spirits go with you on your quest.'

Mara needed no further encouragement. With murmured thanks, she took the box and fled into the gathering dusk. She did not look back.

The next day, realising that she had been foolish to be so frightened, she decided to return to thank the three women for their kindness. It was strange but no matter how hard she looked, she couldn't find the shop. It had disappeared so completely that it might never have been there.

12: Answers

She slipped away in the night, making sure that she did not disturb Geoffrey. He was a noisy sleeper and grunted as she gently lifted his arm from her waist and laid it on the pillow, but to her relief he did not wake. She did not fancy having to spend hours explaining to him why she didn't want his company on a trip to Budapest. Funny, but Geoffrey had become really weird over these last few weeks.

The thousand-franc note she'd taken from Geoffrey's wallet would help, but it would hardly get her to Budapest. Mara wondered vaguely what she was going to do . . . but the first priority was to put some distance between herself and Geoffrey Potter.

The first question was what to do for the rest of the night. She could start walking, but in which direction? She hardly knew the place and she didn't even have a map. So she would have to wait and see if fortune would smile on her yet again – this time in the shape of a passing motorist.

Wandering through the streets of Vannes, she turned a corner and came face to face with an all-night bar. There was little else to do, so she decided that she might as well have a drink before setting off on her journey.

A L'Ami Pierrot was an all-night cafe in the suburbs with an enterprising owner and the blessing of the local gendarmerie – who used the place as an unofficial social club. As she walked in through the double doors, Mara breathed in a blue haze of Gauloises and the mingled stench of garlic and anisette.

A drunken gendarme lurched towards her, bottle in hand and a lecherous grin on his face. He grabbed at her breasts as he staggered past and raucous cheering accompanied his uncertain progress across the room to the bar.

Mara began to wonder if it had been such a good idea after all. A group of American servicemen were drinking in the corner by the pinball machine, eyeing her up slyly whilst pretending to be more interested in a nearby poker game. She edged past them towards the door marked 'toilettes', resolving to tidy herself up and then get out of this place.

The cafe's toilets followed the typical French unisex arrangement and Mara had to walk past a line of men peeing to get to the cubicles. They were used to women in this place but nevertheless they watched appreciatively as Mara passed and one of them – a fat, middle-aged policeman – turned and made an obscene gesture, pointing his rapidly stiffening prick in her direction. His words might mean nothing to Mara, but there was no mistaking the gesture.

She closed the door of the cubicle behind her with a sigh of relief and sat down to pee. There was no point in hurrying – she might as well wait here a while until those drunks had finished and gone back to their equally drunken comrades.

After about five minutes, all had gone quiet outside and Mara judged it safe to emerge from the cubicle.

She opened the door and was horrified to see that three of the men were still there only this time they were waiting – and they were waiting for her. Their flies were unzipped, their penises hard and threatening.

The man who had shown her his erection was still smiling in that disgusting, gap-toothed way which had so revolted her. He stank of cheap wine, garlic and sweat, and the very sight of him turned Mara's stomach. She tried to back off but his two friends were too quick for her. Already they were behind her, blocking off her escape.

The ringleader reached out and squeezed Mara's breasts, so brutally that she gasped with pain. She tried to resist but strong hands grabbed hold of her arms and twisted them round behind her back, rendering her helpless.

Surely someone would come and see what was happening – help her, raise the alarm? But, of course, they'd got one of their mates outside, keeping watch . . .

Events were moving so fast that Mara's mind was in a turmoil. It felt almost as if everything was happening not to her but to somebody else. Brutal fingers bruised her flesh as they ripped off her leather jacket and blouse and squeezed, harder and harder, into her soft breasts – claw-like fingers, tearing her fabric and baring her fragile flesh. The hand was forcing itself between her thighs and sliding upwards, oh so insidiously, towards her crack.

There were grunts of malevolent delight as the hand reached her groin and her assailant realised that this little slut was already naked underneath her skirt, just ready for the taking. Ready? She was begging for it . . .

Strong arms lifted her feet from the ground and – in spite of her struggles – Mara found herself lying spreadeagled on the dirty floor, the chill of the damp tiles working its way through her flesh and into her very soul. Hands held her down; a filthy handkerchief was thrust into her mouth to silence her cries; and overwhelming strength forced her thighs apart, baring her cunt for the assault which she knew must come.

The fat gendarme had his prick out and he was showing it to her, making sure she got a really good look. There – didn't she think it was a lovely one? Well, she would soon find out how good it felt to have it up her cunt, and maybe one or two other places as well . . .

He flung his enormous bulk on top of her and she was powerless to resist him, for her thighs were held fast. His friends were egging him on with hoarse whispers of encouragement and in seconds he was inside her, his fat prick tearing into her softness, his foul breath moistening her cheek.

She tried to dissociate herself from what was happening but in spite of her revulsion she could feel a treacherous warmth spreading through her loins with every stroke of the invading cock. No! He mustn't excite her, he mustn't . . . She wouldn't let him!

Just as she had given up hope of rescue, the door to the toilets burst open and the inert body of a young man crashed in through the doorway and fell to the floor, blood trickling from the corner of his mouth. Confused and distressed though she was, Mara recognised him instantly as one of the men who had been standing at the urinals.

A massive shape filled the doorway: a broad-shouldered man in US Airforce uniform and the blue beret of the United Nations.

'Pardon the intrusion, ma'am,' said the US Captain, touching his cap respectfully. 'But I just gotta sort out this scum for ya.'

So saying, he launched into the three bewildered gendarmes, who were no match for him, their flabby, drink-sodden bodies falling in swift, almost silent succession under the Captain's fists.

His job done, the Captain helped Mara to her feet, offering her his jacket to cover her nakedness.

'Are you all right, ma'am?'

'Yes . . . I think so. Thank you, you were very kind . . .'

'Why, it's all in a day's work, ma'am.' He kicked one of the inert bodies sprawled untidily on the dirty floor, its head lolling in the drainage channel underneath the urinals. 'Now, if you'll just wait here, I'll get someone to take these scum away and I'll ask one of the waitresses to come and tidy you up a bit.' He turned to go, but Mara put her hand on his arm, and smiled up at him.

'Don't leave me, please. I'm OK, honestly I am. And, besides, I haven't thanked you properly for what you did just then, Captain . . .?'

'Steve Wanamaker, ma'am. At your service.'

Seeing the quizzical look on his face, Mara smiled and stretched up on tiptoe to kiss him full on the lips. The force of his desire was like a furnace within him. He was a good-looking, all-American boy, in a hick sort of way: straw-blond hair and open features, broad shoulders and a tight backside . . . and that nice fat bulge in his uniform trousers . . .

'You'd like to fuck me, wouldn't you, Captain Wanamaker?'

He blushed crimson. 'I . . .'

'It's OK, Captain – you can take the fifth amendment on that one. But I'd say, judging from that beautiful hardness I can feel in your pants, that you're just about bursting for a fuck. And here I am, naked in front of you, and I haven't even offered myself to you yet: what an ungrateful girl you must think I am! After he's killed the dragon, the white knight always gets the girl.'

She stroked his cheek playfully, and pulled his face down to hers so that she could whisper in his ear.

'Let me suck you off, Captain. I'm sure you'll enjoy it . . . I'm very good with my mouth!'

Before he had a chance to reply or attempt to pull away from her, Mara was on her knees before him, gently tugging down his zip and feeling inside for the warm hardness she so needed. She needed to touch him, kiss him, fuck with him; to feel his warmth melting her terror and exorcising the memory of her ordeal.

His penis was reassuringly stiff and throbbing with life. Wanamaker stroked her hair and moaned quietly as she pulled it out of his pants and began to run the tip of her tongue along the shaft, very, very lightly at first and then more boldly, as he relaxed and submitted himself to her tender ministrations.

He tasted good: salty and clean and wholesome on her tongue. The prick of an all-American, clean-living country boy. Surely licking such a lively, wholesome prick must be good for the body and the soul . . .? Mara sucked on the Captain's prick and felt the life and warmth flooding back into her body. Yes, there it was: the warmth gathering in her belly, swelling her clitoris, hardening her nipples, sending the juices rushing to lubricate her cunt.

Wanamaker's balls were large and heavy in her hands, and she wondered how much beautiful, white, frothing spunk it took to swell them so wonderfully, to make them hang so pendulous and firm, like golden mangoes on some tropical tree.

She stroked her finger gently over the puckered flesh and felt the curly blond hairs erect at her touch.

'Don't stop . . .' he sighed and spurted into Mara's mouth. She swallowed his gift with gratitude, as a dying man who finds a life-giving spring in the heart of the desert wastes.

Opening his eyes, the Captain looked down at Mara and returned her smile, the tension draining from his face.

'Wanna have some more fun, honey?'

She grinned broadly, and nodded.

He placed Mara's right hand on his shaft, arranging her fingers just how he liked them, and showed her how to wank him back into beautiful stiffness. Mara realised for the first time that his prick was golden, lightly tanned. So, like her, the Captain enjoyed baring his most intimate parts to the summer sunshine . . .

Pushing open the door of one of the cubicles, the Captain sat down on the toilet seat and beckoned to Mara to follow him inside. He took hold of her hips and turned her round, so that she had her back to him, then guided her down as she lowered herself onto his straining penis.

It felt so good to fuck like this, hands gripping the wooden doorposts of the cubicle, pushing down hard on the unseen lover's penis, feeling his hardness burying itself deep inside her belly and then raising herself a little – careful, don't let him slip away – and waiting that agonised split second before plunging down again to swallow him up once more.

The Captain's hand crept round the front of Mara's thigh, worked its way through the thicket of her glossy pubic curls, and felt for her clitoris, parting the fat, juicy lips of her cunt and burrowing inside, into the hot, wet depths of her, until at last his fingers found the mount of exquisite joy and she felt the power of pleasure come crashing down upon her, like breakers on a Californian beach.

He poured his second tribute into her cunt and they stayed there, locked together, for a little while, until they regained their breath and the mists of passion cleared away.

'Honey,' gasped the Captain, helping Mara to her feet, 'you sure are dynamite. And if there's anything I can ever do to help you . . . you just say and, honey, you got it!'

Mara sighed.

'I wish I could stay with you,' she replied. 'But I have to go. I have a long way to go and someone's life depends on my getting there. Someone I really care about.'

'Where you goin', honey? Maybe I can help get you part of the way? I know a lot of guys with a lot of planes . . .'

'Hungary, I'm afraid.'

'Well, whaddya know?' The Captain's smile broadened, and he scratched his head in amiable disbelief. 'Just so happens, me and the guys are flying off to Budapest tomorrow morning – got a little job to do for the UN. Wanna come along? We could have a real good time . . .'

The jeep carried them quickly across the tarmac to the airfield, where the plane was waiting – a big, old troop transport with massive cargo doors.

'Keep your head down and keep real quiet till we're in the air, hun,' whispered Steve, making sure the blanket was completely covering Mara, who was curled up on the seat beside him. 'Don't want the Colonel finding out about you, do we? Leastways, not just yet.'

The sergeant signalled to him to drive on, and he steered the jeep up the ramp and into the cavernous belly of the plane. Mara heard a loud clang as the cargo doors closed behind them, and knew she was on her way.

Once they were airborne, Wanamaker came to fetch her from the jeep, pulling aside the blanket. She blinked in the sudden light.

'It's OK, honey, you can come out now,' whispered

Wanamaker. 'Put on this battledress and follow me. You can ride the rest of this trip with the guys – they won't tell on you, don't you worry none.'

She stepped out of her blouse and skirt and put on the camouflage overalls and steel helmet which the Captain offered her, tucking her hair up on top of her head. As a disguise it was pretty unconvincing but with a bit of luck it would get her past the guards who patrolled the cargo deck.

The 'guys' were twenty or so paratroopers with crew cuts and all-American-hero physiques, sitting in two rows against the rough, curving fuselage. This was hardly a luxury air cruise and entertainment was limited; so they gave Mara an enthusiastic welcome.

'Well, well, what we got here?'

'Geez – what a great fanny!'

' . . . and what incredible tits! Come here, honey, gotta real nice present for you . . .'

Mara watched in amused disbelief as a huge black sergeant grinned broadly at her and unzipped his flying suit, pulling out the most enormous penis she had ever seen. Her pulse quickened as she gazed, fascinated, at the hardening flesh, smooth and black and glossy as a ripe aubergine, its bright purplish tip glistening with slippery juice.

She walked towards him, a little unsteadily, and the plane hit an air pocket, throwing her into the lap of one of the youngest of the soldiers – a mousy lad of no more than eighteen who blushed crimson as his hands filled with Mara's luscious flesh.

His comrades were cheering and stamping.

'Shut it, you jerks!' hissed Captain Wanamaker. 'You want the Colonel to hear? Listen, whatever you and Miss Fleming wanna get up to . . . making your own entertainment, let's say . . . well, that's OK by me. But keep it quiet, or we'll all be court-martialled. And no rough stuff. No roughing up the dame – she's a good friend of mine. Understand?'

A murmur of agreement passed round the plane. The lad

had taken advantage of the diversion to explore the unscheduled gift in his lap a little more fully. His hands were trembling as they roved up from Mara's hips to her flat belly, her tiny nipped-in waist and then higher still, to the gravity-defying fullness of her delectable breasts.

Mara made no attempt to escape or wriggle free from his grasp. After all, where would she go? To the Colonel? She could just imagine what *his* reaction would be. And, anyway, there was something deliciously seductive about travelling on a plane with twenty sex-hungry soldiers and wondering if there would be time for them all to fuck her . . .

'Go on, for Chrissake!' hissed a young soldier opposite Mara. 'She's beggin' for it, Burstein! If you don't know what to do to her, there's plenty here who do!'

As though suddenly realising the threat to his unexpected prize, the lad began to fumble with the zip on Mara's all-in-one flying suit. It was stiff, and took for ever before it finally yielded and slid down to her groin, revealing her complete nakedness underneath.

A gasp ran round the cabin as the lad's hand slipped in through the gap and met warm, naked, female flesh for the first time in its life.

Galvanised by the touch, he began to rip at Mara's clothes, pulling the flying suit down over her shoulders and baring more and more of her wonderful flesh. He pushed her to her feet, so that he could pull the suit down over her hips and thighs, until at last she stepped out of it and stood naked before him.

'I'm cold, soldier,' she was surprised to hear herself whisper. 'I'm shivering. Can you warm me up?'

Immediately, it seemed that hands were upon her from every angle, pawing at her, pulling her down into their midst. She was drowning, drowning in a sea of hands and fingers and lascivious tongues that ran across her quivering flesh, raising goose-bumps not of cold but of expectancy.

She was lying on the floor of the plane now, the rumbling of the engines transmitting itself to her through the vibrations of the fuselage beneath her. She began to vibrate to its own, secret rhythms. The young soldier was standing over her, his penis naked and stiff in his trembling palm. And his comrades were urging him on, goading him: 'Take her, son'; 'Give it to her, boy'; 'Show her what a real man can do . . .'; 'Ain't you never fucked no woman before, son . . .?'

She closed her eyes, and concentrated only on the sensations. Teeth were nibbling gently at her nipples, teasing them into pleasured wakefulness; fingers were exploring her body; a tongue glanced briefly across her throbbing clitoris, making her gasp with sudden pleasure, stolen away. She was no more than a bundle of intense sensations, at the mercy of each one of a thousand different stimuli.

The penis entered her smoothly and without violence, as though to confirm that it was the most natural thing in the world for a penis to thrust into a vagina. This was no poisonous serpent, intent on spitting its deadly venom into her, it was a gentle fountain of pleasure, and she was a rose-garden of delight, waiting for the scented waters to fall upon her and make her blossom into glorious life.

They fucked and the boy – being so young – came quickly to the summit of his pleasure, collapsing onto her belly and lying there, moaning, until someone picked him up and took his place. They fucked once more and Mara came to orgasm again, hardly noticing as one man climaxed in her vagina and climbed off, to be replaced by yet another.

At last she opened her eyes and found that she was looking up into the face of the black sergeant who had been the first to acknowledge her charms so graphically.

'I bin waitin' a long, long time for this, sweetness,' he murmured and entered her with a single, sharp thrust that overwhelmed her senses and sent waves of delight washing over her. 'Maybe I'm gonna die tonight,' he whispered in her ear, 'and maybe I ain't. But I reckon I'll be happy either way.'

His hugeness stretched her to capacity and Mara thanked

her lucky stars that her cunt was already well-greased with the semen of those who had gone before. As it was, his immense size caused her some pain. He fucked with strength and stamina, holding back his ejaculation long enough to bring Mara to the peak of pleasure once, twice, three times. And as she came for the final time, he pumped his load of semen into her, to join the abundance of juice which was already flooding out of her martyred cunt.

The black sergeant kissed the tips of her breasts lingeringly before sliding his still-hard penis out of her. She watched him walk away with a strange wistfulness, a sweet regret. Afterwards, her worshippers cleaned her up and kissed her and shared their food and drink with her, before giving her a fresh set of clothes.

'Here, take this. You're gonna need it, honey.'

The Captain handed her a khaki bundle. It looked like a rucksack. Mara looked at him questioningly.

'No need to look so scared – it's only a parachute, sweetheart. Better put it on right now. The jump's in ten minutes and you sure as hell ain't gonna get down in one piece without it.'

It was then that the horrible truth dawned.

The clear, cold air rushed past her so fast that she scarcely had time to be afraid. All her thoughts were filled with the memory of what she had been told to do: count, release the chute, spread her arms to keep the canopy steady, curl up when you see the ground rushing up . . . don't panic!

She landed with a heavy thud which winded her, but she was otherwise unhurt. She staggered to her feet, not quite believing that she had actually jumped – or rather been pushed – out of a plane and that she had really and truly made it in one piece to the ground.

The jump site was an open patch of ground in the wooded hills near Budapest, a crudely marked X in a small clearing. They were lucky to hit it so accurately. Mara shivered as she looked at the sharp tops of the trees and mused what might have happened if she had been just a little off-course. As soon as they had checked that Mara was safe and sound, Wanamaker and his men picked up their rifles, shouldered their packs and headed off into the forests. She never did find out what their mission was . . .

She checked the rucksack they had given her and was relieved to find her clothes, passport, student card and – most important of all – the box, all safe and undamaged.

The first thing to do was to get dressed and get rid of the parachute – no point in inviting a whole load of awkward questions – and then she must head into Budapest, to try and find out where the box had come from. It seemed like an impossible task – a search for the proverbial needle in a haystack.

She rolled up the 'chute, and chucked it into some bushes, feeling like a partisan saboteur out of a propaganda film, then slipped into sweater, skirt, boots and her warm leather jacket. It was dark and cold, and she was beginning to wish fortune had provided a more conventional way of getting to Hungary when a noise among the trees close by made her jump back in alarm.

'Who's that?' she demanded, desperately looking round to see who – or what – was stalking her.

More noises. Quiet rustling. An animal? No – too regular for an animal. More than one of them . . . Who . . .?

Something touched her arm and, before she had a chance to scream, a hand was clasped tightly over her mouth and she was dragged backwards into the bushes.

'You are lucky, little one, very lucky,' said the gypsy chief, reaching out and grabbing Mara by the chin. 'These hills are full of thieves and vagabonds and murderers. Any of them might have caught you and' – he drew his finger across his neck with a fine sense of the dramatic – 'slit your pretty little throat from ear to ear.'

Seeing Mara still shivering with fright, he slapped his thigh and laughed loudly, his one golden earring dancing and glittering in the firelight as he shook his head.

'No need to look so glum, little one. You are with friends

here. For I see that there is within you the blood of the Romany and the power of the sight.'

Mara looked at him, astonished.

'How can you tell?'

'I too have the power, child, as you do. I am the seventh son of a seventh son, just as you are the seventh daughter of a seventh daughter. Many things are known to me. I see into your heart and I know that there is something you seek . . . and a life you are trying to restore. I look into your heart and I see pain and confusion but also I see goodness. And it is because I see goodness that I will help you all I can. We shall all help you.'

'And what can I do for you in return?'

The gypsy chief smiled and ran a finger down the ample curve of Mara's right breast.

'You are very beautiful, my dear. There is royal Romany blood in you, as there is within me. Will you consent to become my gypsy queen for just one night?'

Mara looked up into his dark eyes and knew that she could refuse him nothing. Already he knew the deepest, darkest secrets of her heart. He had looked inside her, and must surely have seen the force of her desires, the depth of the passions within her. And so he must already know how much she desired this swarthy, powerful man . . .

'I . . . I accept your offer,' she replied, her voice hoarse with emotion. 'Your request honours me. Do with me as you will.'

The gypsies lived a vagabond existence in the hills near Budapest, spending the autumn and winter months in the oak and beech woods around Hüvösvölgy and Kis Hárshegy, where they set up camp with their brightly coloured vans and tents.

The chief, Janos, had a beautiful red and yellow van in the traditional style, outside which sat his three wives and numerous pretty daughters. They smiled graciously as Mara approached and seemed to wish her nothing but good.

'It is the way of our house,' explained Janos. 'As chieftain, it is my sworn duty to take to my bed any true gypsy woman I desire so that the sacred blood of our house may continue throughout generations. And, since you are also of ancient gypsy blood, I am obliged to bed you and share my seed with you.'

Mara nodded and made as though to climb the steps into the van but Janos shook his head and laid his hand on her arm.

'The joining will take place here, in the open air, in full view of my wives and people. Among my people, nothing is hidden. They must see that my potency continues great – for, if I fail my people, they are entitled to depose me and appoint another to be their chieftain.'

Mara waited, rather tremulously, as Janos went into the van and brought out a splendid, embroidered blanket, which he laid down on the ground beside the van. Already the rest of his people had gathered in the clearing, carrying lanterns to light up the ceremony. A violinist struck up a passionate gypsy tune and the spectators began to clap their hands.

'You must dance,' explained Janos. 'It is our tradition. You must dance and kindle the flames of my passion. But first you must take off your clothes. It is an insult to dance before the Gypsy King unless you are naked.'

Rather self-consciously, Mara got up and took off her jacket and boots. The ground felt damp and cold beneath her bare feet and she recalled a similar night, not so long ago, when she and Heimdal had fucked in the woods and he had travelled into the underworld, there to speak with the soul of Andreas Hunt . . .

Remembering her lover's need of her, she tore off her sweater and skirt with a good will and began to dance, dance, dance as she had never danced before. Her beautiful, firm breasts quivered upon her chest as she leapt and pirouetted and undulated on the grass before her master for the night, to the ever-quickening beat of the gypsy dance.

At last, she fell exhausted upon the ground, tiny beads of sweat standing out on her flesh. And she felt hands lift her up and then lay her down, on her back, in front of the gypsy king. He nodded to one of his wives and she took a tiny box from him and came over to where Mara was lying. At once, hands seized her legs and prised them apart, holding them still to prevent her closing her thighs. Mara wondered why they should think they needed to hold her firm.

And then she felt the terrible pain in her clitoris, as something sharp burned its way into her. What were they doing to her? What were they doing to her clitoris?

'No, no!' she screamed.

'Have no fear,' soothed Janos. 'They are not harming you in any way, though the pain you feel is intense. What my dear wife is doing to you is for your greater pleasure, I assure you. All of our favoured women have had their clitorises pierced, as you will see.'

He clapped his hands and his daughters lifted their skirts and pulled apart their cunt-lips, revealing the tiny rings of gold wire passing through their clitorises. As she watched, they began to toy with the wires and she saw how their clitorises swelled with the pleasure they were bestowing upon themselves.

The pain came again, terrible in its intensity, and Mara almost fainted. But within a few moments it had ebbed away and, as Janos's wife toyed with the tiny golden ring, she felt the most exquisite of sensations throbbing through her whole body. She began to pant with the sheer pleasure of it.

'You see, my dear? Did I not speak true?'

Speechless with pleasure now, Mara nodded, her cunt overflowing with moisture as the waves of pleasure dulled her brain – a pleasure far more intense than the pain which she had just suffered. The pleasure seemed to take over her entire being, annihilating all pain and all fears.

The music began again, slow and sensual this time, and Mara looked up and saw that Janos was unbuttoning his breeches and taking out a delightfully long prick, pierced at its tip with a thick golden ring.

A pillow was placed under Mara's head, raising it up, and Janos straddled her chest, thrusting his penis into her mouth. She thrilled to the strange and wonderful sensation of his penis-ring against her tongue and writhed in ecstasy as his wife continued to play with the tiny ring in her clitoris.

Janos half-choked her with his spunk, then turned her onto her belly and set to work on her arse, loosening it with gentle strokes from the hilt of his dagger before plunging his hard dick into her soft flesh and riding her as he would ride some wild, gypsy steed through the forest.

At last, when Mara was almost dying with desire, her clitty pulsating with frustration, he turned her onto her back and fucked her cunt, very gently and slowly, so that she would derive the maximum enjoyment. The tears ran down her cheeks as he thrust in and out of her, his pubis rubbing against her clitty-ring and awakening terrible, wonderful sensations within her that she had never dreamed of before. It lasted an eternity. Perhaps she would never come! Perhaps she would spend the rest of her life in an agony of ecstasy from which she could never escape . . .

But her pleasure would be denied no longer, and they came together in a warm cascade of semen and cunt-juice.

The cards were lying face-up on the upturned barrel.

'There is no doubt,' said Janos. 'I have seen and touched the box, sensing its vibrations, and I have cast the runes and now I have read the Tarot. So many signs cannot lie. This box, whatever it is – and I have not the power to divine such a powerful magic sigil – was recently within an occult shop in the city of Budapest. The traces are still upon it.

'I know of only one shop which would have an interest in such an object and it is on Úri utca – at number lla, close to the entrance to the network of caves underneath the hill. You must seek there, my little one, if you wish to find out more. But it would perhaps be wiser not to seek at all. Some knowledge is best left untouched . . .'

'Thank you,' said Mara, getting up to leave before her resolve weakened and she abandoned herself to Janos and his seductive life of pure pleasure. 'You have been very kind. I shall never forget the delights which you have shown me here.'

Janos smiled.

'Then won't you stay awhile, my pretty? I have only three wives – another one would suit me very well and you could make me many fine sons . . .'

For a moment, she almost thought of saying yes, of forgetting this whole mad crusade, but the memory of Andreas Hunt's screaming, agonised face made her turn her back on the gypsy camp and begin the long walk down the hill towards the city.

Budapest in the weeks before Christmas is a beautiful sight. But Mara had no time for sightseeing and barely noticed the castle, towering above her as she passed through the Buda fortress walls and into the Tóth Árpád sétány, with its rows of chestnut trees. No time to visit the famous public baths or eat sticky chocolate cake in some cosy coffee-house. No time either to rub shoulders with the literati at the Café Korona. She turned into Úri utca and looked for number lla, the key to that vital piece of knowledge.

She passed a variety of houses – romanesque, gothic, baroque – and then spotted number nine, with its entrance to the cave complex and its exhibition on the history of Hungary. So where was number lla?

There: a tiny, half-hidden shack, strangely out of place in this dignified district, and hardly visible amongst the grand houses on either side.

She stepped up to the door. 'Arcady', it read. She took a deep breath, pushed the door open and went in, wind-chimes softly jingling as the door closed behind her.

The shop was dark and filled with the heavy scent of incense. Joss-sticks burned in every corner. To her right, a shelf groaned beneath the weight of garish wooden folk-dolls and occult effigies. At first, Mara could see little else in the dimly lit shop beyond the shelves of shiny crystals and bottles of occult essences. But a shadow, a little darker than the rest, moved to one side and, with a click, switched on a light.

'H . . . hello,' began Mara, suddenly feeling foolish at her total ignorance of Hungarian.

'Good day,' replied the young man in excellent English, much to her relief. 'American?'

'English,' replied Mara. She was amused to see an unmistakable flicker of relief pass across his face. 'I have something I'd like to show you.'

She rummaged in her bag, and took out the box.

'You sold this to a man who was travelling to Vannes?'

The young man looked at her doubtfully.

'I sold it in good faith. If it was stolen, I had no idea . . .'

'No, no; you don't understand,' replied Mara, urgently. 'I'm not blaming you for anything – I'm just trying to find out more about it. You see, a friend's life depends on my finding what was inside this box. You've got to help me, please!'

'I'm sorry. I know nothing about it. It was empty when it came to me.'

Mara's face fell and she slumped into a chair in the corner, underneath a pair of carved voodoo masks. Was this the end of her quest? Was this the end of Andreas Hunt?

'But I do know where the box came from, if that's any help.'

Mara leapt up and grabbed the youth by the lapels of his tatty corduroy jacket.

'Tell me, tell me!'

'It was brought to me by a group of Germans returning to their homeland from exile in Transylvania. They came here from a village called Burzenheim – that is all I know. If there is more to be found, madam, it is there that you must look for it.'

13: Ghosts

Oh shit, thought Andreas Hunt. I wonder if anyone knows what's happened to me. I bet the Editor's bloody livid. I'll have got the sack by now. What's going to happen when things get back to normal? Am I just going to walk into work one day, Mr Laid-Back, and say, 'Hi guys, I lost my body for a while but it's OK 'cos I'm back now'? Am I fuck . . .?

When things get back to normal. Will they ever get back to normal? Will I ever really be Andreas Hunt again and take Mara home and fuck her and make her scream for more?

Andreas was puzzled, frustrated . . . and getting angrier by the minute. If there was one thing he hated, it was being fucked about. Every now and again, he'd almost be getting used to being trapped in nothingness and then – pow! He'd find himself in someone else's body once more. It could last for anything from a few seconds to half an hour but always in the end he would feel himself slipping away and, like water down a drain, he'd be sucked back inexorably to the darkness of captivity.

It wasn't as if it was even the same body each time.

Mara. Can Mara hear me when I call out to her? It makes no sense yet sometimes I'm sure she can. I can feel the surge of energy as her mind meets mine. And yet she still doesn't come.

He remembered that night in the woods, when they had fucked inside the magic circle, symbolising their joining. They were one now. He wasn't going to be defeated so easily, oh no, Andreas Hunt wasn't going to give in.

Hunt raged silently within his crystal prison. I'm not going to let this happen to me, I'm fucking well not. Somehow, just somehow, I'm going to learn how to control all of this. And I'm going to find a way to get out of here, out of Winterbourne, and back to Mara.

The Master withdrew his still-hard penis from the geisha's cunt and nodded to her to stand up and get dressed.

'A most agreeable gift. Your girls are a credit to you, Mr Takimoto. And I am sure they will prove to be a credit to our . . . organisation.'

The Japanese businessman bowed, a half-smile of pleasure on his thin, cruel lips. The tiny puncture-wounds had almost healed now, and there had been no pain since that moment when the Master had admitted him to the ranks of the elect. No pain; only the enormous pleasure of knowing that he was, at last, serving the most sublimely perfect evil.

'What would you have me do now, Master?'

'You must return with your colleagues to Tokyo and resume your research on the Logos project. It is of the utmost importance that the system is perfected and in place before the next General Election. And you must seek out new converts to our cause. But remember the rule: only those who are in powerful or influential positions are to be initiated; or those who are physically beautiful and therefore of use to our organisation. The power is to be used sparingly and with wisdom.'

Takimoto bowed and left, Delgado closing the door behind him.

The Master turned to Cheviot.

'How is our plan progressing?'

'Your name has been put before the standing committee. I, Parry-Evans, Eldridge, Lord Stourbridge and the Bishop have all spoken in support of you, but there are other strong contenders. The appointment is to be announced in one week's time.'

The Master's eyes narrowed and his knuckles whitened as

he clutched at the arms of his chair.

'My candidacy must not be successfully opposed,' he hissed. 'Do you understand? You must not fail. Do whatever is needful to ensure that I am the one appointed to the post.'

Cheviot nodded, in no doubt as to the likely consequences of failure. The Master's anger was undoubtedly to be avoided at all costs. He looked across the desk into the face that had once been Andreas Hunt's – a little cynical, maybe, but open and full of good humour – and saw the twisted mask of impatient evil, lips twisted into a parody of Hunt's ever-present half-smile.

'Master, your success is assured,' replied Cheviot. 'None shall stand in your way.'

The Master relaxed back into his chair and folded his hands in his lap.

'See that it is so. And now I feel in need of sexual refreshment, some pleasurable diversion to revive my flagging spirits.'

Delgado stepped forward, ingratiating as ever.

'We have two pretty youths,' he suggested. 'Fresh from the streets of Istanbul and barely eighteen years old – yet wise in the ways of the flesh. I brought them back with me from my last trip to Turkey, to find new whores for Winterbourne.

'Their arseholes are deliciously tight – and I myself can testify to the efficacy of their moist little tongues. And their cocks! So beautiful, big and hard, and so young that they can stay hard all night long. They are but newly initiated and so very eager to serve their Master . . .'

The Master shook his head.

'I tire of boys, Delgado. They preen and simper like young girls, but they have no tight, wet cunts for me to stretch and their hardy flesh does not redden and bleed so easily when I put them to the lash.

'No, today I have a fancy for some delectable little virgin. A young girl as pure and unsullied as January snow. You shall find me one and bring her to me, Delgado. I have a thirst which only virgin blood can slake.'

Delgado bowed and turned to leave.

'Wait, Delgado. I have a message which I wish you to pass on for me. A message for the Romanian prince. Tell him that the Fleming woman is not to be harmed. She is to pass through the borders unhindered – or he will answer to me. Mara Fleming is my toy and my prize. Her life – and her death – shall be mine and mine alone.'

Delgado closed the door behind him, leaving the Master gently stroking his testicles and dreaming of the undisputed power that would soon be his.

It was easy – too easy. Mara could not help feeling that fortune was smiling upon her a little too readily. Without a visa, carrying only a small rucksack, a passport and a crudely forged student ID card, Mara had been waved through the Romanian border crossing without question.

The car had been parked about half a mile inside the Romanian border, keys in the lock and no driver in sight. A couple of soldiers were chatting on the other side of the road, but nothing she did seemed to attract their attention. It was almost as if they were doing their utmost not to notice that she was there.

Trembling – after all, this was the first time she had stolen a car – Mara climbed into the driver's seat, threw her rucksack onto the seat beside her, turned the key in the ignition and drove away.

Even the sound of the car's engine wasn't enough to make the two soldiers turn round, though they must surely have heard it. Mara began to wonder if fortune wasn't so much smiling upon her as using her . . .

She glanced down at the dashboard. A full tank of petrol. On impulse, she opened the glove compartment and found bread, cheese, a road map and a fat roll of banknotes. A bottle of beer rolled out from under the seat and clinked against her foot as she swung the car round a corner.

She stopped for a while, pulling in to a narrow country lane and falling asleep. When she awoke, she ate the bread and cheese and studied the map. It would take about another day's drive to get into Transylvania and – allowing for stops and getting lost – she ought to be in Burzenheim by early evening.

As she was drinking the last of the beer, a face appeared at the window of the car, making her start with fear.

It was a young man in rather ragged overalls and he was smiling at her in obvious appreciation.

'English . . . English lady?'

Mara realised that he was looking at her passport, which was lying on the seat beside her. Hurriedly, she picked it up and put it into her bag. She wished fervently that she hadn't wound down the car window to get a little fresh air, as a massive, hairy hand slipped inside and began, quite openly and unashamedly, to stroke her breasts.

It was not entirely unpleasant. The young man was gentle and his touch had a certain sensitivity; and Mara felt her nipples stiffen with involuntary pleasure. The farmer obviously saw this too, and chuckled with delight as he tweaked each of the nipples in turn, drawing gasps of pain-mingled pleasure from Mara.

'You want . . . spend night at my farm? Have good barn, good soft straw – better than car.'

Mara didn't know what to say. Here was a young peasant, quite clearly interested in her body, offering her a night's lodging in his barn. She knew she ought to shake her head, wind up the window, stamp down on the accelerator and drive away – but what if he reported her to the authorities? After all, she was still driving a stolen car and she had no visa. And then there was the matter of the forged student ID card . . . And he was rather handsome . . .

Fully aware that what she was doing was madness, Mara got out of the car and extended her hand to the young man. He was tall and strong, and she knew he could break her in two with those muscular arms if he chose to. But he smiled and took her hand, shaking it with the enthusiasm of a child.

'Come, lady,' he announced. 'I Miroslav. I show you where sleep . . .'

Mara followed the peasant up the dark, rutted track, his lantern casting an uncertain, yellowish light on the muddy ground. Miroslav led her through a rickety gate and up a shorter muddy track towards a tumbledown barn, not much bigger than a shed.

He removed the bar holding the door shut and indicated to her to go in.

The inside of the barn smelled strongly of chicken dung and Mara caught her breath as an enormous rat scuttled across the straw. In the corner of the barn, two horses were tethered together in a stall.

'Look, English lady: horses fucking!' Miroslav lifted the lantern proudly, to give Mara a better view of the entertainment he had provided for her. The mare – a slender, piebald creature with a gentle expression – was standing her ground patiently as a powerful chestnut stallion mounted her.

Mara was transfixed, she could not look away from the spectacle of the stallion thrusting into the mare and making her whinny with pleasure.

Mara gasped as, with a neigh of delight, the stallion ejaculated, his massive shaft juddering as the sperm raced up his penis and flooded the mare's cunt.

Mara was panting, and her nipples were pressing hard against the soft fabric of her blouse. Glancing down, she saw the farmer's penis was hard and doing its best to thrust its way out of his tattered overalls. With a start, she realised that she desired him; that she wanted him to play the stallion to her mare.

The farmer, like the stallion, needed no encouragement. Talking softly to her in Romanian, he began to undress Mara. Stunned, she simply stood there as he peeled off her clothes, one by one, until she stood naked before him on the filthy straw.

Then he took off his overalls, his ancient sweater and his pants. Underneath these unprepossessing garments, his body glistened with all the muscular beauty of a Michelangelo sculpture. From between his strong thighs sprang a mighty, sap-filled bough and Mara knew that she must slake her thirst upon his sap.

She knelt before him on the filthy straw and he shuffled his feet a little way apart, the better to present to her the delights of his loins.

She began by running the tip of her tongue over his balls, between his thighs, around the root of his shaft, greatly pleased by the instant reaction she felt as his bollocks tensed and clear drops of a slippery liquid began to weep from the tip of his yearning penis.

And then Mara took him into her mouth, letting him thrust into her throat as hard as he wished, almost choking her as the tip of his thick shaft rubbed against the back of her throat.

He pulled her towards him, greedy for her, and the thick tide of his semen gushed out and bathed the warm moistness of her mouth in a silent tribute.

To Mara's surprise and delight, Miroslav was not so easily satiated. His penis barely softened for a few moments before once again growing hard and eager for the fray. With a grunt of pleasure, he grabbed Mara by the waist and forced her to bend forward, supporting herself by taking hold of an old hay-manger which hung on the wall in front of her.

'Little mare . . .' he hissed into her ear as he pulled apart her arse-cheeks and, without further ado, thrust his penis into her well-greased cunt.

Mara shrieked with pleasure as Miroslav's hardness burrowed into her and he fucked her as the stallion had fucked his mare. She imagined herself as the little piebald mare, standing patient and steady as the stallion mounted her. Had the mare felt the force of the stallion's semen as he pumped his seed into her? Had her cunt blossomed into spasms of delight as the stallion's orgasm tore through him?

Mara braced herself against the rail and imagined that it was not Miroslav but the stallion who was fucking her. It was such a powerful image that she felt her orgasm building up in her loins and she cried out in pleasure as wave upon wave of pleasure rippled through her.

Miroslav came with a savage roar and lunged forward, his teeth bared like the stallion's, intent on biting his little mare's throat.

But, at the very last minute, the voice in his head forbade him that ultimate pleasure.

'No,' repeated the voice. 'She is the Master's plaything. She is not for us. Let her go free . . .'

Mara was surprised when Miroslav pulled out of her, still erect, and seemed not to want to continue with their games of lust. He was polite enough, yet somehow distant, as though he had only just recalled some ancient taboo. He brought her blankets and coffee and then left her for the night, to share her dreams with the chestnut stallion and his little piebald mare.

In the morning, he gave her bread and coarse sausage, wrapped up in a cloth, told her where to find petrol and sent her on her way. As she drove back down the deeply rutted track, Mara could not suppress the powerful feeling that she had just had a very lucky escape.

Delgado knocked on the door of the Master's office, and waited.

'Enter.'

He went in, signalling to the guards to wait outside with their charge.

'Ah, Delgado. You have something to interest me?'

'I think you will be pleased with this one, Master. I picked her myself. It was not easy . . .'

The Master put down the papers he was reading and gave Delgado his full attention.

'She is a virgin?'

'Most assuredly so, Master. And very young, as you instructed. Our agents kidnapped her as she was leaving school. A convent school, in fact . . .'

'Good, good. Bring her in and let me see her.'

Delgado opened the door and called to the guards, who

half-led, half-dragged the girl into the room.

The Master's eyes narrowed with pleasure. Delgado had done well. She was exactly as he had hoped: a slender, almost frail schoolgirl just turned sixteen; small and vulnerable and very, very frightened. Her light-brown hair trailed down her back in a thick plait and she was still wearing her school uniform.

'Excellent,' hissed the Master. 'It has been too long since I tasted virgin blood, defiled virgin flesh.' He strode across the room to the girl, seizing her by the chin and forcing her to look up into his evil, burning eyes.

'What is your name, child?'

'You can't do this to me!' screamed the girl, making a sudden attempt to struggle free. But the guards held her fast and all she succeeded in doing was pulling her neat, white blouse out of the top of her navy-blue pleated skirt.

'She is called Alexandra,' replied Delgado. 'Is she not delicious? Why, I should very much enjoy . . .'

'Yes, yes, Delgado. You have done well. And you shall have her to slake your own desires upon when I have finished with her. But for now, you must go – all of you. Leave me alone with the girl.'

With visible regret, Delgado retreated from the room and closed the door behind him.

The girl slunk back against the wall, arms crossed protectively over her small, pert breasts.

She was whispering 'No, no, no . . .' in a mantra of suffering innocence; she was crouching in the corner now, like the small and very vulnerable creature she was, almost whimpering with fear.

But the Master simply smiled and unzipped his flies.

'My dear Alexandra,' he murmured as he took out his erect penis. 'I'm so very glad to meet you.'

The girl tried to escape him but he was upon her like a jungle cat springing upon its prey. His fingers tore at her clothes, ripping off her pristine white blouse and navy-blue skirt. Despite her protests, within seconds he had torn away her bra and her virginal white knickers.

'Now then, Alexandra,' hissed the Master. 'Have you ever sucked a cock before?'

She shook her head, wide-eyed, as the Master advanced, his fat prick hard and glistening in his hand. Strong fingers prised apart her lips and he thrust into her.

He could not remember a more delicious feeling than the sensation of having Alexandra's warm, wet mouth closing around his cock. And the knowledge that these pretty lips were fresh from speaking a young virgin's chaste prayers gave the experience added piquancy.

What's more, he could tell that the girl's resistance was weakening. She made no attempt to bite him and her breathing was becoming quicker and hoarser – a sure sign of growing excitement. How he loved to corrupt such childlike purity, to sow the seeds of evil within the belly of innocence.

He held off for as long as he could, then allowed himself the luxury of his first orgasm of the day. The poor girl gagged on his semen but he made her swallow it down – every last drop.

As she lay, panting, on the floor at his feet, he wrenched her legs apart and – ignoring her pleas for mercy – ripped through her hymen with a single, violent thrust of his pelvis.

He was rewarded with a cry of terrible distress, followed shortly by moans of pleasure as the girl felt the approach of her first-ever orgasm. She would be an apt pupil, and an enthusiastic whore.

Things were looking good. And the Fleming girl was near to the prize, he could sense it. Very soon, everything would be perfect.

The tiny village of Burzenheim lay far off the beaten track, in the very heart of the lonely, wooded hills of Transylvania. What few signposts there were petered out long before Mara reached the village and she was reduced to asking – in phrase-book Romanian with hand-signals – for directions from the few peasants who crossed her path.

Some were too frightened to speak. Others laughed at her confusion.

All seemed baffled that anyone should want to visit Burzenheim.

As she drove deeper into the Transylvanian heartland, Mara realised that what she had heard about the area was truer than she could possibly have imagined. She passed deserted villages, one after the other, lining roads already half-overgrown with weeds. In the last few months, hundreds of thousands of the exiled Germans who had inhabited these villages had taken advantage of the opening up of Eastern Europe and had returned to Germany, their ethnic homeland.

Even the villages retained German-sounding names: Felzburg, Kassel-am-Weser, Folgesheim . . . And Mara remembered with a wry smile all those old horror films set in Transylvania – where German-speaking peasants stormed the castle on the hill at midnight clad in lederhosen and brandishing burning torches.

Now that this once-thriving area was almost deserted, devoid of human life, Mara really could believe that a place like this might house vampires . . .

Dusk was drawing in as she reached the outskirts of Burzenheim. At first glance it seemed to be a ghost-town, as deserted as all the other villages for miles around: tumbledown cottages whose doors swung crookedly from broken hinges; abandoned farm-vehicles, rusting quietly in the autumn drizzle; empty streets where children had once played. Deadwood City. Mara could almost imagine the tumbleweed rolling down the main street.

She parked the car among some trees, on the outskirts of the village. You couldn't be too careful. Best to cover her retreat, just in case.

Walking towards the centre of the village she realised that there were increasing signs of life. A neatly painted cottage here, a few chickens there. And there, in the middle of the main square, was a curious small wooden building, a little like a church. It was freshly painted and – to Mara's astonishment – surrounded by a shallow, water-filled moat on all sides except in front of the main entrance door, which was reached by a small footbridge.

But this was not the most curious feature of the building. Above the door hung a red banner bearing black insignia – insignia which Mara recognised only too well and which sent a shiver running down her spine.

A red banner bearing a black swastika. The insignia of the Third Reich.

More than that, Mara could feel an unmistakable power emanating from within the building. Something so powerful that it felt like an irresistible magnetic force, dragging her towards it. She glanced down and saw that the crystal pendant around her neck was beginning to glow faintly. Could it be that the Phallus of Osiris really was here? Or was she about to suffer yet another crushing disappointment?

Guards stood on either side of the door dressed in a simplified version of the familiar black SS uniform. Mara knew it was far too late to turn back and make her escape, they were sure to have seen her approaching. Best to put on a brave face and march boldly up to the front door.

At her approach, they crossed their bayonets to bar her way and began to question her in rapid German. Her heart sinking, Mara looked the taller of the two straight in the eye, and replied:

'Englisch.'

'Good day,' replied the guard, lowering his bayonet – much to Mara's relief. 'You have been sent from England to take part in the ceremonies?'

'Yes,' replied Mara, hoping that she had given the correct answer.

'They have chosen well,' remarked the guard, eyeing Mara's breasts approvingly. 'Though you do not comply to the classic Aryan physical type, you have a fine, strong body, worthy to bear the Führer's sacred offspring. Through you, our cause will be greatly advanced in England.'

Baffled by such talk, Mara smiled and thanked the guard,

and allowed herself to be ushered into the building.

Inside, she was surprised to see about a dozen naked women sitting in a circle around an altar draped with a red cloth embroidered with swastikas. A priest was chanting an invocation over something which lay in a golden dish on the altar. Something which Mara recognised instantly, though she had never seen it before . . .

The Phallus! These people were worshipping the Phallus of Osiris! But how was she going to take it from them?

Her train of thought was interrupted by a tall, blonde woman who was introduced to her as Gilde.

'I will look after you, my dear,' she explained, with a smile. 'I can see that you are nervous – so are we all! For how few of us are fortunate enough to be chosen to receive the gift of the Führer's virile penis within our unworthy bodies! Is this not a wonderful day for the Fatherland and for the glorious cause?'

The Führer's penis? Did these people then believe that what they had in their midst was the Führer's mummified phallus? Mara would have laughed, were she not so frozen with terror.

'What . . . what will happen?' she enquired, her voice shaky with emotion.

'Why, you shall take your turn in the circle, with the rest of us. The priest will bless the Phallus and it will be passed to each of us in turn to use upon our bodies. It is said that we shall experience the most exquisite bliss as we couple with our beloved leader. And if the Führer wishes it, our bodies shall be made fruitful so that we may bear the offspring of his sacred loins.'

Mara stared at Gilde, open-mouthed. The woman was assuredly deranged. And yet what she said had a bizarre ring of truth to it. A group of exiled Nazis, up in the Transylvanian hills, believed that they had been granted custody of their dead Führer's penis: what could be more natural than that they should also believe it to have magical powers – especially the power of fertility?

There was nothing for it. She must go through with the

absurd pantomime. If she attempted to leave now they would know that she was an imposter, and they would kill her without the slightest hesitation.

She took off her clothes as bidden and laid them in a neat pile beside the door, then took her seat in the circle between blonde Gilde and a stunning redhead with emerald green eyes. All of the women were beautiful in their own way: some tall and statuesque, others tiny and fragile; but all remarkably lovely. Evidently the agents of this bizarre community had done their work well in selecting potential brides for their deceased Führer.

There were gasps of astonishment and delight as the priest took the Phallus from the dish and held it aloft for all to see. Its shiny, blackish-green surface was glowing with a phosphorescent green light, pulsing regularly, almost hypnotically. Some of the women began to weep quietly as they gazed upon this symbol of all their hopes and desires.

The blonde girl to the right of Mara knelt before the priest and held out her hands, cupped together as though she were about to receive the sacred Host. The priest also knelt, and touched the tips of her breasts, the triangle of blonde curls between her thighs and the furrow between her juicy buttocks with the tip of the Phallus. Then he raised it to her lips and she kissed it reverently.

The priest laid the Phallus in the girl's hands and she carried it to the centre of the circle, and lay down among her sisters with her legs spread wide apart and her knees raised. Her cunt glistened with juice and Mara saw that the girl's pupils were hugely dilated, as though she had been given some narcotic drug to relax her before her ordeal.

The other women began to chant and Mara moved her lips and made some semblance of a sound, hoping that her ineptitude would go unnoticed in the general excitement.

The blonde girl was placing the tip of the penis in her cunt now, just resting its blackish tip against the moist pink entrance to her womanhood. Already she was beginning to twist and turn, as though in agony or ecstasy, moaning wordless nonsense as she writhed. For a moment she paused and Mara wondered if she had lost the courage to proceed. But no: with a supreme effort of will, the girl thrust the penis into her vagina.

As the mighty shaft disappeared into her, she gave a high-pitched scream and began to convulse. A greenish aura surrounded her body, as though she were burning in a green fire. Mara turned to Gilde in alarm.

'What is happening?'

Gilde sighed, patted Mara's hand and smiled reassuringly.

'Unfortunately, the poor girl is insufficiently strong to withstand the ordeal. She will die in horrible torment but it is well that the Führer should reject any who are not worthy to be his brides. Few are strong enough, most of us will die this night. But we are happy to die, joined with the body and spirit of our beloved Führer. What greater glory can there be in death?'

Mara watched in horror as the fire consumed the girl's body, engulfing her in a veil of thick green smoke. The girl's screams grew weaker and fainter, and when the smoke cleared, she lay very still and white on the floor before them, the Phallus still gleaming malevolently in her cunt. When the priest removed it, a foul, greenish-black slime oozed out of her onto the bare stone floor.

Mara was so far lost within herself that at first she did not notice the hand tapping lightly on her shoulder.

'It is your turn,' whispered Gilde. 'Be of good courage, my dear, for the sake of the Fatherland and the Fourth Reich!'

Still dazed by what she had seen, Mara got unsteadily to her feet and walked across to where the priest was waiting, Phallus in hand. There was no escape now. If she did try to run away, she would be torn apart by the guards as a spy. And yet if she submitted, she faced the likelihood of a horrible, agonising death.

Summoning up the power and assistance of her mentor Heimdal, the leader of her coven and all her spirit-guides, Mara sent out a final message to the soul of Andreas Hunt: 'I have done this for you, Andreas . . . if there is any way that you can help me, help me now. Join your soul to mine and help me combat this power, which is too great for me to bear . . .'

The Phallus touched the tips of her breasts and she felt a tremendous energy surge through her, almost painfully, like an electric shock; and yet with a seductive power which sent ripples of anticipatory pleasure through her body. Her cunt grew wetter and wetter as the Phallus slid down and touched, first the glossy black triangle of her pubic hair, then the tight amber furrow between her nether cheeks.

As she kissed the Phallus, she became vaguely aware of a green light dancing around her, isolating her from the rest of the world like a protective cocoon. At any moment she expected to feel the searing heat of the bright green fire raging through her body, reducing her to a cold and lifeless shell.

But she felt no pain, only a strange, sensual warmth which made her long to feel the massive shaft between her thighs, thrusting up into the depths of her belly.

She accepted the Phallus from the priest and lay down in the circle, on the exact spot where the dead girl had lain only a few minutes before. The ground was still sticky with the greenish slime which had oozed out of her cunt.

Drawing up her knees and spreading her legs, Mara abandoned herself to the mindless chanting around her. The forest of swastikas painted on the temple ceiling seemed to dance and spin above her, filling her mind with images of pain and sadism and death.

Taking a deep breath, she held the tip of the mummified penis against the soft, fragile flesh of her vagina and pushed it home. Immediately, a terrible pain tore through her, and it seemed to her that she was being ripped apart limb from limb, her cunt violated by some ravening monster with a fiery prick whose boiling seed would destroy her from within.

She clenched her teeth and stifled the scream that had gathered at the back of her throat. She would be strong. She would not fail. And, even as she told herself to be strong, she almost thought for a moment that the voice of Andreas Hunt was speaking to her through the green mists of her suffering:

'They won't destroy us, Mara. Somehow, I'm going to break free . . . Winterbourne, come to me at Winterbourne . . .'

And the pain began to subside, giving way to a languid pleasure which washed over her like tropical sunshine, or warm Nile waters on a summer's day . . .

The room was lavishly furnished, with a painted earthen floor and walls lined with ornate leather hangings, decorated with hunting scenes. She was lying on a low bed, her head on a wooden head-rest, naked, ready, full of desire. She was waiting, waiting . . .

A woman's voice was calling out somewhere in her head . . . Osiris, Osiris, Osiris . . . At first it seemed very far away, but it grew nearer and nearer, until at last Mara realised that she was speaking the word, over and over again.

And he was there before her – a tall man, with his back to her. He was taking off his robes to reveal his beautiful nakedness. He was beautiful, so beautiful . . .

He turned to her, and she called out to him:

'Osiris! You have come to me at last.'

But his face was the face of Andreas Hunt, full of life and desire and longing for her.

'Isis . . .' he breathed, and lay down on the bed, his hardness seeking entrance between her thighs. She slid her legs apart, so that his tongue could toy with her clitoris. She remembered the touch of that tongue – gentle yet firm, knowing exactly how to pleasure her and delay her orgasm until she could bear the waiting no more.

He brought her to orgasm three times, each successive orgasm greater and more pleasurable than the last, seeming to take hold of her soul and wrench it from her body. Then he lay upon her and fucked her, his massively hard penis burrowing into her flesh with instinctive skill, and his pubic bone grinding against the delicate nubbin of flesh that throbbed between her cunt lips.

As they came together and their juices mingled, dusk fell suddenly on the room and an eerie light flooded in through the windows, turning her lover's flesh a macabre shade of green. As she gasped in horror, a tall, dark figure appeared in the doorway – a figure whom Mara recognised instantly. Her scream of terror dried to dust in her throat as the incandescent coals of his eyes burned into her, showing her no mercy.

The Master!

Powerless to defend herself or Andreas, Mara watched as the Master raised the sword above his shoulders and brought it swishing down upon the back of Andreas's bare neck.

His head fell from his shoulders, like a ripe melon plucked from its stalk, and rolled onto the floor, glassy-eyed and bloody. The Master stooped and picked it up. He seemed pleased with his prize.

As he raised the severed head to show Mara the horror of her dead lover's face, the Master's own face seemed to distort and dissolve before her eyes. Paralysed with fear, she watched as the Master placed Andreas Hunt's severed head upon his own shoulders.

Her last memory was of Andreas's dead face, smiling at her with the Master's evil eyes as the blood trickled down the front of his white tunic.

Opening her eyes, Mara found that she was still in the temple but that she was now surrounded by solicitous women, congratulating her on coming through the ordeal and eager to see that she had come to no harm.

But as Gilde reached out to touch her, green lightning forked out of Mara's body and struck the woman, running up her fingers and her arm, surrounding her with the same terrifying green fire that had consumed the blonde victim. She shrieked in terror and pain as the fire enveloped her, turning her blonde hair into a raging inferno of greenish flame.

Lightning flashed round the temple walls and screams

filled the air as the women writhed in the deadly clutches of the cold green fire that froze and burned and consumed. The guards ran forward to help and were themselves struck down instantly.

Only Mara remained unharmed, inexplicably safe within a cocoon of greenish light which seemed to offer her and her alone its protection.

The fire had caught the rafters now, and the whole building was burning with the same eerie, greenish fire. Soon the rest of the village would be consumed. There was nothing Mara could do now to save these people from the terrible consequences of their foolishness. Wrapping the Phallus in a cloth and picking up the pile of her clothes, Mara ran out into the night air, scarcely noticing the sharp stones as they cut into the soles of her feet.

She reached the car and climbed in, fingers trembling as she fumbled for the ignition key. As the engine started, she looked up and saw an enormous green fireball lighting up the sky.

Burzenheim was no more.

In the seclusion of his office at Winterbourne, the Master was listening to the hoarse breathing of the girl beneath him. He had enjoyed violating her. He would enjoy still more sullying every last vestige of her purity, and then throwing her to Delgado and the guards as an after-dinner treat.

As he prepared to wrench open her lips and thrust his hardness once more into her mouth, he felt the sudden surge of power, like static electricity running over his skin, making the hairs on the backs of his hands stand erect. The sudden meeting of minds, of time and space and destiny, took his breath away for a moment, and his mind reeled with the suddenness of it.

But he knew. At last, he knew for sure.

The Fleming woman had found the Phallus. And now three things had become inevitable: the resurrection of his dead queen, the consolidation of his evil empire, and the horrible, agonising death of Ms Mara Fleming.

He thrust savagely into the girl's mouth. Now, his defilement of her purity had become a celebration.

14: Possession

What a weird dream. Andreas awoke from oblivion and tried to recall exactly what he had seen, heard, felt.

Mara had been there, he knew that. Mara in the centre of a strange round wooden building. It looked like a temple, but it was decked out in swastikas. Swastikas? And he was fucking her, on a cold earth floor, whilst naked women screamed 'Heil Hitler' all around them . . . It'd make a great scenario for some arty French film.

This bizarre captivity was beginning to get to him. And yet he was convinced that, for a brief moment, he had called out to her and she had heard him. Now he must just wait. He was doing a lot of waiting lately.

The Master pulled apart Alexandra's arse-cheeks and inspected the tightness of her neat little virgin hole. The girl lay beneath him, quite still and submissive now, still panting from her last orgasm, and waiting to see what he would do to her next.

She had only just begun to enter the world of lust. Gently, the Master placed his cock against her arsehole and pushed it home. The girl groaned a little but thrust her buttocks out, the better to take him inside her. Just like all convent girls, mused the Master: they love to play the outraged little virgin, but they're all whores at heart.

He grabbed hold of her by the waist and thrust harder into her, and was rewarded by a series of welcoming backward thrusts. There was no doubt about it: this one was young enough, succulent enough and randy enough to make an excellent whore. She'd be a great asset to the organisation.

Whilst teasing her clitoris with his index finger, the Master brought himself to the brink of orgasm, then nuzzled into the crook of her neck, as though to kiss her throat.

'Welcome to the land where death is dead,' he whispered, and bit savagely into the soft white flesh.

Her blood tasted sweeter than honey.

Gavin de Lacy nudged his neighbour with his elbow.

'Do you know why we've been called here?'

Royston Birbridge IV shook his head.

'It's not our place to ask. The Master has his reasons.'

He could hardly believe that he was speaking those words. Why, only a few short weeks ago, he'd been the ultimate lord of his own destiny – a hard-drinking, hard-fucking, autocratic young American dragging an ailing British automobile company into the twenty-first century. He took orders – and shit – from no one.

But an invitation to one of Winterbourne's special evening entertainments had changed his life.

He remembered that cold, rainy October night vividly. He'd been in a terrible mood after a day of bad sales figures and unsatisfactory meetings; and he'd been in two minds about whether to turn up at all.

Luckily, his old Etonian sales manager, Piers Thornecroft – whose effortless English style Royston grudgingly admired – had already spent an evening at Winterbourne. Ever since that day, Thornecroft had seemed brighter, punchier, altogether a more formidable character. Something in the course of that one evening at Winterbourne had altered him, visibly and irrevocably.

Thornecroft was so persuasive that Birbridge had grudgingly agreed to take up the invitation. His chauffeur-driven Rolls had pulled up outside the house at about eight o'clock, and Royston remembered peering out through the rain-streaked windows into the gloom beyond and wondering why he'd ever agreed to let himself be brought to this corner of a Godforsaken craphole that was forever England.

He got out of the car, dismissed the chauffeur, and watched the car disappear down the drive, the wheels making a quiet swishing noise on the wet gravel.

A tall black man was waiting for him at the top of the steps. Powerfully built, muscles oiled and glistening, he wore nothing but a white loincloth and – although he wasn't normally that way inclined – Royston began to experience the first stirrings of interest in his underpants.

'My name is Ibrahim,' said the negro with a respectful bow, his voice silky smooth and seductive. 'I am here only to serve you. Will you permit me to take you to the robing room?'

Quite unaccustomed to such servility – and a little unsettled by it – Royston followed Ibrahim down long, wood-panelled corridors and into what had obviously once been the master bedroom at the Hall. The huge four-poster bed remained as a central feature but the room was now decorated as a comfortable sitting room, lined with rails on which hung row upon row of costumes. Several men were trying on Eastern-looking outfits and Royston thought he recognised one of them as the porn magnate, Alan Freestein.

'Your costume, sir.'

Ibrahim took a set of heavily embroidered robes from one of the rails and handed them to Royston.

'Would you like me to undress you, sir?'

Royston felt an unexpected thrill at the words; and was surprised to hear himself say yes, he *would* like to feel the handsome negro's slender fingers unbuttoning his shirt, unzipping his flies . . .

He slipped off his jacket and tie, and Ibrahim got to work on his shirt, easing open the little mother-of-pearl buttons with agonising slowness. Royston realised with a start of pleasure that the negro was teasing him, deliberately augmenting his desire . . .

And now he was naked to the waist, and Ibrahim was on his knees before Royston, unzipping his flies and helping him to step out of his trousers. His cock felt painfully erect as it pushed its head against the inside of his boxer shorts.

Ibrahim took hold of the elasticated waistband and pulled down Royston's pants. It took him right back to the days of his childhood when Martha, the family's black housemaid, used to take him to the john, pull down his pants and hold his prick over the bowl so that he wouldn't splash the nice tiled floor. His mom and dad had been kinda fanatical about their nice clean all-American dreamhouse.

He'd been a strangely precocious kid. Even then, as a young boy, he'd had erections just thinking about Martha's gentle touch. When he was older − an insecure adolescent with a wallful of pin-up posters and yearnings he didn't know how to satisfy − Martha had started coming to his room and 'helping' him undress for bed. On one occasion her strong black fingers had strayed to his prick and it had hardened immediately in Martha's hand. God, how he'd blushed with shame as she held the fruit of his adolescent desire, too young and inexperienced to understand what was going to happen to him but knowing somehow that it wasn't right to be like this. To his surprise, Martha hadn't laughed or scolded him. She'd simply smiled, closed her fingers about his shaft and begun to slide them very gently up and down, causing him the most delicious sensations.

He could still recall his surprise, terror and delight as Martha had brought him to the very first orgasm he'd ever had at a woman's hand. A pitiful thing by later standards, but a glimpse of a whole new, vaster world for an adolescent boy with an overdose of hormones. From then on, it had been their secret. He had grown to love and crave the touch of Martha's fingers, the warm moistness of her lips.

And, a few weeks later, it had been Martha who had spread her legs for him, lying down on that same tiled floor and letting him enter her − his very first woman. His clumsy fucking had doubtless done little to pleasure Martha; but when she got to her feet and pulled down her dress, Royston was delighted to see a little pool of sticky semen, soiling the clean tiled floor.

But it was Ibrahim who was sucking him now, and it felt like heaven on earth. His tongue was winding round and round the tip of his still-hardening penis, teasing drops of clear love-juice from it, the harbingers of the great flood to come. Royston cradled Ibrahim's head in his hands, stroking the blue-black hair, sleek with scented oils. He wanted to tell him to stop – stop, or there'll be nothing left for later – but his resolve failed him, and he whimpered piteously as the spunk rose in his balls and pumped its creamy-white abundance into Ibrahim's greedy mouth.

Immediately afterwards, he felt disconsolate. What was the point of accepting an invitation to an orgy if he was going to use up all his spunk on a casual encounter with a glorified cloakroom attendant?

Ibrahim must have read his mind, for he smiled and said:

'Please do not worry, sir. You will enjoy great potency and pleasure this evening.'

He went away for a moment and returned with a glass full of a rich red liquid, a little like port, but mixed up with other, headier fragrances.

'Our herbalist, Madame LeCoeur, has prepared this for the greater pleasure of our guests. Please drink it. It is entirely safe and you will enjoy the most potent of orgasms.'

Royston eyed the glass doubtfully, but decided to give Ibrahim the benefit of the doubt and drank the liquid down in a single draught. It had a kick like a mule and his head reeled for a moment with the power of it. Then a warm glow stole over him and he realised to his surprise and pleasure that his penis was hardening again.

Ibrahim smiled.

'Please put on your robes and I shall take you to the Great Hall. The celebrations are about to begin.'

Royston recalled how nervous he had felt as Ibrahim led him, and half a dozen other men, into the anteroom leading off the Great Hall. All were dressed in Eastern robes and they obviously still felt some vestiges of self-consciousness.

Four pretty boys, entirely naked save for an abundance of gold jewellery, led them into the Hall, which had been decorated to resemble a Turkish harem. An assortment of beautiful women were sitting and lying around the central pool, their perfect bodies clearly visible through their diaphanous veils. A dais at the back of the hall had been arranged as a stage, with steps leading up to it from either side, and a dark, bearded man with a lame leg and evil, glittering eyes was standing beside it.

The man Royston knew as Anthony LeMaitre was sitting in the shadows, his robes parted to reveal a lively penis which two naked girls were taking turns to suck. LeMaitre's face stirred memories somewhere at the back of Royston's mind. He could have sworn he'd seen him somewhere before – but not as LeMaitre. He dimly recalled a cynical, indomitable journalist who'd made trouble for him a couple of years ago, sniffing around at the Birbridge factory for the scent of corruption. It was a good job they'd covered their tracks so well. Now, what was he called . . . Hartley? No, Huntley . . . Hunter . . . something like that. At any rate, the resemblance was uncanny.

LeMaitre spoke:

'Delgado, you may begin the festivities.'

With a little bow, Delgado introduced himself, welcomed his distinguished guests – who included several MPs and TV personalities, and more than one senior academic – and then announced that the slave-market was open.

There followed a delightful pantomime, involving a collection of delicious young women, entirely naked, and chained together in pairs. They were to be auctioned off to the highest bidders. Naturally, with so much wealth about, the bidding was lively – but the auction had been carefully arranged so that each guest would end up with a pair of young women to attend to his pleasure.

Royston was unused to bondage but soon caught on to the idea. Supplied with two delectable young slave-girls, an abundance of chains, leather thongs and instruments of torture, he had soon devised a scenario to his own liking.

The first girl, a small dark beauty with flashing black eyes and slender hips, he chained to rings in the wall, so that she hung by her wrists with her back to him. Then he forced the second girl, a tall Nordic wench with heavy breasts, to wield the whip on her sister-slave's back and buttocks. How he laughed with pleasure to see the red welts raised on the dark girl's flesh, and to see her twist and turn in a vain attempt to break free.

He took up the dildo – a fearsome object with hard rubber spikes – and thrust it into the blonde girl's cunt, forcing her to go on whipping the first girl whilst he manipulated the instrument of torture in and out of her cunt. Evidently she enjoyed the pain, for she came to a noisy climax and cunt-juice dripped abundantly down her muscular thighs.

Unable to control himself any longer, Royston pushed her aside and thrust his engorged cock deep into the dark girl's backside, ignoring her cries of discomfort as he grabbed handfuls of her martyred flesh.

His orgasm was even more pleasurable than the first, and he blessed the herbal cocktail which had rendered him so potent and so ferocious.

He barely noticed the blonde girl as she came up behind him and slipped her arm around his waist, nuzzling into the back of his neck in an irresistible, fatal kiss.

The sharpness of her little white teeth was so exquisite that he came to orgasm again, even as the sweet, welcoming darkness closed over him.

When he awoke, he had felt the great change in him immediately. He felt refreshed, renewed, cleansed of the human weaknesses of gentleness, compassion and fear. The kiss of death had awakened him to a new, exciting world where pleasure and power were the law, and where pain was something that happened to other people. He knew he would never be able to thank the Master enough for admitting him to the ranks of his immortal elite.

And now, this evening, he and de Lacy and Pembridge and Cheviot and all the other big cheeses had returned to

Winterbourne: not invited this time, but summoned by their Master, who had an important announcement to make.

They sat in a semi-circle by the side of the pool, in the middle of which a dais had been raised to hold the Master's golden throne. The Great Hall had once again been returned to its Egyptian splendour, for the Master was preparing his citadel for the return in triumph of his long-dead queen.

Elaborate paintings covered the walls, depicting erotic scenes: the Master and his Queen Sedet fucking beside the banks of the Nile; Sedet's initiation into the realms of the Undead, as the Master fucked her and bit into her throat; men and women seduced and bled dry for the greater glory of the Master's evil host; men, women and beasts, all fucking together to supply the Master's legions with the energies they would need to establish their evil empire.

On the dais, on either side of the gilded throne, sat two naked girls, crystal collars encircling their pretty throats and concealing the scars of their initiation. They wore the heavy wigs and kohl eye make-up of dynastic Egypt, and each one was masturbating with a garishly painted wooden snake. As the serpents' heads disappeared into their cunts, they chanted a litany of praise to their Master:

'All praise to the Master, Lord of the Undead, Conqueror of Death, who fills our cunts with semen and our mouths with praise; who strengthens us with the blood of virgins and the death-cries of the unworthy.'

A curtain swished back and Royston Birbridge IV gasped in awe as the Master strode into the room, dressed in golden robes and wearing the golden death-mask of a pharaoh upon his head, covering his face. He was naked save for his cloak, which flowed out behind him, revealing the beauty of his strong, naked body, which age and death could never decay.

Six pretty boys with rings through their erect penises stood guard as he climbed the steps and took his seat on the great throne. One of the girls immediately knelt between his thighs and began to suck his penis.

'My children,' began the Master; and his words sounded strangely distant, muffled as they were by the heavy golden mask. 'Tonight, we celebrate a great victory: the first step on our journey to universal dominion. Tomorrow, I leave for Egypt, appointed – through your many good offices – to the position of Ambassador to Cairo. From this beginning, I shall establish myself as a strong and charismatic public figure, worthy of yet higher office. Your work shall aid me in my endeavours. Children: you shall share in my glory, in the glory of my eternal dominion.'

Delgado gazed up at his master, adoring and yet hating him for denying him his rightful place among the immortals. It was so hard to be patient, when all he longed for was a sound, young body in which to serve the Master for eternity. He looked round the assembled throng and anger surged up into his throat, choking him like bile. So many fat old men, initiated only because they had positions of power. So many pretty boys and girls, chosen only for their physical strength and beauty. How much more worthy would they be if only they held the evil, brilliant spirit of Delgado within their worthless frames!

As the anger blotted out all other emotions, he felt a curious numbness overcome him; and all sense of his self-identity faded away into the shadows of unconsciousness. The invader took control and Delgado lost all understanding of who he was.

Andreas blinked, tried moving first a finger, a hand, an arm . . . he could move! He tried taking a step forward, but a dull ache rippled through his right leg and he stumbled momentarily, unprepared for the jolt as the shorter leg almost buckled underneath him. Well, whoever's body this was, he didn't think much of it.

However, a body with a limp was still a body. He looked around furtively, wondering if anyone had noticed his arrival. But all attentions were focused on the strange masked figure seated on a dais in the middle of the pool. Andreas remembered the pool – so he was back in the

Great Hall at Winterbourne. It looked different. He didn't remember any of this Egyptian mumbo-jumbo.

He gazed up at the strange figure on the dais, hardly aware of the words being spoken. A golden pharaoh on a gold throne. Exhibitionist, or what? Andreas felt his borrowed cock twitch and stiffen as he watched the naked girl sucking the golden king's prick, toying with his balls, almost teasing the spunk out of him. Strange, Andreas could feel every movement of the girl's tongue, experience every caress she lavished upon the other man's prick. And as the golden king spurted into the girl's mouth, Andreas felt his own spunk rise and inundate the inside of his pants.

He glanced around, colouring momentarily with embarrassment and gasping with the pleasure of the orgasm – his first in . . . how long?

How long would his possession of this body last? Not long, if past experiences were anything to go by. He must use this opportunity to gather information, find out something – anything – that might help him to regain possession of his own lost body.

And where the fuck *was* his body? He felt like an unsuccessful shepherd, whistling helplessly on some barren hillside, whilst his sheepdog gambolled away over the fells, never to be seen again.

The man on the dais was speaking. Maybe if he listened, he'd learn something. And he mustn't draw any attention to himself. If they realised what was going on, there was no telling what these crazy people would do.

'I leave tomorrow for Cairo,' concluded the Master. 'And I shall have need of all the sexual energies contained within your bodies, and within this hall, to speed me on my way. So, for tonight, let the festivities begin! Fuck as you have never fucked before, for the greater strength and glory of your Master!'

The curtain twitched aside once again and Madame LeCoeur entered, pushing in front of her a naked girl, barely pubescent and with a long plait of light-brown hair. The girl seemed dazed and disorientated, and Andreas did not doubt for a moment that she had been drugged. As she turned her head, trying to work out where she was, Andreas noticed two small puncture-wounds on the side of her neck.

'This is Alexandra,' announced Madame LeCoeur. 'She was a virgin until a few hours ago. She is the Master's very special gift to you. He desires that you teach her all she needs to know to become one of Winterbourne's finest whores. Do with her as you wish.'

A baleful chorus struck up, the sound sweeping around the hall like a desert wind:

'"Do what thou wilt" shall be the whole of the law.'

They fell upon the girl like ravening wolves, tearing at her flesh and pulling her to the ground, squabbling amongst themselves as to who should be the first to defile her. A young woman whom Andreas recognised with a start as Anastasia Dubois sat gleefully upon the girl's face, forcing her to lap at her cunt. A fat American knelt beside her, wanking over her tiny nascent breasts. A young TV presenter pushed aside his rivals and thrust his cock into the girl, her cunt still soiled with her own dried blood and the Master's sticky semen.

All were gathered round her, struggling to fuck her, to bugger her, to soil her breasts and belly and face with their semen, whilst the masked figure on the dais looked on, his penis thrusting in and out of the slave-girl's eager mouth.

Those who could not reach the girl resorted to fucking each other. Three men were buggering each other, the first pressed face down on the ground whilst the others lay on top of him, ramming into each other's arses. Two middle-aged female executives set about masturbating each other with wine-bottles. And Winterbourne's whores, in the guise of Egyptian temple prostitutes, filed into the hall and fucked whoever would have them, with the fervour of religious zealots.

A girl approached Andreas, semen trickling down the furrow between her breasts. She was laughing, the deranged laughter of the insane, and in a moment she was on her knees before Andreas, fumbling with his flies and taking out his penis. Now she was sucking him and God! it was divine, so unbelievably divine. He had almost forgotten what it felt like to know real, physical sensations. He was going to come! Oh God, he could feel the spunk boiling in his bollocks and he didn't give a toss about anything any more – only that wonderful sensation he had almost given up hope of ever enjoying again.

She sucked him to a climax, and he felt as though his entire being was flooding into her on the creamy tide of his spunk.

'Did you enjoy that, Delgado?'

Delgado? Surely the girl wasn't talking to him! But yes, she was looking up at him, the remains of his semen still visible on her little pink tongue, and she was smiling again and calling him Delgado . . .

Something – the glint of lamplight on gold, perhaps – made him look up. The figure on the dais was standing now, his still-erect penis springing proudly from his loins, a drop of semen clinging to its tip. He was raising his hands to the heavy golden mask, taking hold of it, lifting it up, over his head, to reveal his face.

Unmasked, the Master smiled down upon his people, and blessed the fruits of their lust, for they had refreshed his spirit.

Andreas stared blankly up at the face he knew so well. The stubborn chin that had greeted him every morning in the shaving-mirror for God-knows-how-many years. The lips that had so often savoured the delights of Mara's fragrant cunt-juices.

The face that had once been Andreas Hunt's.

The shock of confronting his own, lost self was sufficient to break the fragile link which held his spirit within Delgado's body. And the vortex gripped him once again, tore him away from the world of pleasure and pain, and back to the bitter comforts of his dark prison.

15: The Return

Mara parked the old VW halfway up a secluded cart-track, and walked the rest of the way.

It had taken courage even to think of returning to Winterbourne Hall; for the memories were strengthening every day, and she often awoke in the middle of the night, terrified by dreams of the Master's burning eyes.

But how could she ignore the message which she was sure she had received from Andreas Hunt? The words had cut through her mind with all the sharpness of surgical steel and their imprint still remained.

'Come to me, Mara, come to me at Winterbourne.'

Was it a trick? She had to accept the possibility that it might be so. But the stakes were high. If Andreas's spirit really was trapped within the walls of Winterbourne Hall, she might well be the only living person able to help free him. She clutched the painted wooden box to her and walked on resolutely towards the gates of Winterbourne Hall.

Andreas felt himself dragged into wakefulness, by what he at first thought was the physical sensation of someone's hand on his shoulder, lips kissing his closed eyelids.

Then, with a silent sigh, he remembered. The world of sight and touch were lost to him. And someone, someone desperately, magnificently evil, was using his body; had stepped into it as easily as he might try on a new suit. Andreas craved another few moments of lucidity within some borrowed body, just so that he might find out more about the power which had dispossessed him. Only in that way might he learn some way of getting his body back.

But the memory of the hand on his shoulder, the lips against his lips, haunted him, tormented him with a conviction he dared not believe was true.

Mara was near. Mara was coming to rescue him. He could feel her presence, getting closer with every moment.

And he cursed himself for a gullible fool. Did he really expect the Seventh Cavalry to come riding over the horizon, just in time to save Andreas Hunt? No one was coming to save him. No one even knew where he was.

Mara saw the gates not far ahead. The sight of Winterbourne Hall, dark and forbidding at the end of a long driveway, stirred memories which brought the tears stinging to her eyes. She fought them back, summoning up all her courage, all the strength of her occult knowledge and powers, all the might of her spirit guides. And she touched the crystal talisman about her neck, reassured by the unexpected sensation of warmth. It felt almost like touching some portion of living flesh . . .

She took a deep breath, reminding herself of Heimdal's reassuring words. Fortune had smiled on her so far, so why should it let her down now? She wondered again whether she ought to have told Heimdal about her plans to come to Winterbourne – why had she decided to keep quiet about it? Had she really sensed that there was something changed in him, something that she no longer felt able to trust? But that was sheer foolishness. Heimdal had been more than a friend to her. And now she wished he were here, to tell her what to do next.

There were guards at the gates, just as Mara had feared. Two youngish men in dark uniforms. Not unattractive. She knew what she had to do. Seduction was the only weapon she had. Still, if her plan worked, fucking the guards would not be entirely unpleasant.

Tucking the box beneath her cloak, Mara walked up to the gates, her speech ready-prepared in her mind.

'Excuse me,' she began. 'My name is Tricia. I have an appointment at the Hall . . .'

She was going to continue, going to tell the guards how she was a skilled whore from London who had been invited up to the Hall to display her skills for Madame LeCoeur. Would they like a little sample of what she could do? Would they perhaps like to give her a preliminary audition . . .?

And then she was going to suck them off, one after the other. And if they wanted more, she would go with them into their lodge and fuck them on the bare wooden floor until they were too tired and too befuddled with sex to think of stopping her from going up to the house.

That was her plan. But as she began to speak, Mara realised that neither of the guards was paying any attention to her. In fact, they seemed to be looking straight past her.

She turned to look behind her, but the road was empty. She spoke again, but still there was no reaction. In desperation, she reached out and touched one of the guards on the shoulder. He did not even notice.

Mara realised the incredible truth: the guards could neither hear nor see her. As far as they were concerned, she was invisible.

Realising that the talisman must be responsible for this unexpected stroke of good fortune, and fearing that the effects of the charm might not last, Mara set off towards the house, half-regretting that she had not had a chance to fuck with the two young guards. If the circumstances had not been so grave she would have delighted in unzipping their pants, taking out their cocks and sucking them, even though they could not see her. And she smiled to herself as she thought of the expressions on their faces as they were brought to a juddering climax by an unseen woman.

It was early morning and Mara knew that most of the whores – and those of their guests who had spent the night at the house – would still be asleep. Winterbourne's security system would be at its most vulnerable. Yet she feared the terrible power of the Master, which had once before drawn her here and made a mockery of her powers. Could it be that he, and not Andreas, had called her to the hall? Had he brought her here to humiliate or destroy her?

She decided not to risk the main entrance. Even if she really was invisible the sight of the front door opening and closing – apparently of its own volition – would be enough to arouse suspicions. Instead, she walked quickly round to the back of the building and slipped in through the open kitchen door.

There was no one in the vast, oak-beamed kitchens. Copper pots and pans hung from the ceiling, spotless and gleaming. The wooden work-surfaces were scrubbed clean and the cupboards were empty. It looked as if little food was ever cooked in the kitchens at Winterbourne Hall. Did anyone ever eat at all?

Hurrying through the kitchens, Mara stepped out into a long, panelled corridor which she recognised only too well. It was the corridor which had once led her to doom and despair. She shivered with recollected misery as she recalled how Delgado had taken her down that same corridor, and then down a flight of stairs into the gloom. The secret door in the panelling had slid silently across at his touch and he had pushed her through into impenetrable darkness.

She remembered the secret workshop, lined with magical artefacts and dusty bottles; and the guilty excitement flooded back into her mind as she recalled how the spirit of a long-dead Egyptian priestess had entered her and joyfully fucked with the Master, who had possessed the body of his henchman, Delgado.

And afterwards Delgado had taken her to the cellars. Her memory of them was fragmentary, as though she wanted to blot something horrible out of her mind. Her hands trembled as she recalled a coffin, naked bodies fucking like animals, the face of Andreas Hunt as she plunged a dagger into his chest . . .

She couldn't go down to the cellars. No, not there. The fear gripped her heart, squeezing all the breath out of her, making her gasp with terror.

But she could sense the presence of Andreas Hunt all around her in this place. She knew that he must be here, somewhere, his spirit trapped and helpless. Only she could find him, help him, release him. And she knew that she must begin with the cellars, if only to exorcise the memory of her own humiliation and despair.

Still dazed by memories, she stepped out into the corridor to be confronted by two naked bodies, still lying where they had fallen asleep, apparently in the afterglow of passion. The younger and prettier of the two women still had her fingers buried to the knuckle in her partner's cunt and abundant juices still glistened on her hand. The older woman had taken the younger woman's nipple into her mouth and lay half-underneath her partner, like a grotesque baby at her breast.

As Mara stepped over the bodies, the younger woman moaned and reached out her hand but did not wake. The air was heavy with the scent of sex.

She turned away and was about to walk down the corridor when she heard footsteps and saw three men coming towards her from the direction of the main staircase. It was too late to run. She must stand her ground and hope that the talisman would protect her.

They walked towards Mara, talking and laughing, and apparently taking no notice of her. Good. So they had not seen her. But as they walked past her, one of the guards – a tall, muscular man with dark eyes – turned his head towards her, and Mara felt for an instant the power of his burning recognition. At that moment, she knew that she was doomed.

Astonishingly, the guard turned his head away from Mara and continued down the corridor with his comrades, who disappeared into a room on the right-hand side, shutting the door behind them.

A few moments later, the door opened and the tall guard emerged. He closed the door gently behind him and took a few slow steps towards Mara.

As she gazed, terror-stricken, into his dark eyes, a wave of recognition swept over her, hardening her nipples and making her clitoris throb with anticipation. She had never seen the man before in her life and yet there was no mistaking the look in those dark eyes.

'Andreas?' gasped Mara; and the tall guard began to undress before her.

The feeling of Mara's presence was all-consuming now. It was destroying his peace of mind. Andreas tried to shut it out, to think of something else – anything else – but it wouldn't go away. It felt exactly as though she were calling to him, coming ever-closer, smiling, reaching out to him, gently and suggestively stroking him . . . He could feel the exquisite touch of her fingertips as they slid over his groin, searching for the tag that would pull down his zip . . .

He must stop fantasising! He must, or he would go insane. Sightless, he fought the overwhelming image of her face, her firm breasts, her warm, damp thighs; and his anger and desire grew immense.

Just as he abandoned control of his emotions it happened again. The swirling colours and the spinning, spinning through nothingness. Until at last the kaleidoscope slowed down and gave way to the ordinary brightness of electric light.

He stood, blinking rather stupidly, outside the door to the guards' rest-room, feeling awkward and disorientated in his military uniform. For a moment, he thought he was alone. But a voice called to him very softly and this time it wasn't in his mind.

'Andreas? Is it really you?'

Mara was standing there in the half-light, the same beautiful woman he had so loved to fuck. And as soon as he saw her, he found himself frenziedly unbuttoning his tunic, flinging it to the ground; ripping off his shirt; fumbling with the belt-buckle on his trousers.

Mara gently prised his useless fingers from the buckle and unfastened it herself, unbuttoning the waistband of his trousers and pulling them down, wrenching down his underpants and baring the swelling branch of his vigorous penis. He felt helpless as a child in her hands, surrendering himself utterly to her tender ministrations.

Please God, he thought to himself. Let it last long enough, just long enough . . .

He wanted to undress her but he was too slow, too clumsy. His awkwardness in this borrowed body frustrated his attempts to unfasten those tiny little mother-of-pearl buttons. He wanted to rip off her skirt, fling himself on top of her, enjoy her before the dream faded and he was back in the dark solitude of his imprisonment.

But Mara made him take things more slowly, stand back whilst she undressed herself for him, peeling off her sweater and blouse with agonising slowness, baring her wonderful, glowing, tanned flesh inch by tantalising inch.

Her breasts bobbed free, their large pink nipples already stiff with desire, like the stalks of luscious twin fruits. Andreas groaned, longing to reach out and touch them, taste them; but she smiled and shook her head. She must be naked first.

The skirt yielded at last and slid to the floor. Mara kicked off her shoes and stood before him in her glorious nakedness.

'Got to have you, got to have you . . .' moaned Andreas, very quietly, for fear of discovery.

Mara put her finger to her lips.

'Hush,' she whispered. 'Someone might hear.'

And she silenced him by pulling his face down to the level of her breasts and filling his eager mouth with a hard, pink nipple. His hands roamed over the surface of her breasts, delightedly, as though rediscovering a lost land of pleasure and plenty. They were not Andreas's hands but it was Andreas's touch upon her flesh.

There was no mistaking the firm gentleness of those fingers upon her breasts, or the exquisite sensitivity with which he sucked at her nipple. Mara slid her hand down Andreas's belly. It seemed strange to stroke this unknown flesh, and yet to sense that somehow, inexplicably, it housed the spirit of her lover.

She teased his pubic curls for a little while, determined not to give in and touch his shaft until she had brought him to the very summit of desire. He groaned quietly as she teased his balls with the very tip of her fingernail, running it oh-so-lightly across the surface of the goose-pimpled flesh, and making it tense in accustomed readiness.

Andreas, too, wanted to explore. He was beginning to learn the skill of this borrowed body. Carefully, he let his right hand drop down and stroke Mara's beautiful flat belly, her tuft of glossy black curls.

She shuffled her feet apart to let him in and he delved into the very heart of her womanhood. Her inner thighs were warm and moist, as he knew they would be. He ran a finger over her pubic curls and rejoiced to feel the slippery juices that hung like dewdrops on an exotic flower.

Her cunt was dripping wet. Parting the outer lips with his finger, Andreas dived into the ocean of her womanhood, sighing with pleasure at the remembrance of her wonderful taste, her own intimate fragrance . . .

He was almost sobbing with desire now, his finger in Mara's cunt and his thumb teasing her clitoris into throbbing wakefulness.

Mara seemed to sense his desperation and sank to her knees in front of him, taking him into her mouth. He could hardly suppress a cry of mingled anguish and joy as her lips closed around his shaft, and he knew for the first time how much he had missed her. His fingers toyed with her breasts as she sucked him off, greedily now, forgetting how she had wanted to make it last.

He couldn't hold back any longer. The sperm was rising in his shaft, it was going to spurt out and it would all be over . . . no, no, please . . .

As though sensing his anguish, Mara stopped sucking his prick and looked up at him questioningly.

'Would you like to fuck me now?' she whispered.

She knew that she need hardly wait for his answer, and indeed she was already lying down on the polished parquet floor, her legs spread wide for him and her black-fringed moistness gaping wide.

He lay down upon her, his borrowed penis searching desperately for her. But she had to take his shaft in her hand and guide it herself to her tight, wet cunt. Andreas gave a groan of delight as his hardness slid smoothly into her.

They fucked not desperately, but luxuriously, suddenly oblivious of the danger, the shortness of time, the fear. Mara had the curious sensation that she was fucking two men at once, and this heightened her desire to such an extent that she climaxed within seconds of his entering her.

He rode her to a second climax, and poured out his tribute as her cunt opened and closed in a series of delicious spasms.

Almost as the last waves of pleasure ebbed away, Andreas felt the familiar pain surge through him and darkness closed in at the edges of his world.

'Mara . . . don't leave me; don't let go . . .'

The words gasped from him as blackness tore him from her sight and returned him to his captivity.

Mara pushed the unconscious body of the guard away from her and onto the floor. She had shared the moment of pain and loss as Andreas's spirit was torn from its body and knew now that the guard had been nothing more than a temporary host.

And yet, Andreas's spirit must still be within the walls of Winterbourne, perhaps disembodied and aimless; or even within some other host. She sensed its presence all around her but the vibrations were coming most strongly from beneath her feet.

She must brave the cellars once again.

No one saw her and no one stopped her. It was easy to find the secret panel and step into the darkness of the magicians' workshop. Gratefully, she saw that the lantern was still there and she switched it on, illuminating the dusty darkness with a dull, orange glow.

Immediately, her heart sank. The hole which had been

knocked through to the cellars had evidently been bricked up again, for only a blank wall greeted her. The job had been skilfully done and it was impossible to see exactly where the doorway had been. An old carved oak cupboard had been pushed in front of it and had been made to look as if it had always been there. Clearly the Master was anxious to hide something down there in the cellars. But what?

She laid the Phallus in its box on the ground and, without much hope in her heart, Mara set about trying to move the cupboard. It was heavy and took all her strength to slide it across until it was a couple of feet forward of the wall and she could slip behind it.

The wall had been smoothly replastered. There was no sign of any way into the cellars. She was far too weak to attempt to batter down the wall. It looked very much as if she would have to give up and leave.

At that moment, Mara heard a high-pitched, almost electrical whine, and turned round to see what was causing it. The painted wooden box which held the Phallus was glowing with the same green phosphorescence which had proved so destructive at Burzenheim, and Mara feared that the Phallus was about to use its power to destroy her.

But, as she watched, Mara realised that something quite different was happening. The high-pitched whine grew louder and more distinct and the wall in front of Mara began to glow a faint green. As she looked on in astonishment, it grew strangely transparent.

Picking up the box and the lantern, Mara knew what she must do. She stepped towards the wall and – with only the slightest feeling of resistance – felt herself walk straight through it. When she turned and looked back, the wall behind her glowed like liquid green glass.

The cellar lay before her, a dark, inhospitable, featureless place in which a thick layer of dust lay over everything. It could not quite obscure the dried blood-stains on the floor and walls, nor the outline of a pentacle, deeply engraved into the cellar floor.

Memories crowded unbidden into her head. She realised

with horror that she was standing on the very spot where the dagger had robbed Andreas of life, her heels grinding into the dried blood that had once pumped through that savagely butchered heart.

But another feeling was enveloping her now. A feeling of welcome, of protection, of joy even. She realised with a start that she could feel Andreas's spirit all around her. It felt as though a thousand hands were running wonderingly over her flesh, exploring her, worshipping her body and drawing her closer in.

'You've come at last . . .'

The words echoed silently through Mara's brain. Andreas was speaking to her, communicating with her with the power of his own mind!

'Come to me . . . I'm very near. Come to me . . . I want you, Mara . . .'

An overwhelming surge of sexual desire hit her, like a surf-crested wave breaking on a tropical shore, warming her, awakening her body once again. Andreas was making love to her with his mind . . .

She looked around her and saw a dusty chair and, beside it, a long-handled whip. She knew immediately what Andreas wanted her to do. Sitting down on the chair, she picked up the whip and turned it round so that its handle pointed towards her cunt.

'Want you, Mara . . .'

With an almost religious reverence, Mara thrust the handle of the whip into her cunt. It slipped in easily, for the guard's semen was still trickling out from between her cunt-lips. She unfastened a few buttons on her blouse, and slipped her hand inside, cupping her right breast and pinching her nipple between thumb and finger.

Slowly, she began to wank herself with the whip. But she was not masturbating. It was not the handle of a dusty bullwhip that was entering her slippery cunt but Andreas Hunt's penis – long and thick and virile, just as she remembered it. Andreas Hunt's gloriously randy, ever-hungry prick.

She could hear him whispering to her in her mind: 'Let me fuck you, Mara . . . Feel my prick inside you. Does it feel good, Mara? Feel me fucking you . . .'

She gasped with pleasure as the whip burrowed into her; and as she felt her desire increasing, she took her fingers from her nipple and slid them down her belly to her cunt, teasing aside her pubic curls and seeking out the throbbing button of her clitoris.

As she brought herself to a powerful climax, she imagined that she was lying on Andreas's bed and he was on top of her, fucking her as he had done so many times before; fucking her and crying out for more.

'Andreas!' she cried, as her cunt tightened about the whip-handle and her juices flowed in triumphant abundance down her thighs.

A strange sense of peace seemed to have descended upon her, and Mara felt no fear as she laid aside the whip and took up the box containing the Phallus. She turned towards the stone sarcophagus which she had tried so hard to blot from her vision, for it awoke so many disturbing half-memories.

But she was not afraid now. There was nothing to be afraid of. All fears of traps and deceptions had left her. Somewhere in these cellars Andreas's spirit was imprisoned; and she must try to free it.

Somehow, she just knew that everything was going to be all right now.

She took the Phallus from the box and held it in front of her, like a talisman, confident now in its will to protect her. And as she approached the sarcophagus, a miraculous thing happened.

The crystal talisman and the Phallus began to glow, pulsating with a greenish light. The crystal grew hot against the bare flesh of her throat and sparks of light crackled from the Phallus in her hand.

The heavy, granite lid began to dissolve, fade, clarify . . . It was becoming as transparent as the cellar wall had become. It glowed a pallid green and grew glass-like as she approached. She could just make out a dark shape within.

A voice in her head was crying out:

'Yes, Mara, yes! Come to me, come to me. I can feel you near now. You are so very near . . . .'

Andreas, sightless within his crystal prison, tried to hold back the excitement, but he sensed Mara's presence all about him. She had known that it was him in the guard's body. She had come to him at last! He didn't know how, but he knew she was going to help him to break free.

As she reached the sarcophagus, Mara gripped the Phallus firmly in both hands and looked down, not quite knowing what she expected to see or do. A strange serenity had overtaken her. The Phallus would guide her. Andreas would guide her.

But the sight that met her eyes did not console or reassure her. She looked down, and the scream tore through her body, unbidden and uncontrollable.

'It's me, Mara: it's me – can't you see?'

Andreas tried desperately to break through the wall of her terror, but she just kept on screaming as she looked down into the coffin and into the sightless eyes of the Master, his cast-off body imprisoned for eternity within the crystal block; his thin lips dragged back, baring his teeth in a cruel sneer.

Memories flooded her brain; drowned her reason, her consciousness. Mara stopped screaming and stood trembling violently, a low moaning escaping from between her clenched teeth.

'Mara! What's happening to you?'

Andreas's thoughts bounced off the protective barrier of psychic energy she had instinctively cast up around her, and there was no way through to her now.

Still clutching the Phallus in its open box, she turned and fled – back through the dark and dusty cellar and away up the steps to the glassy wall, which oozed and yielded as she flung herself through onto the other side. In her haste she dropped the lantern and it rolled noisily back down the steps into oblivion.

Mara turned momentarily to watch its faint light disappearing as the wall darkened and solidified into its former impenetrability. Still shaking, she dragged the cupboard back to its original place. Now there was nothing to suggest that anyone had ever been here.

Breathing deeply to try and calm her terror, Mara stepped back into the corridor, closing the secret panel behind her. The corridor was empty. If she hurried, she might yet escape before the Master's evil power fell around her like a blanket, suffocating and imprisoning her, robbing her of her psychic powers and her identity.

She half-ran, half-stumbled along the corridor, back towards the kitchens. Voices from an open doorway alarmed her, and she flattened herself against the wall. A naked woman emerged from the room, laughing. She had peroxide blonde hair and a butterfly tattoo on her right breast, and there were little trickles of red liquid drooling from the sides of her open mouth. Now she was wiping her hand across her lips, smearing face and hands with sticky redness.

Mara held her breath and the woman passed the alcove where she hid without even glancing in her direction. A couple of guards came out of the room, dragging the body of a naked man. His flaccid penis was still dripping a glistening trail of semen, mingling with a mass of sticky red on his groin.

They went off after the woman and Mara was alone again. She crept out of her alcove and hurried on, glancing momentarily through the doorway of the deserted room. Inside, red-stained silk sheets spilled in disarray from a heart-shaped mattress, clashing with the candy pink of the walls and the deep-pile carpet. The door hung open, its name-plate coy and concise: 'Marilyn', in sugar-pink lettering on a white ceramic plate. Mara shuddered, and moved on.

She reached the kitchens safely. The back door was closed and to her dismay she saw that a key protruded from it. Did someone know she was here? Did someone want to prevent her from leaving?

Footsteps in the corridor outside. She fumbled with the key. It was stiff and rusty and wouldn't turn.

The door from the corridor creaked open. Mara swung round, defenceless yet ready to fight for her life and freedom in any way she could.

It was a guard she had never seen before: short, thick-set, with a deep scar running down the right side of his face. He was walking towards her, slowly and inexorably, as though relishing the sharpness of her fear, the unmistakable scent of growing panic.

'Don't come near me!' screamed Mara, wrenching the key so violently that it at last turned in the lock.

The guard just kept on coming, silently and slowly. He took a knife from his belt, held it up so that it caught the light, and Mara could see its wicked blade glint with malevolent intent. The front of his uniform trousers bulged obscenely and there was no doubt what he planned to do with her. He would have her there, on the kitchen floor, and then he would kill her. He would thoroughly enjoy both stages of the process.

Mara rattled the door-knob, desperate to get out of this place, to run away, anywhere, just to escape.

The guard turned round, suddenly, to see another man standing behind her. He smiled, a broken-toothed leer lighting up his brutish face.

'Bit of fun, eh, Mister Delgado? Wanna join in? You can have her after I've finished, then we'll cut her up a bit and say she was stealing the silver . . .'

His expression turned momentarily to one of astonishment as Delgado took a pearl-handled revolver from his waistcoat pocket and calmly shot him through the temple. The silencer reduced the sound to a dull thud and the guard sank to the floor in a crumpled heap.

Mara gazed in amazement at the man who had once so cruelly abused her, possessing her body again and again and afterwards casting her to his minions as casually as he might cast a lump of rotten meat to the dogs. Why would he want to protect her? There was something different about him – a look in his eyes . . . a look of . . . Andreas?

'Mara . . .!' There was pain in the voice, and a hand was reaching out to her, clumsily, tremblingly.

But there were other footsteps now, coming up the corridor towards the kitchen door. Time had run out. There was no time to stay around. Maybe this was a trick anyway.

Ignoring Delgado's desperate pleas for her to stay, Mara wrenched open the door and ran, ran, ran into the nearby woods. Ran for her life and kept on running.

In his borrowed body, Andreas watched Mara run from him, cursing the lameness that prevented him from pursuing her. She had gone. Terror had torn her from him and now she might never return. In a few moments, darkness would come again and rob him of the little life he had in this imperfect, evil shell. In that darkness, he must find a way to help Mara. In that darkness, he must somehow learn how to free himself from this agony that was neither life nor death.

The cries of desperation died in his throat and almost choked him. For the first time in its odious, calculating life, the body of Delgado wept.

16: Envoys

Heimdal was feeling pleased with himself. Ever since he had met the Master, he had experienced a tremendous flowering of his psychic powers. Together, they had undertaken astral travel and had spied upon the white witch Mara Fleming in her quest for the Talisman of Set, the breathtakingly powerful Phallus of Osiris.

Strange, it had taken the awesome power of the Master to reveal to Heimdal the folly of his former ways, the insignificance of the Fleming girl. For so many years he had felt he owed her a debt of respect and gratitude for helping him to discover and develop his psychic potential. But the Master, in his infinite wisdom and mercy, had helped Heimdal to see that the girl had been but a trifling diversion, an inconsequential source of useful information on his natural progression towards the fulfilment of his psychic and spiritual destiny.

And all of this felt and sounded good to Heimdal. For he had never felt easy with the thought that a slip of a girl might carry within her the seeds of a power far greater and more mature than his could ever be. It was fitting that he should now understand that she had been no more than a useful stepping-stone.

Yes, the Master had brought him enlightenment. Enlightenment and the gift of immortality. Small wonder, then, that Heimdal's obedience to him was now total, beyond question.

And now the girl Mara had succeeded in obtaining the Phallus. There had been a few anxious moments when she had managed to shake off the hopelessly amateurish acolyte

Geoffrey, but they had soon picked up her trail again. The Master's agents in Romania had been most helpful. By all accounts, the silly girl was back in England now, still looking for the body of her lost lover. He smiled as he pictured her likely reaction when at last she found it. The stupid little bitch was in way over her head.

She did have a nice body, though. Heimdal thought about her luscious, firm tits and felt his massive cock stiffen in his skin-tight leather pants. The things he'd like to do to her . . . He longed to humiliate her, to make her perform unspeakable obscenities – maybe tie her up and make her fuck with some hideous, pox-ridden old man. He wondered vaguely if he could perform a ceremony of conjuration, and watch her being fucked by a fiery demon . . .

But these pleasures must be for some later time, perhaps when the Master had enjoyed his plaything and cast her aside for his followers' pleasure. For now, the Master had instructed that the Fleming girl must not suspect that anything was wrong. The next stage of the operation was vital if his queen was to be located and the ceremony carried out successfully. Heimdal must therefore confine himself to more ordinary lusts.

Doubtless Mara would now seek her dear friend Heimdal's help and advice in her misguided quest to resurrect the unwary – and irredeemably dead – Mr Hunt.

And Heimdal, needless to say, would be only too ready to help. He'd be happy to give her as much time as she wanted. Why, since he'd met the Master, Heimdal had all the time in the world.

'Show it to me,' said Heimdal, genuine excitement making his voice tremble. 'I must see this wonder.'

Mara laid the painted wooden box on the floor, and opened the lid. Inside lay the Phallus, greenish-black and shiny, like some strange polished wood-carving, smooth with the patina of age.

Heimdal stroked it gently with his fingertip.

'Amazing!' he breathed. 'Never did I think I would live to see this. Scholars and magicians have quarrelled for thousands of years about whether it even existed! And you, my dear Mara, have succeeded where all others have failed.'

Mara sighed.

'You have told me that only the Phallus can save Andreas, and I have seen its power myself. But it serves no useful purpose unless I can find Andreas's body.' She looked across at Heimdal, beseechingly. 'Will you help me to find him?'

Heimdal smiled broadly, benevolently. He was enjoying this. Mara was in his power and she knew it. She could achieve nothing without his special abilities.

'Of course I will help you,' he replied. 'I'll do anything I can. Don't worry,' he added. 'I won't leave your side until you find him.'

Mara wondered why she felt a little cold shiver run down her spine.

'We must carry out another ceremony of location,' announced Heimdal. 'But not here. This place is too secluded, too empty. We must carry out our ceremony in a public place, so that we can employ the energy of those around us to add to the power of our evocations.

'Get your coat, Mara. I'm taking you to the pictures.'

The entrance to the cinema was halfway up a grubby side-street, on the unsavoury side of town. Its crumbling facade retained a certain elegance, reminiscent of more affluent days, but a quick glance at the billboards outside destroyed any lingering hope of respectability.

'Hot Nuns,' announced the posters. 'Watch them teach those monks some dirty habits!'

Mara looked at the poster and felt sick. Was she really going to allow herself to be taken into this place? A couple of tramps were reading the other poster. One of them had his hand in the pocket of his grimy duffle coat and was obviously wanking himself off as he looked at the stills of a nun with her habit up round her waist, her glistening pink crack clearly visible to all who cared to look.

'Two please.'

The ticket-seller was a fat, middle-aged woman with dirt under her fingernails and fine, dark hairs on her upper lip. She handed the tickets to Heimdal with a conspiratorial smile.

'Enjoy yourself, dearie,' she sneered as Mara pushed through the ancient turnstile.

The auditorium was a regular flea-pit, all flaking paint and elderly bucket-seats with frayed upholstery, stiff with dirt and God-knows what else. There was a strong smell of Jeyes fluid, cigarette smoke, stale urine and dried semen.

To Mara's dismay, the cinema was pretty full. Heimdal led her to the back row and dragged her along to the end. There was no one on either side of them, but she had to push past a couple of disgusting old men on the way to her seat and they had a good feel of her tits and arse. She sat down on the rough moquette and realised that her blouse was gaping open. Those old men were quick workers.

There were several men in overalls in the row in front, presumably factory-workers or garage mechanics, taking some well-earned leisure after a hard day at work. The smell of engine oil rose from their overalls and mingled with the pot pourri of fragrances already filling the cinema. Mara felt vaguely nauseous.

'I don't understand,' Mara hissed to Heimdal. 'How can we perform the ceremony here?'

Heimdal put his lips to her ear and whispered:

'We fuck, darling. We fuck.'

'But . . .'

One of the men in front turned round and glared at Mara.

'Will you fuckin' button it, darlin'? Some of us is tryin' to watch!'

Mara sank into her seat, feeling thoroughly miserable. Heimdal continued, more quietly than before:

'We fuck here, my darling, and in that way we shall tap into the sexual energies of all the people sitting here. At the moment of maximum power, there will be a sign. That is all I know.'

'What if someone sees us?'

Heimdal shrugged his shoulders. God, he was enjoying this. The silly bitch would do anything he told her, just to save her precious Andreas Hunt. And to think it was all a complete bloody waste of time! It was a good joke and he almost laughed out loud, only just managing to check himself in time.

The film had already started, but it didn't make much difference. There didn't seem to be much of a plot. A couple of nuns were about to have a bath together. They'd stripped off their habits but were still wearing their starched white wimples – plus rather more eye make-up that you'd expect to see on the average holy sister.

The women were touching each other up now – running their hands over each other's bodies, slipping fingers between each other's thighs and up into slippery cunts. They must have been enjoying themselves because one of the nuns took out her finger and it was dripping with clear juice.

Now they were getting into the bath. The taller one was kneeling at the end with the taps and the other one was standing up in the water at the other end. The tall nun was holding a long, rough loofah. Now she was running it over her flesh, rubbing it hard so that her skin blushed deep pink. Her breasts were small but perfect: like roses just before the bloom opens fully – full of sap and promise.

The taller nun was reaching out with the loofah and – oh no, surely not! – she was inserting it between the other girl's thighs. How could she possibly hope to . . . ? As Mara watched in frank astonishment, the tip of the loofah disappeared upwards, into the smaller nun's cunt. She was crying out and gripping the taller girl's shoulders so tightly that her knuckles gleamed white with the tension. Yet her cries were not of protest but of passion. She was loving every minute of it.

As Mara watched, Heimdal took hold of her hand and

guided it to his flies. With a shiver of pleasure she felt his naked penis, already protruding massively from his open flies.

'Place this over my shaft, and wank me.'

Heimdal handed her something cold and hard. Mara looked down at it and saw in the flickering half-light that it was a ring, fashioned out of clear white crystal. Its many facets flashed multi-coloured fire as she slipped it over the tip of Heimdal's enormous penis and slid it – with some difficulty – down to the base.

She began to masturbate Heimdal with slow, regular movements. At the same time, she felt another hand – not Heimdal's – creeping slowly across her thigh and searching beneath her short Lycra skirt for her intimate furrow. She glanced up in alarm, to see the grimy, lined face of a man who had sat down in the seat next to her. Her heart sank. She recognised him instantly as the tramp who had been wanking himself off outside the cinema. As soon as she turned to look at him, she got the full benefit of the all-encompassing stench which travelled with him, and almost gagged as he grinned at her, lascivious and unashamed.

She tried to close her thighs but Heimdal stopped her.

'No. Let him do whatever he wishes,' he said, with authority. 'It will empower the ritual.'

In an agony of shame and humiliation, Mara submitted herself to the tramp's lewd caresses. His calloused hands ran up her legs, into the hot moistness of her inner thighs; and she felt the quiver of excitement run through him as he realised that she was wearing no panties.

'Sexy little slut,' rasped the tramp, clutching at her fanny so suddenly that Mara gave an involuntary gasp of discomfort. 'I'll plough your furrow for you.'

Silently he got to his feet and eased himself, with difficulty, in front of Mara so that he was facing her with his back to the seat in front. His filthy, evil-smelling body loomed over her like some malodorous demon and, in a moment of utter horror, Mara realised what he was going to do to her.

Still clutching Heimdal's prick, Mara felt the tramp's hand on the back of her head, forcing her forwards so that her lips were almost brushing the front of his greasy trousers. Fumbling in his haste, the tramp unfastened his flies and out sprang a lively prick, hard and serviceable, but as filthy and unappetising as the rest of him. It was obvious what he intended her to do.

'Suck him off, Mara,' hissed Heimdal. She realised instinctively that it was a command.

Almost tearful with revulsion, Mara parted her lips a little and – before she had time to resist – felt the tramp's foul hardness enter her mouth. Nausea almost choked her but bravely she sucked at the filthy flesh, knowing that never again would she forget the terrible taste, the foulness of his smell.

He thrust into her greedily, and quickly defiled her throat with a tide of salty semen which he forced her to swallow. Then he withdrew and Mara thought he would leave her alone. But instead he returned to the contemplation of her cunt, sinking back onto his seat and thrusting grimy fingers up into her most intimate parts.

To her shame, his rough caresses awakened her lust, and she began to wank Heimdal harder and harder as she felt her own orgasm approaching.

The warm tide of Heimdal's spunk, gushing out all over her fingers, sparked off her climax, sending her cunt into spasms of guilty pleasure which sent her juices cascading all over the tramp's filthy fingers.

Her stifled moans of desire must have disturbed the row of workmen in front, for they left off gazing at the naked nun who was sucking off a supremely well-endowed priest in a confessional, and turned round, craning their heads to see what was going on behind them.

They were delighted by the scene which met their eyes: a slender, pretty young woman, her gorgeous fat tits bursting out of her blouse, was being masturbated by a filthy tramp, whilst some blond guy in tight leather trousers was creaming himself all over her hand.

'Well, well, well,' remarked one of the workmen. 'So this is a live sex show, is it? Can we all join in?'

Mara's head reeled. What was happening to her? Why were the three men getting up out of their seats and coming towards her? What were they going to do to her? She stared at them, wide-eyed with terror, too bewildered to cry out.

Silently, without any of the other cinemagoers noticing, the three men dragged Mara out of her seat and into the cramped space behind the back row, where – in times gone by – the usherettes would have stood to watch the show. In their place, Heimdal sat and watched, wanking himself gently and making a magical sign with the fingers of his left hand. The crystal ring encircling the base of his shaft seemed to glow a delicate phosphorescent green.

A hand was clamped firmly over Mara's mouth and she could hardly breathe, let alone cry out. Dark shapes were looming over her as she lay on the sloping floor, the lusty nuns still disporting themselves on the massive cinema screen in front of her. She tried to struggle, but it was no use. The first of the workmen had already unzipped his overalls and was lying on top of her, his colleagues holding her legs apart so that he could enter her without difficulty.

They fucked her in turn, as though she were an inflatable doll, her juicy orifices just there for the taking. And on more than one occasion, to her immense humiliation, they succeeded in bringing her to orgasm.

As the last of the workmen poured his seed into her cunt, Heimdal stood over her and let his semen spurt out in giant gobbets, all over her face.

As the last droplet of semen fell, the pictures on the screen changed dramatically and a howl of protest ran around the auditorium. The garish pictures of naked monks and nuns gave way to black and white footage of a tall man in a trilby, boarding an aeroplane. As he reached the top of the steps, he turned to wave to a small crowd of dignitaries below, and Mara saw his face.

'Andreas . . .!' she gasped, struggling to sit up.

A voice rose above the general hubbub of discontent:

'Mr Anthony LeMaitre, the new British Ambassador to Cairo, left today for Egypt . . .'

The scene faded. Mara blinked up at the screen, where once again the two nuns were taking it in turns to fuck with Father Abbot. The images were gone and yet the scene remained fresh and unmistakable in Mara's mind. That had been the body of Andreas Hunt – the eyes empty of Andreas's humour, true – but Andreas's body, nonetheless.

Mara struggled to her feet, abandoned now by the three workmen who had returned to their seats to watch the film. Heimdal helped her to button up her blouse.

'Cairo, then?'

Mara nodded. What other alternative could there be?

Mara packed her bags quickly and joined Heimdal at the airport. At least by travelling with him, she automatically rid herself of any lingering worries about money. Heimdal had enough to charter a whole squadron of aeroplanes.

As they got off the airport bus and prepared to climb the steps to the plane, Mara felt a sudden twinge of pain in her head, as though something – or someone – were stabbing a needle into her brain. She put her hand to her head and paused for a moment, but the pain did not return.

'Are you all right?' demanded Heimdal, taking her by the arm.

Mara nodded and began to climb the steps.

Once on the plane they sat together in the first-class cabin and Heimdal was more than usually attentive. Mara felt the pain again, so she closed her eyes to escape the noise and light.

The pain subsided to a dull ache and was replaced by the very distant sound of a voice in terrible torment. A voice she knew only too well.

'Mara! Mara! No, no, no! Danger! Can't you see? I'm *here* . . . come to me Mara . . .'

Mara listened intently, trying to decipher the meaning of what Andreas was trying to tell her. He was alive. He was afraid. That much she knew.

'I don't understand, Andreas,' she telepathed to him. 'Try to explain.'

One word only came in reply:

'Danger.'

'I know there's danger, Andreas. I'm being careful. Heimdal is helping me. I'll be all right, don't worry.'

'DANGER. Come back to me. Winterbourne.'

Mara sighed inwardly. If Andreas's soul really was trapped in the underworld and could only communicate with the outside world through Winterbourne, perhaps he didn't understand that she must find his body in order to free him.

'I'm doing this for you. For us. Coming back to Winterbourne won't help you.'

'Danger . . .'

The same word, repeated over and over again. Hysteria? Maybe. Andreas must be terrified in the dark world of lost souls and disembodied spirits. It was ironic, really, that he should be trapped by something he didn't even believe in. Or was he really trying to warn her of some danger she didn't even know of?

She tried to make a last attempt to contact Andreas, but the link was broken. His voice faded away into silence in her head, and she sat for a while, very still, wondering what to make of it all and what she ought to tell Heimdal.

A voice broke through into her thoughts.

'Are you OK, Mara? You're very quiet.'

She opened her eyes and looked into Heimdal's resolutely solicitous face.

'I'm fine,' she replied, with a little smile which belied her inner turmoil. She thought for a moment and then added: 'I've just got a bit of a headache.'

'Let me examine the talisman,' said Heimdal. 'It has been a long time since it was consecrated and empowered, and I'm worried that its power may need to be renewed and refreshed.'

Rather reluctantly, Mara allowed him to slip the crystal

talisman over her head. He turned it over and over in his hand, examining it minutely and intoning quiet words in an unfamiliar tongue. Finally, he held it like a pendulum, over a piece of paper, and watched as it revolved slowly until its tip pointed towards the black sector of the circle.

'Its power is almost spent,' he concluded. 'If it is to allow us both continued protection we must renew its power now. If we leave it any longer, it will be too late and the talisman will be useless.'

'But how do we renew it?'

'Through sexual energy, as before. We must have sex.'

Mara looked at him, aghast.

'What – here, on this plane?'

Heimdal patted her hand reassuringly. He really was enjoying playing the benevolent uncle to her gullible child.

'It's a matter of life and death, my dear Mara. Yours, Andreas's . . .'

But not mine, he thought, with a warm glow of satisfaction. Death is an unknown country to the Master's blessed disciples.

'Yes, yes, I'll do anything,' replied Mara, realising the seriousness of the situation. 'Just tell me what to do.'

The pain of sight was almost more acute than the pain of utter darkness.

Since the moment when he had shot the security guard and watched Mara run away from him, perhaps lost for ever, Andreas had felt a gradual change come over him. It was almost as though the taking of that one, unremarkable life had returned to him a little of his own . . . or someone else's. He didn't like to think about it too much. There are some people whose lives you'd rather not have a bit of, however small.

Andreas thought back over the transformation. It puzzled him, and he didn't like that. Things he didn't understand always freaked him out – that was what Mara always said. He tried to think about it logically.

Gradually, over hours or days – it was difficult to tell, for in his dark prison he had little sense of time passing – Andreas had felt the power of certain extraordinary senses being absorbed into him, like water trickled slyly into a pile of sand.

The periods of bodily possession were growing longer. The dark man with the lame leg – Delgado, they called him – seemed to be a particularly good subject. His unpleasant little mind simply opened like a flower to Andreas's more substantial soul, and he had found himself returning to that same body, again and again.

Even whilst he was trapped and helpless within his crystal prison, Andreas found that he was beginning to acquire strange powers – perhaps powers that were inherent in the prison itself, or which he had inherited from . . . whom, exactly? A . . . former occupant?

From time to time, he would find himself floating, disembodied, in the cellars at Winterbourne – able to see and hear and smell even though he had no physical existence. It was the oddest feeling and not particularly pleasant at that.

He had looked down many times upon the dusty granite lid of the sarcophagus, knowing it to be the place of his imprisonment, and wondering with a kind of dark fascination what he would find if he were able to see through the unyielding stone. And then one time he had looked at the bricked-up wall of the cellar and to his astonishment it had begun to liquefy, to swirl and flow and clarify like butter in a pan. Good God, it was impossible! He could see through to the other side!

This weird experience – or was it just an illusion? – had lasted only moments; but something within told him that he might be able to develop the power, perhaps use it one day to escape . . .

And then there was the gift of sight.

The gift? Andreas wished he could manage a hollow laugh. It was a curse, no more and no less, to be able to see what Mara was doing, and to know that she was being led horribly astray. He knew now that his own body had been stolen from him by the one they called the Master; and in fleeting astral journeys he had seen Mara move ever-closer to a confrontation with the Master himself.

He did not quite understand why the Master wished to lure Mara to Egypt but once a journalist, always a journalist. He had a nose for danger. Andreas had the inescapable feeling that Mara was being lured to her doom.

He had spoken to her and she had heard him. He was sure of it. So why wouldn't she listen?

There was something phony about that man Heimdal. Something horribly cold and unfeeling and insincere. And now she was fucking with him again – fucking because of cruel lies and deceptions.

Helpless but horribly aware, Andreas lay locked within the cold embrace of the Master's discarded body, forced to watch Mara move ever-closer to the centre of the Master's evil web.

At the back of the first-class section, opposite two mercifully empty seats, Mara and Heimdal were fucking.

Mara hardly dared move, for fear that someone would realise what they were doing. She was astride Heimdal's lap, his prick disappearing into her cunt, its tip nudging against the crystal talisman which Heimdal had carefully lodged against the neck of her womb. She was grateful for the long skirts of her dress, which fell in discreet folds about their legs – but there would surely be no doubt of what they were up to if anyone should happen to pass.

'Any drinks?' asked the stewardess, walking towards them down the central gangway.

'Oh God!' gasped Mara. 'Let me get off – she'll see us!'

'It's all right – don't panic, Mara.' Heimdal held her fast on his lap and called out to the stewardess, who was only a few seats away now, 'Nothing for us, thanks – my girlfriend's not feeling too well. Could you leave us quietly for a little while?'

'Is there anything I can do to help?' The stewardess frowned solicitously.

'No, no. She'll be fine. I know just what to do to relieve her pain,' replied Heimdal, pinching Mara's nipples so hard that she gave an involuntary gasp of discomfort.

Mara's heart pounded as the stewardess at last made her way back up the aisle with her jingling trolley of drinks.

They fucked very slowly, very carefully. The hard edges of the talisman cut into the soft flesh of Mara's cunt, and tears escaped from underneath her closed eyelids and ran silently down her cheeks. She dared not cry out.

And yet her pain was also pleasure. For Heimdal's finger was on her clitoris and his hardness filled her, stretched her, excited her in ways unimaginable to anyone who has not fucked in the face of danger.

Heimdal rubbed Mara's clitty and pinched her nipple between fingertip and thumb, knowing that it must cost her dear not to make a sound. Feeling her cunt quivering with the first spasms of her pleasure, he allowed the anticipation of his own climax to swell his balls and stiffen his shaft. He poured his frothing semen into her with a satisfied grunt, his arms tightly clasped underneath her to stop her falling forwards in her moment of passion.

Moments later, when they were sitting side by side in their seats once again, zipped and buttoned and apparently quite respectable, the stewardess returned.

'Everything all right now, sir? Madam?'

'Oh yes,' replied Heimdal with a satisfied grin, casting a quick glance across at Mara who was sitting with eyes closed beside him. 'Everything is going to be just fine now.'

17: Luxor

They awoke to the shrill cries of street-vendors and the warmth of the early-morning sunlight filtering in through the shutters. Cairo awoke early.

Mara opened her eyes and blinked, forgetting for a moment where she was. Egypt. Egypt? She glanced around her. It didn't look much like Egypt. The room was disappointingly Western, with all the usual five-star luxuries – the television set and the complimentary shower-gel. But Heimdal hated slumming it now that he'd made it to the big time.

They showered, ate breakfast and took a taxi to the Egyptian Museum. It felt more like a holiday than a life-or-death quest.

They spent the morning mingling with a party of embarrassingly enthusiastic Americans and gazing dutifully at the treasures of Tutankhamun, then went back for lunch at the hotel. Heimdal kept frustratingly quiet and in the end Mara could stand it no longer:

'Heimdal, we've got to do something, and we've got to do it soon. How are we going to find Andreas – or should I call him Anthony LeMaitre now? Do we just turn up at the British Embassy and ask to see him?'

Heimdal shook his head and smiled, a little patronisingly, thought Mara.

'Not much point in doing that,' he replied. 'At best, we'd get to see some underling and that would be it – we'd get no further. Even my name has little influence here. No, my dear, tonight you're going to have dinner with the cultural attaché.'

Mara gaped at him, and he patted her hand reassuringly.

'It's all arranged, don't you worry. By a great stroke of good fortune, it appears that the cultural attaché is something of a connoisseur when it comes to beautiful women. He is also a rather influential man. If he arranges a meeting for us with Mr LeMaitre, the Ambassador is unlikely to question his judgement.

'I have arranged for you to meet him at eight o'clock this evening, at the Ramses Hilton. I understand from my sources that he has rather . . . specialised tastes, whatever that's supposed to mean. Well, whatever it is that he's into, I'm sure you can handle it, can't you, Mara?'

He stroked Mara's cheek and she felt the cold chill of his gaze enter her soul, like a creeping paralysis.

'Conquer the slave, my darling Mara, and you are sure to conquer his master.'

Mara waited in the foyer of the hotel, nervously smoothing the folds of her dress. She'd made sure she looked her best. She seldom wore make-up but tonight she'd applied glossy crimson lipstick to her full lips. It made her feel like an upper-class tart . . . but then again, wasn't that what she was supposed to be tonight?

That afternoon, Heimdal had taken her to a designer store and bought her the dress – a daringly low-cut gown in emerald-green raw silk which clung to her curves and emphasised the swell of her magnificent breasts. Her mane of black hair was piled high, with little tendrils left free to straggle carelessly across her tanned shoulders. She felt out of place, unwillingly moulded into something that she was not: a custom-built vamp.

She found herself wondering which of the tuxedo-clad men coming out of the lift would turn out to be the Honourable Tony Wentworth, Cultural Attaché at the British Embassy in Cairo. He was sure to be a grotesque old roué.

The group of men moved past her without pausing, though several of them cast appreciative glances in Mara's direction – mentally undressing her, wondering what it would be like to run their parched tongues over her juicy breasts, down over her belly and in between her thighs.

A fountain played in the centre of the foyer, small golden fishes flitting to and fro in the bubbling depths: a touch of purest kitch in this sanitised Western oasis. Mara looked away and out into the cool of the night, watching small boats glide past in the royal-blue dusk, their lights twinkling in the dark waters.

A voice jolted her back to reality.

'Miss Fleming?'

She looked up, instinctively raising her hand to her throat, checking that the talisman was still there.

'Mara Fleming, yes.'

'Tony Wentworth. Delighted to meet you. Shall we go in to dinner?'

He was a middle-aged man, perfectly respectable as far as Mara could tell and not the least bit odd in appearance. About forty-five, dark-haired, with touches of distinguished grey at the temples. Not ugly – in fact, quite nice-looking. Medium height, slim waist, nice tight backside. Mara quite fancied him already, in spite of her misgivings. Perhaps Heimdal had exaggerated, out of malice. Perhaps he had just got hold of the wrong end of the stick.

She followed Tony into the restaurant, where half a dozen grinning waiters fought to outdo each other in ingratiating politeness. He shunned a table by the window, opting instead for one of the booths in the corner furthest from the door. The booth was partitioned off from most of the restaurant and only dimly lit by a single wall-lamp. Perhaps that alone ought to have alerted her.

The food was good if stereotypically European and Wentworth was an interesting conversationalist. Mara began to relax a little, forgetting for a while what she had been brought here to do. It wasn't until she felt his foot exploring the inside of her thigh that she remembered that she was here as his whore. Only, instead of money, she was going to be paid in something far more valuable: information.

She glanced up at him and saw that he was smiling, but cruelly now, like a cat who has caught a mouse and intends to play with it thoroughly before killing it.

He leaned forward across the table and slid a finger down her cleavage.

'Take off your dress.'

Mara stared at him, incredulous.

'I . . . what did you say?'

'I said, take off your dress, sweetheart. Pull down the top. I want to see your tits.'

'Someone – a waiter – might see . . . !'

He grinned broadly.

'Yes, indeed they might. Don't you think that adds a little spice to the game, Miss Fleming? Now, be a good girl and do as I say. I'm getting a little bored with your conversation, fascinating though it is.'

Trembling with apprehension, Mara slipped the straps of her dress down over her shoulders, wriggled her arms out of them, and took hold of the embroidered silk top of her green evening dress.

'Do it.'

She could refuse. She could get up from this table and walk out, go back to the hotel, tell Heimdal she couldn't go through with it. But there was something about Heimdal that frightened her, something she was sure hadn't been there before. All the genuine softness and understanding had gone out of him, replaced by a phony attentiveness which frankly made her flesh creep. If she refused him this, maybe he'd refuse to help her any more. He might abandon her here in this strange country, without money or other resources save her body. Besides which, she had left the Phallus with him at the hotel. What if he took his revenge now by leaving with it, hiding it from her?

She tugged at the silk bodice and it slid down with a whisper of silk, leaving her naked to the waist, her breasts thrusting free. The muted lamplight played on her flesh like a lover's caress and Tony Wentworth settled himself back in his seat to watch.

'What . . . what do you want me to do now?'

'Well, let me see . . . Have you ever heard of body piercing?'

Mara stared back at him, sick at heart, unable to speak for fear of what he would say to her, what he would make her do to herself.

'You haven't? I hear it's very popular. Young ladies like yourself tell me that they so enjoy having their flesh pierced. Would you enjoy that, Miss Fleming? I must confess that the idea quite excites me. And a little bird tells me that you have already taken the first steps towards experiencing this delightful art-form.'

Mara stared at him, wondering how he could have found out about that night on the hillside in Budapest, when the gypsy king's wife had pierced her clitoris. It was obvious, of course. Only Heimdal could have told him.

The memory of the pain was still fresh in her mind, even now: the terrible intensity of the burning as the sharp golden wire pierced her tenderest flesh. She wouldn't let him lay hands on her . . . not on that most intimate and sensitive and precious part of her womanhood! No – not on any part of her!

'Now, now, don't fret, my dear. I'm not going to pierce your clitty for you again. Well, not yet, anyway. The night is yet young. Let's start with something a little less difficult, shall we? How about your nipples? You'd like that, wouldn't you? A little golden thread through your nipples that you could play with? Just think of the wonderful sensations you'd feel.'

Mara sat in speechless misery as Wentworth reached inside his waistcoat pocket and took out a thick, pointed darning needle, threaded with fine gold wire.

He placed it in the palm of Mara's outstretched hand, and she sat staring at it for several minutes.

Tony leaned across the table again and hissed:

'You'd better get on with it, my dear. The waiter will be here any moment with the dessert.'

As she still did not move, he continued.

'Do it now, Miss Fleming. Push the needle through your right nipple.'

Terrified, she pressed the tip of the needle against the sensitive flesh of her nipple. A sharp pain shot through her and she hesitated.

'Push it in; right through the flesh, from side to side. I want to hear you describe every sensation as you pierce your flesh.'

Mara obeyed, tears welling up and spilling down her cheeks as the sharp point burrowed into her flesh and she clenched her teeth to stifle her cries of anguish. She pushed it in, slowly and inexorably.

'Speak,' commanded Wentworth. She saw his arm moving and realised what he was doing. He was unzipping his flies and wanking himself off under the table. 'I want to hear your pain, feel your pain, share the pleasure of your pain.'

'It . . . it is like a terrible burning,' gasped Mara. 'As though a burning dagger were piercing my flesh, not just the flesh of my breast but the whole of my being. I can feel the pain everywhere – in my breasts, my belly, my thighs, my cunt . . .'

She gasped, unable to speak any more, as the needle emerged from her flesh and she drew it through, pulling the golden wire behind it. A little trickle of blood was winding down her breast, like a crimson thread, matching exactly the colour of her lipstick.

'Good, good,' sighed Wentworth, evidently much excited. 'Now I want you to tie the gold wire into a little ring and manipulate it – tell me what that feels like.'

Mara removed the needle and formed the golden wire into a ring, as he had instructed. Already, the burning of her pain was beginning to turn into a very different warmth. Wentworth was smiling, knowingly now.

'It feels . . . like the whole of my body is on fire, with such a delicious warmth.'

'Lift up your skirt and spread your legs,' instructed Wentworth.

She reached down under the table and pulled her skirts well up onto her thighs.

Immediately, she felt a bare foot climbing her leg again, and remembered that time in the library – it seemed so very long ago now, like a scene from another world and time – when she had masturbated Andreas with her foot and he had pulled her, laughing, onto the polished wooden floor, where they had fucked like guilty children, terrified of discovery and yet stimulated by that very terror.

She was terrified now, too. And excited, beyond belief.

The foot was between her thighs now, exploring her cunt-lips and forcing its way between them. She was wet and he slipped into her easily, his big toe finding her clitoris and skilfully rubbing the tiny gold ring which still pierced it.

Footsteps sounded behind them. The waiter was returning, with their dessert. Wentworth smiled at Mara's confusion, offering no words of encouragement. Still he was wanking her, teasing her into paroxysms of desire.

There was no time to pull up the bodice of her dress. She seized the white velvet stole she had worn when she arrived, and wrapped it hurriedly around her shoulders, hiding her martyred breast. But she could not quite so easily conceal her unwilling excitement, unable to escape from the power of the all-conquering, despotic foot.

The waiter noticed Mara's halting breath and tear-stained cheeks.

'Is Madam unwell?' he enquired, solicitously.

Wentworth made no attempt to bail her out, so Mara replied, rather jerkily:

'Madam is quite well, thank you. Please leave us.'

The waiter set down the dishes and went off again, no doubt puzzled by the sight of a tearful white woman, clutching a bloodstained white wrap to her bosom.

Wentworth brought himself off with a low grunt of satisfaction and, in their silent corner, Mara heard the quiet splash of his semen onto the tiled floor. A few seconds later, she felt her own orgasm approaching, and sank back into her seat with a sob of guilty ecstasy.

Afterwards, Wentworth allowed her to dress and took her to his room. There, in the darkness, he stripped her and tied her to the bed with leather straps. To her surprise, he did not fuck her but summoned the boy who cleaned the shoes.

He arrived, an unprepossessing sixteen-year-old clad in the hotel's dark-red livery.

'I wish you to fuck this Englishwoman,' Wentworth instructed him. 'There is money in it for you if you do well. And you need not show her any undue gentleness. I wish to derive pleasure from the spectacle.'

The youth grinned. He had evidently carried out Wentworth's commissions in the past and was accustomed to his unusual tastes. Without further ado, he took off his belt and used it vigorously on Mara's defenceless body, raising red welts on her tanned flesh.

Wentworth settled himself in an armchair, took out his penis and began to masturbate as the Arab boy laid down the strap and took off his trousers and pants in readiness for his conquest.

He fucked clumsily and Mara winced as he forced himself into her, like some over-eager young animal moved only by the thought of his own pleasure. But he fucked with self-restraint and did not allow himself to come until he was certain that his master had derived full enjoyment from the spectacle.

Afterwards Wentworth fucked the boy, clearly deriving even greater pleasure from the tightness of the lad's arse than he had done from the contemplation of Mara's humiliation and discomfort.

When it was all over, he cut through the straps which held Mara to the bed and gave a humourless smile.

'Women in general displease me – all but the most alluring and the most lascivious. You have not displeased me. Heimdal spoke the truth when he told me of your beauty and your enjoyment of unusual pleasures. I shall therefore give you the information you seek.

'LeMaitre is no longer in Cairo. He has gone on a journey to Luxor, to view the ancient ruins of the Theban necropolis as a guest of the Egyptian government. The day after tomorrow, he will be visiting recent discoveries in the Valley of the Kings. If you seek LeMaitre, you must seek him there.'

Luxor was a disappointment to Mara: jammed full of tourists and ugly hotels, and hardly in tune with her idea of a noble and ancient civilisation.

The letters of introduction which Wentworth had given them got them through the security cordon, but they arrived at the hotel too late: the official party had already left for the mortuary temple of King Seti I, a couple of hours earlier. They must make their own way to the Valley.

The notorious 'people ferry' across the Nile was crowded, not just with people but with chickens, boxes of dates and even the odd goat. Heimdal complained incessantly all the way across and even Mara was feeling disgruntled by the time they reached the other side.

Because of their official documents they were spared the traditional tourist ordeal of queuing to buy tickets at the kiosk. But nothing could spare them the horrors of haggling with the car-drivers and donkey-boys who pestered them from the moment they stepped off the ferry.

'I'm not travelling on a donkey,' thundered Heimdal. 'And neither are you. Let's find someone with a decent car.'

Unfortunately, the best the locals could manage was a battered saloon of indeterminate age and make, though Heimdal did manage to negotiate a very fair price. Crammed into the back, they lurched from side to side as the driver wove his merry but uncertain way along the road, swerving at regular intervals to avoid small boys, livestock and cars moving towards them, equally erratically, from the opposite direction.

It didn't take long to reach the Temple of Seti but again they were too late. According to a group of American tourists, the official party had moved off for the Valley of the Kings about half an hour previously.

A few miles further on, they hit the burning white

expanses of the Valley of the Kings: a steep and completely barren valley, with innumerable royal tombs cut into the limestone hillside, their numbered doorways like neat puncture-wounds in the flanks of a mummified carcass. A line of gleaming-black official limousines reflected the morning sun off well-burnished chrome.

Their driver parked near the rest-house, and they paused gratefully for a drink of water before paying him half his fee and telling him to wait for them.

They set off up the valley, having discovered that the official party were being given a tour of the tomb which had recently been discovered at the very far end, halfway up the steep rock face, between the tomb of Tuthmosis III and two other, unfinished tombs.

As they reached the far end of the rising valley, they saw what they were looking for: a flight of rickety wooden steps covered with an impromptu scrap of tatty red carpet leading up to the sightless eye of a recently opened tomb, about halfway up the hillside. Two armed guards stood outside the entrance, their sub-machine guns slung across their arms in readiness for any attempt on the lives of the Prime Minister and his aides, who were talking in a group to one side of the tomb entrance.

Mara and Heimdal showed their passes and were saluted respectfully.

'Where is Mr LeMaitre?' asked Mara. 'We have an important message for him.'

'Mr LeMaitre and his personal assistants have gone back into the tomb, to take a closer look at the very fine wall-paintings,' replied the guard. 'You will probably find him in the furthest chamber, the Pharaoh's burial vault.'

He handed Heimdal an electric torch and they stepped gingerly into the gloom.

'Be careful,' remarked the guard. 'It is very dark, and you might have an accident.'

The entrance led into a narrow passage, unlit except for one or two very temporary inspection lamps slung from pins knocked into the ceiling. The roof was low and even

Mara had to stoop to pick her way along the rubble-strewn passageway. Evidently this was a very recent discovery indeed and few tourists had as yet passed this way.

Mara glanced at the paintings as she passed: white stars on a dark-blue background; pots of green papyrus; Pharaoh in his sailing-barge, gliding down the river that led through the underworld; Isis and Osiris, fucking together on the banks of the Nile. The Eye of Horus glared down upon her from the ceiling, as though keeping a special watch on her.

She heard voices – at first faint, but then gradually getting closer.

'We're catching up on them,' she whispered. 'I must hurry.'

Nervously, she patted the canvas bag slung over her shoulder, in which the Phallus lay, safe in its box. What would she do when she finally came face to face with the body of Andreas Hunt, under the sway of this new and very powerful persona? Would she have the courage and the strength and the instinct to use the Phallus on him, to cast out the usurper and return Andreas's soul to his body?

She cast the thought from her mind, aware that she must act first and think later.

They carried on down the corner, Heimdal leading the way with the torch as they crossed a rickety footbridge over a sheer forty-foot drop to a pit below.

'Glad you're not a tomb robber?' whispered Heimdal as they reached the other side and looked down into the vertiginous ravine.

The corridor took a sharp bend to the left and led down a flight of stairs into an antechamber. At that moment, a figure emerged into the antechamber through an arch at the side of the room. A tall, rather thin, blond figure like a half-grown labrador puppy. Luckily, she recognised him before he noticed her.

'Oh my God – it's Geoffrey Potter! What's he doing here?' Mara took a step backwards in her panic. There was something not quite right here. Something very much not right. Twice she had shaken off Geoffrey and twice he had reappeared, with that same amiable and yet slightly malicious smile. And then there was the incident with the white deer.

I've got to get out of here, thought Mara, turning to flee. It was stupid, she knew that; but she knew something terrible would happen if she came face to face with him again. He'd changed and the change wasn't for the better. He would do something to prevent her rescuing Andreas.

She dodged back into the shadows and Heimdal followed her, grabbing her arm and forcing her to look at him.

'What's the matter?' he demanded.

'Quiet!' she beseeched him. 'There's someone out there – someone I mustn't meet. I think he might be dangerous to us. We've got to find somewhere to hide until he goes away.'

They couldn't easily go back the way they'd come without crossing Geoffrey's line of sight – besides which, Mara was afraid of falling if she tried to hurry back across the narrow footbridge.

She looked around desperately for some other place to hide and as she slid along the wall of the chamber, in the shadows, she stepped into an alcove.

It was a short side-passage – a dead end, perhaps fifteen yards long, curving to the right and ending in a rough rock face. Mara slipped inside, out of sight of Geoffrey, and Heimdal followed her.

'Look – a door. We can go through there.' She pointed to an archway on the left side of the passageway, dark and forbidding but offering some prospect of a better hiding-place.

'What doorway? There's no doorway there – just a blank wall! Have you had a touch of the sun or something?' Heimdal shone his torch on the wall, revealing nothing but smooth limestone, marked here and there by the workmen's chisels and axes.

Mara reached out and touched the wall. He was right. The place was solid, cold, smooth, just like all the rock around it. But she could still see the outline of the doorway with perfect clarity: a square arch, with hieroglyphics painted in red above the lintel, and leading through into an utter blackness which the torch-beam could not penetrate.

'I can see a door,' she replied, her voice trembling. 'There *is* a door.'

She heard a voice in her head – Andreas's voice, very far away now – crying 'No, no, no, no!' over and over again.

But another voice, smooth and seductive and far more powerful, whispered softly in her head, stifling Andreas's cries and pushing all thoughts of him far, far back into the deep, airless darkness.

'The Phallus, Mara. Use it now . . .'

Half-instinctively, her own will suddenly drained from her like blood pumping from a severed artery, Mara reached into the canvas bag and took the Phallus from its box. It was warm and lively in her hands, pulsating like living flesh and yet glowing with the same bright green fire that had wrought such destruction at Burzenheim.

The world around them, the world beyond that tiny passageway, fears of pursuit: all faded away as Mara held the Phallus of Osiris in her trembling hands and watched the lightning fork from it, engulfing all – herself, Heimdal, the corridor – in a blinding green light.

When the light faded, Heimdal and Mara found themselves looking through a square arch into a cold chamber. In the centre stood a small stone altar, on which burned a sodium-yellow flame.

A flame that had burned alone in the darkness for four thousand years.

Slowly, Mara walked into the chamber, Heimdal following close behind.

The walls were decorated with paintings, as bright and perfect as they had been on the day the artist finished them. The first showed a young woman and a tall young man in priest's robes, fucking before the altar of a temple. Another painting showed the priestess fucking a naked man, blood oozing from his throat where her teeth had pierced it. In the next scene, the woman was shown being captured and tortured by a dozen priests, who were stripping and violating her as she lay on a stone slab. And the final scene depicted her tightly wrapped body, being lowered into a coffin.

Mara's mind reeled, overcome by the memory of the recurring dream she had had, those months ago before Andreas's disappearance. The dream of a young woman, violated and buried alive in a room just like this one.

And, propped up against the far wall of the room, stood an ornate wooden coffin. On its lid, it bore the portrait of a young woman.

A young woman who bore a striking resemblance to Mara Fleming.

Mara stood in stunned silence, lost in the contemplation of this other self from four thousand years before. This young woman who had been buried alive and in terror, in punishment for some crime which Mara could not even begin to understand.

A voice behind her made her turn round suddenly. The smooth, seductive tones froze her blood and the Phallus fell from her hands, rolling away across the floor.

'Hello, Mara,' said the voice she knew only too well – the voice of all her sufferings and torment. There was a universe of hatred in that voice. 'I've so been looking forward to meeting you again. Don't you remember me? I'm the Master.'

She gazed into the cruel, unsmiling face that had once been Andreas Hunt's, and sank to the floor, merciful unconsciousness veiling the spectacle of victorious evil.

18: Renewal

'Run, Mara, run!'

Andreas's silent screams of anguish filled earth and heaven, the spiritual expression of his impotent rage and fear. He yearned for physical power to scream and destroy and run and run and keep on running, until at last he could reach Mara and drag her away from the danger.

But he was powerless to help her.

The gift of sight, the curse of awareness, had brought the knowledge of danger to him; and he had watched, unable to turn away or close his eyes, as Mara walked as meekly as a lamb to her own slaughter.

He understood now. The truth imprinted itself on his brain with horrible clarity. He wondered why he hadn't realised it before. The Master was going to force him to watch the death of Mara Fleming. Andreas's torment would be sure to bring him the most immense pleasure. Yes, that must be it. He had robbed Andreas of his body and now he was going to rob Mara of her life.

Andreas screamed, and his soundless anguish filled the brooding skies over Winterbourne with heavy storm-clouds. Nearby, a dog howled its discomfiture, and others joined with it: a modern-day wolfpack, baying at the moon.

All nature, all life, felt the force of Andreas Hunt's rage. Thunder built up in the darkened skies, a thunderous heaviness that made Delgado's head ache as though it were about to split open. He rubbed his temples and glanced out of the window into the apocalyptic darkness, sensing the storm closing in on Winterbourne. A sickly moon had cast its pallid light over the black clouds. A dull flash and a distant rumble signalled the beginning of the storm.

Puzzled by such unseasonal weather, Delgado loosened his collar. It was winter, and yet there was a sulphurous heat in the room, a stifling sensation that dried the throat and constricted the windpipe.

He took a quick drink of water, and got up from the Master's favourite leather armchair. He must get a grip on himself. He turned to look at the sleeping girl slumped on the settee, her legs still splayed obscenely wide and all her juicy treasures on display. It had taken him only a few days to turn prim little Alexandra into an accomplished whore. A trail of semen had spilled out of her, soiling the costly leather. He made a mental note to get it cleaned up before the Master's return.

Mustn't let the Master think he'd been abusing the power he'd delegated to him during his absence.

A wave of terrible anger and pain washed over him and he clenched his fist in frustration. A chance to serve, that's all he was asking. A chance to serve his Master's sublime evil throughout eternity. A chance to vanquish death, as he and so many others had done. Was that so much to ask in return for his loyalty, the gift of his life?

He opened the desk drawer and took out the crystal ring. No one knew it was there, save the Master and Delgado. And Delgado would not have known, if he hadn't seen the Master putting it in there shortly after the ceremony which had brought him into his new body.

He picked up the ring and caressed it. It was cool, smooth, and yet full of inner fire. He knew that the ring had something to do with the gift of eternal life-in-death. If he wore it and fucked one of the undead whores – say the ice-maiden Joanna Konigsberg, or impressionable little Alexandra – mightn't its power persuade her to bestow upon him the Kiss of Death?

And once he was in the ranks of the undead, once he had shown such initiative, the Master would recognise that he had been wrong to deprive him of the discipleship which was his by right.

The Master would not punish him. He was sure of it.

Andreas raged in his silent torment, and the latent power within him burst to the surface in the only way it could, sending out shock-waves into the threatening, black skies. Lightning forked to earth suddenly, lighting up the sky and the skeletal arms of the trees surrounding Winterbourne Hall. Delgado drew the curtains, slipped the ring onto his finger, and went out of the room.

'My darling, my own and only queen, my princess, my Sedet . . .'

Mara opened her eyes, still dizzy and sick from the faint. The voice was soft and smooth and exquisite, filling the room with a silken web of whispering evil.

She tried to get up, but could not. Struggling, she realised that her wrists had been attached to two iron rings set into the tomb wall, at about waist height. A dark-haired woman was gazing at her, her lips curled in a pitying half-smile.

Wait. She had seen that face before. A picture . . . Recognition dawned. One of Andreas's photographs – some society girl he'd been trying to trace. Ann . . . Anastasia, that was it. Anastasia Dubois. Very dark, very beautiful, with scarlet-painted lips that reminded Mara of the bright wetness of fresh blood.

And beside her, a tall, fair-haired man with blue eyes.

'Geoffrey . . .!'

'Silence!' He spat out the words, and slapped her across the cheek so hard that her eyes watered. She hardly recognised him as the innocent youth who had befriended her, only weeks ago.

The Master was kneeling, caressing the naked body of a dark-haired young woman, which lay amid the discarded wrappings of a mummy. And yet, this was no mummified corpse, brittle and dry as dust. The flesh was perfect yet pallid, strangely bloodless, and the woman lay lifeless as a wax doll on the hard stone floor.

'Sedet, my queen; soon your loyalty shall be repaid, and you shall reign once more by my side. Patience, my queen, and I shall bring you back from the wastes of death into your own glorious inheritance . . .'

Mara watched in blank incomprehension as the Master picked up the Phallus of Osiris. He held it aloft for a moment, and Mara saw it glowing in the half-light.

The Master then turned to Heimdal and offered him the Phallus.

'You have done well, my son. You have outwitted the white witch and brought this priceless treasure to me at last. Yours shall be the honour of initiating the ceremony.'

He undressed, and Mara recalled with pain how often she had seen that same, naked body; how often she had caressed those large, firm balls and taken that hardened shaft into her mouth. The body of Andreas Hunt stood before her, transformed into an empty shell, inhabited by an evil heart, a cruel parody of the man who had so often fucked her until she screamed with pleasure.

The Master braced himself against the wall, his backside thrust out towards Heimdal. Heimdal stepped forward and pulled apart the Master's arse-cheeks, pressing the tip of the Phallus against his arse-hole.

The thick shaft of the Phallus disappeared into the Master. He gasped, clearly feeling pain as his flesh stretched to accommodate the intruder. Heimdal reached round in front of the Master and took hold of his stiffened shaft. He began to thrust it in and out, at first gently, but then gradually harder and faster, until at last the Master's semen spurted out onto the painted wall of the burial chamber.

The Master took the Phallus from Heimdal's hand and spoke once again. His voice seemed to come, not from the lips of Andreas's old body, but from the very depths of an ancient and evil soul:

'By the power of almighty Osiris, I shall end your imprisonment and bring you back to life!'

He took a knife from his belt and drew it across his wrist, letting the blood flow freely from the wound and over the shaft of the Phallus. Mara watched in amazement as the wound began to close and heal. Within seconds, all signs of its existence had been obliterated, and only the blood-stained Phallus remained to bear witness to its transient existence.

The Master knelt down beside his Queen and caressed her body with the Phallus, running its tip across her waxy flesh; touching nipples and lips and fingers and belly with the bloody shaft.

Gently, the Master pulled the young woman's legs apart to reveal the surprising pinkness of her cunt. It was as though all the life that remained within this frame had been distilled into her womanhood, as pink and moist as any living flesh.

As the tip of the Phallus nudged into Sedet's cunt, all life seemed to freeze within the burial chamber. Everything was enveloped in a bright green light; and Mara watched in terror as the scene was enacted in slow-motion before her eyes.

It was as though at that moment she, too, was an immortal, with no need to breathe, no need for the blood to pump through mortal veins. There was only the overwhelming compulsion to watch and the unbearable sensation of pleasure as Mara realised that, through the strength of her own psychic powers, she too could feel the power of the Phallus thrusting into her . . .

The Master was fucking his Queen: fucking her with the mighty Phallus of Osiris, the Phallus that had, even after death, impregnated the goddess Isis and brought forth the sun-god Horus. The Phallus, which generations of sorcerers and savants had sought to find for their own ends, had at last been found, and its mighty powers were being harnessed to the ultimate evil.

The Queen's cunt grew moister as the Phallus thrust into her again and again; and Mara realised that the woman's flesh was growing less waxen, as the warmth of blood brought a rosy tinge to her limbs and belly.

The Master slid his finger between Sedet's cunt-lips and began to toy with her clitoris, rubbing rhythmically in time with the thrusts of the mummified penis.

And something miraculous and terrifying happened.

As Mara watched, the Queen's body began to move and a low moaning seemed to issue forth from her lips. At first the sounds were incoherent but then they began to resolve themselves into words:

'Master . . . my Master . . . you have come to me at last . . . How I long for you to fuck me . . . Master . . .'

The Master withdrew the Phallus from the Queen's cunt, and the waxen doll was transformed into the living, breathing body of a young woman with long, dark hair and violet eyes. A woman who bore more than a passing resemblance to Mara Fleming.

Mara gasped in horrified fascination as the woman got to her feet, at first unsteadily, but then more confidently. She was fine-boned, full-breasted, her fertile thighs dripping mingled blood and cunt-juice. She reached out her slender hands, red-tipped like talons.

'Master . . .!'

But as their fingertips touched, the Queen gave a terrible screech of fear and pain. Her body began to tremble and she tried to clutch at the Master's arm for support, but her hand passed straight through him as though he were a ghost.

Grey appeared in her hair. Her skin began to grow flaccid and lined. The Queen was ageing fast. Decades, centuries, millennia flooded in on her, tearing her apart, desiccating her flesh, snapping her bones with a hideous cracking.

And as Mara watched, the Queen's body crumpled up like a paper bag and fell to the ground, where within seconds it had dried away almost to nothingness, leaving behind it nothing but a small pile of dust and bone fragments.

'No!' screamed the Master. 'I will not be cheated a second time!'

He paused for a moment, deep in anguished thought;

then picked up the Phallus and, with a horrible, thin-lipped smile, advanced towards Mara.

Delgado stroked Geena's hair. She really was a most impressive young woman – a tangle of glossy dark-brown hair, smooth olive skin and dramatic, emerald-green eyes. She reminded him of a very beautiful, very dangerous jungle cat.

The large Victorian conservatory at Winterbourne had been an excellent choice for a jungle scene. Delgado himself had supervised its installation and fitting-out: a controlled heating-system, to produce just the right amount of hot steaminess; lots of lush vegetation and thick-stemmed vines hanging from a canopy of dense green foliage. Parrots and a gaudy bird of paradise flitted about in the branches, their cries adding that final touch of authenticity to Delgado's masterpiece.

It was hard to believe that, outside, a terrible storm was raging, though flashes of lightning occasionally lit up the interior of the conservatory.

Delgado stretched out on the soft green grass beside the sunken pool in which gaily coloured fish swam lazily back and forth in endless, joyful idleness. Beside him lay Geena, the leopard-skin she wore leaving one breast bare, its brown tip already puckered with desire.

He bent to kiss the little scars on her throat, with a reverence born of desperate, yearning ambition.

'Want to fuck me, little wildcat?'

She bared her teeth playfully and he noticed with approval how perfect and white and sharp they were.

She cut two lengths of strong creeper and bound his wrists to the pillars which Delgado had had transformed into jungle trees. His cock reared in joyful anticipation of one of Geena's savage little games; and the crystal ring sparkled enticingly on his finger. Would its power lure her to defy the Master's commands and bestow upon him the precious kiss of death?

The whip was made from strands of pliable hide plaited

together and studded with animal teeth to give it a deadlier sting. Delgado flinched as she swung it down upon him, unable to cry out for she had gagged him with a strip of leopard-skin, tied tight across his mouth.

She whipped his belly and his chest, carefully directing the lash so that it fell just short of his penis, its tip just gently stinging his balls. He rolled about in a delirium of pain and pleasure, fearing he would spunk off before she had even ridden him. How he longed to feel his semen jetting out and into the welcoming belly of this hot little jungle-cat.

He need not have worried; for as soon as she was satisfied with the welts she had raised on his skin, Geena pulled up her leopard-skin, revealing powerful thighs and a shaven pubis. Delgado was crazily excited by this sight of her bare cunt-lips, marking the shameless entrance to her palace of pleasure. If only his hands were free and he could reach out and thrust his fingers into that divine wetness . . .

She pulled apart her cunt-lips, the better to display to him the delights within. He groaned quietly as she gradually slid first one, then two fingers into her tight hole, stretching the flesh, showing him how difficult it would be to penetrate her, for she was so, so tight . . .

Grinning, she pulled back the little pink hood which hid her clitoris, and the hard button of flesh sprang into view, engorged with blood and eager for the fray. She began to sing to herself – some barbarous jungle song – whilst she rubbed on her clitoris; and Delgado moaned as he saw the juices collect at the entrance to her vagina and begin to trickle down her leg.

At last she took pity on him and straddled him with her powerful thighs. Taking the knife from her thigh-strap, she slit the gag and he began to babble nonsense, desperate to feel the silken warmth of her flesh around his.

She silenced him by bending forwards and thrusting her bare nipple into his mouth; and whilst he was thus occupied, she took the opportunity to seize his penis and guide it into her hole. It was a tight fit, but with one mighty thrust of her powerful hips she took him deep inside her.

The thunder outside the windows joined with him in a great roar of pleasure and the whole world seemed to tremble as Geena rode her captive to orgasm.

Delgado felt the sperm rising, and thrust harder with his hips to bring Geena off with him. As she fell forward in orgasm, she caught sight of the crystal ring and the light from its many facets seemed to hypnotise her.

'Do it, Geena!' cried Delgado. 'Bite into my throat, give me that one, last pleasure . . . Think of the exquisite taste of my warm blood, gushing into your mouth, gulping down your throat, trickling down your chin . . .'

She seemed to struggle for a moment, as though fighting back the urge. But the scent of fresh blood filled her mind and, with a ferocious growl, she bared her teeth.

Just as she bent to kiss his throat, a terrible flash of lightning struck the conservatory, shattering the glass and sending a gale-force wind swirling around, ripping the leaves from the plants, making the birds shriek with terror and flee for shelter.

The second fork of lightning hit home only feet away from the metal pillar to which Delgado was tied. Geena forgot her bloodlust and leapt back in alarm. Delgado tried to wriggle free, but to no avail.

'Cut the bonds, Geena! Cut me free, I command you!'

But Geena simply threw her head back and laughed, oblivious to the lightning fizzing and crackling around her.

As lightning struck the pillar, it seemed to Delgado that the entire world was pain – nothing more and nothing less. His last thoughts framed a curse – a curse on the greed that had brought him to this terrible fate – as the fireball flamed out from the crystal ring and engulfed him, consuming him and purifying him of all his unclean desires.

Rain drove into the conservatory through the broken windows and fell silently upon the blackened shell that had once been a man.

Only the crystal ring remained untouched: a ring of sparkling white light upon Delgado's charred finger.

★ ★ ★

No one thought to look for Delgado until the following morning, when they found his charred body, still chained to the pillar, and the body of the whore Geena beside him. The woman's body was strangely unmarked but her face was a mask of sheer terror.

A freak accident, obviously. And a tragic loss to Winterbourne. But, after all, a whore is just a whore; and Delgado's death would not linger long in the memory.

There was, however, one intriguing fact which no one could quite explain. For some reason, there was a single band of perfect, white, untouched flesh about the third finger of Delgado's left hand: the only flesh on his body that had not been charred by the fire. Only a ring could have protected his flesh from the lightning.

But if he had ever worn a ring, there was no sign of it now.

19: Rebirth

Mara screamed as the Master approached her, the light of triumph in his eyes.

'A fitting end for you, my sweet,' he hissed. 'A fitting end for one so meddlesome and so beautiful.'

She tried to kick out, to fight him off, but Heimdal and Geoffrey held her thighs apart, preventing her from evading his terrifying desires. The vampire-woman Anastasia looked on, a secret smile playing about her lips as though she felt a very special hatred for this young witch-woman whose pursuit had so preoccupied her beloved Master.

'You cannot . . . You cannot use the Phallus on me!' she gasped, as she felt the Master's fingers opening up the flower of her womanhood, ready to pierce and violate her. 'It has protected me! It will not harm me . . .'

The Master sighed and shook his head.

'Poor, misguided child,' he replied. 'The Phallus will protect only the one who has the power to possess it. All others, it will destroy. Since my powers are infinitely greater than your second-rate talents, it will now protect me and destroy you. What could be more natural and more logical than that?

'Farewell, Mara Fleming. In death, your body will be infinitely more beautiful and more useful than it was in its miserable life. Your insignificant death shall restore glorious life to my Queen.'

The Phallus entered her like a burning brand, searing her delicate flesh and making her cry out with the terrible, delicious pain of it. The Master's finger was on her clitoris, rubbing it, making it swell in spite of her terror and pain.

She realised, in the midst of her confusion, that she was more excited than she had ever been before in her life. She yearned to be penetrated and violated and fucked by this inhuman, disembodied penis, whose fiery-cold and ancient power was seeping into her, making her tremble with the anticipation of unholy, unearthly pleasure.

Mara felt the juices flowing from her cunt, moistening her cunt-lips; and a single tear-drop of cunt-juice was trickling down the inside of her thigh. The walls of her cunt were pulsating gently, in anticipation of her orgasm. Their taut velvet rings tightened gently about the monstrous shaft of the Phallus, and she began to moan quietly, knowing that she was lost – now and for ever.

The Master's triumphant gaze was burning into her and she was unable to turn away, was forced to look deep into those pitiless eyes. As she watched, a picture began to form behind those eyes. The figure of a woman – very tiny and very distant. But she was walking towards Mara, getting larger and more distinct with each step she took. Her slender nakedness glistened, her tanned flesh smoothed with a thin film of oil, and she was running her hands lasciviously over the taut flesh of her firm but heavy breasts.

She spoke, and there was a bitter irony in her voice, in the curl of her full red lips, in the glint of her large, violet eyes.

'Mara, sweet child. So very like me, and yet so unlike. Did you think that the Phallus could harm me, that in killing my body my immortal soul would also be destroyed? Did you perhaps think that you might take up the place which is rightfully mine, at the right hand of my beloved Master? How fitting that your frail and unworthy goodness should be made whole and powerful by the Master's grace.

'Mara – I shall utterly destroy your pitiful little soul, but your body shall live on for ever, ennobled by the beauty of sublime evil. This, child, is a far greater immortality than you deserve. Take comfort in that thought as I end your miserable life.'

As Mara watched, helpless, the figure of the Queen seemed to come nearer, seemed no longer to be contained within the compass of the Master's burning gaze. She unfastened her crystal collar and Mara clearly saw the two little white scars on the side of her throat.

As she stepped forward from within the encircling tongues of flame, Mara saw that from the dense black hair at the base of her belly protruded a bizarre limb of flesh: the greenish-black Phallus, with two massive, blackened testicles hanging obscenely between her thighs.

Mara screamed, but it was too late. And no one who heard had any intention of helping her. The Queen's death-cold, encircling arms were already about her, suffocating the life from her body; and the Phallus was thrusting into her, again and again. And with each thrust, her orgasm grew nearer; and a little more of her soul drained away, until at last it seemed that she was no more than a shadow, clinging on to life with the last of its strength.

A final thrust brought her to orgasm and her cunt contracted in a long series of delicious spasms. She cried out her ecstasy and terror as the life was wrenched from her body, and her soul was cast out into the void.

'Andreas . . .!'

The darkness lasted for a long time. Darkness and silence that were not quite oblivions. It seemed to go on for ever. Was she dead?

And then she saw it, coming towards her from out of the blackness. A scaly, snake-like monster with the face of a woman. The face of Anastasia Dubois. The woman's mouth opened, to reveal wicked fangs, dripping venom, and she hissed and lunged at Mara, evidently bent on killing her.

The serpent had short forelegs covered with iridescent scales – blue, red, green, violet . . . The colours flashed and gleamed as the monster reared up and tried to slash Mara's throat with its wickedly curved claws, crystal-clear and sharp as daggers.

Mara looked for a way of escape, but all around her was

blackness. She knew that if she turned and ran, she would be running towards certain death and destruction. What was she to do?

A voice, clear and strong, spoke from behind her.

'Use me, Mara. Use my strength.'

It was the voice of Andreas Hunt. She turned, but there was no one there. On the ground beside her lay a dagger – pure, white crystal, with an engraved silver hilt. She bent and picked it up, ducking swiftly to avoid the swipe of the snake-woman's talons.

And Mara lunged at the monster's throat, slitting it from ear to ear. The blood that poured out was not the crimson of life, but a foetid, greenish-black liquid whose stench made Mara's head reel.

The monster slumped to the ground, and a great magnesium-flare of white light burst around her, annihilating the darkness and dazzling her so that she no longer knew who or where she was. The ground began to tremble beneath her feet; cracks appeared, and she stumbled, falling onto her hands and knees.

The earth yawned wide, like the maw of a ravening beast, and she fell, fell, fell into the heart of the burning white light.

When she opened her eyes, she was back in the tomb. But something was different, very different. She looked down at her body and saw that she was wearing the clothes of Anastasia Dubois – the same red shoes, short white skirt . . . even the same bracelet: a gold circlet depicting a snake with its tail in its mouth.

And she looked across at the pale figure, still chained to the wall; and realised that she was gazing at the dead body of Mara Fleming, a greenish fluid oozing from her cunt and the Phallus still lying between her thighs.

If that was Mara Fleming, who was she? Who had she become?

She felt a hand on her shoulder and found herself looking into the concerned face of Heimdal.

'Are you all right, Anastasia? You look as if you've seen a ghost.'

She nodded silently, only too sure now of the role that she must play. And she must be word-perfect – or die. The pain of realisation hit her like an express train. Her body was dead. Somehow, in the void between life and death, her spirit had overcome that of the vampire-woman Anastasia Dubois; and now she had taken possession of her body.

Would she now also become a vampire, forced to feed on sexual energies and the blood of innocents?

The Master was stroking the face of the dead Mara Fleming, intoning soft and gentle words, in a language she could not understand. He removed the Phallus and hastened to unlock the manacles about the dead girl's wrists.

The dead lips were moving soundlessly. Colour was coming back to the pallid face, animating the bloodless limbs.

The eyelids flickered open, violet eyes glinting with the cold, hard light of evil. The full red lips curled into a smile and Sedet, Queen of the Undead, spoke once again:

'My Master and my eternal lord,' she sighed, pressing her lips to his in a joyful kiss. 'At last you have found me, released me, summoned me to your side.'

The Master took her hands and helped her to her feet, steadying her in her weakness.

'See with what joy your subjects greet you!' he cried, and Geoffrey and Heimdal fell to their knees, Mara following suit for fear of discovery. He turned to them and commanded:

'Celebrate the rebirth of your Queen. Fuck, my children: fuck and deny all that is good and contemptibly frail and mortal. Fuck, so that the energies of your copulation may strengthen and refresh your Queen.'

Mara scarcely knew what to do, but Geoffrey and Heimdal made her decision for her. They tore at her clothes, rending the fabric and stripping her down to her pale yellow silk bra and French knickers. Not even bothering to take off her underwear, Geoffrey reached into her bra-cups and roughly pulled out her breasts so that they hung over the top. He bit into the flesh, making Mara gasp and flinch.

In a moment, they had laid her down on the cool stone floor, amid the dust of ages. Geoffrey unzipped his pants and straddled Mara's chest, his thighs and arse pressing down hard upon her martyred breasts and his weight almost squeezing all the breath out of her. He took out his prick, supporting Mara's head in his hands and thrusting his hardness between her lips. He tasted strong, potent, the flesh of his prick strangely cool and inhuman. But wasn't she inhuman now, too . . .?

Heimdal did not even think to take off her panties. Instead, he unbuttoned his flies and, taking out his magnificent penis, simply pulled aside the gusset of her French knickers. Mara knew that she must not resist. She must seem to be enjoying this as much as Anastasia would have enjoyed it. With terror in her heart, she sucked at Geoffrey's cock and spread her legs wide to let Heimdal into her cunt.

Two men were fucking her. Or were they fucking Anastasia Dubois? Tears glistened between Mara's closed eyelids as she experienced the bittersweet pleasure of copulating within the body of another woman.

It felt so strange, to have a different cunt throbbing and pulsating around Heimdal's shaft; different breasts, the long, pink nipples hard and eager against Geoffrey's thighs; different lips, closed so tightly around Geoffrey's eager prick.

She came, and as her body convulsed with pleasure she felt Heimdal's spunk jetting into her tight new womanhood, inundating her with its pearly abundance. Geoffrey was not long in climaxing and she swallowed down his semen with an eagerness that was not entirely feigned.

To her surprise, neither Geoffrey nor Heimdal needed

more than a few seconds to recover. Within a minute, they were hard as iron again, and seeking new ways to take their pleasure.

And the strange thing was that she, too, felt more eager than she had ever done for sex. She not only wanted to fuck: she needed to – needed the taste of semen and the feel of a hard prick inside her. Was this more than just desire? Was this the beginning of a terrible need which she would never again be able to control?

Already Heimdal had rolled her onto her belly and was exploring the exquisite tightness of her arsehole. She felt the flesh stretch with an undeniable frisson of pleasure.

'You're a divine fuck, Anastasia Dubois,' he breathed in her ear.

The pictures had first distorted, then disappeared. Andreas did not know whether to be distraught or relieved. He had watched in helpless horror as his lover, Mara, was horribly violated with a macabre severed phallus – and at the moment of her greatest agony, the link had gone. The sight had been taken from him.

Something had happened to Mara. Something he couldn't quite understand. But he knew it was something bad, very bad. He had called out to her to take his hand, to let him help her – but had she heard him? He had no way of knowing. Her terror echoed through the emptiness, reverberating incessantly in his brain.

He lay in a limbo of darkness and frustration, wondering how he was ever going to get out of this mess.

And then a picture began to form again. It was Mara! She was walking towards him, her arms outstretched, in all the glory of her nakedness.

'Fuck me, Andreas. Fuck me now.'

His spirit entwined with hers, and he felt a wave of tranquil ecstasy surge over him as they were joined together. At the summit of their ecstasy, her face seemed to blur and fade and distort, and he cried out:

'Don't leave me . . . not now . . .'

But as her features swam into focus once again, Andreas realised that they were radically changed. He was no longer looking into the face of his lover, Mara Fleming.

He was looking into the face of the vampire woman, Anastasia Dubois.

He tried to push her away but she held onto him with desperate tenacity, her lips framing the same words over and over again, urgently, desperately:

'It's me, Andreas! Can't you see? It's me, Mara . . .'

They lay together on the floor, limbs entwined. Sticky semen dried to flaking whiteness on martyred flesh. They were exhausted but still enflamed with desire, waiting only for the command for the ceremonies to begin again.

The Master looked down at the pile of dust and bone fragments and smiled grimly.

'You were a useful toy, Mara Fleming, but now you are dust.'

He gave the pile a little kick and walked away towards the glimmer of afternoon sunlight, his new Queen imperious and beautiful by his side.

20: Epilogue

An uninvited guest within the body of the negro slave Ibrahim, freed for moments only from the darkness of his captivity, Andreas Hunt watched with mounting anger and grief as the three figures emerged from the main doorway of Winterbourne Hall.

The Master led the way, his Queen radiant and youthful on his arm. They made a handsome pair, mused Andreas with irony, as he recalled how – short months ago – things had been so very different.

Andreas Hunt and Mara Fleming, now the empty puppets of the Master and his Queen. Now Andreas was a captive disembodied spirit and Mara . . .

He bowed respectfully as the Master and Queen Sedet got into the car and Anastasia Dubois emerged onto the front steps of the Hall.

She turned to Andreas and he knew that what he had hoped for was true. Mara's spirit was not dead. It lived on, within the body of this beautiful vampire-creature, Anastasia Dubois. She looked at him and smiled.

'Thank you, Ibrahim,' she said, momentarily touching his hand. There was a hint of sadness in her voice. And was that a glimmer of recognition in her lovely emerald eyes?

He bowed again, this time whispering words for her ears alone.

'Don't give up, Mara. I'm coming back for you. It won't be long now . . .'

As the limousine drew away, its wheels crunching on the frosty gravel, Andreas surrendered to the dark.

But not for long. He was going to crack this one, no

matter what it took. Andreas Hunt was back on the case.

Above and around the sightless, silent spirit of Andreas Hunt, locked deep within the crystal, loomed the dark shape of the granite sarcophagus, the walls of Andreas's forbidding prison.

And on the lid lay something innocently small.

Nothing ornate, nothing of any great significance. Just a ring, cut from a single, flawless crystal. A ring, sparkling defiantly amid the dust.

More Erotic Fiction from Headline:

Lustful Liaisons

Erotic adventures in the capital city of love!

Anonymous

PARIS 1912 – a city alive with the pursuit of pleasure, from the promenade of the Folies Bergère to the high-class brothels of the Left Bank. Everywhere business is booming in the oldest trade of all – the trade of love!

But now there is a new and flourishing activity to absorb the efforts of go-ahead men-about-town: the business of manufacturing motor cars. Men like Robert and Bertrand Laforge are pioneers in this field but their new automobile has a design defect that can only be rectified by some cunning industrial espionage. Which is where the new trade marries with the old, for the most reliable way of discovering information is to enlist the help of a lovely and compliant woman. A woman, for example, like the voluptuous Nellie Lebérigot whose soft creamy flesh and generous nature are guaranteed to uncover a man's most closely guarded secrets...

FICTION/EROTICA 0 7472 3710 7

A selection of Erotica
from Headline

FONDLE IN FLAGRANTE	Nadia Adamant	£4.99 ☐
EROTICON DESIRES	Anonymous	£4.99 ☐
LUSTFUL LIAISONS	Anonymous	£4.50 ☐
THE ROYAL SCANDAL	Anonymous	£4.99 ☐
FRENCH FROLICS	Anonymous	£4.50 ☐
EROS OFF THE RAILS	Anonymous	£4.99 ☐
CREMORNE GARDENS	Anonymous	£4.99 ☐
ECSTASY ITALIAN STYLE	Anonymous	£3.99 ☐
MY DUTY, MY DESIRE	Anomymous	£3.99 ☐
IN THE MOOD	Lesley Asquith	£4.50 ☐
KISS OF DEATH	Valentina Cilescu	£4.99 ☐
THE LUSTS OF THE BORGIAS	Marcus Van Heller	£4.99 ☐

All Headline books are available at your local bookshop or newsagent, or can be ordered direct from the publisher. Just tick the titles you want and fill in the form below. Prices and availability subject to change without notice.

Headline Book Publishing PLC, Cash Sales Department, Bookpoint, 39 Milton Park, Abingdon, OXON, OX14 4TD, UK. If you have a credit card you may order by telephone — 0235 831700.

Please enclose a cheque or postal order made payable to Bookpoint Ltd to the value of the cover price and allow the following for postage and packing:
UK & BFPO: £1.00 for the first book, 50p for the second book and 30p for each additional book ordered up to a maximum charge of £3.00.
OVERSEAS & EIRE: £2.00 for the first book, £1.00 for the second book and 50p for each additional book.

Name ..

Address ...

..

..

If you would prefer to pay by credit card, please complete:
Please debit my Visa/Access/Diner's Card/American Express (delete as applicable) card no:

Signature ...Expiry Date